CHICAGO PUBLIC LIBRARY

R00672 49495

D1372596

FIC   Cruz, M.

October in Cairo

$18.95

DATE			

LITERATURE & LANGUAGE DIVISION

JUN   1989

© THE BAKER & TAYLOR CO.

OCTOBER IN CAIRO

by

M. CRUZ

THE PERMANENT PRESS
SAG HARBOR, NEW YORK

Fic

R0067249495

The West should disabuse itself of the idea that Muslims are ready to sacrifice themselves for Islam at the drop of the hat.

However much this movement brandishes the flag of Islam, we should never forget the fact that this is a social revolution, a reaction against certain deep social ills and victimization.

Fuad Dessouki
Egypt

And when a person owns nothing, or has nothing to lose, he will resort to any mean, ordinary or extraordinary, even though that would destroy both his adversary and himself.

Muhammed Hussein Fadlallah
Lebanon

Copyright © 1988 by Sue Dangler

All rights reserved, including the right to reproduce this book, or parts thereof, in any form, except for the inclusion of brief quotations in a review.

Library of Congress Number: 87-62807
International Standard Book Number: 0-932966-84-5

Manufactured in the United States of America

THE PERMANENT PRESS
RD2 Noyac Road
Sag Harbor, NY 11963

1

Even though the hour was late the whole warren of seedy twisting lanes off Pyramid Road was jammed with noisy throngs of people, women walking with babies on their hips and chattering like magpies, scrawny boys on bicycles, berry brown men and gray donkeys pulling carts piled high with burlap bags or bundles of logs; even an occasional honking car braved the obstacle course. The din was fierce and no one paid attention to the short spark of a person making his way through the confusion. The lane was awash with an open gutter filled with piles of garbage which drew flies, maggots, and alley cats and it had many a missing stone as well. He walked with a springy step in the middle of it, having decided that simpleminded security agents would be expecting a fugitive to tread timidly, clutching at the shadows; they wouldn't notice anyone strutting about big as life. The convulsed area through which he strode was full of tailor shops and grocers and open-air cafes where chickens revolved on spits and butcher shops where sides of lamb hung covered with flies. Above the shops were flats where people lived ten to a room and were lucky to have a toilet.

The man stood quietly in the doorway of a laundry for several minutes, peering up and down the street, watching for signs of trouble. Because the traffic was so heavy and the lane so crowded with animals, carts and people, he had to concentrate carefully to see if he were being followed. He wasn't and he sighed. To keep his confidence from sagging he told himself, whatever I lack in size or material possessions I make up with an incisive intelligence. He said it three times, as if it

1

were a magical incantation, then he spun around and swiftly
sped up a passageway leading to the arched entrance of a
small cafe. It had been vacated and shuttered for the rest of
the evening not by accident, but thanks to a proprietor sympathetic to their cause.

As he approached the entrance, a large figure, easily six feet
tall, emerged suddenly from behind one of the pillars. "Ali, is
that you?" demanded an anxious voice in Arabic.

There was enough light from a passing motorbike for Ali to
recognize Mustafa. The grueling life in the underground had
not yet eroded Mustafa's youthful appearance; his hair was
still thick and bone black, his complexion clear. He was normally a genial man in his coarse way, spirited and friendly as a
canary, but tonight's assignation was hazardous and melancholy business, and his nerves were on edge.

"Yes, it is me." Ali flashed a provocative grin, hugging the
bigger man to him.

"Dammit, you are late again," Mustafa scolded, enfolded
by Ali's muscular embrace.

It was on the tip of Ali's tongue to retort that only the
bloody fascists care if trains and people run on time, but he
refrained. Mustafa seemed, however, to read his mind and he
grimly opened his mouth to confront Ali. The hot words died
on his tongue, however, when he saw that the motorbike had
made a U-turn and was roaring towards them.

"Who in the Devil is this?" piped Mustafa weakly. His heart
tumbled to his shoes, and he would have fallen in a heap if Ali
had not swept him up in his arms and pushed him hard against
the wall, shielding him inadequately with his smaller body. As
the biker sped by, they caught sight of the garish likeness of
movie star Najar Assaghira on a poster attached to the rear
fender. The man was advertising a film. Mustafa glanced with
relief at his retreating back, silently apologizing to him with
his eyes for not understanding his harmless purpose.

Ali reached up and patted Mustafa's cheek. It felt damp. He
took his hand and led him to the doorway. "Careful," Ali
warned as they made their way around a half-hidden stack of
burlap bags. Mustafa gave the obstacle only a second of his

attention as he listened to Ali say contritely, "Forgive me for being late, brother. I must have lost track of the time."

"That's all right," Mustafa responded in an offhanded manner as though the apology or the scare hadn't mattered one way or another; the main thing was that Ali had made it here safely. But the casualness didn't ring true. Mustafa knew of Ali's dare-devil way of coming to meetings, no matter how many times he had warned him to be more circumspect. By contrast, no earthworm ever moved more invisibly than Mustafa when he ventured outside in the hostile world. He had a mania for secrecy. "It is dumb to take chances," he admonished Ali in a voice that sounded like wheels spinning earnestly on gravel.

Hearing the sound of a truck's engine, the two comrades moved apart and flattened themselves against the wall once more, painfully alert to movements. Satisfied that nothing was amiss, they separately ducked down to enter a tiny room off to one side of the main dining area. A stocky, white-bearded guard in a brown robe scrutinized them closely before letting them pass. Once inside, Ali and Mustafa found a half dozen other men already huddled about a rickety wooden table. The streaked windows had cobwebs on them, and there were dead flies on the sills. The only moonlight that entered the room came through slim cracks in the wood where the boards were separated, shrunken by the weather, and the individual faces were barely distinguishable. Ali sat down next to Fathi, even though he couldn't stand him, an emotion reciprocated by Fathi, who offered no greeting.

Fathi's bright blue eyes looked as if two glass coins to ward off the evil eye had been set into his sockets, and he turned them now on the leader of the group, a tall man who appeared to be somewhere between 35 and 70. He wore silver-rimmed glasses with thick lenses and a three-piece tweed suit. His relationship with the Jamaati-il-Islam, the Muslim Brotherhood, had forced him into a life of deception and the clothing was not of his own choosing. Once the Islamic Republic was in place, physicality was going to be demoted, and all men would wear garb through which the outlines of the body could not be discerned and a full beard would mask the face. Now, the man's smooth, shaven face had its usual querulous cast. His sharp features seemed always fixed in tension and concentration, radiating deeply-held beliefs. Known to the others as "Ibrahim," his *nom de guerre*, he had the humorless air of a dedicated schoolmaster. His brown face folded onto itself like a camel's bag, but there was an assurance in the set of his lips and a penetrating grasp in his steady eyes. It was those qualities that bound the young disciples to him. Soon as the two newcomers found themselves stools, he glanced impatiently at his digital watch and complained, "Why isn't Talaat here?"

Nobody spoke, not even Ali who was always swift to defend Talaat. Fathi bit his nails. Ibrahim was never wrong, but Mustafa continued to study him, his expression gradually growing less certain until he ventured hesitantly, "An hour ago, you sent Talaat to the airport to pick up an American reporter, Master, or don't you remember? You said we might be able to use her to our advantage."

"I did?" Ibrahim was shaking his head, his face a blank of incomprehension.

"An American reporter?" There was a quick start of interest from Ali, and he cast an imploring glance at Mustafa who shook his head almost imperceptibly. When Ali ignored the subtle warning by asking, "Why wasn't I told?" Mustafa trod heavily on his foot.

Ibrahim was shocked at this breach of etiquette, but he determined to maintain his own civility and his own authority. Even before last week's police raid, members of the Brotherhood were haunted men who were beginning to show the strains of too little sleep and too few meals, of being forever on the run and in hiding, of living with the constant fear of the knock on the door in the middle of the night. Now more than ever, Ibrahim feared his own little cell was out of sorts, increasingly out of order and at times even out of control. His problem, he suddenly decided, was that he was too easy, too kindhearted. He tried to help these youngsters, and it was backfiring in his face. An iron hand was called for. He sat rigidly at the head of the table, his back straight, his chin up, and gazed coldly at Mustafa. "Of course, I can remember my orders. I am not senile yet. Never mind, we cannot wait for Talaat. We will talk about tardiness later," he concluded, looking piercingly at Ali and in a tone that made it clear the discussion would not be a pleasant one. There was a muffled giggle.

Ali thrust out a belligerent lip; he hated being publicly embarrassed. "Go on, Master," Mustafa encouraged, maintaining the pressure on Ali's foot.

Everyone turned to Ibrahim like compasses attracted toward a pole. Underneath the stern facade, he was jittery with excitement. They could see it in the glowing eyes and in the touch of vanity in his voice. "Yes, yes, we must get on with it, so listen carefully, my brothers. Eleven years," Ibrahim cracked out the words, referring to the number of years of Sadat's rule, "it is enough! For years our task was to try and be invisible, to find out what was on people's mind and relay it back to our superiors and let them decide what to do. Our work has paid off. Now we have help from the mosque, from the schools, from ordinary citizens. I am talking about the people in this squalid neighborhood who have no money, no jobs, no security, no dignity, and no hope for the future. We are about to turn the tables and change all that. Yes, by God, we will."

Ibrahim laughed with delight, showing tobacco-stained teeth. He waited a moment longer, to give emphasis to his announcement. "The moment we have all been waiting for has finally arrived. We are going to strike at Satan himself and soon. For a long time now we have watched people trying to outdo one another in venality. We have seen decency far outweighed by villainy, uninhibited ambition, and rampant carnality. What more can we say about the black, crass soul of a leader who must have 101 palaces at his disposal, about his vain and ambitious wife, a gluttonous cat with claws tearing our Holy Scriptures to shreds. This harridan with her nose forever up the rumps of the rich and famous, she has hated our faith from day one! I am not the only one to suspect she got herself wed to Anwar Sadat simply so she could attack all True Believers from a position of power."

Ibrahim glared at his followers as he thought, How shameful! Sadat was middle-aged and already had a pious village wife who had stood by him loyally during his long imprisonment, supporting the family by selling off her property—when, unblushingly, he decided to cast her off and marry a scantily-clad, flirtatious 19-year old girl. Jihan: the offspring of a diseased camel and a bald headed woman! Jihan: whose name and nefarious activities—birth control clinics, veil burnings, divorce bills, women's rights—crop up like chicken pox wherever Western imperialists manage to gain a toehold. It all seemed somewhat diabolical, as though an evil jinn had taken a hand in it.

"What can we say," Ibrahim continued in a crescendo, "about the huge fortune that Esmat Sadat has amassed by criminal means? That it goes right on under his brother Anwar's nose and he cannot see it? What can we say about Osman Ahmed Osman, except that he is making billions of pounds in construction and real estate and buying palatial homes in Mirabella on the coast of Spain, as well as a yacht and a villa in Saint-Jean Cap Ferrat in France?" Ibrahim had spent his whole life giving speeches and he was giving one now, his voice rising and falling like a village sheikh's in a religious thrall.

Eyes that were lively and attentive a moment ago started to glaze over. How many times had they all heard The Master speak of Egyptian society as the new *Jahaliyya*—the state of idolatry and corruption that existed in pre-Islamic Arabia? Ali Salah tugged restlessly at his beard, his brown eyes lapsing into peevish opacity. Did Ibrahim think he was in front of a blackboard teaching them geography? Didn't he understand the risks of this gathering? Ali was so agitated that he could hardly control himself. Holding his voice down to keep from shouting, he beseeched, "Can we get on with it, Uncle? You are preaching to the converted, you know."

Mustafa exchanged a quick, tolerant smile with the man on his right. Fathi was watching Ali intently, scowling, and the aversion in Fathi's face stung Mustafa all at once. He vowed to tell Ali later to edit himself in Fathi's presence. Ibrahim's face was flushed with shock and anger for no one had ever so openly challenged him. It had to be Ali Salah, of course. His American education had ruined him, had caused him to forget that real Egyptians wear a mask of courtesy and courtliness even when they are thinking unspeakable thoughts about each other.

Ibrahim went on pedantically, "What I'm saying is this: putrification has become so embedded in the upper class that the whole social system has become infected. The evil at the top has filtered all the way down the ladder because this man Sadat has vast powers of evil." He paused to let his eyes drift around the circle, collecting the full attention of each man. "But we can take heart, Allah will recompense us well for our patience." He paused. "Soldiers are ready to turn their guns on their commanders. We do not know how or when, but it is certain they are ready. Do you follow me?"

Most of his disciples were wide-eyed, gasping in surprise. Rashed stared at him, completely lost. Fathi leaned forward, gazing at the Master with mouth slack, flatteringly impressed. He understood by Ibrahim's burning eyes that his leader had been let in on the planning of an important mission, but what was he to make of the word "soldier"? Did Ibrahim mean soldiers of Allah like themselves or men of the army? Fathi whispered inquiringly to Ibrahim, but he shook him off imperiously. Mustafa raised his eyebrows and waited. The others, too, were perplexed and annoyed by being kept so much in the dark. After all, weren't their necks destined for the hangman's noose if the plan failed? None had a willingness to shed blood to no purpose.

Ibrahim didn't wish to reveal too much. His mouth tightened and his words came out reluctantly and with asperity. "All right, my sons, I can tell you that the brother of one young officer was thrown into prison and not a word more. Sadat's American cronies may think him a god, but this grieving lieutenant knows him for a scorpion. Only this time Sadat's stung himself with his own tail. A family's honor will be avenged."

Ibrahim paused once more to gaze fiercely around the circle of expectant faces, staring in turn at each man's alert eyes as if he were checking the plan for flaws, and just when

the silence would have forced someone to speak, he added in
a louder voice that Allah should be praised, for at last there
were men well-placed and willing to commit *ghadhbah lil
Allah*—an outrage for God and thus become *shahid*—martyr.
"And we are ready to give them all the support we can. Once
we have our freedom, we can work together to make a better
life." Ibrahim's deep voice had risen to a shout by the finish.

Shahid! The thought of martyrdom made Fathi's heart race,
though his eyes remained outwardly steady on his leader.
Ibrahim pressed Fathi's arm, an unprecedented familiarity,
and Fathi's heart raced even faster. Ali watched passively, his
eyes fixed on the worm of a vein at Ibrahim's temple.

"Have they targeted Mubarak, too? And Al Ghazala?" The
questions fluttered toward Ibrahim like a shuttlecock across a
badminton net from Rashed, a 19-year-old student with a
cupid's mouth, long eyelashes, and quivering brown eyes.
Ibrahim tried to wave him off, but Rashed had grabbed center
stage and wouldn't let go. Sensitive about his weak voice, he
was set on showing himself as the strongest character on the
premises, the one with the most resolve. "They should," he
insisted hotly, moving to the edge of the stool and spreading
his arms with energetic movements. "Theirs is the un-
scrupulous ambition of men who would kill, steal, and injure
babies if they could order other people to do it for them and if
it would advance their careers a centimeter or two. We should
put a—"

The sound of frantic footsteps approaching at a run through
the darkness of the cafe halted Rashed in mid-sentence, chill-
ing the group. Ibrahim sprang to his feet. A rotund woman
who had been posted as a lookout at the head of the street
filled the doorway. Her scarf pointed upward in such disarray
that it might have been struck by lightning, and she was
breathing deep sucking breaths as she pointed behind her.
"Police van! Hurry, quickly!"

The others rose without a word and darted one after another through the door. Within seconds the little room was
empty. As Ali pulled Mustafa along the edge of a wall away
from the cafe, he told him, "Let's circle the area, you to the

left and me to the right, and later we will meet at Bab el Luk. Fathi's is the safest place for us tonight."

"No," Mustafa protested. "Fathi is fed-up with you, and besides, I am expected home—"

"If they come to your mother's house in el-Zaytan, we are lost." Ali cracked the last word like a nut. A flush appeared at Mustafa's throat and moved upward. Ali spoke rapidly before he could be stopped, "You know perfectly well she is against us."

Traffic roared around them while the sounds of Cairo's poor masses rose in awesome cacophony. The truth of the accusation cut deep, for Mustafa clearly remembered his mother's betrayal, her blabbing about his clandestine activities to Uncle Saleem, a brother whom she knew to possess no more discretion than a town crier. The dragnet was growing tighter by the day and even his own home was not a safe haven. A brief, bitter smile twitched Mustafa's lips, but was instantly replaced by an expression of such sorrow that it broke Ali's heart. He started to say, I'm sorry, brother, I didn't mean to hurt you, but at that moment a woman walked by. A silken *yashmak* covered her face below the eyes and draped to her chest. Mustafa gave her veil an envious look; if only he had one to hide behind right now.

"Forget Fathi," Mustafa told Ali, who answered him in a rush of words. He couldn't be sure whether Ali said "See you at Ragaa's" or "See you at Rashed's," but whichever it was, Ali meant it to end the conversation, for he whirled around and took off without a backward glance.

Mustafa shuffled off, braving the crowded dirt lanes. He tried to hide his face under his old army hat, peering from under the green brim. He would have to walk back in the wrong direction until he could cut down a side lane and head back to the center of town. When he got to the lane, it was so small that it was necessary to press tightly against the walls of the buildings as cars and carts went by. After several hundred yards, he turned into a wider thoroughfare. There he met up with a large donkey laden with kerosene tins, and he put one hand on its rump, following alongside for a distance, using the beast and its burden to hide behind. The night air smelled of diesel exhaust, roasting lentils and coffee, human sweat. Mustafa came to rest in front of a souvenir shop, in the window of which was a crudely lettered sign reading, "Will Male Free to Japan." Directly across the street a joyous crowd was pouring out of a puppet show, and he made himself a part of it, jostling along the way, but he was too busy searching for enemies to enjoy the colorful sight and the press of warm bodies. He prayed for Allah's mercy, which he knew should be a request that he might die and go directly to Paradise if he were caught. But what he really meant was, God, please don't let them get me.

In a few moments, Ali reached a squat house surrounded by a mud brick wall. The rusty iron gate was open. A radio blared nearby, but there was no one in sight. He made straight for a wooden ladder and climbed up to the roof, which was connected to a neighboring roof by a plank. The moon, pale as a chicken's egg, hung like a small lantern above his head. Tentatively, he rested his weight on the plank, picking his footing with care and started to navigate the abyss between the two buildings. A groan of protest came from the plank and he weaved unsteadily. Hearing voices below, Ali continued swiftly to the other side. Rather than search for a ladder, he decided to use the strong, low branch of a tree to get himself safely down. But the bough was not as strong nor as low to the ground as he had thought, he discovered once he had made the fateful move.

Now, Ali hung there, his hands clinging frantically to the branch, his feet swinging high above the earth. He tried to move his hold, to swing himself backward onto the tree trunk, but he couldn't make it. He heard the branch crack, making him queasy with fear that he would twist his ankle when he hit the ground. A goat bleated in the distance. There was a more ominous sound above Ali's head as the tree shuddered, the bough broke, and a microsecond later he was hard upon the ground. His feet were so tender that he winced when he felt the sharp stones through his sandals' thin soles. Valiantly, he fought not to let go with a howl big enough to freeze the balls of anyone within earshot. Bent over under a sinister lean of houses that seemed to meet three stories above his head, grimacing the pain he dare not express, he thought he heard hoof beats, though it could have been his own heart.

Suddenly, there was a yell directly overhead, immediately followed by a potful of liquid flung unceremoniously on his head. A chamber pot! Chastened, Ali straightened with effort and shook himself vigorously. Then he grimly picked a course that had him crawling like a lizard along the wall in the shadows. A donkey brayed behind him. He stopped and looked around desperately for a place to hide. Nothing but blank mud walls on each side of a lane covered with pressed melon rinds and dirty straw. He whirled around and limped on until he reached a spot where a shallow earth lip extended into a muddy ditch. Tall reeds arched like a green roof overhead, but the sand was hard and wet, and his sandals left crisply outlined impressions on the surface. Half-sliding, half tumbling down the bank, his jaw clenched in a stoic denial of pain, he plunged into the ditch and began wading awkwardly through the stagnant water toward a drain pipe. Once there, he bent low to crawl through it.

When Ali came out onto Pyramid Road, he paused to wring water from his shirttail. Ruffling his wet hair to make it stand on end, Ali watched as a Rolls Royce pulled into the circular driveway in front of a gaudy nightclub and discharged two Arabs in flowing *thawls*, their white *khaffiyeas* clamped on with black ringed *agals*. Sleek and sophisticated, with little moustaches echoing their slitted eyes, they were Saudis—rich Saudis. Rage engulfed Ali. Despite their country's official boycott of Egypt, rich Saudis continued to descend upon Cairo and Alexandria in droves. For centuries they had come riding in from the deserts, smelling of camel dung and cardamon; now they flew in smelling of money, to make sport of his people's poverty. Like sailors on shore leave, like devouring locusts, they grabbed everything in sight.

And that everything included the two shapely Egyptians on their arms. One was wearing a low-cut ball gown scattered with colorful embroidery that looked, from a distance, like diamonds. The other harlot was decked out in a skirt like the drapes in a bordello and seemed to have no eyebrows at all above her greedy raisin eyes. Her full painted face was framed by a dangle of precious metal from her ears. The taller Arab, a smug-faced bastard if ever Ali had seen one, sprung one of her curls, and she laughed coquettishly, her teeth shining blue in the neon light. Ali stared at the women and the desert nomads and their fancy automobile with such concentrated rage that if there were any justice under heaven they would have gone up in a big mushroom cloud of orange fire. A mini-Hiroshima. The harlots were muttering excitedly in coarse Arabic about their orchid corsages.

Ali Salah wished the waters of the Nile would rise up and take them all—the harlots, the camel dung nomads, every last person in the nightclub. Shaking with a wet chill and enraged by the evil before him, he leaned weakly against a utility pole. His body began to ache all over, and he felt as if his head were being blown up with more pressure than it could take. Action was called for, the anger told him. Restraint snapped and he bellowed forth with all his strength, "*Haaarrrammmm!*"

Sin, forbidden in the eyes of God: it was a bitter howl and it had come from his heart. The Saudi turned to face Ali, as stunned as a sparrow that had flown into a wall. The Saudi's driver bolted around the Rolls Royce, coming menacingly toward Ali. The breeze ruffled the Arab's dark brown robe, revealing a long, J-shaped *jambiyah* at his waist. One glance at that dagger was sufficient to warn Ali that here was not only danger, but danger of a highly lethal kind. His feet hurt ferociously, but once again they didn't fail him.

2

The late afternoon sky over Cairo was fading as the TWA 747 hummed toward the International Airport, lulling many of its passengers into catnapping. In a seat in economy class, a Chicana closed her book and leaned back against the head-rest. Washed out in the unflattering glare of the overhead reading light, her face looked older than its 27 years, but nothing could hide the outlines of a deeply Latin beauty in the regular high cheekbones, the coppery skin tones. Her ivory lace ascot collar was decorously pinned with a cameo brooch, but her coarse raven hair looked comfortably out of control.

The woman's name was Maria Luz Gracida, and she was thinking about the conversation she'd had during meal service with her seat-mate, a small, effeminate, and deferential South Korean businessman in a Valentino suit. In his case, appearances were deceiving for in his approach to promoting Korean firms abroad this self-confident graduate of U.C.L.A. exhibited the timidity of wild things—sharks and killer bees came to mind. "We Koreans have had a hard row to hoe," Hwan had said to Luz, speaking around a mouthful of tasteless custard, "a very hard row. But I think we are a strong and sophisticated people now. Our country is prosperous and ready for democracy. There are so many obstacles to overcome when you have been a poor nation devastated by an endless war, and not everyone's going to latch onto the brass ring. These Egyptians certainly won't," he added without lowering his voice, "but that's the breaks."

Luz's big brown eyes seemed to scrutinize the face—the face of a Mandarin in an Oriental print—then she glanced around. "There's an Egyptian sitting in front of you, chico," she warned in a low voice.

Hwan sniffed at her nervousness in disdain. "This plane is crawling with Egyptians. You can't swing a cat without hitting one."

Luz didn't like the way the man was staring at her. "The U.S. is giving Egypt five billion dollars," she said. "That's B as in boy." Not waiting for Hwan's retort, Luz turned to the window to stare down at the broad, slow-flowing river and the circles and radiating avenues at the head of the Nile Delta. All the buildings were light brown, as if camouflaged to blend in with the desert. It was the color of the local stone, to be sure; but it was also the dust of sand storms that was never washed away. Turning back, Luz asked the Korean what he advised in the way of sightseeing for a first-time visitor.

Hwan ran his thin hand across his face. "I suggest you take the elevator to the top of the Sheraton," he began. "This is where I went immediately on my arrival in 1977 to get a quick visual perspective of what the city is all about. The Sheraton is one of the tallest buildings on the banks of the Nile, and you will be treated to a view that's—well, uninspiring. There below you, you'll see unharmonious tangles of fake pharaonic, oppressive Victorian, and dull modern blocks. The flat roofs are so covered in refuse you'll think the sky just rained down garbage. You won't be inclined to linger. But return to the streets below and you'll find yourself in one of the friendliest capitals in the world. Allah has never been especially kind to Cairo. First, he sited it on a tract of land that is featureless and gave it a climate in which scorching heat and rainless days play an all too prominent part. And then, as a final indignity, Cairo has suffered from the terrible neglect that's a result of having half the national budget devoted to defense for the past 30 years. But as a compensation, Allah peopled the city with Cairenes. Other cities might have St. Peter's or Manhattan or Oktoberfest, but Cairo has wonderful people."

The plane shuddered slightly as it went through a bit of turbulence, and Hwan fell silent. Looking out at the lights, he marveled, as he always did when he returned here, how paradoxically it was that the Egyptians could be the sweetest people you'd ever hoped to meet—and yet have one of the dirtiest capitals. No, unlike the Republic of Korea, Egypt would not bloom even with the present massive infusion of U.S. dollars because there was no sound foundation to build upon. Large investments were being squandered, and the American aide officials you met couldn't mask their frustration. Hwan turned to say as much to Senorita Gracida, but her attention was caught by her other seat-mate, a large man with sagging skin, lined eyes, and a touch of gray in his dull locks. The two Americans had been chatting up a storm from the moment they boarded the aircraft.

"Washington is a very hard town," the ex-Congressman was saying morosely to Luz. "You lose office and you're referred to as a former person. It is tough on the ego. And to be beaten by a Methodist! Holy Mother of God, it's just incredible."

Hardly more incredible that Dooley himself, thought Luz as she regarded him sympathetically. Among journalists, Thomas Joseph Dooley's name connoted rough and tumble politics—that is, Boston Irish politics, the old Kennedy Mafia. During his years in Congress this son of a saloon keeper was much disliked by some, passionately applauded by others. Some very humane legislation bore his signature, and until recently, elections had gone well for him. With a mother who never missed daily Mass and a brother in the priesthood, he had the Catholic vote sewed up. Then The Boston Globe printed an exposé about his affair with the wife of a fellow Congressman, and it was all over. "I'm sorry you lost," Luz murmured.

"Are you now?" Dooley responded, pleased. Then he backhanded the air. "Well, you needn't be. It happens even to the best of us. Call it Kismet, the wheels of God, changing times. But this is a deep subject, lass, and one that needs plumbing when I take you out to dinner. You will be saying yes now, won't you?"

Luz nodded enthusiastically. "I'd be honored."

The clattering rumble of lowering flaps and the landing gear shattered everyone's sleep. Hwan stood up and opened the overhead luggage compartment. Luz opened her eyes and glanced at her watch. The loudspeaker crackled and a thickly-

accented female voice came on the air to say that they would
be landing in ten minutes, *Ins'challah*. She was turning the
whole matter over to the Almighty, and her comment drew
about an equal number of boos and claps. The plane was
inching along under wispy clouds like a gekko walking on the
ceiling. Luz pulled the red blanket up over her head. But the
voice of the stewardess was sufficiently commanding to convince anyone ticketed to Cairo that failure to disembark there
would lead to being hurled into the sea from 35,000 feet.
Reluctantly, Luz tossed aside the blanket and took the carry-
on bag Hwan was handing her. She ran a brush through her
unruly hair before donning an elaborately embroidered black
bullfighter's jacket. The aircraft touched down smoothly and a
great cheer arose from the Arab passengers. The plane slowed
as the engines fired in reverse thrust. Luz unfastened her seat
belt and reached inside her shoulder bag for her passport.
Stuck inside its pages were the photograph and name of the
stranger who was to meet her: Mustafa.

Entering Cairo International, Luz Gracida felt as though
she were in a very male space. Under the flickering flare of
single florescent lights, three uniformed soldiers cursed a
mob of Egyptian workers returning home from Libya in their
unwashed striped *galabiahs*, urging them to form lines and
proceed through the formalities in an orderly fashion. Un-
heeding and moving like slugs, they bumped into and off each
other, making it a long time before anyone got through immigration. Luz collected her suitcase at the rotary pickup and
cleared customs without incident. A long corridor led her out
into the night where she slowed her pace to pick her way
carefully through a horde of tour guides and hotel drivers
displaying cardboard signs filled with names: Thompson, Pe-
trocini, el-Guindi, Ben Ezer. She paused for a long time, her
eyes searching the signs for her own name, but it was not
there. Apparently, she'd been stood up.

Through the sliding glass door Luz stepped into the mid-
September warmth outside the terminal. A southern wind
blew strong across the asphalt, carrying with it a sharp odor of
high-octane fuel. A young urchin almost knocked her off

balance with his zeal to carry her bag. "Hey, *bandito!*" Luz pretended outrage. "Not so fast."

After her Boston Irish companion, as he now was, came up behind her and gave the boy several *baksheesh* coins, Luz regained both her footing and full custody of her bag and continued to the taxi stand. There she stopped. Onto the pavement beside her rolled a huge baggage cart with 12 bags, big ones, and countless smaller ones. Then appeared an ample Egyptian lady of regal bearing almost entirely enshrouded in mink—mink enough to carpet a room. Diamonds glittered on her plump fingers. A Lincoln Continental drove up and quickly took possession of Madame and all the luggage. Then it roared off, leaving Luz standing on the curb enveloped in exhaust fumes and nursing resentful notions of joining the Socialist International.

The few hundred passengers from TWA and Tunis Air had swollen in number from other arriving flights during the brief period it had taken Gracida to get through the terminal, many of them carrying huge cartons secured in twine, filled with goodies obtained in European shops and supermarkets. By coincidence, she and ex-Congressman Joe Dooley were staying at the same hotel—the New Shepheard's—and Luz, light-heartedly, asked Dooley if he would care to share a ride into town. Someone was supposed to meet her, but if he didn't show, they could split a taxi fare.

Dooley wore a Russian-style synthetic fur hat with the side flaps swinging gently in the breeze, making him look like a World War II bomber pilot. He knew exactly where he'd like to go, to some place that served up cold drinks and hot hostesses. You can ask a taxi driver for directions, but you can't admit as much to a nice young lady who was obviously educated by nuns. Joe's powers of invention had dulled, however, and he blurted out, "The trouble with the New Shepheard's is they don't allow you to have booze or dames in your room. Guess I could get a couple here."

Leaving his bag in her safekeeping, Joe went off to buy two bottles of beer, and while Luz waited she noticed two men engaged in quiet conversation. They seemed to be assembled out of an all-purpose Mediterranean ethnic kit: dark, glowing brown-black eyes, deeply tanned skin, and both yelling at the top of their lungs, using parallel hand gestures. The one with a lilac swashbuckler shirt unbuttoned to midribs had been on her flight from Madrid to Roma. He had brooding eyes and unruly black locks, several of them spilling across his forehead. His jaw was twice too long for his face and off-center, as though his mother had once let her flatiron slip and broke it, but mostly Luz remembered him because she had thought it highly unusual for a Latin to turn up his nose at the wine, then go for hours without saying a word to anyone, not even making moon eyes at the dishwater blond stewardess. He was staring at her now in a friendly fashion, his dark brows highly arched, but she felt uneasy. What did he want? Mystified, she clutched her bag close against her thigh and tried to determine the length of the taxi line.

Instead, on the far side of the parking lot, she glimpsed a bright yellow Fiat 126 as it scurried along the perimeter on its way to almost running over Dooley as he sprinted to the curb. A moment later it screeched to a stop in front of her. The passenger door flicked open and a slender young man jumped out. He wore rubber thongs, white cotton pants, and a blue cotton shirt that made him look like a Greek fisherman. He bore a vague resemblance to the man in the photograph as he skimmed toward her, airily as a bubble. "Welcome to Cairo, Miss Gracida," he greeted in a blunt, serviceable English that came out in a rumble, pitching her bag into the seat he'd just vacated. He opened the back door and boldly ordered, "Get in."

"Nice," Luz commented admiringly of the painting on the side of the Fiat—a pyramid standing against the inflamed backdrop of a desert-sunset—before she motioned Joe to crawl in back first. He didn't want to, but Luz insisted and he finally gave in. Lowering herself into the back seat, she said to their rescuer, "This is very kind of you to pick us up, Mustafa."

"My name is Khalid," he corrected, leaving Luz to wonder if that was his first or last name. He didn't give her time to ask. Waving his hand at the driver, he introduced, "Talaat, my cousin who owns Sun Tours. Actually we are both better

looking than Mustafa, who is 17-months older than me, my
closest cousin in age and a good friend. He wanted to fetch
you himself, but he is tied up." Khalid had a strong, guttural
voice, a face lean and fine boned. He was hanging over the
back seat, beaming.

Luz smiled at his manner. "That's all right. Mustafa's being
my guide for this week was arranged by an old college classmate by the name of Ali Salah. Do you know him?" When
Khalid didn't answer, she assumed he did not. "You see," she
went on to explain, answering Khalid's unasked question, "I'm
here to cover the anniversary of the October war of 1973, the
festivities and the parade."

There was an aura of aggrieved common sense about Khalid
as he repeated, "You are going to the parade?"

"Yes," Luz nodded. "The big one on the Sixth of October."

"Ah, well, that parade ought to be a can't miss proposition
but believe me," Khalid said firmly in the here-are-the-facts-
take-'em-or-leave-'em manner he brought to almost everything, "you can miss it and with a happy heart. Actually, the
biggest parade we have takes place in Alex during the summer
months. It is made up entirely of the sons and daughters and
grandchildren and great-grandchildren of King Ibn Saud."

Talaat winced, but Khalid laughed heartily, delighted with
his sally. He continued to hang over the seat studying Luz.
His genial mask dropped for a more calculating expression.
There was no doubt about it; her guide was weighing her as
carefully as a goldsmith.

When he discovered that Gracida was a reporter, Dooley
admitted, "I don't read the damn papers anymore. Which one
do you write for?" Luz told him *El Fronterizo* and *Hoy.* "I'll
read them," he promised, popping the cap on a brown bottle
of Stella beer. He tried to pass it over to the Egyptians, who
refused. Luz thought it most unlikely Dooley would ever read
the newspapers for which she wrote, since they were in
Spanish. After a few moments of silent rumination, Joe added
sourly, "That is, if they aren't your usual left wing rags."

Amazement showed on Luz's caramel face. "Do I look like a
leftist?"

Up in front, Talaat smiled, his squirrel eyes bright. "You are lovely, whatever your politics," he praised. His mellow voice came across warmly, but in thickly-accented English, creating a need on Luz's part to pay close attention. The 40-year-old native of Luxor had the grace of a Southern gentleman, dark good looks—and best of all, he was a cautious driver. As Talaat pressed down on the gas pedal, the soft-sterned Fiat lurched forward on its burdened rear springs, groaning under the weight of the bags and bodies.

Lulled by the hum of the engine, Luz nestled into her seat and gave herself over to the swaying motion of the car. She thought back to the unlikely series of events that had brought her here, of the University of California at Santa Cruz and of an intense man of 20 with ice-blue eyes, a compact yet imposing build, a goatee, and the name of Ali Salah. Luz had been walking along the beach the day after his live-in girlfriend had moved out on him. In a grand, romantic gesture typical of someone who had spent his adolescence overdosing on Arabic poetry, Ali loaded his pockets with sea shells and threw himself into the pounding surf. Luz dived in, fully clothed, to save him from the waves; and, although sparks didn't fly between them at their first sea-soaked meeting, Luz was attracted to him.

Ali was leprechaunish, intelligent, macho, crazy, and Egyptian, which allowed Luz to look at him across the glamorous abyss of the exotic. He was an extraordinary man in many ways. Fresh out of his A level exams, he had arrived in California in 1972 with four dollars and twenty-nine cents in his pocket and an obsessive dream nurtured by the comfortable modernity that he had glimpsed in American films. Ali, one of thirteen children of a mechanic in Assyut, had found his way to a 76-year-old English lady's inspirational knee, but despite the influence of Hollywood, he was so deficient in the basics of English that his benefactress had to work long and hard to lift him to a competent level. The dream Ali had inherited from his movie-going youth was to create a world where even the poorest could share in the good things: a nice house with books on the shelves, food stocked in the pantry, and electrical appliances everywhere you looked. "My dreams for my country?" Ali used to ask rhetorically. "Oh God, Luz, sometimes I hate to wake up."

The foreign student scene was full of strange characters and Luz had laid hold of an epic one in Ali Salah. They would sit together with their friends in the Student Union while Jerry Lee Lewis' full-throated celebrations fell in a torrent from the loudspeakers—Jerry Lee and Ali roaring out in unison, "A Whole Lot of Shaking Going On," and Ali wearing an old Army jacket, smoking incessantly, and pounding away madly on the table top with plastic spoons. It was like watching high blood pressure. He could be an earnest lunch pail sort of a guy, a budding geologist bouncing around the hills in a beat-up Nash Rambler with a pick and shovel, baloney sandwiches, and Kool-aid until the night fell, and then he'd shed his shell of propriety to reveal the zany personality of an Eastern Chevey Chase: a voluptuous eater of pork paprika and crab salad, a compulsive womanizer, a maverick free-spirit who wore green socks and look-at-me pink patterned ties. He shunned the other Muslims on campus because they came on as shy and uptight, and they were always throwing up the weight of a dead Islamic past to him.

Later, despite their many intimate moments, Luz realized she had never gotten to know Ali. His feelings about anything and anyone were never full blown and easy to recognize. Obviously, he was some kind of a nationalist, but she never had the slightest idea of what he planned beyond "shaking things up, getting people angry." "Egyptians," he claimed, "weren't angry yet. I think they are without hope. When you are really in despair, truly in despair, even anger is an impossibility."

Once, pressing her head into his muscular shoulder where she whiffed deeply of chili pepper, Luz ventured, "Life isn't like the movies, Ali. It's a lot messier and complicated. You can sting the old order once or twice, but sting it a third time and it might crush you like a mosquito."

Ali had refused to accept this. He would tilt at windmills because someone had to tilt at them. Caught up in the sweet euphoria of the moment, Luz had told him, "You're my kind of man, Don Quixote." Then she'd lifted her head off his chest to gaze into lively, yet unrevealing eyes. Over their mattress on the floor hung two huge picture, one of Nasser in uniform, the other of Bob Dylan with psychedelic hair. Both were Ali Salah's heroes.

Ali had buried his head further into the pillow, but their faces were still close. "What kind of man is that, *habibti*?" he asked.

Luz had clutched him hard, then released him. "Romantic but temporary," she'd replied with the air of someone who has drawn a line for her career and plans to stay on it. Ali went to the English dictionary and found out that romantic means, "Not grounded in reality." He insisted he wasn't a romantic and they got into a fight; then they made love passionately and afterwards fought some more—a familiar cycle.

It was Ali who had started Luz on her way to learning his mother tongue, and it was a working knowledge of the language that had brought this assignment in Egypt her way. Now, she peered closely at Talaat's reflection in the rear view mirror. He had the same deep-set blue eyes and wide mouth of Ali Salah, and it was startling to see so much of Ali's face in his.

3

The flag was limp. The sun beat down and the damp air from the Nile was rising. Cairo was languishing like a main sail in a calm. The Consular officers and secretaries, the entire staff of the American Embassy, headed home where the martinis were dry and the domestic concerns bore no shadow of international crisis. Two stories above the parking lot, considering an editorial in the semi-governmental Egyptian newspaper *Al-Gomhouriya*, sat a man in what appeared to be a semi-official American uniform: gray slacks, rumpled blue shirt, a loosely-knotted gray striped tie, and black oxford shoes. Of medium height and build, with sandy hair and a silky moustache he kept tugging at, deep lines around his eyes, and a worried forehead, he was in many ways a classic case for a textbook on the Foreign Service Officer or, if you hoke it up a bit, a novel of foreign intrigue. A mid-career Arabist, not very high in the grand scale of things in the State Department, he had spent ten years amassing an encyclopedic knowledge of the nitty-gritty of the Middle East and America's policy herein. His reports on a host country were not only filled to the brim with useful detail, but as entertaining as any Graham Greene ever sent to Whitehall from his African post. Yet it was unlikely that anyone could pick him out in a crowd.

The quintessential, faceless bureaucrat was Political Officer Leonard Berg, and sometime in the next two days he had to churn out a report that might make or break his career. Apparently, he had caught Secretary Alexander Haig's eye with his downbeat forecasting. According to the Ambassador, who never read anything his staff wrote, but merely pushed reports upward through the bureaucratic maze—thus leaving him free to pussyfoot around contentious matters of which he had no knowledge—Haig had hit the roof when he saw one of Berg's depressing reports and he called demanding clarification. From behind his desk—a surface laden with the latest copy of the radical Arabic journal *Rose 'al-Yusuf, Ma'ariv* in Hebrew, pads of yellow legal paper, memos, cables, letters, a pack of Life Savers, a coffee mug and a warmer, and a dozen black ballpoint pens—Berg tiredly cupped his chin in his hand and squinted at the photograph of Haig. The more Leonard squinted, the more he felt as if he were being readied for a firing squad.

"I hate to be the sugar in your gas tank, General Bonehead," he told the Secretary of State's pugnacious likeness. "And please understand, I'm not writing any attacks on anyone. It's just they picked me, a nebbish, to break the news—good or bad. *Nu*, a witness who gives evidence? I didn't think it would get me straight to heaven,"—his voice filled with mock-piety as he leaned back in his swivel chair—"but I didn't think it would get me canned, either."

Berg glared at the photograph as though in confrontation with General Determination himself. The man had wanted to become President. When he didn't get it, he tightened his crampons and started stomping all over the world's lesser peaks. Leonard spoke wearily above the mass of paperwork that lay strewn across his desk. "You know, Al, it's damn frustrating sometimes to talk to people about this situation. Even the CIA types who say everything's coming up roses admit that it helps their digestion to believe that. I gotta tell ya, Al, your friend Ronald Reagan is engaging in the worst example of fantasy that I've ever seen in a President since Nixon pinned all his hopes on the Shah. I'm not sure he'll ever face reality. Phew, color blindness, that's the trouble. The only colors you bats can see are red and black. But not Islamic green."

"Sorry to barge in on you, Len, but tell me, is this conversation about art or optics?" Though the voice was hushed, Leonard knew it was Ambassador Roland Tucker. Berg was visibly startled by his sudden, unannounced presence in the doorway. Roland Tucker's slate gray eyes narrowed when he saw Berg was alone. "Talking to yourself, huh, Lenny? That's a mighty bad sign."

Berg hesitated, embarrassed. Then he pounced on the portable recorder on his desk, jabbing at the buttons as if to stop the tape. "Just making some notes," he managed to say thickly.

Tucker's eyes blasted into Leonard. "Boy, aren't we jumpy today."

Leonard smiled at the Ambassador, a man of grizzled mien and snowy mane, with a tuberous nose and a voice full of sheared metal and groaned italics. Leonard's hazel eyes became welcoming as he said, "What can I do for you, sir?"

Tucker sat down, moving his right leg with difficulty. Arthritis was setting in. Looking at his Political Officer, the Ambassador couldn't help feeling a bit of envy. Lenny had an extravagance of what Tucker was so amazingly feeling the lack of: promise. Len was in his mid-30s, on the upward trajectory of his career, and oh so serious, while Tucker was 59—or was it 60?—and burned out. The Ambassador began with a broad smile of camaraderie. "You can do us both a favor by knocking off right now. Those bags under your bloodshot eyes make you look like something washed ashore by Hurricane Dorcas. Apparently the poster I gave you hasn't done any good"—he pointed to the sign on the far wall that said, Angels Fly Because They Take Themselves Lightly. He was talking to Leonard in a cajoling voice, as one might to a recalcitrant child. "I see that you're still without a terminal at your desk."

Tucker's impenetrable self-assurance could make him an intimidating presence, but Berg brushed the remark aside with his best stick-in-the-mud tone. "I know you're trying to be helpful, sir, but take it from me. A pencil is better than a computer. You can stir your coffee with it and scratch your back. You can chew on it instead of your nails or twist a tourniquet with it in case we get attacked, like we did in Islamabad."

Tucker stared at Berg with a kind of weary disgust. "Holy Mackerel, you are as cheery as Typhoid Mary."

The comment was faintly accusatory, but Leonard took no offense—wasn't, in fact, listening. He was scavenging through the litter on his desk, muttering, "Come to Papa," at some unseen document or cable.

The Ambassador was as mentally whipped as everyone in the Mission, but he'd be damned if he'd show it. He raised his voice, his mouth twitching. "Hear me well, Cassandra, the last thing I need in my life at this point is your doomsday scenarios. Spare me the gloomy portents. Cheerless forecasting has a way of becoming a self-fulfilling prophecy. You tell people the Miami Dolphins aren't going to the Superbowl this year and what happens? The fans quit going out to the stadium to cheer them on, the players get depressed and start losing games."

Berg glanced up at the Ambassador, wrinkled his brow and pretended to weigh the matter. The political officer was pushing hard for a more enlightened policy, and he had no intention of changing his reports, even for the treacle-besotted homespun philosopher/jock in front of him. Scooping up the paperwork he'd take home with him tonight, he replied with as little deference as he dared, "Are you making a point, sir?"

"I seem to be trying and failing." Tucker rose from the chair in a state of acute frustration and went over to the window. He stared out into the garden toward two huge trees from which a faint saffron twilight seemed to emanate, and willed the tension in his neck and back to dissolve. "Half the staff is out with the flu," he complained, ticking off his woes on his short, stubby fingers. "And the other half isn't back from home leave. I feel like the Dutch Boy with his finger in the dike. And that's just the job. On the domestic front, Paulette's going through a miserable menopause. Son Jim's been expelled from St. John's for selling marijuana on campus, and daughter Jackie, the Honor Roll student at Sacred Heart, is pregnant—by her Medieval history professor, she claims. I wouldn't think anything of it, only the father is a Father."

Leonard snapped his briefcase shut. "You mean he's got other children?" he said, preparing to be amused, for Tucker only referred to the Catholic Church for the purpose of entertainment. Years ago his wife had made her acceptance of his

marriage proposal conditioned on his conversion, and he'd
been getting even ever since.

"No." Tucker sucked in his cheeks and it sounded like water
emptying out of the tub. "He is a Jesuit priest."

Berg laughed heartily as he took his blue jacket down from
a hook. Flanked by the Ambassador, he headed for the lobby,
their footsteps echoing through the marble corridors. Tucker
was saying, "Worse yet, this Jesuit Romeo who seduced my
daughter has written a book about how we blundered into the
Southeast Asian quagmire. The reason for the Vietnam war,
he says, was because Cardinal Spellman was gay. Spelly had to
show us he had the biggest balls in town."

"Well, it's a theory," said Leonard, laughing.

"You think you've got worries?" Unstated, but implied by
Tucker's focused glare, was, Unless you've got a wacky Jesuit
priest seducing your daughter, Lenny, shut up.

Berg had worked for six different envoys, and he particulary
liked Roland Tucker. So what if he sometimes showed up in
mismatched plaids and wide ties. Let's just say he doesn't read
Gentleman's Quarterly. Along with his substantial build, he
had a ready sense of humor and laugh lines that belied his
claim to being incredibly sober-sided. A good-natured soul,
Tucker was well-liked by the equally good-natured Egyptians.
And he was certainly head and shoulders above his predeces-
sor Nedham Lewis, a New Englander with a confrontational
disposition. Not for nothing did his staff call Lewis "The Nazi"
behind his back. When you heard Lewis' footsteps coming up
the stairs, slashing his jodhpurs with his rawhide whip and
calling for his Doberman Pincers, you knew what to expect!

Now, Berg asked Tucker if he wanted them to reply to an
article critical of Carter and Camp David in last week's issue of
Journal d'Egypte. Tucker waved his hand and turned his head
away, brushing the question aside like a gnat. "Joni should
probably do it," Berg suggested modestly. "Her French is
better than mine."

"Nonsense," Tucker boomed as he patted his back affectionately. "Your French is as good as Mitterand's."

As far as language ratings went, Tucker had a 4/4 in German
and a 3/3 in Dutch, but he couldn't order soup du jour from a

French menu if his life depended on it. Leonard rubbed his blond moustache anxiously. "You didn't send in my last cable. That's the only reason you're flattering me, is it not?"

Leonard was absolutely correct, but Tucker denied it indignantly. "We could make a fine team, Lenny. You lie and I'll swear to it."

Leonard heard himself exclaiming, "Three hours I spent on that cable, and it ends up *bubkes*, beans,"—with a decided edge in his voice.

Tucker assured Berg his words had been well-chosen. "I want to commend you for your insightfulness."

They came suddenly to a standstill. The heavy doors of the Embassy were locked. Berg motioned to a black Marine Guard standing stiffly inside a glassed-in cubicle, who reached under the counter and pressed a hidden switch. The doors hissed open.

"Thanks." Berg's mouth was drawn to one side, giving a knife-like crease to his cheek. Tucker felt his own forehead puckering. What was happening to the previously unflappable, impassive, often Sphinx-like Political Officer? Up until very recently, Tucker had been glad to have Lenny on the scene, short stopping the ground balls with the bad hops, but lately Len often seemed trigger-happy and short-tempered, less patient than in the past, less fun to be with. He seemed like a man throwing caution to the wind. Was he about to ask for a transfer? If he didn't pull up his socks before the next rating period, Tucker would be forced to describe him as a brilliant young man whose sterling qualities were presently obscured by the state of his emotions, and that he didn't want to do. He liked Len too much to damage him so professionally that he'd end up sharpening pencils in Ouagadougou.

Forcing brightness into his voice, Tucker lectured, "Criticism can try the soul—if you let it." The Ambassador knew that getting things accomplished in Cairo's high-stakes game of international diplomacy took more than caning editors, arm-wrestling reporters, and shouting across a conference table. "Forget the article, Len, and fuck the critics. They pass like the wind, so why should we spend our time defensively addressing these attacks, answering back, denying? Cairo is

Cairo; its cafes, tea stalls, and parlors pump out their day's supply of gossip, and that is never going to change. Such goddamn nitpicking! So what if in the heat of battle we sometimes forget to brush our teeth? We let the pissant opposition gain control of the debate when we keep saying Sadat is not an outcast, not unpopular, not a traitor, not a crook."

"Took the words right out of my mouth," Leonard began, but Tucker broke in over his words and said, "Open up and I'll put 'em back."

When Berg frowned uneasily, Tucker put his arm around his shoulders with the elaborate informality that older men use with their juniors. "Camp David," Tucker sighed; the playfulness was gone from his voice. "I used to say those words to help me fall asleep at night. Camp David—it worked better than a glass of brandy. But now I'm not sleeping so well. And I think you're to blame, Len. Your appetite for gloom and doom verges on the insatiable."

Leonard was about to say something, but Tucker rolled right on. "So I keep asking myself, is Len giving me objective reality, or is he down in the dumps? Be honest with me now, are you happy?"

Leonard flushed darkly, ready to object to being put on the couch like a Soviet dissident who opposes government policy. But he grinned as he admitted that he could be relatively happy if he didn't lose his mind and get married again. "Sane?" Tucker moved along, touching Lenny's back. He seemed to force his voice to be less concerned.

"Basically." What Leonard said next seemed to confirm that opinion. "I can still dress myself and I don't froth at the mouth."

Tucker stumbled on a loose tile and found himself holding on to Lenny's arm again. "Optimistic?" he asked, softening his voice even more.

Berg laughed, a bitter, scatter gun laugh.

Tucker looked pensive. Perhaps the times did warrant some alarm sounding, and certainly there were other analysts in the various European legations who were to be heard decrying Sadat's growing in-country unpopularity. Just the other night at an intimate dinner party in the British Residence, the First

Secretary had offered the observation that a bunch of resentful chickens are apt to come home to roost—and on Anwar's dead body, they hope. And among the Egyptians themselves, the rosy-eyed optimism of 1977 had evaporated, and the faces of certain top officials were marked by the strain of showing a confidence they no longer felt. Friends found themselves at loggerheads with one another. Family members started feuding during the big midday meal. Arguments now flared up at the cocktails parties diplomats attended. But the politics here were nowhere as wild as in Lebanon or Syria or Iraq, Arab countries with permanent parking places in the Twilight Zone. There, they kill each other. Thank God, that's not the Egyptian way.

The Ambassador's driver was posed next to the shiny custom-built limousine, its windows smoked to shield its occupants from onlookers. Tucker glanced down at his gold Piaget watch, thin as a communion wafer, and found that it was nearly seven o'clock. He barely had forty minutes to make his appointment with the Finance Minister. But he listened while Berg complained that the home office is afflicted with some misconceived notion that our favorite Egyptian is loved by his people. "I'll eat petunias if that's true," Leonard said rapidly. "There are so many problems here that you can't live to tell them all. And what's dangerous is the Egyptians think Sadat does not see them. They think he is blind and corrupt and dictatorial, and they do not appreciate his outspoken wife, their cosmopolitan lifestyle, their abiding affection for the mega-rich."

"Excuse me for intruding," said Tucker, reaching into a Berg pause, "but it seems timely to point out at this juncture that Mrs. Sadat is one progressive-minded individual. Yes, she is. If only this country had a million more just like her."

"If?" Leonard repeated deliberately but without malice. "If my sister had a moustache would she be my brother?"

They were speaking now in overlapping monologues—a tense, passionate, but disconnected description of a land not their own. Two photographers with the same camera, but entirely different snapshots of the same object. "I won't debate the accuracy of these charges," Leonard continued as if

Tucker hadn't spoken. "What's notable here, sir, is that Washington appears to be stunned by them. Responses to our cables all have this curious undertone of surprise and shock. Fairy tales they want? My reports are meant to alert them to a potential catastrophe." He paused to see if the Ambassador had appreciated the importance of this remark. There was no sign of comprehension, only the anger accorded a bearer of bad news. "So my reports don't comfort? I'm serious."

"I know, Len," said Tucker with a Doctor Kildaire croon. "We're trying to get you something for that."

They were looking into each other's eyes, descending the steps. They almost bumped into the Head of the Science and Technology Section who was demonstrating his backhand to the AID Director, but he sidestepped them with a graceful movement. Tucker opened his mouth to speak, but took in a breath instead. Lenny's rantings, no matter how well-intentioned, were wearing thin. Tucker smiled emptily and said, "I find it difficult to go along with your assessment, Len. Not that I'm dismissing what you're saying. I plan to take it up with Haig when I go into Washington next month. You might not wish to hear Al's views; they aren't much in accord with your own. But let me remind you that he does have input from other sources, the CIA, the National Security Council, the Pentagon. He knows more than we do, so why should we try and second-guess him?"

Leonard recognized the signal of dismissal, but he plunged on, "Haig is the only person I know who hasn't changed a thought in his head on the Middle East in 45 years, and now—God help us!—he's running the show. Does Washington really believe that once we anoint some guy and send out papal emissaries like Shelley Winters and Charlton Heston to sing his praises, the peasants will automatically genuflect? Frank Sinatra's dropping in. Next thing you know, he's standing in front of a pyramid crooning 'Jihan with the laughing eyes,' and you got slugging matches with the *paparazzi* at the airport. You call this a peace process?"

Tucker almost laughed at the idea, but he made a stop signal and found himself saying somewhat sententiously, "Hold it, my friend. Even if you assume, which I don't, that

Sadat is not the best there is, he is certainly the best of what we have to choose from. Without him this place would collapse into chaos and communism. And I don't see any rejection locally. Sadat is acceptable to most people here, even if he doesn't have star potential, and they'll never love him the way they did Nasser"—he said the name with contempt. "Polishing dull acceptance into something brighter is probably impossible, Len, but it's not a Somoza situation, far from it. So will you stop looking for Sandinistas on the horizon?"

The Ambassador's display of optimism was to be expected, of course, but Berg thought Tuck had just given new meaning to the word monotone. He'd sped through it so fast that you couldn't help but wonder if the envoy was being paid to run the Mission in words per second. Did he really believe what he was saying?

Mrs. Tucker appeared and came to rest beside her husband, who took her arm. Roland Tucker was moving away, walking confidently to his waiting limo. A smile that bordered on smugness curled on one side of his mouth. Nothing shakes you, you son of a gun, Berg cursed silently as he followed behind the Ambassador. The whole frigging Embassy could burn down around our ears, and you'd report it as a marshmallow roast.

"We," Berg pressed on, employing the editorial pronoun, "seem rather oblivious to the obvious: before Camp David, Egypt was a poverty-stricken, desperately overcrowded country that saw itself as the hub of the Arab World and a first rank supporter of the Palestinian cause. Three years and several billion dollars later this country is still faced with a multiplicity of problems that remain unsolved. Sadat hasn't halted the national disintegration and the bulk of the people are still desperately poor, still multiplying like gerbils, and they're still fervently pro-Palestinian. For the student population, especially, what's happened with Begin seems an embarrassment, a blot on their heritage that's rubbed in nightly on the news. Be a campus activist who mentions The Post-Sadat Era and you get a standing ovation. They don't stand on their feet, they stand on their chairs and whoop and holler."

The Ambassador nodded acknowledgement of facts that

were too well know to him and responded in the same reasonable tone as Berg's. "The Egyptians are super-fine people, and
they're not without resources: oil, cotton, the Canal, ancient
monuments the whole world would give its right arm to see.
Eventually, they're going to make it. And if they don't, well,
they'll endure. They've been doing it on the banks of the Nile
for as many years as the human race has been around. Their
peace of mind is tried daily by hunger and hardships that are
mercifully beyond our imaginings, and yet they endure. A
very fatalistic people. I'm convinced Sadat will rule as long as
Hussein. That little King, that little twerp, he's off his rocker.
But eventually he's going to dump the Palestinians and sign a
peace treaty, take my word for it. And Sadat will be welcomed
back into the Arab League with open arms."

It would have been the perfect last word, but Berg wasn't
finished. "Risky assumptions," he said. He was standing with
his arms akimbo, looking as fierce and belligerent as the
students he'd been describing. "Eventually, sir, is not today."

"Enough!" Tucker made the hard clicking sound that signaled the end of his conversations. "The way we're arguing we
sound worse than a married couple. You're a trip, Lenny, and I
love you dearly, but enough, go home. And when you get
there, the first thing you do is tell your cook to have his nubile
daughter take a bath; then send her to your bed. It's just what
you need."

Gottenyu, thought Leonard bitterly as he tilted his head
and answered with a sigh that left him deflated, "You're probably right, sir."

Tucker was enormously pleased. "If you and your pencil
don't come in tomorrow, Lenny, you won't be missed. Sepa-
rating fact from fiction is a cottage industry in this country."

After that cryptic remark, Tucker turned his attention to his
wife, and Leonard had no opportunity to open up the subject
of his indispensability for it was at this point that he was
greeted by a salvo of hellos. The Economic Officer and his
Egyptian secretary had just come out the door. They paused
to invite him to join them at the Marine House for Happy
Hour. "Let's have a gin or three," they proposed. Leonard
could've used four or five, but he said no thanks and went on
his way.

4

Luz Gracida glanced down at her watch, wondering just how long it would take Sun Tours to reach the hotel. From what she could see in the twilight, arriving in Egypt might have been arriving in Houston: warehouses, oil storage tanks, and all the signs for Agfa film, Air France, and Marlboro cigarettes in English. Khalid leaned over the back seat to ask Luz about her agenda. Luz told him she'd have interviews starting immediately after breakfast each day, then for an hour or so before lunch she'd like to be taken to visit a college, to see what was on the students' minds. After lunch, more of the same. She asked him if he could wrangle an invitation to Mrs. Sadat's tea party on Tuesday; she didn't relish the idea of standing outside the doors, cooling her heels while waiting for VIPs to come out, and running up to them with a question shouted out over the usual pandemonium.

Khalid told the Chicana to leave everything in his hands. He was a study in long-term tenacity, having helped every journalist who had set foot in this town for the past 200 years, bagging all the biggies, the Cabinet ministers, the military's general staff, and opposition politicians, even if he had to camp outside their compounds or prostrate himself before their drivers. To determine precisely how to get to them he had developed a network of sources that a Mossad agent would give his right arm for. Luz sought more assurance. "Then I will get to talk with Mrs. Sadat?"

"That," Khalid said, rubbing his thumb and the side of his first finger together in the universal sign language for a bribe being passed, "has already been arranged."

34

Talaat seemed in a bad mood, but Luz hardly noticed. Her
mind was on what she could pack in during these next two
weeks. The radio was on; Sadat was speaking to some uniden-
tified gathering whose only response was silence. Talaat finally
said something that attracted Luz's attention by making the
reason for his sullen silence clear.

"Damn speeches!" he barked. "This is another area of
wretched excess. They come at you like vitamins, one a day.
Friday there were three. That is what I hate about television.
When that miserable tub of lard Farouk was not hurling bolts
of sonorous words from his balcony, we didn't hear him. But
the bloody cameras and microphones follow Sadat from the
palace to the village and back a hundred times every year."
Talaat swerved when a Pontiac almost sideswiped him. He
flashed a well-deserved but obscene gesture at a woman in a
cashmere coat—who turned out to be a long-haired young
male.

A huge flying beetle committed a splattering suicide on the
Fiat's windshield. Talaat swore under his breath, then pressed
a button on the dashboard. The wipers began a sluggish
march across the glass. He lashed out at Sadat once more, this
time in pungent Arabic. Luz was nodding, but it was hard to
tell whether she was really interested. Talaat rushed on, too
caught up in his own anger to care if her interest was genuine.
After all, she was to be used for their holy purposes rather
than swayed to their point of view.

A fervent admirer of Sadat's, Luz was thrown off balance by
Talaat's comments. Like a tidal wave suddenly intruding in on
a beach party, they caught her in the gut and drew her up
straight. What she learned was that the President was rarely
in the city these days. Sadat, by all accounts a very brave man,
had sensed the cold stare of the Cairenes and was spending
his time in more congenial surroundings.

"He had a fairly high beginning in classical *fus'ha*," Talaat
was saying about the President's televised speech, "but then
he stumbled into street Arabic and stayed there croaking and
bleating about how we are a nation of science and religion,
Nahnu dawlat el 'Ilm wal Din. We will stay out front in the
world's technological race and still hold fast to our traditional

values. There was much talk about eternity, which, at four hours, made his speech a perfect marriage of form and content."

They were in the center of Heliopolis and the darkness was engulfing them. In the rear view mirror Talaat caught sight of a pair of blue headlights approaching at high speed. He moved to the right hand lane as the vehicle closed in on them. Talaat always had a calm presence despite the dangers of their clandestine work, but it deserted him now. In the glare of the street lamps he could see that it was a 1955 Chevy. At almost the same instant, he saw a barrel protrude from the side window; his skin pricked at the glint off a 6mm deer rifle. A blast shattered the pane around him into a million needles of glass. He felt faint, as if his bones had turned into noodles.

The Fiat lurched onto the shoulder, its smooth tires unable to hold on the gravel, and Talaat heard Luz scream, "*Madre mia!*" She grabbed Joe in panic, digging her nails deep into his arm, and Khalid thrust his fist into his mouth to keep his own cry in check. Luz pulled Joe away from the window and craned her neck to the side so that she could see out. The Fiat and the Chevy were both moving now at a dangerous speed, shaving corners with the screech of tortured tires, overtaking vehicle after vehicle, whose occupants were left gawking at a sight straight out of a cops-and-robbers movie. Khalid clutched at the edge of his seat with white-knuckles, watching the flickering needle of the speedometer with bug eyes. The world outside the car had receded into whirling darkness. The traffic slowed for a stoplight, which turned red just as they approached. Both the Fiat and the Chevy went barreling through.

Another round tore through the pyramid logo on the side of Talaat's door. He heard the tearing of metal, then another thud beside his leg. He hunched forward and jerked the steering wheel, forcing it to the right. Unconsciously but violently, he jammed his foot on the brake. Luz was hurled to the side and struck the sharp handle with her elbow so that she almost swooned. Khalid was sent crashing into the dashboard. Peeling himself off, he turned angry, blinking eyes to Talaat and ordered him into full power. "Keep going, you fool!"

Talaat trusted Khalid's judgment more than his own. The Fiat bounced off the curb, careened to the left, then catapulted forward ahead of the Chevy. Talaat wrestled the shift stick into second and brought the taxi under control. He pressed the gas pedal to the floorboard; five seconds later he was into third, then into high. Joe gave Luz a rude tug and grunted, "Get down, girl." Then he slumped forward and spat through his teeth, "Jesus, Mary, and Joseph!"

Khalid turned gingerly in his seat and peered carefully out the back window. Glancing at Luz and Joe, he inquired, "You two okay?"

Dazed, Luz huddled half on Joe and half on the floor and tried to understand why the universe was exploding around her ears. "Yes," she replied, her voice shaky as she asked, "Who are they? What do they want?"

"Funny, I was about to ask you if they were friends of yours." Khalid smiled grimly, a deep crease between his brows.

Joe's eyes glittered as he wailed, "Not even my ex-wife would want to do this to me." He looked up and saw Luz framed against the moonlight, tension in every line of her flushed face and taut body. He reached for her arm and she turned in an instant. Joe's eyes stared from their shadowed sockets. "Faith, lass, and this tomato sauce I'm sitting in is me own blood."

Deftly, Luz tore open Joe's shirt and lifted up the material carefully. When she saw the blood gushing from deep gashes down his back, her stomach tightened. "Is he hurt?" She heard the question from the front seat and forced a reply through trembling lips, "Is there a doctor on this rocket?"

Luz took Joe's hand, dry as bark, and looked into his face. His eyebrows were arched and his mouth was open in a baffled expression. "We'll get help right away, Don Jose," she promised, "don't you worry."

Dooley suspected that she was minimizing his injuries in order to lull him into a false sense of well-being, but he didn't argue. Instead, he closed his eyes and envisioned himself sitting peacefully with his fishing pole amid a framework of birch trees by a tranquil lake full of trout.

Luz felt her hand and wiggled it tentatively: nothing broken. She ran her tongue over her teeth to make sure they were all there. But the nightmare wasn't over. The Fiat whipped between a donkey cart and a cement truck, avoiding both by a hair's breadth, then flashed by a Mercedes and missed a VW beetle by a matter of inches. "It would seem we've gotten into a spot of trouble with some people," Khalid said with tight-lipped irony as he clutched the seat.

Surely he was stoned! Luz's throat was so tight she felt she was being strangled, but she forced out one word: "Loco!"

Talaat braved a few wending side streets. The Chevy was only two car-lengths behind and again bearing down on them menacingly. The distance to the nearest protection, the Umm Ali's Fast Foods Restaurant, was 50 meters. Talaat turned for it. A few meters from safety, he was hit by a bullet. His right shoulder was blown to bits; blood gushed all over his gray sweater. His foot slipped off the accelerator and the car veered crazily. Heart beating wildly, Khalid grabbed for the wheel. Talaat's hand held it in a steel grip.

Joe groaned unexpectedly and tried to sit up. Luz shoved him back down. He shrank against the upholstery, his breath coming short. She took his beefy hand and placed it gently in hers, cooing Spanish admonitions that soothed even in their incomprehensibility. Dizzily, he fought to keep a clear head by focusing on the two tiny flames burning in the centers of her bright eyes, but the tapers blew out and everything faded into oblivion.

The bumper came to rest against a pile of brick. Talaat fell back hard against the seat, breathing laboriously. His eyes began to cloud over. He turned his head toward Khalid. For a short moment they gazed at each other. Khalid saw his right hand holding his left shoulder, the trickle of crimson between the stubby fingers. Bolting out of the car and in deepening fear, he rushed around to the driver's side, pockmarked now with bullet holes, and threw open the door. He slipped his arms behind Talaat and tugged at his body, using his own body as a counterweight. Talaat moaned softly as Khalid laid him down on the ground. Eyes shut tight against the pain, he waved Khalid closer and commanded, "Listen to me."

Khalid's heart was beating wildly. "Save your breath," he ordered, kneeling beside him.

When Talaat looked at Khalid, he was fighting to control tears. "It is too late," Talaat mumbled through a mouthful of blood. Khalid couldn't bear to hear the words and started to deny them vehemently, but Talaat stopped him with a strange warning: "Beware of Ali. He can beguile you—"

Khalid's head jerked forward, mouth open, eyes squinting. What in the hell was Talaat saying? Did he mean Ali Salah, their relative and a comrade who had proven himself capable of endurance and loyalty to the cause time and time again? Yes, it must be. What other Ali did they know? Reeling with disbelief, Khalid grabbed Talaat's hand and squeezed it hard, as if to wring an explanation out of him.

"He is a very complicated person." Talaat's voice became so low Khalid could barely hear it. "So mixed up inside," Talaat went on feebly, "pulled in different directions. We don't know him." But Khalid hardly heard him; all he could think of was the pool of blood growing wider on the ground. Drawing Talaat's hand to his lips, Khalid kissed the hard lines and rough spots that were more from hard labor than age. Talaat's brow furrowed deeply as he struggled with his thoughts and words. "Ali doesn't know himself," he whispered. He was slipping fast; red spittle bubbled at the corners of his mouth.

"Please, please, you must not leave us," Khalid begged, his lips gently brushing the salt-and-pepper eyebrows. "We need you, Talaat."

For a long moment the bent figure of Khalid knelt, looking down in anguish at the still face of his cousin, an indefatigable fighter and one of the most dedicated men in the Jamaati il-Islam. Losing the battle to hold back the tears, he buried his head in his hands.

When Joe Dooley came to a few minutes later, he couldn't remember where he was, but then slowly it came back, the Chevy, the rifle. He stretched out on the back seat of the Fiat, his back bloody and warm. He would have lifted his beer to his parched lips, but the bottle wasn't there. As he lay still, his breathing shallow, he heard Luz and Khalid arguing in the

front seat. She wanted to get to a hospital right away. Doors
were opened, then angrily slammed.

Khalid, standing outside beside Luz, took a deep breath
and appealed for sympathy. "Look, lady, I need medical attention, too. See these cuts. I got them crawling on my hands and
knees to where Talaat was lying. And see the tooth I cracked
when my head hit the dashboard." He opened his mouth a
fraction.

Luz saw only a few infinitesimal scratches on his knuckles.
His brown eyes were no longer limpid with tragedy, but alert
and guarded. In spite of the ache in his soul and his body,
Khalid forced himself to look cold and unbending and to show
little concern for Joe. His uppermost thought at the moment
was to reach Ibrahim who might well be in danger from the
gunmen in the Chevy.

"What an ignorant woman you are," he scolded Luz.
"Where have you lived that you've never heard of police who
shoot first and ask questions later?" He opened his arms and
lifted his palms up in a conciliatory gesture. When he spoke
again it was with a voice of sweet reasonableness. "You have no
idea at all what it is like to get ensnared in a police investiga-
tion here. Trust me when I say we have little choice but to
take care of this on our own. We can't go for help without
identifying ourselves as having been attacked by unknown
assailants, and that, in turn, would invite an uncertain but
unpleasant fate from authorities who who can malign and
manipulate you to their hearts content."

"But we're innocent victims," Luz flared. Sweat glistened
through her makeup.

"Makes no difference," snorted Khalid, his face as pale as
that of a man who has just passed through the eye of an
emotional storm. Luz staggered forward to lean on the hood.
She was shaking so hard that she could barely stand and
Khalid was no better. They leaned into each other. A small
knot of passersby swiftly congregated around them. For a
moment Khalid stood in silence, looking deeply and threateningly into the eyes of each who dared to join his glance;
then, turning to Luz, he said intently, "Let me tell you about
the Egyptian fox who presented himself at the Libyan frontier

one day. He was stopped and interrogated: 'Why are you leaving Egypt?' The fox explained that in Egypt these days they're putting camels in prison. 'But you're a fox,' said the Libyans. 'Yes,' the fox agreed, 'but God only knows how long it'll take them to work that out.'"

Luz responded bitterly, "They told me that you people have a real sense of humor, but Holy Mother of Christ, I had no idea how bad it is. To stand here making jokes while your *companero* lies dead, and Dooley is bleeding like a stuck pig in the back seat is—"

Khalid's eyes twitched impatiently. He stepped in front of Luz and took a menacing stance. "You are a tourist; you have nothing to fear." But his low, threatening voice said otherwise, and she realized this was not the time nor place to vent her indignation. Khalid was pointing to a pharmacy just down the street and ordering sharply, "Get bandages and whatever else you need. Tell them you are a nurse if they ask. Look cheerful," he added, using his fingers to keep his smile in place, urging her to do likewise for the pharmacist's benefit. "Remember, you are a carefree vacationer from the Spanish Sahara."

"Sure I am." Luz laughed harshly.

"Luz." Weakly, Joe called her name, and she leaned over to hear him ask, "Did they nail Talaat?" Luz blinked and looked away. I wish I were dead, said a little voice inside her head. Khalid turned once more to Luz, and, half-coaching, half-warning, he said, "Don't let them know you are an American or you will be a dead woman."

When put so succinctly, Maria Luz Gracida discovered that she didn't want to die after all. She made the sign of the cross and walked off without another word, leaving Khalid to hide Talaat's body in the trunk of the car.

5

Leonard Berg turned down Latin America Avenue, then halted uncertainly after a few paces. There was a heavy, airless feeling and the sounds of the city, the traffic jams, the river, and the people came to him clear and strong, not floating, but exploding upon him as if they had been shot from a gun. He watched a Ward bus go by preceding a rooster's tail of exhaust fumes. They were so called because the Ward Company of the U.S. had supplied them. After their mufflers fell off, the noise they made was widely referred to as the Voice of America. Like most of the buses in town, this one was threatening to burst at the seams with the pressure of people scrambling through the doorless doors and windowless windows or clinging precariously to the sides and the roof. While some foreigners might find it madcap, Berg loved it. Although upset by his fruitless exchange with the Ambassador and appalled by what Cairo had become, something of the allure which the capital had for him when he'd first come here lingered on. It was like running into an old friend again and remembering just how much you liked her, and noticing how much she has changed, and yet how little.

Everyone was going somewhere, all night long, doing something, scurrying, darting between the speeding cars and talking at the same time. Strolling along the cracked pavement with the desert welling up from below, Berg was aware of a pleasant sense of fascination with the spirit of Cairo, the historical thickness in the cityscape. You were surrounded by it and felt it stretching back. Cairo is what it was from the very beginning, a sprawling caravanserai on the edge of a sea of sandy desolation, alive with vibrant people, hot and dusty, smelling of incense, dung, musk, and glowing coals. There was about it a restless uneasiness which taunted one's senses to the verge of breathlessness.

Berg knew, of course, that there was a steady stream of activity in his own hometown of Toledo, Ohio, but Toledo was too familiar to be intriguing. Here everything was strange and mysterious, and part of the thrill of being here was related to that in a big way, to the fact that he could imagine all sort of secret messages being carried under the women's *abayas*, cryptic notes being passed to the barber or the butcher, like in The Battle of Algiers, conspirators meeting in dark basements, conniving, plotting, their faces stubbled with three days' growth and floating like oblong moons under shaggy masses of dark Trotskyite curls. "Cut it out," he chided himself. Life was not a Cecil B. DeMille spectacle; but try though he might to suppress it, there was an infuriatingly romantic streak in Leonard Berg. And sometimes, after he had been dealing too long with the prose that crossed his desk, the poetry took over.

After the light changed, Berg crossed over to the other side of the street where boxes of green bananas and avocados, yellow and red apples, and pineapples were piled high in front of a fruit store. He purchased a red apple, then ambled past a small group of Japanese tourists, heavily camera-laden behind a guide carrying a white banner. They all wore Peck and Peck cottons that suggested they had been out on the golf course until just a few hours ago. Leonard turned into Doctor Hakim's immaculately clean pharmacy. It gave off the sharp essence of a hospital ward, a spectacular mix of Dermasol, grain alcohol, and Vicks Vaporub.

Berg was surprised to hear an American voice speaking Arabic to the clerk behind the counter, asking for iodine, sterile gauze, adhesive tape, antiseptic, and tweezers to pull glass shards out of skin. She had her back to him and almost simultaneously two thoughts went through Leonard's mind. The first was that he'd heard that voice before; the second was that hers had been a strange request. Was she studying surgery at night school? When the clerk went to fill her order, she moved over to a cabinet and stood with her arms folded, gazing at an advertisement for suppositories guaranteed to shrink hemorrhoids the size of walnuts. As yet she wasn't conscious of his presence, and for several minutes Leonard soaked in the sight of her—the dishevelled frizz of black hair, the black leather Charles Jourdan boots, the throat soft as a rose petal arching from the collar of a bullfighter jacket specked with stains of—what? Real bull's blood?

At first sight, she was stunning, like a Goya model pouring wine into a gold goblet with deep red stems or some portrait hung in a Viceroy's palace. Up close, she was even more so, with coppery skin and a bee-stung mouth. Her brown eyes were large, but appeared larger still because of the smudge of fatigue surrounding them. Leonard polished the apple on his sleeve and made it shine a deep, waxy red. Could he offer it to her without seeming suggestive? He put the apple in his pocket. Seeing no gold band on her finger, Leonard decided to edge into her perimeter of vision by taking a closer look at some bottles inside the cabinet. He reached the imported medication section, the stuff that Doctor Hakim usually offered to you with the assurance it was the latest, which was synonymous in his mind with the best, and paused. She was still oblivious to the attention, lost in her own head.

Then she raised her face to him. Leonard furrowed his brow with the effort of recollection and Luz's mouth turned upward in a token smile. She was the first to break the silence. "What is this for?" she asked in a voice that rolled its r's just a little, pointing to a powerful anti-cancer drug. "People who think they've got a touch of leukemia?"

His eyes approved the wit. She was a Hispanic in the California mold, her soft and easy voice told him that, but he was struggling to remember everything—the pert and perky personality, a sunny disposition, and a rather tenacious attitude about life. But he wasn't sure. Exhausted, wracked by the emotion of Talaat's violent death and Joe's injury, Luz could have hardly appeared a copy of the optimistic creature of his memory. As the shock wore off, Luz became more aware of her injuries: a badly bruised arm, a sprained neck, a body that ached in every pore. But she forced herself not to show the pain.

"Anything you might want is available over the counter here," Leonard explained. "AMA? FDA? Forget it, this is deregulation at its finest. Get government out of people's lives and all that jazz." He laughed and his laughter was easy and exhilarating, as though he enjoyed the sensation of laughing almost as much as whatever it was that triggered it. "You're an American, aren't you? The accent seems to indicate that." Suddenly, he looked more directly at her. "Haven't we met?"

He waited for the Aha of recognition, but it didn't come. The eye contact broke as she moved away, but not before Leonard caught sight of a reddening of her high Indian cheeks. He followed a few paces. Then he stood still as abruptly as if someone had placed a hand on his chest, then flung his arms out and roared, "This is a reunion!" He realized how bold he had been. "Excuse me, but you look the spitting image of a girl I met at Columbia University at a talk given by Zalmay Khalilzad. I bumped into your table in the cafeteria, water glasses sloshed, and six of us ended up going out for *hummus* and *falafel*. For being a real klutz I got such a nice reward!"

Luz looked at him blankly, and Leonard was embarrassed by offering a joke and a compliment that hadn't succeeded in making their presence felt. Abruptly, Luz cried out in amazement, "*Madre mia!* That was 2,000 years ago, and your memory bank of faces has me on file!"

"You haven't changed a bit," Leonard went on excitedly.

"Then you must have the wrong girl." Luz tried to look exasperated, but a slow smile defeated the effort. Then her expression grew serious. "What are you, CIA?"

Leonard looked at her in astonishment. "How can you suggest that when I'm out here seeking my fortune as trumpet player in a small rock and roll band while moonlighting as the political officer at the American Embassy across the street." He shook her warmly by the hand. "Bella Berg's favorite son, Leonard Schmuel, at your service."

Luz smiled in turn and shook her head in wonderment at

the coincidence. Behind the amiable mask, she was thinking rapidly and decided it might be more prudent to withhold the facts. "Luz Gracida, tourist."

Her handshake was light and crisp at the same time, but Leonard got the sense of a calm exterior hiding a deeply troubled interior. It was the turbulence in her deep eyes that gave her away. "Well, you're back in my life," she said in a jerky and difficult voice, trying to convey the unspoken, "and it feels I'm coming down with measles for the second time."

Leonard ignored it. "It's not my normal custom to ask a girl out to dinner after only 60 seconds," he began, then in a throaty, almost sexy voice, he growled, "but you and I go back a long way, senorita, to a Lebanese cafe in Greenwich Village. When I asked you why you were so friendly, you told me your father was an army officer and you'd learned to connect immediately with people. You had to, you moved every two years. Then you and your girlfriends went back to your hotel, and I went back to mine. So much for connecting." By now, he was laughing delightedly, a musical laugh that raced up and down the scale. The cold knot of misery and fear that had gripped Luz since the Talaat's violent death began to ease, thawed in some mysterious way by this man who was saying with authority, "When shall I pick you up? And where?"

Luz looked at him but only for a second, as though she wasn't going to risk being entangled in his gaze again. "Ah, the things I do for my readers!" she said dramatically. "I've been shot at, ate rotten food, stood out in the snow and sleet and the burning sun. But I draw the line at cavorting with diplomats. You *hombres* never tell it straight."

For a moment Leonard appeared scandalized by the charge, then he shrugged, making no attempt to defend the corps. "Please don't try to put me off by saying cruel things. Besides, what if we bend the truth a little? You're smart enough to piece it together." He grinned appealingly.

Luz was tempted. "Trouble is things are a bit Raggedy Andy at the moment," she said evasively. Out on the street a car backfired, and Luz jumped as if an electric charge had passed through her. The tip of her tongue showed as she moistened her lips. "I'll give you a call at your office when things get sorted out, if that's okay."

"Here you are, Miss." The booming voice of the clerk resonated across the pharmacy as he motioned Luz to a cash register at the end of the counter. The clerk was a little man with bird-like head and shoulders, a body as tiny as his voice was big. His protruding eyes gleamed like a symptom of a kidney disease. With healthy doubt in the big voice and the bug-eyes, the clerk asked, "Are you really a nurse?"

Their eyes met and they stared at each other uneasily. Easy does it, you can manage this, Luz told herself, cutting him off by asking where's the iodine. He reached into the shelf behind him and withdrew a small dark brown bottle, which he blew on to remove the dust. He twisted his face into a smile of apology and offered, "Mercurochrome, just as good." Luz asked how much she owed. "Ten pounds, eight piastres," he replied, bagging the items.

After she had settled her bill, Leonard took the Chicana by the elbow. "I'd like to help you in any possible way, so don't hesitate to ask," he said as they moved out the door, and she looked up at him, her mouth forming a smile, but her brown eyes wary. He reached into the inside pocket of his jacket and pulled out his wallet. He extracted one of his cards and swiftly wrote on it with a slim gold pen. He handed it to her. "Here's my home phone number. Phones here work about as often as Prince Charles; so if you can't get through, leave a message at the Embassy. I'll be over in the twinkling of an eye."

Luz walked on a few steps, then turned to face him. Full, generous lips were parted in a smile to reveal glistening white teeth. "Gracias, amigo. I appreciate this." Shoving the card in her bag, she headed for the Fiat waiting at the end of the block. Suddenly, she experienced a loneliness unlike anything she had every known before.

6

"We did it," Ali croaked, pride and amazement in his voice as he embraced Mustafa at the busy terminal.

"Let's run for it!" Mustafa shouted, pulling Ali by the arm.

They encountered the usual air of frazzled disorganization on the train to Helwan as the ticket seller screamed at nonpaying passengers across an unbridgeable sea of heads and arms. No sooner had the two comrades boarded than they had to prepare to get off by pushing their way through a dense, sweating, wiggling mass of people. Ali couldn't see his shoes, but he could feel them trying desperately to keep their shine though stomped on by dozens of other feet. The corner of a briefcase cut cruelly into his back, and he felt as if he were being held hostage in a can of tightly packed chunky tuna.

Part of Ali Salah's strength, his capacity to endure, was that he forgot very little. When his immediate circumstances threatened to become unbearable, he could shut his eyes and drop back to almost any period of his life and run it through his mind like an old movie. Right now he was back in Santa Cruz, stretched out on the lawn in the front of the bandstand at a Bonnie Raitt concert. He remembered Raitt as a woman with a sinful mane of red hair, singing raw and snaky R&B songs, but he liked her social conscience, her stands against nuclear weapons and the forcible eviction of native tribesmen. Ali was profoundly grateful to the benevolent Deity who'd made him a man; but if he'd had to come into this world as a female, he'd have wanted to be born Bonnie Raitt. Then he would save the Mediterranean Ocean from death by pollution and the children in the City of the Dead from malnutrition.

48

The briefcase jabbed Ali once more and brought him back to the miserable present. He looked around him. Most of the passengers stood staring ahead blankly, slack-jawed, like sheep on their way to the slaughterhouse.

But not Mustafa. "Look, Ali," the large, ebullient man ordered, perspiring profusely. "See that beauty near the window."

Ali turned obediently, but it was difficult to know about whom he was talking. "The goddess over there," Mustafa pointed frantically with his chin at a pretty girl who looked susceptible to male attention. Her veil was worn under a sequin-studded pillbox hat and covered her hair, neck, and bosom; her long-sleeved dress was a dazzling fuchsia extending to a pair of matching high-heeled pumps. Her eyes met Mustafa's and suddenly her glum face was radiant. Mustafa, who looked inappropriately lecherous and engagingly disheveled in a opened-neck shirt and dirty sneakers, was grinning broadly, flashing a gold tooth.

Ali fixed Mustafa with a gelid stare, arched his eyebrows mockingly and said, "Didn't anyone ever tell you that the only beauties are those who don't call attention to themselves?"

"Right," Mustafa answered without feeling. He was captivated by Miss Pillbox Hat, whose gaudy outfit hardly fit the austere ideal of Muslim Sisterhood.

"You are impossible." Ali's tone was cantankerous. "You are so frothy at times you make the foam on a milk shake look heavy."

"I do?" Mustafa's brows shot up in a perfect parody of Ali's and he said accusingly, "You have insults to last all day. You are always so quick to let us know how right you are and how wrong everybody else is."

Ali tried to cut in but Mustafa wouldn't let him. He rushed on, wishing that Ali would disappear into thin air and stay there for a long time. Ali seemed so disembodied at times, like a man with no sense of his own physical reality. To top it off, he was frequently inclined to pompousness, and if you heard him holding forth on the subject of Islamic purity, you might well get the impression that, in his mind at least, the entire Faithful consisted of impious backsliders with the singular exception of Ali Muhammad Salah. Mustafa's eyes focused on Ali and his voice dropped slightly. "Well, I will have you know I did not join the group to make my getting into Paradise easier, but to bring a bit of Paradise to this earth. Your superciliousness is wasted on me."

A blush appeared on Ali's face. "So, you are a heretic as well as everything else."

Just then Mustafa's dark eyes were caught by a totally unveiled woman whose dress was cunningly contrived to show more than it revealed and he whistled, "Ali, do you see that?" He raised his clasped hands above his head and shook them in glee.

Ali looked at him more sad than surprised. He prayed to overcome Mustafa's evil because he himself had once loved women, the sight of them, the touch. Having to go without them left its scars for a long time after he had joined the Jamaat. "All for Allah and Egypt," he kept reminding himself until the need and longing faded away. Salah, the vessel of pure sexual heat who'd unsexed himself, was now asking himself, how in the world did the unrepentantly lustful Mustafa ever get into the Brotherhood when he was at such a wide variance with its ideas and ideals? Could he survive in a society that fiercely protected the image of the virtuous woman? A society, moreover, that would not allow the sexes to get disgustingly squashed together on a horrible train like this. Mustafa was too relaxed—you wished someone would light a bonfire underneath him. Yet even Ibrahim had tried and failed. Haughtily, he told Mustafa that the shirt that covered his big belly could profit from a good scrub.

"I know," Mustafa conceded, trying to placate him, but he didn't take his eyes off the doxy, and Ali's disgust gave way to a stabbing youthful memory.

Excitement for 15-year-old Ali Salah had been a childhood trip from his home in Assyut, 235 miles away to Cairo, the fairy-tale place that filled his romantic young mind so much of the time. He had gone to the zoo and up the tower on the island of Gezirah and then to the cinema. To the intense, impressionable Ali there were few delights that seemed more wonderful. For days afterwards he fantasized his seduction of

Sophia Loren. Walking down the streets of the city he had passed her face, ten times life-size, on the posters. Now, twenty years later, Cairo was the nightmare in which he and millions of others struggled to survive. But the bittersweet thoughts fled; he had other things to think about—a strike at the Satan who was doing next to nothing to save his beloved country.

"What was the plan exactly?" he asked Mustafa, who shrugged and answered, "From Ibrahim's portentous tone, I guess he will have some poor chap shoot poison arrows at Sadat from a flying carpet."

Ali imitated his sarcastic cadence. "I hope Ibrahim never finds out what a cheeky bastard you really are." Spying a vacant seat, he dove for it.

Ali was so absorbed in the idea of a unit of soldiers carrying out Mission Possible that it wasn't until they were getting off the train at the Maadi station that he remembered Mustafa mentioning a reporter that Talaat was collecting from the airport. "Where did you say the reporter is from?"

Mustafa was squinting at the crowd, moving his eyes from face to face, looking for a policeman and he didn't answer right away. When he finally gave the reporter's nationality, Ali stiffened. "Do you know her name?"

Mustafa's manner at once changed. He peered keenly at Ali for a long moment before he understood. Giving Ali a look of disgust, he said with a more militant effect than he had intended, "Well, well. Are you not cured of a fondness for the *ajaanib* women?" Getting no answer, he went on, "Yes, it is Luz Gracida."

The shock was tremendous. It overwhelmed Ali for a moment. "Luz Gracida." He said her name as though he were rolling it around in his mouth tasting it. Luz meant light in Spanish, so he had called her Noor, which meant light in Arabic. Ali narrowed his eyes suspiciously. "You were snooping around in my things, weren't you, you thief? That is how you knew where to find her, isn't it?" He paused, conscious that his hands were gesticulating wildly and he was yelling like a demon.

Mustafa walked with his head bowed down, kicking at

stones and clods of dirt. He hesitated, wanting to brush over the sticky matter of their planning something behind his comrade's back. But when he saw Ali meant to stick to the subject, he gave a testy shake of the head. "You oughtn't to shout at me like that, Ali. God be my witness," he declared, lifting his large frame into a posture of conviction, "I never touched your junk. It was Talaat. He found her picture in an album and where she worked in your address book. He typed her a letter and signed your name to it." *

"He wouldn't," Ali hissed, not able to make himself believe it. His heart pounded into high gear.

Mustafa showed discomfort. "She wrote back, saying the paper she writes for would love to have her come here and do some stories."

Ali's hard eyes raked him, but he didn't speak, so Mustafa stumbled on, trying to maintain a note of sweet reasonableness in his voice as he explained, "It was all Ibrahim's idea, so don't be mad at Talaat. Ibrahim says reporters have this luxurious freedom of movement, and Khalid can attach himself to her as her guide. He can get around easier, get into places we can't; facilitate things. We save our own people by offering up others."

"And so this, ah," Ali's throat caught, his voice trembled. He couldn't say her name, "this reporter, she is to be the sacrifice?"

"If you wish to call it that." Mustafa smiled, trying to clear the atmosphere. To avoid Ali's gaze for a while, he turned to watch a decrepit Renault go chugging by. They turned down an unlighted side street. As his eyes adjusted to the dark, Mustafa looked to see if they were being followed. They weren't. That should have undercut Mustafa's anxiety, but instead the unease intensified. He took Ali's arm, pulling him along. "Let's hurry."

Ali's emotions were in a turmoil as he struggled to take stock. There was to be an attack on the President, a chance to pass through the crucible of a great event, to define himself against tremendous odds. He had never faced a challenge of this magnitude, and just when he was beginning to focus all his attention and energy on it, he was being pulled here, there, and everywhere. Why in heaven's name was he being kept in the dark about so many important matters? Why did he have to suffer such indignities at his leader's hands? It infuriated him that Ibrahim treated him like a puppet on a string, sometimes as a peon, sometimes as a disciple—while never letting him in at the center of things.

Out of the corner of his eye, Mustafa could see Ali's jaw working furiously. Mustafa took a handful of sunflower seeds out of his pocket. His front teeth cracked the shell, his tongue extracted the kernel, his breath blew the husk from his lips, all in one swift movement. In a honeyed tone, he asked, "You're sure you're still not sweet on this Gracida?"

"Don't be ridiculous!" A flush began at Ali's throat, moved upwards, a tension at his jaw. "Noor is a harlot who—"

But Mustafa spoke before he could protest further. "That is good," he said in a flat voice as he looked up at the night sky. The moon had an ashen quality to it. A harlot, eh? Ali's words had real bite, as if he believed them. "That being the case, we won't feel badly if anything happens to her."

Ali stopped breathing. "Will she be harmed?" he asked quietly.

Mustafa shrugged disinterestedly. "Who knows? If she co-operates, no. But you know Talaat, he has never been particularly fortunate in his choice of women. There is something about him that brings out the worst in them."

"I wouldn't know about that." Ali coughed nervously. The vertical lines in his forehead creased and his hand went to his beard. "There is something about Ibrahim that has been annoying me lately, a certain insecurity. Do you not sense it?" When Mustafa did not reply, Ali reached up and patted his back gently. "Don't get me wrong, I admire Ibrahim. But, dammit! he's so bloody patronizing the way he refuses to cut the strings and let me fly."

"Easy, easy," Mustafa cautioned. "Your impatience is one of your worst faults."

"Faults?" Ali couldn't seem to figure out any response other than faked indignation. "Sorry, but I haven't any."

Mustafa reached into his shirt pocket and produced a pack of Marlboros. He lit the last one and took a reflective drag.

Then he passed the cigarette to Ali, warning, "Don't under-estimate him, as Sadat does. Ibrahim is tough, he is brave, he is—," he paused, searching for a word. His amiable face wrestled with something he did not want to say.

Ali supplied, "cunning."

Aware of how deeply troubled Ali was, Mustafa put a hand on Ali's shoulder and crooned, "You know that Ibrahim only recruits the best. He will pick a body to shreds, but only for good reason. He doesn't want us to get tripped up by our own arrogance. As he says, 'Let's not run too far too fast.' Tonight you did the rest of the group no service by acting disrespectful to our leader. If your thought was to build yourself up by tearing him down, mind the impulse. It will be the ruin of you."

A small silence fell between them. Ali bristled inwardly at the rebuke, but he forced a laugh. "You make Ibrahim sound as if he has been around since the Fifth Dynasty."

Mustafa raised an eyebrow at Ali, a good-humored gesture. "Do I now? Truth is, Ibrahim may be preposterous as a person, but he is an incredible leader. He was a way of kindling fervor in an audience, getting people to sit up and take notice. And when it comes to brewing plots and grand strategies and desperate maneuvers, well, Ibrahim has been doing it for more years than we have been alive. So please, Ali, be glad we have him. Nothing is going to go wrong with him in charge."

They were passing the telecommunications building. Ali suddenly thought it might be wise to give Rashed's house a call, to see if he made it home safely. The two men went in and approached the counter directly. While Ali dug down for his wallet, Mustafa called a clerk over. He began, "Please give me 826—"

Before he could complete the number, the clerk cut in crisply, "Sorry, all 800 numbers are out of order."

Thinking to call a friend in Dokki, Mustafa said, "All right then, try 701—"

The clerk raised his hand, palm out like a traffic cop and cut him off. "Sorry," he repeated, backing away. He was a little man with a shifty eye and a nervous sniff. "The 700 exchange isn't functioning either."

Noticing a line of six callers all talking animatedly into phones at a bank of instruments on a long shelf against the far wall, Ali demanded of the clerk, "Who are those people talking to?"

With a frown, the clerk answered, "They are all calling London."

Mustafa had a brother in London. His look now was one of contentment. With a wide smile, he told the clerk. "Put me straightaway through to London." Turning to Ali, he elaborated, "I'll have my brother phone Rashed."

7

During the next 24 hours, Joe Dooley went in and out of consciousness. He remembered the taxi stand where he had been arbitrarily annexed by two Arabs and a Mexican; he remembered a soft female voice, the smell of rubbing alcohol, the bandages. He had nightmares, raving on for short periods of time. In them, he would be looking through a gun sight. He'd focus on a target so precisely that he could see the cross hairs on its back. He'd awake with a cold, crawling apprehension of fear. That was his back. Once he yelled for Luz and told her breathlessly that even though the Dooley clan didn't go around with shamrocks in the middle of their foreheads, he never missed Mass as a child. But, he confessed, in his young and lusty manhood he had been a rogue of the first order. "So if I'm dying, lass," Joe pleaded, "I'd like ya to get a priest here on the double, just to cover my tail."

"What about a doctor instead?" asked Luz, who was sorely tempted several times to take Dooley to the hospital. Each time Khalid stepped in with a reminder of the risks she would be taking, saying when the police can't find the culprits to imprison they will settle for the victims. Innocence has no application when the police decide to close a criminal case.

Luz's life seemed to speed by during the next few days, her time constantly filled by nursing Joe Dooley back to health. Up at the crack of dawn, she raced about the hotel room, taking his temperature and pulse, changing his dressing, going out to shop, and coming back to fix him a simple meal of yogurt, fruit, orange juice, and warm cocoa, helping him wash up, sitting by his bedside and reading to him or telling him jokes to perk up his spirits. "At a cockfight, how can you recognize the Pollack? He enters a duck. How can you recognize the Mick? He bets on the duck. How can you recognize the Italian? The duck wins."

Joe lifted his head, and as Luz puffed up his pillows, he got a warming glimpse into the unbuttoned top of her blouse, into the northern swell of her breasts. "I'm probably one of the last idiots to vacation in Egypt," he said disconsolately. "But at last I'm admitting defeat. The Arabic language has always been a mess, what with the Z's and S's being backwards and some of the U's and N's upside down. But now the Stella beer's beginning to taste like camel piss." That, for Dooley, was the last straw.

Yesterday, Luz had woken up on the couch to the submachine gun rattatattat of a Dirty Harry movie. Joe had drifted off, leaving the TV on. She unpacked her portable typewriter and rolled in a clean sheet of paper. But after several mysterious phone calls—no words, just heavy breathing—no one could blame her if her enthusiasm for this assignment was no longer fresh. By the day's end there was nothing on the sheet of paper in the typewriter.

At six a.m. a familiar voice on the telephone broke through to Luz's consciousness. "Miss Noor," said Khalid, pronouncing each English word slowly and with considerable difficulty, "this is Ahmed, driver of your friend Hoda el-Abdelbarazy. Can you be ready in front of hotel in half an hour?"

"Ready as rain, Ahmed," Luz answered smoothly. She and Khalid were speaking as if they were unacquainted, yet they understood each other perfectly. Both were playing the little game of those well-trained in the ways of tapped phones. Khalid had instructed her in this matter when he'd deposited her and the wounded Dooley at the hotel.

Luz showered quickly, grabbed her notebook, and hurried downstairs, a journalist in baggy red overalls that covered her body yet called attention to it. Khalid drove her to Dokki to meet a man he deemed "of profound intellectualism," one Ragaa Qaddus of Cairo University. To hear Khalid tell it, Qaddus was the only avowed Marxist ever believed to have received a pat on the back from Khomeini for being a thorn in the Shah's side, but he was terribly reticent about giving interviews since he had fallen under Sadat's hatchet on the fifth of September.

"We do not talk to strange women," Luz was told by Qaddus' daughter through a crack in the door. The woman was hissing frantically in the English she had acquired after watching hours of "I Love Lucy" on TV and exhibiting the rolling-eyed tremors of an angel-dust junkie. So who, thought Luz, she calling strange?

"But Doctor Qaddus agreed," Khalid said in amazement, his eyes flashing. "We give our solemn promise not to quote him or mention Cairo University." The woman shook her head a determined no, and Luz's appetite was whetted. Some of the best interviews are with people who are irritated by the intrusion of the press.

"It is probably illegal for my father to talk to an American reporter," the woman said, the tension in her voice plain. "It is possibly dangerous and certainly, it is insane." For the next 20 minutes Khalid used his powers of persuasion with the consummate skill of a lawyer trying to save his client from the electric chair. Unable to listen longer to his pleading, the woman reluctantly gave in and unchained the door.

"I am embarrassed to have to begin every sentence with I," Qaddus said disarmingly in Arabic, sitting across the table in his son-in-law's flat. "But there is no way to avoid that in an interview." He was a frail man with skin as pale as uncooked filet of sole and piercing black eyes. His thick gray hair was disheveled enough to suggest he rarely combed it. In his twenty-three years of teaching, Ragaa Qaddus hadn't built a reputation as one of the profession's street fighters. In May, however, he showed his backbone when he publicly protested the automatic advancement of those students from prominent families with failing grades. Somebody had to speak out. A colleague had been sacked when he refused to give Jihan Sadat a master's degree in Islamic Studies just because she was the First Lady.

"Favoritism is very hard to get rid of once you start down that path," Qaddus worried. "People are joking that if you are well-connected you have to ride through campus with your windows rolled up, or they'll throw you a diploma."

Since she had gotten him talking, Luz decided to use the opportunity to clear up the rumor that the Professor had once been exiled to Iran. Qaddus suddenly stiffened. "Rubbish!" Then he leaned back and sniffed donnishly, "The Shah was a peacock who was convinced that the sun rose just to hear him crow. He was like a ten-year-old who thought he had a lifetime supply of Lego blocks, zipping around the country to tell his peons to put a school here, a dam there, and a factory over yonder. He was constructing a whole new Iranian landscape and that was the problem. All of it was imposed from above. People of little import stood no chance with him, but the high and the mighty were charmed."

Qaddus had spoken of the Shah as if he were the last of a long line of heads of state whom he'd counseled, to no avail. "Many leaders are afflicted with that same movie director quality," he continued. "They have the idea that life is a movie they can script at will, and they're forever climbing up onto the film platform to survey the set of their political fantasies. It is the path to folly and disaster."

Okay, but Luz was still primarily interested in Sadat. She took an indirect approach. "What you're saying then, is that men like Sadat don't recognize natural limits?"

"Exactly." Qaddus grinned and the wattle under his chin flattened as it pulled up toward his ears. "He is the autocratic Rais, the Pharaoh, the Caliph. He thinks if only he wishes it hard enough, he can make it happen and nothing can stop him. Ah, if only the world were as subject to complete creative control as *Gunsmoke*." He paused while his daughter brought them small cups filled with thick Turkish coffee. Then he went on, "Sadat is a product of the army. He believes you can solve any problem if you get twelve smart majors and one colonel in a room and stay up all night arguing. Self-evidently, something has broken loose in Egypt that is out of his control. He is in much deeper water than he is accustomed to. Please don't take this personally, Miss Noor, but you Western reporters have heaped such adulation on him that it has turned his head. He no longer discusses; he and Allah announce. What makes his regime stink in the nostrils of those of us who are Westernized and his natural allies is that he ignores us and spends his time sending candy and kisses to the Americans, to keep your romance alive."

Luz didn't take it personally, but neither did she follow up on it. Rather she inquired about the Muslim fundamentalists. Qaddus, working his way through an explanation that said he never thought of himself as a sympathizer until this moment, answered, "When we look at these young men and women, we must understand what motivates them. Considering some of the nonsense in the press, we don't really understand their motivations. We are told they hate their fathers, that their classrooms are overcrowded, badly ventilated, and poorly lit, that they suffer from brain tumors; they use barbiturates and opium. They say, *Il ziyy el Islaim*, the Islamic dress of the young women, is only worn because they cannot afford dry cleaning and panty hose. This suggests to me an innocence we can ill afford."

Ragaa Qaddus said all this about ten minutes into their visit. During the next three hours, the erudite intellectual rattled off a mesmerizing monologue that critiqued every Sadat failing he could lay hands on while Luz took notes. Before Sadat embraced the West there were 200 millionaires; now there are 5,000. His Open Door policy, or *Infitah*, has inflicted terrible hardships on the little neighborhood stores, the small entrepreneurs who are trying to contend for a place in the sun with the big multinational firms. Although the practice is not new in Egypt, the detention of individuals suspected of subversion is widespread today, and the offense now appears to be defined broadly to include any active opposition to the regime. You can be incarcerated without charges or due process of law. Some have been tortured or killed while being interrogated.

Luz's ballpoint faltered, and she stared at Qaddus for a long moment, her face pinched. "You will swear to this on a stack of *Das Kapitals*?" she said in a small, frozen voice. Qaddus nodded vigorously.

Then he went on to enumerate Egypt's other problems: the

population explosion in terribly restricted land space—
"Remember that 96 percent of Egypt is barren desert"—the
failure of family planning to take hold in an illiterate people,
the brain drain, the immigration of our best people, poor
administration, the bureaucracy that sits on our faces like a
fifth pyramid, the fatalism of *"Mallesh,"*—he huddled his
shoulders in a gesture of resignation to demonstrate. "And
then there is Begin who insists on going at high speed to fill
up the West Bank with Jewish settlements in total disregard of
its Arab inhabitants. This will spill more blood."

Luz was confused. "But you're not—"

"Arabs?" Qaddus finished for her. "With our 7,000-year-old
civilization we are Egyptians first, but we are also Arabs. We
cannot bear the indignity of the Israelis' treatment of the
Palestinians. When we see Arabs being treated badly and
humiliated, we feel it. A wiser, less ambitious man would not
need to be instructed that there are emotional limits. They do
not change just because they get in the way of his success."

"But," Luz protested, "those settlements were not pros-
cribed by the peace treaty. They're not illegal."

Qaddus jumped in, "That the whole point, Miss Noor.
Where Palestinian rights are concerned, the treaty is pretty
weak."

Luz was starting to get annoyed. "Why are you people
trying to shoot Anwar down before he even clears the tree-
tops? Camp David isn't the final answer to the difficult business of the Middle East; nobody in Washington would say
that. But it's a step in the right direction."

"Is it?" Qaddus calmly ladled a spoonful of sugar into his
coffee. "That is the most extravagant claim of all, my dear.
Kissinger's notorious step-by-step approach, however lauda-
ble its purpose, is proving more of an obstacle to peace than a
lubricant. Poor, inept Carter! He couldn't budge Begin, who
has your Congress in his hip pocket, and Sadat ended up
having to sign an agreement with loopholes big enough to fly a
jumbo jet through. That is why he has lost the people's trust.
Our envoy in Tel Aviv says his phone rings off the hook, and
he is all puffed up with this and that invitation. On the other
hand, the Israeli ambassador could leave his embassy here in

Cairo and go live like a hermit in the Sinai, and no one would notice. You can't start or stop a conversation in Israel without mentioning Camp David. But here? Dead silence. The cold, cold peace." He paused. Like a good public speaker, he let the silence gather before going on. "We Egyptians are not a people to be stampeded. Let Israeli tour buses come here by the thousands. We are not going anywhere."

Khalid was subdued throughout. The debilitating stress that came from Talaat's dying in his arms was doubly hard now that Ali was against him. "Would you care to explain this mistake of yours?" Ali had asked him in the angry, disappointed tones of a coach asking his star player why he'd missed the goal. Ali had come over to Khalid's place to comfort him only to end up banging on the floor, screaming hysterically, holding Khalid responsible for the whole miserable incident and threatening to drum him out of their cell. Khalid had bolted from the house to spend the entire night walking up and down the streets, crying and talking to himself. Luz could see his sadness, although she was not fully aware of what had caused it.

Qaddus' daughter was almost constantly at her father's side with tea and food and would not budge until he cleaned his plate. When his mouth was full, she fed the reporter information, at one point remarking gleefully on the President's recent bout with impotency, which she accepted as Allah's punishment for granting Playboy magazine an interview and allowing Menachem Begin to kiss his wife in front of the whole wide world.

"What's the matter with—" Luz bit her lip to stop herself from saying, "better to have your opponent plant a kiss on your wife's cheek than a bomb on your children's heads." Still, she was intrigued as to how the woman had come by the juicy impotence tidbit. Khalid explained, "Here there is an emphasis on personal contributions to national matters. It is something of a cliché, but we say that everybody knows everybody else's business. If you don't know someone personally, you will know someone who does. Egypt is like a big village."

Qaddus started to expand on this point, but his daughter, concerned that he was growing tired, stood up, hands on hips,

irate, formidable, and ready to bounce his guests out the door
on their ears. They forestalled her by standing up too. Dis-
mayed, but obedient to his daughter's command, Professor
Ragaa Qaddus bid them good-bye.

The sun had burned out the freshness of the morning, and
the Mokattam Hills seemed smeared with heat when Khalid
and Luz climbed down the stairs and walked through a se-
cluded courtyard. They turned down a busy street, past a tall
gate decorated in the Italian manner by a pair of unpainted
cement lions. They crossed the divided highway, coming
through a row of scruffy palm trees bare as the telephone
poles next to them. By the time they reached Khalid's car she
was sure they were being tailed by the man on the airplane,
the one with the jaw like a gourd and the eyes of a hunter
observing his prey. Why, Luz wondered, was he following
them? She came to a dead stop and asked Khalid. The question really tumbled him. He said nothing for a minute—the
time it took Gourdjaw to duck behind a fence. His baggy
eyelids drooped at Luz sadly. "Who knows?" he shrugged,
baffled but still game. "Let's just keep on going."

8

By the time Luz returned to the hotel, Joe Dooley was
gone, departing with all his belongings without as much as a
note of good-bye. Part of her was relieved: after all, she hadn't
come to Cairo to play nursemaid. Still, she was upset by his
abrupt disappearance, wondering why that ungrateful slob
had skipped out? Despite the guilt she felt for having brought
harm upon him by her insistence that he ride along with Sun
Tours, Luz felt resentful. Irritably, she gobbled down a tuna
fish sandwich and a Coke, then headed out to the USIS
Library and an appointment to see a film. It was September
26th—11 more days until the big parade.

Khalid and Luz settled back in their seat in a little side
room off the main reference library to watch a video on an
oversized television screen. The Great Pyramid at Giza appeared. The camera panned across the stones, stopping for a
moment to register a women with a guidebook under her arm
and sensible shoes on her feet. Shading her eyes against
searing heat to look beyond bare dunes to wave after wave of
windswept sand or seated primly, smoothing the skirt of her
seersucker dress, she resembled the fourth grade teacher
everyone loves. The camera moved onward, slowly in reveren-
tial deference to the high solemnity of Giza, past a van selling
cold drinks, and a few tour buses that looked as exhausted as
the Ursuline nuns boarding them. The sand was soft pale
brown, and the dozen camels standing about were browner
still. But their saddlebags were dazzling flashes of color: red,
orange, purple. The tone was set by the Rimsky-Korsakov
soundtrack: *Molto pretentioso*. The camera caressed the

Sphinx, moving by inches up its paws and chest to its face. Now, moving out so the entire figure could be seen, one word was superimposed. The word was "Egypt."

"Jesus," Khalid snorted. "Do they think we're idiots?"

Luz reminded him it was made for the US market by Americans who specialize in framing current events in visual and dramatic terms their countrymen can understand. It wasn't designed to offend local yokels like himself, nor to have much to do with recognizable human experience. On the tape there was more of the scenic material, the mosques of Sultan Hassan and El Rifai, peasants toiling in the fields in Wadi el Natrun, a wooden water wheel turning in Al-Fayyum, palm fronds waving in the breeze at Bani Suwayf. Then the history lesson began. Old photographs flowed together till they appeared to be movies too, and lushy romantic music bound the images. There was Anthony Eden seated in Ismalia as if he were royalty posing for commemorative coins. Nasser did a cameo next. Barrel-chested and erect, he was all magical voice in 1954 as he informed the British they must quit the Suez Canal, moving from a growl to the whistle of a strong wind, obedient to explosive rhythms wholly his own. The huge crowd started to roar, but there was a quick cut before the master orator could steal the show.

"By God!" Khalid's voice was barely a breath against her ear. "Nasser had it, the gift."

They watched a newsreel excerpt, fuzzy with age. It was at a military base of some sort in the 1940s. A holy man raised his hands high above his head, an inspiring gesture, and bestowed upon a crowd of soldiers his blessing. Khalid identified him for Luz as Hassan el-Banna, founder of *Ihwan El Muslimin*, the Muslim Brotherhood. Khalid set his chin and thrust out his lip. "A truly great man," he instructed Luz in a soft voice and she looked at him—one quick, alert glance, measuring. Could Khalid be a follower? Off to the side of el-Banna, a figure in khaki grinned briefly and turned away, and for an instant you could see it was Sadat. He was still a rather attractive, but utterly obscure, newly-minted young army lieutenant. More than twenty years later he would be the President, and, with the aim of striking a mortal blow at the

Nasserites, he would empower the Muslim Brotherhood, the Jamaat. "Fascinating," murmured Luz, who was captivated to see the past before it got edited into history.

There was an awkward zoom, a bit of cloddish composition, then came a clear shot of Sadat in one of his mosques dressed in a white *galabiah*, bowing his head down to the ground in prayer. When you saw him up close, the first thing you noticed was the blackness of his skin, the callus in the middle of his forehead that came from years of prayer. In a voice-over, he was describing himself as *khabir el aylah wal mu'minin*, head of the family and of the believers.

"This devotion thing, it is packaging," complained Khalid, who thought Sadat treated the Faith like a publicity stunt. Now the President was standing by a primitive water sluice in the middle of an irrigation ditch and prattling on and on about his total identification with his birthplace, the conservative little village of Mit Aboul-Kum in the Nile Delta. Khalid told Luz that the President traded in a fellahin connection in that consistent and smarmy fashion so often that the latest joke asks how many Sadats does it take to replace a light bulb: the answer is five—one to screw in the bulb and four to complain about electricity spoiling traditional village life.

"*Bueno*," Luz chuckled in spite of herself. Her fingers were flying across her notebook: If Nasser was the Teflon man to whom no failure stuck, then Sadat is the Velcro man on whom everything fastens.

Khalid roared as though his fingers had been smashed in a door and her head jerked up. "Where is your sense of shame?" he inquired sourly of the President who was shown on the screen brushing his teeth in his underwear, being massaged, resting in his pajamas in his bedroom.

Luz could see that Khalid didn't like these tactics at all. He looked, in fact, like a mullah watching an x-rated version of the six o'clock news. To calm him down, she tried to draw a parallel with Jimmy Carter wearing cardigan sweaters in his effort to look likeable and friendly. You loosen up, let down your hair, and get your picture taken in your nightie. You put on your boots and baseball cap and jump the fence to hold a baby lamb for the camera. A polo shirt registers as Just a

Regular Guy and what you want to wear if you and Walter Cronkite are filmed in a speedboat in Aswan being charismatic. The awshucks image of outdoor wholesomeness says, "I'm the boy next door; don't think of me as an Arab terrorist. I'm going to build a universal peace center for everybody's religion in Mit Aboul-Kum." Cronkite was getting dewy-eyed over that. And why did two homespun rustics like Jimmy and Anwar give Playboy an interview? To show they were just another pan of cornbread and another plate of stuffed grape leaves, not commanders-in-chief who might blow up the planet by their actions. You wring your hands over whether you got a fair solution to the Palestinian problem and whether food subsidies are better than bread riots and whether Qaddafi should be bumped off or not and what happens? You end up roasted.

Luz fell silent as Elizabeth Taylor came on the screen singing in a soft, but determined voice. "Friendship, friendship, what a perfect kinship." Near the end of the refrain, Jihan Sadat joined her, their arms around each other in a show of affection. What with the hugging and kissing and jostling to create a clean view for the cameras, it looked like a family reunion, which is just what Taylor said it was: "We're cousins. This quarrel between us should never have happened."

Khalid had had it. Abruptly, he switched off the video machine, not caring whether Luz saw the rest of the film or not. Whoever produced it had a mind like a food processor stuck on puree. When he turned his head to look directly into her eyes, she could see that his face was stiff with unconcealed hostility. Why, he demanded to know, was she a defender of this sleazy fakery, this blatant chicanery?

When it came to talking media, the reporter was never at a loss for words. "Anwar's no different than Jimmy Carter and Dick Nixon," Luz protested mildly. "Jimmy was forever coming up with a lot of hard-scrabble nonsense about learning how to endure in Plains, Georgia, and Nixon has told us a million times that his family was so poor they couldn't buy a horse for his sickly brother Arthur. And while there may be some charm in Southern Baptists and Quakers and Muslims who believe in quiet suffering, I must confess it's lost on me.

Too bad they don't do it a little more quietly, I say, but then I think, hold on, Gracida, if they do, you'll be out of a job. All that Abe Lincoln in a log cabin stuff makes good copy. Besides, presidents have to try and be all things to all interested parties. What really matters is these two very courageous statesmen are, against all odds, trying to give peace a chance, reaching out as far as they can, and realizing that it is probably not far enough, but refusing to give up and I love them for it. *Dios mio*, if they can pull the white dove out of the hat, they're entitled to the full Beverly Hills treatment: gold Rolex watches, a dazzling array of Pierre Cardin suits on their hangers, and hot tubs in their limos."

Khalid's lidded brown eyes rose to hers. "Trust my judgement, Noor. This man is two-faced and for himself, not for Egypt. If you're counting on him, count fast."

Luz scowled at Khalid. Wasn't he a sullied witness, refusing to see how substantial the rewards of his President's behavior have been for himself? Here was a draft-age male who was not at war today, and still he would rebuke the man who made it possible. It seemed a rather ungrateful attitude to Luz and she asked him, "What's wrong with a peace treaty? Would you rather be in a fallen infantryman's grave in the Sinai this time next year?"

Khalid clapped his hand to his mouth to hold back his response, which was thoroughly profane.

Later, from the ninth floor of the hotel, Luz could look out this September 27th night into a light mist rolling in on Cairo. Where was Dooley tonight, at a bar or a bordello? Where was Ali? And Leonard Berg, why did thoughts of him fill her all day long? Out there in this mysterious city hovered the questions that sent her mind leaping back over the past week. The weird incidents that swirled around her seemed random at first, but were they part of a pattern? The streets below were dappled with dim circles of electric light over pockets of darkness. Her eyes roved up and down the street until they spotted the man who'd followed her and Khalid all day long. He was sitting on the steps of the building opposite the hotel. His face lifted slowly to her window. His back was to the light from a street lamp and his face was in deep shadows, but she could see the line of his mouth and jaw. It was the same man who had been with her since Madrid, and she wondered what this could mean. Should she send herself a telegram and take the next plane out? She was nervous and skittish, and angry at herself for being so.

Luz sat down at the table in front of her typewriter, slipped her feet out of her shoes, and breathed a sigh. The gin and tonic in her hand and *Kiri te Kanawa* singing "O don fatale" on BBC's Verdi hour would, she was sure, restore her spirits. But it didn't. She leaned over and switched on the TV picture. It had been another trying day, with a batch of interviews and a press conference. Then, there were the routine stories to scoop out: a member of the rubber-stamp parliament alighted from his car several days ago in Alexandria and was promptly gunned down. Government forces stormed a Coptic household where they claimed to have found a large arms cache which they said was being prepared for an attempted overthrow of the regime. In Ismalia, a mullah was being prosecuted for sedition on charges of inciting other sheiks to destabilize the Canal Zone. Political instability was rife.

An engine backfired just below her window and Luz jumped. Was she going to let her imagination run away from her? She had once climbed mountains and terrorized ski slopes with a boldness that Karen Blixen might have envied, but in time she had learned there were ample reasons to be apprehensive. She was aware of the dangers of working in the Third World long before gunmen in a Chevy came out to welcome her to Cairo. There had been a harrowing experience while covering the war in El Salvador when the hotel she was staying in was attacked by rebel soldiers who mistook her for a spy and imprisoned her for ten days. After choking down a couple of Scotches at her homecoming dinner, she got up in front of her co-workers and said, "*Asi es la vida*, so goes life." As a Latin, you accept whatever comes your way as the cost of your education.

Luz had not been scared when she found Joe Dooley gone. Mad certainly, shaken by the unexpected suddenness of his departure, but not with fear. At one point she tried to ring up

Leonard Berg; then realizing the time, she hung up. She had
wanted to confide in him, but she feared his help could only
be purchased with a full confession. What did she think she'd
find in Cairo? Certainly, it was not the Sadat who was speaking
now on prime time. Clenching his fists and stomping his feet,
braying and screwing up his dark face, his skin so greasy it
looked like he sweat Coppertone lotion, he appeared to be
doing an impersonation of Papa Doc Duvalier at a voodoo
ceremony. *Madre mia*, Talaat had been right after all! As a
flight of oratorical fancy, the speech had all the grace of a
gooney bird, crashing on takeoff and spending the next hour
fluttering in a tizzy on the ground. What can one utter but an
exasperated "Ugh" unless, perhaps, a mortified, "Say it isn't
so?"

Luz raked the screen with a belligerent eye. Where was the
charismatic leader whose tongue was touched by fire? The
speech ended. A solitary voice in the crowd yelled out, "Hear,
hear!" Could it be lost on the President that he had only one
vocal fan in that large assembly of stony faces? Hear, hear:
perhaps that one voice was harder to bear than no supporters
at all.

Slowly, Luz picked up a thick folder of Xeroxed articles and
background files she'd put together before leaving the States.
Nobody famous in the Arab world had been treated as rever-
ently as Anwar Sadat, she thought as she leafed through the
pages. Time, Newsweek, and U.S. News sent him valentine
cover stories. The dailies were uniformly kind. Some editors
rhapsodized so effusively that it might have embarrassed Anwar's mother. But if Sadat was the darling of the US media, his
people were not equally enchanted, at least, if Luz's infor-
mants were correct, and she uncomfortably suspected they
were. Coolly meticulous of eye and passionate in dislike, they
had spoken up knowing that their outspokenness could land
them in jail. Gracida didn't shy away from complicated issues
either, but if she wrote honestly, she would probably find
herself accused of trying to chip away at Sadat's halo. It would
win her few friends among the paper's readers and a lot of
enemies. Americans are an oddly blaming kind of people,
hostile as much to the bearer of bad news as the bad news

itself. On the other hand, we have all watched this scene—the heroic saga of the misunderstood reformer who pushes too far too fast and bombs out—that we almost know how the story is going to end. But is this saga really Sadat's story?

"*Madre mia!*" Luz cried softly, conjuring up the petulant scowl that she was sure would be on her editor's face once he read her copy. "You're a digressor," he'd once complained; "try and simplify." Now, she worried, "it might even cost me my job." Slightly spooked and with this far from happy thought nagging at the back of her mind, she flexed her fingers over the keys and bravely started to type.

"A persistent theme sounded by President Sadat," she wrote, "is the superiority of the peasant ethos to that of the city dweller whose soul has been warped by all the worms in the Big Apple. Since the government can only hope to save an exploding population of 45 million poor Egyptians from sinking in its demographic swamp through more assembly lines and urban expansion, Sadat is in danger of sawing off the branch on which he sits."

Luz leaned back in her chair, her eyes moving rapidly across the lines. Did I really write that? Tearing the sheet of paper from the typewriter, she crunched it into a ball and threw it against the wall. Tires squealed in the street below. She dashed to the window. Pushing the curtains aside, she saw a silver sports car careen around the corner, barely decelerating at the stop sign, and zoom off. The man who'd been watching her was no longer there. The Nile flowed on to the sea, uncaring. At that moment, the numbing horrors of late caught up with her and Luz felt alone and scared. "This place is beginning to give me the willies," she said to her lonely room. Suddenly, she remembered the prayer of Medieval pilgrims: "O Lord, heavenly father, let the angels watch over thy servants, that no evil may overcome them. Protect them from the perils of fast rivers, thieves, and wild beasts."

Her serenity renewed, Luz sat down at the typewriter and began her article again. "History will credit Anwar Sadat with great achievements—a peace treaty, dismantling Nasser's secret police, modernization—all that could not have come about without his skills. Moreover, what hope there is for industrial expansion goes back to his deals with the multinational corporations. They will bring jobs and income for the common people. But there is a dark side to his government. Critics say, correctly, that he relies too much on paternalism, secrecy, deceit, and violence—all dangerous means that carry the potential for a terrible end."

9

In the taxi that took them out to dinner, Luz Gracida sat apart from her escort Leonard Berg in one corner of the back seat, staring out at Sharia el Tahir, Liberation Street and at the Sheraton in front of them. Neither said much at the moment. She was preoccupied with an editor who was refusing to run her copy. He was preoccupied with his fear that she might not come back to his flat after dinner. The driver peeled left into Sharia el-Giza, and with one hand on the steering wheel, drove past the huge Soviet Embassy. Next to it was the presidential residence most often occupied by Jihan Sadat, guarded by soldiers and several squat armored cars, their machine guns pointed at the street. The security measures were well-warranted. For the past few weeks the country seemed to be seething with sedition and conspiracies. On the fifth of September the President suddenly issued arrests for 1,536 alleged enemies. Soldiers dragged many of them out of their beds in the middle of the night. University professors who had criticized the Camp David accords or corruption were dismissed from their posts. Journalists who hadn't portrayed Anwar as the son of George Washington by Mother Teresa abruptly found themselves among the unemployed.

Egyptians, Berg knew, pride themselves on their freedom of expression. That freedom is exercised here in Cairo with an exuberance and at a decibel level rarely heard outside of Paris. Where other cities have oil refineries or seaports or more cotton per square mile than any place in the Arab World, Cairo has the open mouth. Thanks to its hot and humid climate, you can plant a word in one ear and be sure it'll grow

73

into a rumor. A dozen dailies and newsweeklies and hordes of film makers have their wild verbiage patches proliferate along the Nile River. Words and images grow year-round and automatically replenish themselves when they are picked. Sadat apparently didn't understand his people's penchant for harvesting opinions in every tea stall, taxicab, and on every street corner, or he was unwilling to bend his policies to accommodate it. This morning he threatened to put an addition 7,000 real or imagined adversaries behind bars.

In the preceding month of August, there had been three plots to kill Sadat, one revealed by Israeli intelligence and the other two by Egyptian security. Colonel Qaddafi continually sent in hit squads from Libya. Every one had been caught, but there's always a first time. Some mullahs were attacking the President during Friday prayers. Not to be outdone, Ayatollah Khomeini dealt himself into the action by saying there's more than one way to skin a cat; the Faithful among the Egyptians ought to rise up and replace their corrupt pharaoh with a true Islamic Republic by whatever means God will provide. Of late, the President had shown himself to be passionately inarticulate in his rage against his tormentors.

A magnificent sun slipped from beneath a bank of clouds like the yolk of an egg breaking over the Nile and bathed the shimmering river in crimson and gold. On a stone wall, bougainvillaea was bursting with bright red blooms. Cairo did nothing so well as October. But Leonard tiredly shielded his eyes. The wave of arrests, he thought glumly, had done nothing to deter those of us bent on being fond of Anwar forever. However, he was pressing his luck. You pour seven million people into a city built to hold four, add a new baby every three seconds, season generously with a treaty that provokes a fire storm of criticism, stir charismatically for years, then add your favorite opponents from every political stripe to the politics of paranoia and wait for the explosion.

And what did Ambassador Roland Tucker think he was doing by ignoring the elephant in the bathtub, refusing to transmit Berg's cables to Washington while recommending casual sex as an antidote to a few forceful criticisms? Did Tuck subscribe to the stereotype of Sadat's countrymen as dim cynics resigned to corruption, serfs who wouldn't know a genuine free man if they fell over one? Supposedly, Egyptians have a 4,000 year habit of imperial rule by Pharaohs, Persians, Turks, Greeks, Romans, Mamluks, Arabs, and Europeans. They've had almost 30 years of military strongmen imposed on them after the overthrow of the despot King Farouk, and they've put up with it all—Nasser's feared Ton Tons Macoutes (which Sadat, to his credit, disbanded), censorship and loss of the right to travel abroad, arrests without charge, imprisonments without trial. But is their famed passivity without limit? Ask the British, who went too far in 1906. When some pigeon-shooting British officers accidentally wounded a local woman, the villagers from Dinshaway attacked them and one officer, who fired at them, was hit in the head with a rock and died. The Brits hanged four Egyptians and sentenced the others to a public flogging and hard labor. It was never the same after that.

Berg moved the hand that was shielding his eyes and watched Luz. The jacket of her suit lay across her lap; her breasts moved invitingly under a silk blouse. He suspected she'd led a lot of guys a merry dance since she put on her first bra. Taking her hand, he turned it over so that her palm was up and covered by his own. He was surprised to see how sweaty his hands were. "Junior prom time again," he blushed. "Stomach's doing flipflops, the pimples are popping out."

Luz, who'd been an ugly duckling, confessed to getting nervous before all her dates in high school—both of them. Leonard insisted on knowing what her two dates had looked like. She said, "What Andy Rooney on 60 Minutes would look like if he were a Chicano," and was rewarded with a smile. She wondered, "Does this restaurant we're going to serve authentic Egyptian cuisine?"

"No," Leonard answered, "but they say the food is good enough to eat. So we'll give it a shot."

When they passed under University Bridge and came up on the road which runs along the Nile, Leonard spoke to the driver, motioning him to their destination, the Swiss Chalet Restaurant. Even after they were settled in their seats at the table, Luz remained subdued. She studied a menu as big as

Moses' tablets for a moment, then put it down with a sigh. "I can't face another decision today," she said apologetically. "You order and I'll say, same here."

Leonard, sensing that she wished to be left alone with her thoughts, didn't attempt to intrude. Instead, he flipped open the menu and got on with ordering some *Batarikh*, the Egyptian caviar. When the wine was poured, he toasted, "*L'chayim*," and she responded with, "*Salud*." Several times he caught her watching his knife as he buttered a roll, and whenever their eyes met he gave her a warm smile. But these invitations to open a conversation were not taken.

The waiter was bringing their Chicken Kiev before she spoke. "I'm sorry to be such a bore, Lenny," Luz apologized, reaching across the white linen tablecloth to take his hand in a conciliatory gesture.

"Lenny it is?" he said with exaggerated surprise. "Aha! So we've come this far, and it's only our second date."

She hung her head theatrically. "Sorry, but I've gotta work fast. You only come around every ten years."

Luz was a picture of studied graciousness as she sat regally on the edge of her chair. Resplendent in a deep purple suede suit held together with pearl snaps, she looked more like a regular Mrs. Fine Arts League than the girl he'd met at Columbia who was given to offbeat Annie Hall getups, baggy dresses, and embroidered jackets. Her decorous manner, however, was contradicted by those expressive lips. There was an alluring atmosphere of sexual struggle about her. Leonard wanted to tell her if she ever entered the Miss Texas Contest, she'd retire the trophy, she was so outrageously gorgeous. But he cranked himself down and said, "I hope you won't take this the wrong way, Luz, but you're one woman I don't mind being seen with in a well-lighted place."

Luz thought he was being too kind. "Here I am," she said, her distress obvious, "feeling frustrated and cranky and played out, and I've only been here a week and a half. Do you think if I ordered a new head it'd be here by tomorrow?"

"That's all right." Leonard covered her hand with his own. It was understandable that she might be ambivalent about her assignment, Egypt in general, and perhaps, life as a whole.

"Cairo has this effect on newcomers." He sought out her eyes with his, found them, tried to see behind them, but it made him catch his breath just to look into them. With their long lashes, they held a smile that revealed a multi-faceted woman: lace and iron, as tender as she was tough, a liberated woman who's quite capable of taking care of herself and a *muchacha* in need of a big brother.

"It's safer for me," Leonard confessed, "if you don't come on like a hot and heavy challenge to my own smoldering passions, batting your eyelashes at me."

Luz looked prettily confused for a moment, not quite sure how to answer, not sure she wasn't coming on, or if he was hitting on her, or who was doing what to whom and how. Then the sunny, sexy smile broke out. Leonard went on, joshing, teasing, and putting her in a mellow mood with his sweetness and raunchy laughter. "I've suffered," he lamented, "from extreme susceptibility to Hispanic women ever since a Puerto Rican stole my cherry in the eighth grade."

"Eighth grade?" Luz could not believe it, unless he'd flunked a few grades. "Besides my brown skin, I can't imagine what else you see in me." She tossed off the remark with the confidence of a seductive woman who knows damn well what men see in her, Leonard in particular.

"Oh, excuse me, Senorita, I have an advantage over you. I know you're a fine newswoman but—" Leonard bent forward to look at her intently in the glow of the citronella candle, as if trying to assess something mysterious about her. "Can you keep a secret?" he asked in an undertone.

"I think so," Luz answered with a hint of laughter, her response to his conspiratorial whispering.

Leonard touched her gently on the shoulder and said, "You seem to hallucinate from time to time and think you're Nurse Jane." He thought he caught a shadow in her eyes at the word Nurse. He grinned, but his hazel eyes were serious. "If you're interested in what Ambassador Tucker or the AID Director has to say about things, perhaps I can arrange for you to meet them."

Luz wondered why he'd brought this up, but he seemed so uncalculating about it and so demonstrably kind that she answered, "I'd love to, if you're sure it's not too much trouble."

"On the contrary. Friends must be ever alert to each other's interests."

"Personally, do you get along with Ambassador Tucker?" asked Luz, throwing Leonard a quick curve.

He ducked it with practiced ease. "The Old Man doesn't seek out my company, but he's civil enough. He thoroughly enjoys being posted here, as I do. He's enthusiastic, which is always a good quality in an ambassador, especially in a Third World country like this."

For a while Luz spoke about what had struck hardest: a population growing bigger and poorer every day. "Before I left Washington, I talked to a high-level colleague of yours in the State Department who said he wasn't worried about the population explosion because Egyptians need very little to live on, and they've always muddled through. Besides, the pro-lifers in Congress have made birth control a very touchy subject."

"Do-nothingism from Washington know-nothings!" Leonard declared, his face ruddy with anger whenever this particular subject was brought up. "Ai, don't get me started on that one."

Berg had enough experience with journalists to know how they usually operated—flying in for a few days and getting what they could in the way of local color, some good quotes from a couple of press office functionaries, a taxi driver, and an undersecretary of transportation, shopping once at Khan el Khalili to pick up some lapis lazuli jewelry and a gold *kartosh* with their name in hieroglyphics, then back out again. Gracida, he could see, was digging deeper. He touched his wine glass to hers. Then he said, "Let me ask you something. Are you one of those people who can't tune things out?"

Luz picked up her fork once more. The long room was noisy with chatter and the chink of glasses and cutlery, and she raised her voice slightly. "Yes and no. I can stand and ignore the context which I'm in, and at the same time, I feel invaded by the surrounding situation."

"Especially, if it's not what you expected." Leonard leaned back in his chair. "Fill me in, will you?" he directed in his best foreign service officer voice. "What brought you here? Where did you learn to speak Arabic? And what made you become a journalist in the first place? Answer them in any order you like."

Luz, who normally had a quick and cogent reply for every question tossed her way, was momentarily stymied. Initially, Cairo looked great to her. It's one of those assignments she'd dreamed about when first she'd become a newswoman. "It sounded difficult," she said simply. "I looked at the list of reporters who are here to cover the parade on October Sixth, and mine was the only name I didn't recognize. It terrified me, and when something terrifies me and makes me say, 'I could never ever do that,' then I know it's the right thing to do."

"Sounds like you're very goal-oriented," said Leonard looking at her directly. "So am I."

"I have to be," Luz explained, trying to impress him with how hard it is for a woman to get a job as an overseas correspondent. "I'd go to all these interviews and make them sit up and take notice of my knowledge of world affairs and my credentials. I have to tell you that I won almost every award known to man and beast in my class, editor of our yearbook and on the daily. There was no reason to dismiss me lightly, but the interviewer would say, 'Sorry, honey, it's a job for a man. I can only suffer so much rejection, so in 1979, I took fate in hand, sunk my life savings, all 1,965 dollars, into a ticket to Davao in the Philippines. As it turned out, the book I wrote on my four months with the Moro National Front won me a prestigious award and a permanent job on the staff of *El Fronterizo*."

"The Moros?" Leonard leaned his knife and fork on his plate and looked at her with new interest. The notion of the elegant Dona Maria Luz traipsing around the steaming jungles of Mindinao with battle-hardened commandoes came as a surprise, but Berg didn't laugh, as others had, at her audacity.

"For me, it was a very tough experience," Luz admitted honestly. "But sometimes tough experiences teach you more about life and yourself than nice and easy experiences. Cover-

ing a guerrilla war is as good a place as any to learn the nuts
and bolts of the profession and to learn how to see yourself as
an explorer and reporter of the human condition in extremis—
and not make judgements where others do."

"And what did you learn from the Moros?"

"Not to hang out with Muslim freedom fighters anymore,"
Luz answered, spooning into her fruit dish.

Leonard put his fork to his chicken, then set it down again.
She had just given him the opening he sought. "That's too
bad. I was hoping you might know some Muslim freedom
fighters here. That you could, *yanni*, be sort of a go-between."

Luz swallowed the contents of the spoon that had been
poised in front of her mouth and hesitated, as if appraising the
figs. "I don't know any Egyptians," she responded at last,
lying without knowing why. "Fighters, lovers, or in-between.
You're an hombre who doesn't seem to have a whole lot of idle
thoughts," she added hastily. Too hastily, perhaps. They both
sat tight, facing one another.

"And you're a woman who has a nice way of calling me
stuffy," Leonard rejoined in a placating manner. A smile was
lurking at the edge of his mouth as he told her he'd been
called worse. While attending Northwestern he'd earned the
title "The Boy Named Sue" from the Johnny Cash song,
usually shortened to Sue, because one evening he was reading
a history book and asked his roommates, "Where's Suez?" His
friends thought that anyone who reached 17 years without
having heard of the Suez Canal deserved to be reminded of it.
And Leonard thought Miss Gracida's memory needed refreshing as well. "What about your old Santa Cruz lover?"

"Lover?" Luz repeated flatly. She felt queasy, as though she
had swallowed not a fig, but the whole world and could not
digest it.

"Can I get you more wine?" Leonard lifted a finger for the
waiter, and when he had the man's attention, he pointed down
to her empty goblet. Then he leaned forward, inviting confession, and prompted, "Ali Salah."

"Ali who?" Luz tried to look up at him, but her lips were
frozen tight, and her eyes found a point in the middle of her
plate from which they couldn't move. The air in the room was

moist. Her clothes felt glued to her skin. She was finding
Lenny's questions made her breathless.

Leonard glanced up at a waiter hovering inconspicuously in
the background. Was the man out of hearing range? Leonard
poured some water from the carafe and slowly drank it. When
he set the glass down, he whispered, "Salah."

"Ali Salah?" The disbelief registered upon hearing that
name, combined with the wild-eyed look on her astonished
face, was monumental. Still, Luz had made the denial with
such force that Leonard lowered his eyes. She turned away
and stopped suddenly, her posture rigid.

Leonard, following the direction of her fixed gaze, saw that
she was staring at Pete Sanchez. It was obvious that she had
noticed him before, although Pete, if challenged, would un-
doubtedly swear, "I've been tailing her ever since Madrid
without her knowing it." At that moment, Sanchez looked up
at Luz and drew back a little. His lovely Egyptian dinner
partner, noticing this byplay, asked him a question in Arabic,
which Pete ignored. He threw his napkin down on his full
plate, then took out his wallet and counted out the pound
notes like a croupier balancing his table receipts at closing
time. Leonard noticed the strained, preoccupied way he was
acting.

Luz had turned in her chair so that she could examine the
Spaniard with the gourd jaw carefully. He was pulling his
companion out of her chair, hurrying away from the table. Was
he trying to avoid a confrontation? Luz looked at him for a full
minute, and then she swung around to face Leonard. "That
bandito's never going to let me out of his sight," she lamented. Her voice sounded frail now.

Leonard didn't even look up. He calmly sliced a piece of
asparagus, pushed it on his fork with his knife, and said,
"What bandit are you talking about?" He put the asparagus in
his mouth, and Luz watched his lips under their busy blond
umbrella begin their rhythmic movements. Torn between
good table manners and assertion, Luz prodded, "That man
who just got up and walked out, do you have any idea who he
is? Or why on earth he should think I'm worth the effort?"

"No," Leonard half-choked the reply, his eyes downcast,

and for a second she continued staring at his lips as though hypnotized. Leonard raised gruff eyebrows. "Why would anyone be following you?" he asked, spearing the last stalk of asparagus. "Isn't that pretty far fetched?"

Leonard had been so nice to her that Luz had almost failed to notice how carefully he was choosing his words—pretty far fetched instead of paranoid. A nice nuance and pre-eminently tactful, just what you'd expect from a diplomat. Luz laughed, a light tinkling laugh that gave the impression that she was both disturbed and angry. One of Berg's fingers was pushing crumbs into a tiny pyramid on the tablecloth; he refused to look up. Luz pushed her plate away abruptly, grumbling, "No, it's far out in left field, but it's true. You must think I'm a real *estupida*. Please don't play games with me, Len! Tell me by what perverted logic is that goon over there stalking me?"

"That's Peter Sanchez," Leonard answered quietly when the waiter had finished removing the last of the dishes. He'd spoken the name of the man casually, as though she should know who he was talking about. "He's not a goon, and he briefed me only this morning. It seems your old Santa Cruz classmate has gotten himself tied in with a bunch of Islamic radicals. He got caught and was in prison for a while. His house was searched and maybe some letters or a diary was found."

Luz stiffened where she sat. Leonard raised his hand to prevent interruption. "Your name," he reasoned, "could've popped up on the computer. The spooks got curious and they're having you followed." He thought he'd covered himself masterfully.

Luz gave a high, limpid laugh. "*Dios mio!* That excuse has whiskers on it."

Leonard took a small sip of wine, then quipped, "Pete's is a thankless task, so you don't have to thank him." He looked into her eyes and tried to read the expression in them, but there was none at all. They seemed opaque. Dropping the joshing manner, Leonard begged, "Please, Luz, I know you two are not strangers. Can't you tell me a little bit about Ali Salah? I assure you, I mean him no harm." He continued to search her face anxiously, waiting for her response.

This was one subject Luz had no desire to pursue. But her serene and artful self-concealment had been shattered. "I don't know." She opened her hand in an appeal to be let off the hook.

It was nearly ten years ago and difficult for her to summon up memory from that distance. His disbelieving eyes, demanding, insistent, never left her face. Her arms dropped limply to her side. Should she confide in Lenny, tell him about the gunmen and Talaat's death, about patching Joe Dooley together and his disappearing? Berg was the usual mix of official guile and good skate, except Luz knew he had more decency in him than most. She'd watched him closely all evening. Her journalistic training had given her an uncanny knack for reading people, for taking a measure of their spirit. Lenny wore a diplomat's mask, but his hazel eyes were the clearest of windows—alternately warm, gay, searing, and troubled. A perfect Father Confessor, but it was a full moment before Luz spoke. "Okay," she nodded numbly, realizing there was no choice. "What do you want to know?"

Leonard flagged down their waiter and ordered Turkish coffee—sa'ada or bitter for her, ziyada or sweet for him. The waiter immediately returned with two cups, both mazbouta, medium. He accepted it with a resigned "Mallesh" before asking Luz, "Where's Congressman Dooley? You two were spotted leaving the airport together, but no one can find him. They've been looking for him in a hundred different places; it's like playing pin the tail on the donkey. Dooley's an ole buddy of Jimmy Carter's, a Democrat who went down to defeat in the same election. But no one suspects the Republicans of hiring some local muscle to make him disappear."

Her voice innocent, Luz asked, "What does this Dooley look like?"

"Picture Tip O'Neill," Leonard instructed. Luz nodded her head. "All right," Leonard continued, "now picture a Tip O'Neill with a snoot full." He leaned forward. "You said, no games. Okay?"

His voice was low, but it contained a note of authority which Luz didn't question. Speaking brokenly and with a few omissions, she found herself telling Leonard what had transpired on that insane ride into the city. When she finished, he sat down his cup and looked at her. It was a long, measuring look that held the same curious hint of speculation and protectiveness that she'd seen in his eyes in the pharmacy. Leonard was taking in the significance of her information; his mind was registering a warning: don't let her out of your sight! One of his fingers was pushing crumbs into a pyramid on the tablecloth. He looked up at Luz and asked her, "Was Ali very religious? Was Ali Salah *meshuggenah*?

Crazy? The other Arab students on campus had called Ali, *Majnun*, the crazy one. "When I knew him, Nasser, the Tiger of Faluga, was his god. He thought Nasser hung the moon." Luz pushed her plate aside and blotted her lips with her napkin. "But Ali was a creature of enormous contrasts and complex enough to go from one extreme to the other. His moods changed all the time. One day he was excited and full of energy, the next day, depressed and fatalistic. There was a great variety of color to him. And even though he had a strong, moral imagination, you might say it lacked a sufficiently stable philosophical base. Stories, *por Dios*! I could tell you stories."

"What sort of stories?" Leonard prompted.

"When you're older, *nino*, you'll know." Luz smiled, but there was a sadness in the lines around her eyes. She drank her coffee slowly. Ali was great in bed, but lousy on his feet—how could she edit that for Lenny's benefit? "Even though he didn't have money enough to paint the town a pale pink, Ali built quite a reputation racing motorcycles and getting into fist fights. As the Arabs say, when you're in a place where you are not known, do as you will. So he was a little wild perhaps—he liked strong spirits and soft touches—but sweet. We were in the same Latin American history class when he got thrown in the slammer and I bailed him out." She paused, then added with an arresting little trace of shyness, "and he asked me to spend the night with him."

"Aha," Leonard exclaimed, eyes dancing, and his soft Midwestern drawl slowed slightly for effect. "The plot moves along predictably."

Blushing, Luz demolished the remainder of her coconut

cream pie in one large bite. After a last sip of coffee she
brought her napkin to her lips again in a gentle dab and
philosophized, "Life is like the words on the back of a sham-
poo bottle: Lather, rinse, repeat. It never says when to stop,
just use your own judgement. And my judgement in those
days was haywire. I'd been educated in parochial schools,
Sacred Heart of Jesus Elementary, Holy Innocents, Loyola.
But I didn't see why I had to be chained to that cherubic
image of men. I'd have jumped head first into a volcano for the
chance to be Steve McQueen's main squeeze. I mean, who
wants a clean-scrubbed altar boy? I didn't and what I got was
Ali. He was in Technicolor while everybody else was in black
and white."

Leonard offered a silver dish. Taking a pale green mint, Luz
continued, "We'd go out to a party and I'd be busy fending off
other women. When it came to scoring, Ali made Casanova
look celibate. Overcharged emotions, excesses—he always
attributed them to being a hot-blooded *Safagi*, an Upper
Egyptian. But I wasn't supposed to get jealous over his flings.
He once held a gun to my head."

"Sounds like fun," Leonard said skeptically. There was a
line in the report Pete Sanchez had shown him—"Salah is
given to vociferous displays of temper and aggression, but
friends insist they usually are just performances,"—and it
came back to Berg now. He went on probing, "Was Salah anti-
American? Pro-Palestinian? Did he hate us, the government,
our policies?"

Luz crossed her legs and admitted that the relationship had
been rather volatile. "We were a mismatch. It was just a
matter of who was going to kill whom. And the answer to your
last question is yes and no and how in the hell should I know?
Yes, he was for the PLO and quite without illusions about its
prospects. But you can say much the same for the Prime
Ministers of Ireland, Greece, Cyprus, Japan, Austria, Spain,
Italy, zub, zub, zub—and the Pope. Imagine it! John Paul
considers the PLO the legitimate representative of the Palestinians. Does that make him a terrorist?"

"Yes!" Leonard's palm smacked the table. "Sorry 'bout that,
but it does."

Luz sat placidly, keeping a mild tone. "Cum'on, will you get off it?" It was obvious from the hollowness of his words that Lenny was mouthing the company line. "You want to talk about people who've taken an actively unappreciative view of U.S. meddling? You have any idea how long that line would be?"

Leonard looked at Luz soulfully. "A man only knows what other people tell him."

"It'd probably stretch from here to Venus and back. If that fact takes time to soak in, *señor*, then soak away."

Leonard had raised his eyebrows in real or affected astonishment at the vehemence of her tone. Like many diplomats, Berg had mastered the art of gentle self-deprecation, the kind that disarms others without really threatening one's own position. Leaning forward so that his face was more clearly in the glow of the candle, he continued doggedly, "So what you're saying is Ali doesn't like us?"

"Not exactly," Luz answered with pardonable irritation. She was starting to debate with herself whether she'd been wise to admit to knowing Ali so intimately. But she went on, "I remember one time in a supermarket when a clerk accused him of taking a yogurt without paying for it. Ali got a burr up his tail and told the guy, 'When your people were swinging through the trees and talking ugga-mugga, my people already had inflation.' The clerk was a Chicano, like me, and I felt like crawling through a hole in the floor." Luz put her head in her hands now, just as she had when all hell had broken loose at Safeway. Then she looked up at Leonard. He said nothing, waiting.

Torn between indignation at remembered outrage and annoyance that Berg had her raking over cold ground, Luz snapped, "But most of the time Ali loved living in Santa Cruz, loved the university. He'd say, 'When I left Egypt I emerged from a dark theater into a bright and disorienting sunlight.' One night we were watching a movie about Chinese Gordon. It was filmed in Khartoum. There's a scene where they show the shacks by the river bank, those awful hovels. Ali said to me, 'Noor baby, I used to live in a house like that.' I said,

'*Madre mia*, how'd you get from there to here?' And he said, 'Luck, I'm not all that ambitious.'"

Leonard still looked doubtful, but he didn't press the issue except to say, "Some people seem to think Salah has gotten politically ambitious with age. Is that possible?"

Luz did not answer. He looked over at her. Her eyes were shut and her breathing was growing louder as memories of the past flooded over her. Her affair with Ali had been an intense melodrama filled with episodes of fighting, break-ups, other loves, jealousy, frustration, all of it played out against a background of student discontent with the never-ending Vietnam War, civil rights, Chicano liberation, the women's movement. In bed with Ali, none of this seemed to matter. His love-making could make her forget her own name and it did, until the moment she became conscious of his term papers that he expected her to type and the laundry and the dishes that he was always leaving for her to do. Educated in the sexual caste system of the Orient, he expected women to bow and scrape to men and be ever so grateful to Allah for the opportunity. The Egyptian Salah had forced the Hispanic Gracida to think about the meaning of the sexual transaction as she had never thought about it before: was it energizing or debilitating? Am I less or more when I'm with him? Ali made her change, in a way, because she did become a person other than who she'd been, harder to fool and truer to herself. He was one of the most pivotal persons in her life.

"But you can believe me," Luz said to Leonard, "it was a relief when it ended. I'd lived through that affair with an intensity I'd never experienced before or since. Times when the hurting was awful, I'd tell myself I'm going to live through this if it kills me. But finally, there came some bursting point where I had to end it—*Basta!*—or go under. I lost contact with him after he left the States. But anything is possible. Ali was unpredictable, if nothing else. He had me bamboozled, or perhaps I should say, he had the 19-year-old girl I once was bamboozled."

For a moment Leonard was silent. When he spoke, his

words were deliberately spaced and clearly enunciated. "So what you're saying is Ali was a con artist."

"If you stop to think about it, what's so bad about a con artist? The Oval Office has never been without one." A trace of anger sparked her words as Luz went on to tell about the time a friend of theirs was dying of cancer. She expressed a wish to see a sunset on the Pacific Ocean one last time. Ali Salah came to the hospital with a stretcher and two muscular friends, all disguised in orderly greens. They kidnapped her, put her in the back of their pickup on a mattress and drove her down to the beach. Her family was livid at first, but Ali's gesture was so obviously well-intentioned they let it go.

Leonard nodded his head sympathetically, and Luz felt a sudden rush of tenderness towards him. "Ali sounds like a tenderhearted soul," Leonard observed, silently wondering: is she letting her fondness for Ali blind her good judgement? He lowered his gaze and thought about what she'd said. Was it honest? Perhaps she'd been more heavily influenced by the experience of being educated by nuns, being taught you're supposed to do good deeds and Christian works of mercy. Catholic role models aren't corporate presidents and rock stars; they're saints who dedicated their lives to others. Individuals who are often rabble rousers instill in their followers the sense that a political system needs changing, that city hall must be fought, authority defied—somewhat as Ali Salah is doing now.

Leonard puffed out his cheeks in a little wheezing sigh and speculatively looked at the Chicana: if he could get her as far as Ali's house, could she get them through the door? Could she get Ali to talk? Luz Gracida obviously had the background, the former connection, and the beauty that gave her whatever tools one would need to get to Ali Salah, to gain his confidence and be with him without much difficulty. But Berg was seized by a sudden pang of jealousy. Did he really want her anywhere near an old boyfriend? Leonard had been leaning comfortably on the armrest of his chair, but now he raised himself to an erect sitting position and stared unwaveringly into her eyes. "But Ali's still a magnet."

Luz stared, shocked, yet aware that Leonard had put his

finger on a truth she had, until now, refused to acknowledge even to herself. "No, it's not that. It's just—" she tried to find the right word, knowing that her eyes already betrayed an interest that made her hesitation fraudulent. "All our friends used to wonder what Ali would be like in ten years. A man to be reckoned with, I'd say, and I never got an argument on that score. What we didn't know is how big the average Egyptian is—how they prefer their leaders to be physically imposing men. Ali's dream was, well, like wanting to be a flight attendant and not being able to reach the pillow in the overhead compartment. He's a born loser."

Leonard's reply was a noncommittal "Perhaps."

Luz pursed her lips. "You might say Ali's a far better man in short spurts than over the long haul, yet he had a kind of madman's charm. And if he hasn't lost that, he might be a story. The problem is finding him."

Leonard was gazing blankly at his own reflection in the silver water carafe when he said softly, "Pete over there thinks he knows where Ali is."

"May I have his address?" Luz asked, fighting down the agitation inside her.

"I'll take you there, *ma petite*," Leonard signaled the waiter to bring the check. "Pack your bikini and be ready early Tuesday morning. We're going to the Red Sea."

Luz was not aware of staring at him or that he was staring at her. It seemed natural that the clock stopped while they looked at each other. "When?"

Lenny brought them back to stark reality. "Since time is the controlling factor here, at once." It was what Luz wanted above anything and didn't want at all. Her big brown eyes with their finely etched brows were confused. There was Minister Maguib to interview in his office and the U.S. Air Force element to visit at their Cairo West base. There was Mrs. Sadat's tea party; Khalid was particularly insistent that she attend. A bird beat in her throat. "Hold on, Lenny," she begged, "I don't think I'm cut out for this Egyptian scene."

"Are you kidding? You've been shot at and banged around on a Sun Tour, nursed a wild-assed politician, then misplaced him, found Jihan's least favorite professor in hiding and got him to spill his guts—and all in nine, ten days. I'd say you're a natural." Leonard rose and took her hand. It was soft and warm. He hadn't coaxed an acceptance out of her. Then their eyes met and held. Luz let out a breath she wasn't even aware of holding in and smiled. Seeing he was on a winning streak, Lenny added, "But before we hit the Red Sea, mate, may I suggest a sail closer to home?"

10

Leonard and Luz climbed down the stairs and walked out on the little dock, right over the black water of the Nile. Two small wooden row boats were rocking gently in their moorings. The traffic on the street had mysteriously disappeared for the moment, and the only sound was the soft lapping of the waves against the dock. Hand in hand, they were standing and looking out at the waters of the ancient river, talking automatically and about nothing when across a narrow stretch of ripples a huge sail loomed, whipping like laundry. Neither of them spoke as the *falucca* came gliding smoothly towards them. At first, Luz resisted the idea of a moonlight cruise on the Nile saying, "I'm not a Titanic type who's into perilous journeys," but Leonard finally managed to persuade her. "Trust me," he crooned, his lips just brushing her cheek, his smile a tease and a promise. "You'll have a ball."

"Ball?" Luz clapped her face in exaggerated alarm. "Why do I get the feeling there's a double entendre hiding somewhere in that sentence? Why am I here? We don't know each other that well, Mr, ah, what is it? Mr. Steinberg? Bergdorf?"

Leonard glanced at her entirely blank face, then slipped his hand through her arm and drew her close, his chin grazing her cheekbone. She could feel his breath warm and moist against her ear. "Fortunately, my dear Lucy, that's a minor problem that can be remedied in no time at all." Luz's mouth went dry.

A potbelly Egyptian came out of a small wooden shack and when the boatman tossed him the rope, he held tight to it while Luz took off her high heels. "Ah good, safety in numbers," she remarked as they climbed into the *falucca*. The boatman bounded over to them and gave Lenny an open-handed clap on the shoulder that staggered him. The boatman wore a sailor's Dixie cup one finger over his eyebrows, two-thirds of his face was nose, and there was a permanent squint to his eyes from years of looking into the sun and the wind. He stared at Luz with friendly curiosity while Leonard introduced him to her as "my old friend Masoud."

All Luz could see was the sailor hat and the gleaming white teeth in a dark face burnt darker by the sun, but Leonard gently touched the man's beard and told her, "Masoud looks just like my Aunt Sophie before electrolysis. You'll love him, as I do." What he didn't tell her was that trustworthy Masoud was on the payroll, exorbitantly paid—by local standards—to keep his mouth shut, avert his eyes, and do whatever else might be required of him.

The sail needed adjustment. "Here, Len Bey, stop acting like Allah took away the use of your limbs," said the boatman, offering the tiller to Leonard.

He grinned, wolfish and keen, and Luz saw he was thrilled. "Where'd you like this battlewagon to take you, darling?" he said, popping his hands together. "The Sudan? Madagascar?" Taking charge of the rudder, he skillfully manuevered them around a long barge laden with oil barrels. He was sitting with his profile to her, looking out over the water.

"You look like a figurehead on a ship, Don Leonardo," Luz said admiringly. She was close to him on the varnished bench, her hand on his knee, listening to the rustling wash of water along the sides of the *falucca*. Praising his skill, she asked how he got to be the Embassy's chief interpreter, alarm-raiser, and analyzer when he obviously spent all his time sailing.

"Jack of all trades," Leonard whooped. "What can I do for you? Unstick your stuck zipper, repair your watch, fix the broken lock on your suitcase, remove the cobwebs from your diaphragm, you name it. My talents are endless. If, by chance, you've brought your Rubic cube along, I'll demonstrate how I solve it in two minutes flat."

"*Madre mia!*" Luz said in quiet amusement. "And here I

had you pegged for a bookworm who didn't know which end of the lawn mower to push."

"You had me pegged right," Leonard admitted ruefully. "Butterfingers is my middle name. The reason I wear loafers is because I've never learned how to tie knots." He kicked his heels in the air for emphasis. "A gold-plated klutz."

Luz grinned at him when she exclaimed, "Chico, you are a very weird piece of work."

He gave her a big toothy grin. "I try." Then he turned earnest once more. "The most fascinating thing about analyzing the Egyptian scene is trying to catch something which is really different from your own attitudes, your own world. If you can latch on to that, it's very important. A lot of my colleagues spoil that possibility because they're projecting their own bias."

Passing on his knowledge of and joy in the Middle East was a serious and agreeable business, and Berg the diplomat could wish for no more attentive pupil than Gracida the journalist. But he let go of the thought. The night was too pleasant for mental exertion, and his beautiful companion was making him feel nervous and reckless at the same time. He touched her hair with his lips, inhaling the scent of soap and perfume. He put his arm around her shoulder and lazily stretched his legs out in front of him.

Luz began to feel fuzzy from the wine and his tenderness. Looking up at the Meridian Hotel, she recalled what Mr. Hwan had told her about tidy views from lofty vantage points. But she was beginning to discover it was a colossal illusion to view this country from afar. To look at Egypt from a distance, whether it be across an ocean and a sea, from an airplane or atop a modern hotel, is to deceive yourself. Egypt had to be touched, smelled, sucked in. She reached over the side to dip her hand into the Nile.

"Don't!" Leonard's hand shot out and grabbed her wrist, hard. "Unless you want to die of Bilharziasis."

Luz's voice came back sharp and anxious. "What's that?"

The explanation tumbled out, and the expression on his face told her she'd been saved from doing something very stupid.

"A killer, health problem *numero uno* here in Egypt." He kissed her forehead. "You've got to be more careful, *bubeleh*. I'd better take you home with me, where I can keep an eye on you."

"Am I to consider that a proposition?"

"I'd be pleased if you would." Leonard took her in his arms and felt her settling in against him.

The bow of the boat slapped its way southward with an insistent rhythm. The suburban streets of Ma'adi were quiet, a late night dampness heavy in the air. The swaying of the moon and trees, the roll of the boat, and Leonard's slow hands and soft voice were slowly hypnotizing Luz. She felt like closing her eyes, but she knew she ought to remain watchful, to see if Pete Sanchez was following them. Masoud was slumped against the mast, throwing quick glances at the shore and talking in bursts. The pearly moon was high now, sharing an indigo sky with a zillion stars. Luz told Lenny that she enjoyed listening to him expound on his areas of expertise, even as an awareness was dawning in her that they knew each other on some level far deeper than words. She looked out at their reflections on the black water and felt the edge of sadness that comes when life is too perfectly beautiful to contain. "Kinda—kind of pretty, isn't it?" she stammered.

Kind of pretty? No, much more than that. The Nile was unlike anything you'd find east of Eden in its enchantment, its seductive power. His lips moving against her throat, Leonard was saying in a husky voice, "The trick is to be able to think like an Egyptian, to take the Arab World on its own terms, and I can do that better than most."

Luz woke to a start. "You?" She knew better than to laugh though she wanted to.

Today's Arab World was hardly a branch of the Quaker Church. An opera of tormented passions and sudden, violent death, it makes Bizet's *Carmen* look like *Sesame Street*. Manipulative personalities were always pressing instinctively for specious advantage, and manhood was too often displayed by one's desire to kill one's enemies. Luz couldn't recognize a thoroughly nice person such as Lenny Berg inside its contours. He was more like a CPA with a calculator-precise mind

than a dashing desert prince on a white steed who could throw
you on the deck with wild abandon, lowering his bearded face
dangerously close to yours. And would Masoud the boatman
dive overboard and disappear, so as to give them a chance to
consummate their love?

"We'd better go back," Luz told Leonard, though she'd
have preferred that Masoud be the one to leave. Lenny kissed
her lips, awakening some intensity until now quiescent. Pulling back, she reminded him in a husky voice, "We are not
alone. I'd have thought you'd have more respect for con-
vention, sir."

"Don't mind me," said Masoud cordially. He casually
reached under his *galabiah*. As Luz closed her eyes she heard
the releasing of a hard stream into the river. Masoud shook his
organ dry, then tactfully twisted around until he'd given them
the back of his head. He picked up a chamois and started
polishing brass.

Luz was lying back against the cushions. She had unpinned
her hair, and it hung loose to her shoulders. Desire rose in
Leonard, compressing his chest, and he had trouble
breathing. His fingers moved to push a few wind-tossed
strands of hair out of Luz's face. What a godsend, he thought,
gazing at her with a look of open delight. Heavy fragrant air
engulfed them. Her head lowered shyly and suddenly
Leonard felt an aching need to have her lying in his arms, to
press his lips into the curve of her neck. His heart was
bounding so hard he thought it might show through his shirt.

As if divining his thoughts, Luz lifted her eyes to meet his.
"Can't we be friends, *companero*? Can't we be each other's
two-week supply of comfort and solace and dinner engage-
ments?"

"Not on your sweet life!" Leonard said straight out, then
laughed, as if at a ridiculous suggestion. "It's not enough." He
had never imagined he'd make such an admission and in such
an emphatic way. He shivered, feeling his armpits sweaty
underneath the navy blue blazer. He ducked his head down in
an effort to get her to look at him, and he heard Masoud grunt
as if to acknowledge an unspoken communication.

None too successful in her earlier affairs, Luz was reluctant

to give in to her feelings for Lenny. There was a tenderness to
him that was genuine. Children and furry animals would turn
to him naturally, sure of kindness and protection. Still, he was
a Foreign Service Officer trained to manipulate people, sharp
and hip and a fast man with a quip. And hadn't he shown
himself willing to use her just to get to Ali? She disengaged
her hand when he tried to hold it and started to splinter the
wood with her thumbnail. "The problem is you live here in
Cairo and I pay rent in El Paso. Long distance love doesn't
work, *caro*, it is too ephemeral. It's good for your fantasy life,
but the heart really doesn't grow fonder over the long haul."

Luz stopped and looked down at her feet as though she'd
forgotten the next line and was hoping an invisible prompter
hidden somewhere in her toes could give her a clue. Ease up,
Gracida, she admonished herself. You both have an integrity
about how you deal with people, so why can't you just let it be
that you're a man and a woman who are attracted to each
other, and you want to sleep with each other? Love in the
afternoon, a transitory dalliance, time out of time with no past
and no future. An interim attachment for people who take
work for granted and lovers for fun, who know that getting
roped into anything complicating is to be avoided at all cost. It
will be your regular one-night stand, no more no less. Luz
sighed and started, "Well, I don't suppose there's any rules
for—"

The river murmured all around them. Leonard bent towards her, kissing her in mid-sentence on her lips and then
her cheeks and temples. She was as calm and easy as the
falucca moving through the waters. "Come stay with me." His
eyes pleaded with hers. "I want to make love to you, go to
sleep holding you, wake up with you in my arms, eat and read
and watch TV and everything else with you."

"*Un momento, caballero.*" Eyes closed, voice a whisper,
Luz protested, "You really shouldn't say those things to me.
You'll feel differently when you get back on land. There must
be something about this river that makes you want to make a
grand gesture, like building a pyramid or falling in love."

Leonard stirred against her, and she felt him undoing the
clasps on her jacket. He bit her earlobe very gently, and she

let his hands play over her breasts, tracing the curves, touching the nipples. Her body was responding all by itself, without asking permission. "Besides," she faltered, "I'm out here on assignment."

"Our being together won't interfere with that," Leonard promised. His voice was calm, but the words dragged, as if voicing them was an effort. "We can mix business with pleasure while we go look up your ex-roommate."

Leonard wished he hadn't said that. Luz was curled up in his arms and he could feel her tense up, and this wasn't the mood he wanted her in. He wanted her as relaxed as she'd been a moment ago. "We'll see," Luz said hesitantly. Her forehead puckered into caramel creases, and he left it at that.

As they pulled up to the dock a light slashed a diagonal line across his crotch, leaving his face in darkness. Luz knew how to make every moment count, but did she want another aimless adventure that would, when it ended, leave her feeling rootless and alone? Still, she felt a strange and disorienting intensification of Len's unique powers. He wasn't handsome or sexy in a Tom Cruise big box office way, but he was suffused with an intense aura of sexuality that he seemed to know how to use for his purposes. He was a man who worked hard and laughed easily. Isn't that what life's all about, toiling with dedication, looking for the humor in things and trying to enjoy yourselves in spite of the odds? She loved the effect he had on her, and so did the perceptive boatman.

A broad smile cracking his rough face, Masoud set about stretching a canvas awning chastely between two metal frames. Then he took a rolled-up mattress out of a wooden box and positioned it modestly on the deck underneath the canvas. Without a backward glance, he climbed up to the street where he parked himself at the top of the stairs, a vigilant sentry.

"I don't want Masoud to get down on me," Luz said, her arms huddled around her knees. "The Muslim attitude toward women is already bad enough."

"Among the Muslims' ideals of honor, discretion ranks first." Leonard bent and kissed the arc of her neck lightly. "Relax, Masoud likes you so much, you can't do any wrong.

And if you do, he won't tell a soul; you can bet your life on that. He's an Egyptian Sunni, not an Iranian Shi'ite—there's a whale of a difference between them. Poor Shi'ites, they've really been cursed by God in the religion He's given them."

Leonard tugged at her ankle, but Luz was still reluctant. "As a guard," she decided, "Masoud looks like a good nursing home inmate."

"A whole platoon of Marines couldn't get by him." Leonard spoke with assurance, rubbing her legs, reaching out for her hungrily. He could feel her shuddering.

Luz wasn't totally convinced. She heard the wash of barges slapping against the shore as she lifted a flap of canvas, gazed out over the lacquered surface of the moonlit river, and wondered if the resolute Pedro Sanchez counted "frogman and underwater infra-red cameraman" among his spying talents. But darkness brought abandon; excitement struggled with fear and quickly overcame it. Their mouths found each other.

Leonard had undressed and was standing naked while she let her skirt fall to her ankles. She started to free herself of her blouse, but he said, "Let me do that," and finished unbuttoning it and placing it carefully on the bench. Then he pulled her down next to him on the mattress. She closed her eyes, yielding to the pressure of chest, stomach, and legs tight against her own.

It was late and very dark, but in the slices of starlight filtering through the tears of awning like strips of neon lighting, Luz could see the fire in Leonard's eyes. Urgently, he brought his mouth down to hers. He could feel her breasts against his chest, then her hands—pushing him away. Luz was savoring the delicious moments of anticipation, trying to prolong the pleasure, but Leonard, unable to control the onset of passion, was hard against her, hands and mouth everywhere, pulling at her bra and panties. Leonard was through being gentle. The fire that he roused in her flamed and she turned half over. Her legs opened and he pushed into her.

When Leonard's breathing had calmed down, Luz asked him, "So how many *faluccas* does Masoud own by now?"

Leonard's legs were spread out on the deck, his arms extended over his head. The coil of his organ rested in the matted hair of his crotch. He looked hurt. "Are you trying to find out how many times I've done this? Oh, Linda, dear Linda, how could you? Indirection will get you nowhere." Luz jabbed him and he stopped short. "Oh migod! It's not Linda. How tacky and inconsiderate of me. I'm sorry, Miss ah—"

Luz's irritation was released in a sharp cry. "Bastard!"

"You sound like my ex-wife," Leonard grumbled, reaching for his slacks. His quiet tie lay like an eel by his feet.

"You're divorced?" Luz stopped abruptly, though she had the feeling that if pressed, he would confide in her. "I don't mean to pry, but why ex?"

Leonard was tired and the gentle rolling of the *falucca* invited sleep. But he lay back down. She moved into the hollow of his body and he began the sad tale. "We were in Val Gardena, happy as two clams, skiing, drinking *vino blanco*, and this sleazy Eye-talian ski instructor asks Karen to meet him at the train station next day. He just stops dead in the middle of the slope and asks her to run away with him, just like that—" he snapped his fingers. "And damned if Karen didn't go to the station and to Roma with him for six whole weeks. From what I hear, they had a fantastic time until his wife and her brother showed up at the pension."

Leonard was turned toward Luz, his blond head propped up on one palm, while with the other he cupped a soft brown breast. He had lived that scene on the ski slope a thousand times: shocking, a bolt out of the blue scorching him with humiliation. For days afterwards he'd worn the pain and confusion on his face. Every expression seemed to betray the thought: what did I do to cause her to do that? With Karen, love and the urge to strangle had run neck and neck, with guilt not far behind. Many was the time he'd close his eyes and see himself doing some kind of violence, like putting a bullet in his temple or jumping off the roof, but there was no more luxuriating in agony. Luz's coming had changed that; it was now in the dead past. Leonard felt lightheaded, as if he were floating above the Nile, drifting toward the stars. Luz pushed the curl of her body back against him, then turned

inside his arms. He kissed her neck and murmured something
in a tongue Luz didn't understand. Abruptly, he pulled away
and stood drawing her up after him. "Karen came back to
Qatar where we lived, but by then I'd filed for a divorce."

Luz slipped her skirt over her hips. "Those Arab Gulf states
can do that to a girl, send her into Flipsville. I once spent ten
days in Riyadh and never saw another woman. I figured a
quiet atomic bomb had been dropped, and the men were the
only ones with the protective shields."

"It wasn't the Arabs' fault; it was that bastard Sandro Pe-
tronelli." Leonard spat the name out like a watermelon seed,
then bared his teeth, "Goddamn Latins! There ought to be a
law against them." He drew Maria Luz to him. "I'll take you
anywhere you want to go, sweetheart," he said fiercely, moving his head back to see the curve of her cheek, the brown
skin of her neck. "But not Italy, not ever."

11

Just after dawn, Zenaib el-Din of Boulak District, sister of Hikmat el-Din, positioned herself on the south side of the massive Security Building to await news of her brother's whereabouts. Tall and heavy, with slanting eyes and an elegantly long face that looked as though it had grown up between two obelisks, Zenaib had come here to demand answers. "You didn't notice Hikmat doing anything hurtful to these policeman, did you?" she called to others who had also travelled from the City of the Dead to see their idol. "You know as well as I that Hikmat wouldn't hurt a fly, don't you?"

Fathi Rajab, faithful disciple and cell member, could hear the panic and pleading in her voice all too clearly. But his own fear-fueled anger was very near the surface. Foolish woman, why didn't she shut up? Stifling an urge to lash out and slap her across the mouth with great force, he studied his shoes. Zenaib had always thought Fathi a nice person who was kindly disposed toward her.

Suddenly, Zenaib had a suspicion she'd badly misjudged the young man's character. Twirling to face Fathi, she asked him directly, "So why do they bother my brother?" Fathi shrugged.

A German tourist who'd run afoul of a pickpocket came up and inquired in English, "Is this the police?"

"Please what?" Zenaib said, mocking his accent. Then she turned to answer a reporter from *Al-Ahram* who was asking her to tell him something about Hikmat. "He has been acting so crazy lately I cannot tell you what he will do next," Zenaib supplied in her forthright manner, then stopped. The reporter waited, knowing that an Egyptian woman cannot be silent for long. "He was so difficult, even as a baby," Zenaib continued, reminiscing. "Always angry about something and usually something that doesn't matter at all, like a pretty girl advertising Cadbury's fruit and nut bars. If he didn't have anything to be angry about, I swear he would invent something."

Al-Ahram prompted, "He is paranoid then?"

Zenaib didn't know that word, but she knew her brother. "Hikmat was the only boy among six girls, and Mama believes he is the center of the universe." There was a touch of sadness in the observation, but no self-pity. "Hikmat thinks so, too. When he closes his eyes, he believes it's night."

When the reporter asked if he could take her photograph, Zenaib patted her thin braid as if she were coiffeured by Vidal Sassoon. "Do I look all right?" she fretted. She had on a floral cotton dress covered by a long, black velvet gown. After the reporter had snapped her picture, she said to no one in particular, "Just because you are mad at life, that is no reason to put you in jail." She turned once more to Fathi, thinking his male voice must publicly be heard, or it would soon be too late. Since he hadn't said a single word in Hikmat's behalf, she wondered aloud at his presence here today. "Am I to believe that you came out of the goodness of your heart?"

"You are to believe whatever you must, Auntie." Fathi's eyes flicked across the crowd, as if looking for someone.

Some men, Zenaib knew, did their allotted tasks in life out of duty and need, while others had a craving for excitement, as if it were opium or hashish. Was Fathi just another troublemaker, searching for the spark that might detonate an explosive situation? Pointedly, she asked him, "Do you intend a hideous scene of some sort?"

Fathi Rajab could adjust his behavior when he had to, and his irritation at Zenaib's outspokenness and her probing, showed itself in a quick glance and a shark's smile. "The less said the better," he muttered, his nostrils flaring slightly as though the cell's troubles could be sniffed in the humid air. But Zenaib went right on talking, telling everyone in sight that she had worried about Hikmat from the time he was born. "Ever since he joined the Jamaat, he has been uncompromis-

ing in his aims. He has an incredible talent for rousing others
to action, for making them think that his plans promise them a
big feast every day of their lives, but having him around the
house can be pure hell. Even when Papa tells him, 'Maybe
our expectations are too high, maybe we ought to take one
step backwards before we can take two steps forward,' even
then Hikmat does not pay attention. Not even to his own
father!" Zenaib shook her head helplessly, as if all her certain-
ties were flaking away like dried skin.

Listening at the edge of the circle, Rashed Madi nearly fell
over in shock. Was she stark raving mad? His chocolate eyes
seemed to be on the verge of melting, and he advanced as if to
throttle her. He started to yell at her to get the hell out of
here, but his voice wavered. Looking beyond Zenaib's shoulder, Rashed encountered Fathi Rajab's deceptively lazy glaze.
Fathi shook his head fractionally, but the gesture was plainly
readable in the circumstances. Rashed was to put sunshine
between Ibrahim's sister and himself. The woman was beyond
the reach of reason, with no more common sense than a
melon.

Nearly a week after he was last seen scrambling into a
three-wheel Piaggi in a dirt lane off Pyramid Road, mystery
continued to surround the whereabouts of Hikmat el-Din,
a.k.a Ibrahim. His popularity among his followers had soared
during his absence, turning him into a legendary figure. His
photograph could be seen in car windshields and storefronts,
and people were frequently invoking his name as a saintly
hero who will return victoriously to take the reins of lead-
ership and steer Egypt away from secularism. The Security
forces appeared undecided about what to say about el-Din's
fate. "He might be alive and then again he might not," they
announced blandly. "Witnesses tell us he was gravely
wounded during the fight near the Mena House, in the leg
and the abdomen."

People took that statement with a grain of salt. The authorities were clearly impatient to be done with the whole
affair and get back to lining their pockets. Every college
graduate in the country was guaranteed a job with the government and how did they spend their days, packed into offices

with six people to one ancient desk? They spent them devising Byzantine procedures to drive decent citizens out of their minds and selling their signatures for cash on the barrel head, that's how. The police files were undeniably crammed to bursting, full of unsolved crimes involving murderers, arsonists, thieves, robbers, adulteresses, fornicators, Zionist and Libyan spies, opium dealers, hashish sellers, smugglers of Japanese watches, drunkards, and runaway wives. And yet they would dare to treat Hikmat el-Din as a criminal! People were bitter and frustrated. Once upon a time there were otherworldly answers for everything. But people were starting to see that not everything was beyond their understanding and control. The police had an easier time of it when they could say, "Ins'challah," and have the masses echo, "God wills," on cue. But Egyptians were discovering the world of human responsibility and direction, and they demanded an end to pinning the blame on God.

Rashed's eyes darted from one unfamiliar face to the next. Fear and uncertainty had invaded his mood, replacing the confidence and bravado he had been voicing at the last meeting. He stood with his toes pointed in towards his ankle-bones and cursed Zenaib's big mouth. He cursed Talaat for getting himself shot dead. He cursed Ibrahim for the carelessness that had gotten him into this fix until he'd worked himself into such a state that he feared he was going to be sick. To distract himself he tried to observe what was going on around him. The stale air of cooking food and wastes brushed by him as he gazed across the street. From buildings that defied both the laws of physics and hygiene, doorways offered up batches of bare-bottomed toddlers. Aggressive women in black *abayas* and scarves, many with bare-bottomed infants on their hips, were milling about in front of a rationed food store, gossiping or quarreling. Above it all were the old men leaning out over balcony railings and the long banners of laundry fluttering from thin plastic ropes.

Rashed, whose entire family had fled Serapeum during the 1967 war, still felt discombobulated by the teeming metropolis on the Nile, by the 24-hour traffic jams, by monuments scarred by graffiti: names, epigrams, political slogans, and blunt sexual invitations crudely carved into ancient stone. You might not have to be crazy to live in Cairo, but after a few weeks you will be, he thought with some bitterness. He shut his eyes, wishing he could go back in time and be a child again on the Great Bitter Lake, but all he heard was his father's voice saying fatalistically, "You have got to eat what is on your plate, my son. Otherwise you will go hungry."

Zenaib, her patience strained to point of teeth grinding, broke through the barriers and ran to the entrance. "What are you doing to my brother?" she shrieked at the top of her lungs. "Where is he? Is he hurt?"

A uniformed guard, his eyes shimmering with the blue hardness of glacial ice, gave her a shove that almost propelled her backward and over a guard rail. "Go home, woman, where you belong."

Zenaib tore at her face and struck her billowy breasts with clenched fists. Tears poured down her faded checks. Rashed Madi dashed to her aid. "Please don't shove, we'll go," he said to the policeman with all the deference of a born loser looking for a streak of luck. "We are just leaving—" his eyes slid towards Zenaib—"aren't we, Auntie?"

"Where is my brother Hikmat?" She wailed and wept noisily, rocking her big body to and fro. "He is innocent, I tell you."

Fathi Rajab looked up at the sky, closing his eyes. He sensed the danger of all of them gathered here. The guards were hurrying on with the business at hand, and there was more shouting at the entrance way to the building. A lawyer in pinstripes emerged, looking as if he had that moment been unpacked from a Harrod's band box. Spectators crowded in, talking in unison. He held up a hand for silence and when he got it, he reported in his aristocratic baritone suavely, "In our discussions about Hikmat, the major referred to him in the present tense, saying at one point, 'He is still a menace.' I honestly don't know what that means. It was all very vague, with the major being very careful not to lead me to the conclusion my client was killed and at the same time leaving the impression that they know his whereabouts, but are simply not disclosing it. Be that as it may, we are in no position to demonstrate and behave stupidly."

Everyone watched the lawyer shape his report with his long, spear-like arm, his bushy eyebrows, and his reassuring smile—a smile that was constant, but never reached his eyes. Rashed's mind and eyes registered that the lawyer's mouth continued to move, but all he heard was blah, blah, blah. "I would," finished the counsel pompously, "advise all of you to go home now and let me handle it." His advice had no takers and to get to his car he had to wade through the mass of people holding his briefcase against his midsection like a Mameluke's shield.

Now, Rashed turned to Zenaib. "The counselor's right," he said, obviously happy that the air had been let out of her balloon. "Go home now."

"But—" Zenaib started to protest, but she had no more strength.

Rashed saw the capitulation in the weary bowing of her head, and he gave her a gentle push. Then he went automatically to Fathi who was staring at the wall, his lips drawn back over tightly clenched teeth. "We had better go find Ali," Rashed announced out of the side of his mouth as he brushed by Fathi's elbow. Fathi nodded his head ever so slightly. Then he turned to watch Zenaib The Protestor change into Zenaib The Shopper.

Whenever a woman sees a mob forming outside the *goumhoreyya*, she joins it. The *goumhoreyya* is the government store, the place you come to with your ration card to buy subsidized items. Hundreds of stores had been set up after the terrible food riots of 1977. Without such outlets, the poor would starve to death—if they didn't bring down the government first. "What are they selling today?" Zenaib inquired of an elderly lady with her little tousled-headed grandson in tow.

"I don't know yet," the grandmother replied stoically. "But it will be something I need."

Today Zenaib was hoping she could get a plump American chicken (which was always half the price of local chicken), a five kilo bag of rice for 25 piastres, and a tin of Danish butter. There had been a soap shortage for over three weeks, and like

the other women around her, Zenaib had all but given up
hope of ever seeing soap again in her lifetime. Waiting to push
her way through the door, Zenaib thought about Hikmat's
angry speech about food distribution in the city. "Egypt is a
nation of hoarders and black marketeers on one hand and
government officials on the other," he'd said in his bombastic
way. "The former function far more effectively than the latter.
I can promise you, my friends, that after the revolution is
won, we shall have neither." How his listeners had cheered!

There was a small commotion at the front of the line, and
Zenaib craned her neck to see what had caused it. Those
women fortunate enough to be the first inside the shop when
it had opened had been able to purchase four boxes of soap
before the supply ran out, and now they were selling a box or
two to those unlucky ones outside. One woman was so enraged by this craven act that she slapped a soap seller's face,
then grabbed a box and started to walk off without paying for
it. The women from whom she'd stolen the soap, chased after
her and tried to grab the box back. It ripped open, sending
soap particles flying through the air. Instantly, the female
crowd split up, some tearing soap away from those who had it,
while others ripped open the boxes. In no time, the atmosphere around the *goumhoreyya* looked like a snowy day in
Switzerland. Fathi and Rashed knew it was time to quit the
area. Checking a natural impulse to run, Rashed moved down
the street with Fathi sauntering beside him with his hands in
his pockets.

After the two comrades were far away from the Security
Building and no one could see them, Fathi broke down. Each
day, it seemed, brought harder, more painful sacrifices. No
sooner was one test overcome than something else would
strike. First, the bighearted and charitable Talaat, now the
brilliant Ibrahim. "I knew it would come to this," Fathi said
bitterly, his face lily-white. "It always does. We are a people
who can go from tumult to slumber in the blink of an eye." He
trailed off, choked with tears.

There was no use looking ahead to the overthrow of Sadat,
for without Ibrahim that dream had no future, nor could he
look back, because that was unbearable. Ibrahim had been

their sanctuary. Rashed didn't know what to say, so he hugged Fathi and let him cry against him. After a while, Fathi raised a tearstained face and announced, "I do not want to see Ali. I do not trust him, never did." His speech was blunt and pregnant with aggression and Rashed stared at him, both appalled and disbelieving. Fathi rushed on, "Well, tell me, Rashed, how do we know Ali didn't have something to do with Ibrahim's troubles? You saw how keen he was at the meeting to take command, didn't you?"

Rashed looked at him in alarm. "My God, Fathi, what has gotten into you? Are you out of your mind?"

Fathi, taken back by the vehemence of the question, gazed bleary eyed at his comrade. "Perhaps, but you go to see Ali alone."

12

A pair of donkeys and a flock of chickens dozed companionably throughout the dusty yard under the shade of the juniper bushes. In the middle of the field of cotton at the apex of a small hillock, a single perfectly shaped palm tree broke the horizon. The heat was heavy, and the whitewashed building glared too brightly to be looked at. Inside the two-room stone house on the outskirts of Cairo, it was darker and cooler. Onions hung in bunches from ceiling hooks. One corner of the larger room was all but filled up by an ancient metal bread stove, like an octopus with its maze of duct works. There was no electricity or running water and pieces of tile were missing from the floor, exposing black adhesive that stuck to your feet. An old woman was squatting on her haunches, denuding corn cobs of their kernels. Her face reflected years of toil and troubles. The corner of the eyes were deeply etched into her leathery skin, as if her worries had been chiseled there permanently. Her granddaughter Lobna came in, her black hair damp with sweat from a morning of pulling onions, and flopped wearily on the floor. Grandmother handed her a cob and commanded her to get on with it.

Ali Salah was sitting by the rear window, his head bowed, his dark eyes fixed on a page of his well-worn *Qur'an*. Above his head, on the rooftop, was a cylindrical tank with holes that sent water seeping through the ceiling and down the walls. Listening to the drip, drip, drip on the floor, Ali could easily imagine he was in a mine shaft—or a torture chamber. From time to time, Ali looked up from the *Qur'an* and repeated a passage to explain its meaning. It was his way of saying that

since becoming a Muslim Brother five years ago, he had left
behind the first 30 years of his life—years when he had gone
to the United States, years when he had drank liquor and
danced with members of the opposite sex, years he now
regarded as sinful; *haram.* When he spoke about these things
to his grandmother and his niece, they watched him with a
puzzled, almost incredulous look, as if he were an explorer
back from Antarctica trying to tell them about glaciers and
snow.

To Ali's eyes, in the dim light, his grandmother bore a
striking resemblance to his dead mother. Still tough in her old
age, she put in a sixteen-hour day. Ali had been very angry at
his mother for dying and leaving him in his grandmother's
indifferent care until he realized that dying hadn't been his
mother's intention. She had simply miscarried during her
fifteenth pregnancy and died of a common and yet incurable
ailment: she gave up her will to live. Today Ali could hardly
bare to hear his grandmother speak of her dead daughter. He
was filled with grief for her, for himself, and for the family life
that had been squandered when his father left to work in
Jordan, parceling all the children out between the various
relatives.

Ali's new life had given him a mission: to prevent his sins
from becoming others' sins, to rise above the temptations and
hedonism that had characterized his old life, to give every one
of his 45 million countrymen dignity. He had found his voca-
tion. After all the false starts, the recklessness and desire for
instant gratification that had flung him into the arms of
Monica and Luz and all the others, he was on the right path.
Ali looked at the sharp-featured little face of his niece Lobna
and gave her another saying of the Prophet's to ponder.
"Whoever of you sees an abomination, he must remove it with
his hands."

Lobna was humming the melody of a popular Lebanese
song, and Ali barked at her to pay attention. "I am, Uncle,"
she yawned without bothering to close her mouth.

There was silence in the room. Bowing his shoulders as
though physically carrying a great weight, Ali complained to
his grandmother, "It is like talking to a wall." Then with the

self-righteous fervor of an ex-sinner, he proceeded to preach to the girl.

Finally, the old woman pinned Ali with an intense stare. "You know, Ali, for someone who has gone to university you have a hole as big as the Quantara Depression in your knowledge about human beings. Can't you see how young Lobna is?"

Then to the girl, Grandmother soothingly counseled patience. "Your uncle has been under pressure since he was released from prison. Furthermore, he cannot find a job and that makes him high-strung. But, praise God, he does not gamble or run after tarts. If he cannot be grumpy at home, pray tell, where can he be?" Ali was on the verge of interrupting rudely when he heard a car coming up the road. He stood.

His niece repeated the sutra, word perfect. "That's more like it," he approved as he went to the front window.

Mustafa parked the yellow Fiat under the fig tree beside the house and walked inside. "Peace be with you," Ali greeted Mustafa, hugging him. Then he noticed Rashed behind Mustafa. From their expression Ali could surmise that it was not good news they were bringing, and he motioned them to go outside where they could talk privately. As they sat on the veranda amid huge green tomatoes spread out on newspapers, Rashed told them he found out about Ibrahim. Ali's impulse was to throw himself upon Mustafa and yell, "Stop it! You are lying! But he sat still as a statue without looking directly at his friends. He was facing pain and loss with the brisk familiarity of one who has amply known both, but to Rashed he appeared a bit cold and unfeeling.

"Ibrahim is as solid as a rock." Mustafa breathed deeply, then repeated, "Solid as a rock," as though the phrase were a magical incantation. He spoke very softly, either summoning up the courage to go on even if their leader were dead or searching for the bright side of a dark turn. "No, Ibrahim would never divulge any secrets to the authorities. Even in captivity, he couldn't be made to talk." Mustafa's voice was ringing with conviction now. "If Ibrahim is not in jail, he is in hiding or—" Mustafa checked himself, as if he had said too much already.

Ali gave no sign that he had heard him. Rashed said in a
regretful tone, "Fathi refused to come with me today because
he has his doubts about you. He thinks you could have betrayed Ibrahim." Betrayed: the word whipped forth like an
arrow from a taut bow. Rashed had used the word betrayed on
purpose, knowing it would wound.

Ali's short frame trembled with rage, his jaw so tense he
could barely move it. He knew he was dangerously close to
losing his poise. "Fathi has pretty blue eyes, but nothing
upstairs," he growled, his own eyes narrowing for combat.
"Which goes a long way to explaining why he does all this
thinking with his asshole."

There was an intake of breath behind him. Standing in the
doorway was his grandmother, with an open show of quizzical
irritation. Ali stifled his own irritation and apologized to the
old woman. "We must face up to life and everything in it," she
replied in a chiding, cautionary tone that was exasperating.
"Allah will put all things right."

Conversation broke off immediately as Ali strode over to the
vegetable garden. Mustafa jumped up after him, grabbing a
tomato as he went. Ali was facing East, the tears coming. He
stood erect, ignoring them. What desolation, Mustafa
thought, staring at Ali's wet and haggard face, and he decided
to refrain from any mention of Talaat's wife. Ignorant of her
late husband's clandestine activities, she had reported him
missing and now the police were sniffing about. Gaining
control of himself, Ali decided, "I shall have to leave right
away, much as I hate to. This place is so peaceful, so serene."
His face had softened a bit.

Mustafa pushed the bite of tomato to one side of his mouth
and scoffed, "You can call it peaceful. I call it boring."

"A little, maybe," Ali conceded.

"Get your things together, Ali," Mustafa ordered. "We are
leaving."

Where to? Ali faced Mustafa abruptly, amazed. Mustafa
didn't care to say. Ali's face fell into wry lines. "We rebels are
like parachutists," he mused. "We are always plunging out
without knowing where we are going." He paused. In the face
of a conspiracy whose outlines he could only glimpse and

whose ramifications he could not begin to guess at, Ali felt fearful. But the feeling didn't last. Panic was chased off by a cold, deep resentment. "And friend Ibrahim is always making plans without consulting me. It makes me feel incredibly stupid and naive."

The reference to their leader nettled Mustafa into replying crisply, "He hated to do it, Ali, but this time it was unavoidable."

"Ibrahim always hates it," Ali retorted with a tinge of exasperation, "but he always does it." Mustafa replied by shrugging eloquently and raising his eyebrows in confusion. Ali refused to let go of his anger, exploding, "So much for the new democracy we hope to bring about. How much were you told?"

"Not much," Mustafa said in a dry voice, a little ashamed of Ibrahim's lack of trust in their comrade.

Skeptically, "That 'not much' sounds like 'a lot' to me."

"Ali, Ali, what more can I say to make you understand, eh?" Mustafa relented, "All right, when it gets dark, I will drive you to your Uncle Dakik's place in Hurghada. Then I will go on to Assyut." Out of the corner of his eye, Mustafa saw the disapproval in Ali's expression, and he rushed on. "We leave at twilight. As Ibrahim would say, in a sleeping country, some of us must suffer insomnia. It will be no more than a short holiday for you, that's all." His manner made the point efficiently, It's a change of plans, but nothing to get agitated about. "But first, I must fill up the tank with petrol. I intend to take along a gun, too."

That statement was so unlike the gentle Mustafa that Ali managed a feeble laugh. Mustafa added, "And lots of *leban zabadi* for my upset stomach."

Mustafa had finished with more than a touch of steel in his voice. Ali nodded, admiring his resolution, and recalled, "The last time you had anything that might generously be called a stroke of genius was in June of 1967, on that outing to Suez, when you insisted we turn around and go back for the *leban zabadi*. We missed the war in the Sinai, thanks to you." It used to embarrass Ali that he hadn't been at the front during his country's terrible ordeal, but now, with their present mission, it all made a clear and redeeming sense. Allah had spared them for bigger things.

Ali had heard some talk that the Brotherhood might be trimming its sails slightly with Ibrahim's possible capture. Lowering the sights, moderating the rhetoric, curtailing their ambitious plans to reform this corrupt society by eliminating the malicious monster at its head.

"Lies, all lies!" Mustafa's reflective smile flashed and disappeared. He had never before looked at Ali the way he was looking at him now. "Tell no one where we are headed. It seems that we are going to be taking several soldiers who have suddenly fallen ill and need to be on holiday until after the big parade. The rest of the various groups will be leaving Cairo too, going off in different directions. There is already too much police activity in this city, but it may be possible to get them to sniff after another scent. We hope we will be followed, we don't know, but we'll try. We have to get as many security agents chasing wild geese as we can."

Mustafa had an impulse to tell Ali that he must take care not to get too close to any foreign women, they were his weakness, but he pushed the anxiety into a silent corner of his mind and gave him a quick embrace.

The sun went down, but the light was still fine. Mustafa started to walk back to the car, and Ali fell in stride. There was a very pretty redheaded woman sitting in the back seat and as soon as Ali noticed her, a renewal of his initial skepticism about Mustafa's sincerity returned in force. "Who in the devil is that?" Ali flamed, drawing himself up. He was not impressive in stature, but he was muscular in his chest and shoulders. When he got no reply he screwed up his face, shut his eyes and took a little stamping, circular walk. "Dammit, tell me!"

Mustafa, perennially good-natured, was opening the trunk. He shrugged innocently, but his smile was close to a leer as he said, "You have got a mind like a, like a—" he gave up.

Ali licked his narrow lips. "A sewer? Go ahead and say it."

Mustafa laughed reproachfully. "It is a friend of my sister Hind. Good boys that we are, we have offered her a lift home."

Mustafa was too easy with flip expressions. Ali started to swear, but Mustafa waved a hand as if flicking away a fly and said, "When I am not pondering the state of the universe and the transcendental meaning of the religion, I am actually quite human." Mustafa's lips buckled and a whoop of laughter escaped. He reached down into the trunk of the car and came up with a large yellow backpack, the kind that Sherpas wear on Mount Everest expeditions. He gave it to Ali, along with a swift and affectionate pat on the back.

Ali tried to lift the pack, but it was heavier than an elephant. "Are the two soldiers inside here?" he asked Mustafa, who was still laughing, a prankish schoolboy laugh. It was rice, sugar, tea, and cooking oil for Grandmother, to keep her away from the marketplace where women are so apt to indulge in idle, but dangerous gossip. Mustafa pulled the damp air into his lungs and dove into the driver's seat.

As the car pulled away, Rashed stuck his head out the window and gave Ali a sign, a combination thumbs-up and a benediction. "Take care, Ali. Go with Allah's hand on your shoulder." Waving, Ali suddenly remembered that Rashed's name meant upright in Arabic. It suited him.

After his comrades had left, Ali made a few notations. Like many in the Jamaat, he wrote constantly, filling innumerable little plastic-covered books with notes on what should be done with industry and agriculture after the revolution was won, social observations, plans for saving the world, snatches of overheard political talk, and imaginary dialogues with people he felt he ought to meet and set straight, Margaret Thatcher and Ronald Reagan, for example. Then he went for a solitary walk. A bird was singing somewhere within the grove of coral trees behind the house, floating notes from the darkness out across the luminous twilight. A star shot a brilliant arch across the sky, and Ali tracked it absently, his thoughts on his future. His first act as the Governor of Cairo, he imagined, would be to bring prosperity to this area, an act witnessed by all his relatives, who would stare with rapt interest, initial skepticism turning to deep admiration and everlasting gratitude as the extent of his powers to do good dawned on them. With a flourish, he would cut the red ribbons, as whole villages broke into lusty cheering. The President would hang a medal around his neck. "Has there ever been a more devoted and courageous son of Egypt than this man who has courageously devoted himself to Egypt?" he'd say—or words to that effect.

Ali heard a dog barking in the distance, melancholy and introspective. He stepped off the dusty path to let a donkey go by. A young girl, small, and scrawny, slapped the rump with a thong to make him trot. Her small son clung to the animal's mane. This, thought Ali bitterly, is what is wrong with us. We tolerate child labor and children giving birth to children. It has got to stop! In the chill of the evening there was a loneliness arising from the fields and the canal, and he was glad when his niece came out to join him. He threw an affectionate, protective look at Lobna and told her he would not give permission for her to marry until she was at least 17. Then he spelled out precautions she should take while he was away: say nothing to anyone about him, do not talk about me even to your best friends, help Grandmother with her tasks for her health has never been of the best and she is in poor spirits lately, be prepared for any eventuality. His voice was a trifle croaky as he spoke. "You probably won't miss me very much," he finished bitterly.

Lobna said nothing, so near to truth were his petulant words. The absence of her nit-picking Uncle would come as a welcome relief. Already the place felt lighter, the air clearer. But fearing another scolding, she tried to smooth things over by looking up at him with innocent interest and asking solicitously, "Is anything wrong, Uncle? They're not going to send you back to prison again, are they?"

Frowning down at her, Ali answered in a lofty tone, "God never pays His debts with money, little one. Much can happen in the next week."

Lobna, a child with the all-seeing eyes of someone at the other end of life, gave him a bittersweet smile. "Much can happen in the next minute. That is life." Lobna started running across the field with her arms out flung, as if she were flying, the sound of her own laughter surrounding her. Suddenly, Ali realized he wouldn't mind at all marrying the carefree woman she would one day become, and realizing this he felt the pain of another loss: Lobna had been born too many years before him. And he was promised to another.

13

The little town by the Red Sea was cramped, sun-beaten, and almost ready for a siesta. Squat cinder block and stucco houses reached right up to the dirt lane. Mattresses and rugs hung over the edges of the roofs. A spavin horse pulling a buggy almost trampled them, but swerved at the last minute. "It is good to be back," Ali Salah said with a gentle smile as he fielded yet another hug from a well-wisher. He was on his way back from Hurghada. His cousin Nafeisa Salah was trotting beside him, carrying green peppers, zucchini, eggplants, lemons, garlic, and *pita* bread in a cloth sack on her arm. A woman was leaning from a window, pinning laundry onto a clothesline strung between buildings. She called out a greeting.

Nafeisa replied without looking up. Her eyes were fixed in clear adoration of Ali. The whole town was talking about him. Everyone was intrigued with everything he did—even though he didn't do much that she could see. The morning was as steaming hot as her mother's copper laundry pot. Nafeisa could feel the itchy rash where her thighs rubbed together when she walked. The sharp rocks jabbed and bruised her feet through the thin plastic of her soles. She stumbled over a rusty shock absorber. "Ouch," she cried as the blood flowed from her big toe. She lifted her face to Ali, her eyes liquid in the dark of her face.

Ali took the sack. Nafeisa smiled at him as they continued on down the street, passing by small merchant stalls and alcoves covered by corrugated shutters. "Do you want to stop and get a Coke?" she asked him, pointing to a street vendor up ahead.

"All right." Ali shifted the heavy sack as they turned down a narrow lane and came upon a vacant lot littered with bricks, scraps of lumber, and rusty metal pipe—their future home, when they wed each other. Construction had stopped years ago, ostensibly for lack of funds.

Afraid that Ali was going along with her idea only to humor her, Nafeisa pressed for more. "Do you really want a Coke?" she asked, love-addled, looking at the lot, and wondering for the millionth time when Ali and she would be able to marry and start their family. She suffered grievously from the poverty which had plagued her since birth, a destitution from which only an educated husband could save her. Her daily life seemed nothing but constant anticipation with no possibility of surcease—and paralyzingly dull. You could take care of your sisters' children just so long, then tedium set in, and tedium Nafeisa bore with ill grace. She wanted to be a mother, not an auntie. To find herself in possession of a finished house would be true bliss.

"Goddamn!" Ali exploded. He was tempted to tell her to stuff the Coca-Cola bottle, but he restrained himself. News of the outside world was hard to come by in a fair and faraway place like Hurghada, and Nafeisa would hardly understand why he was more than a little short-tempered. Before he could say he was sorry, Nefeisa let out a shriek of pain. She had just then noticed that the foundation was fractured in a million pieces, as if a small bomb had been dropped square in the middle of it. Suddenly Nafeisa was everywhere at once, in the rubble, all around it, crying for help. Ali stood, immobile.

"Al-eeee, do something!" Nafeisa's high-pitched voice called for his attention. Damn, what could he do? He cursed beneath his breath, but pivoting to face her, he said quietly, "Ins'challah." God wills it.

A cruel God if He wills this, Nafeisa thought, her eyes moistening. As she left the ruins, pain spread to fill her small body with anguish.

"Sit down, Cousin," Ali prompted gently, but Nafeisa turned to him instead, burying her face against his chest She was holding on to him tightly, disconsolate, her mind grasping what had already penetrated her heart: her future had been blasted to smithereens. No one was watching them, so Ali put an arm around her and kissed her hair. He kept crooning, "*Mallesh*," never mind, whispering protestations of a love which he knew in his heart he didn't really feel, trying to comfort her as best he could. Inwardly, he reproached himself for coming here. He had imagined his Uncle doing some work on the place in his absence; after all, fathers are always anxious to marry off their daughters? He should have anticipated how Nafeisa would feel. While she subscribed with an uncritical devotion to his ideas of an Islamic revolution, she couldn't escape from a yearning for gentility which came from her narrow upbringing. Possession mattered to her more than pride, but she was a woman, after all. A woman with a shrunken look about her, as if life were leaking out of her pores. Ali felt kinder toward her. "We will pour another foundation, Cousin," he promised as he picked up the sack of vegetables. He knew he was lying, but he squirmed away from examining his own motives too closely, shaking off the guilt like salt water on his shoulders.

"Of course," Nafeisa said, striving to reassure herself, to take consolation from his promise. "Everyone needs a roof over their heads, you, me, our children." But Ali—she grasped this viscerally without understanding why it could be so—seemed to need nothing, at least nothing that she or the village had to offer.

An old man perched on an ox cart came by and gave them a grave *salaam*, touching his bony fingers to his crocheted skullcap. Ali looked Nafeisa over, his eyes lit with anger. Permitting his voice to go cold, he admonished, "Cover your face next time, cousin. You should not put your body on display for all to see."

Nafeisa had an anger of her own. "But that is our Uncle Tariq." When Nafeisa threw up her hands in defense she got a whiff of her armpits. Ali could have brought her a little vial of jasmine or musk or balsam from the perfume *souq* in Cairo, but did he ever? She cast a resentful glance at him. "Do you not know your own family any more? Are you not glad to be here?"

"Of course." Ali turned his face to her and forced a smile.

How could he say, "please understand I feel like an outsider,
cousin, ill at ease and alien?"

"I am glad, glad, glad," he chanted, petulantly, forcefully
dragging her off their lot.

"But you are so hard to get along with." Nafeisa dug in her
heels and faced him. Her brown eyes were full. Her cheeks
looked like someone had stamped them with a waffle iron.
Was it sinful of her to be such a scold? She didn't care. "You
blow up for no reason at all, Ali, or there is a sneer in your
voice, or you're speaking to me as if I were not a day over six.
Why don't you come right out and say it? I find your conversation, Nafeisa, as interesting as bird twittle."

Ali had turned a dangerous red color. Neither her tears nor
her remarks had been well received, although she spoke no
more than the truth. Couldn't the bloody bitch see that he
was a man profoundly in mourning without his having to tell
her in so many words about his dead and missing comrades?
Unconsciously, Ali wanted to withdraw into himself without
having to account for anything. He was tired of having to put
on an act in front of the family who thought him an irresponsible child or in front of comrades who thought he'd betrayed
them. He heard a sniffle and turned to see Nafeisa wiping
away a tear. Guilt hit once more. This was wrong, to deceive
her about his true predicament as a fugitive, to constantly lash
out at her. He had an impulse to come clean.

Ali checked it. No one must know what was going to happen on October Sixth. "You had better straighten up and fly
right," he warned, his pointed beard held forward like a spear
aiming at Nafeisa's chest. "Or else I will go back to Cairo, and
then where will you be?"

Silently she lifted her palms upward, appealing to Ali as if
to say, "am I unreasonable?" He spun around on his heels and
stalked off.

Nafeisa didn't straighten up, of course, but she did try and
watch her tongue more. Ali's situation when he had been
compelled to flee Cairo might be described as ignominious:
his career as a geologist ended before it began, his prison
record ensnaring him every time he turned around, and later,
his cousin Talaat murdered by unknown assailants. And he

was received in his uncle's house grudgingly. Hurghada was a typical provincial town. If you cough one morning, the word is out by noon that you are dying of TB, and your enemies have you buried by sunset. Naturally, as a Cairene, nephew Ali swiftly became the subject of stories that had more embroidery than a woman's wedding dress by the time they reached the local tea stalls.

Uncle, who was the *omda*, the village mayor, quite understandably didn't like to sit among his cronies and hear them. His aunt treated Ali with a note of cavil and suspicion, less for his big city ways than for his failure to marry her daughter. She listened to his version of why the wedding had to be repeatedly postponed with profound distrust, and then she was on her feet, squawking like a rooster, telling him he'd have to sleep on the beach at night. Ali shrugged, a bitter gesture. "So what are you are really saying, Auntie? That you would let us get married even though I do not have the bride-price? Fine by me."

Seeing his purpose, Uncle struck him on the cheek so that he reeled away, while Auntie swore with a fervor and more than a touch of hysteria that she meant nothing of the sort. An Egyptian woman does not give herself to a man, even if he is related, without exacting tribute for her vulnerability. Cousin Ali was a financial fiasco who could easily up and leave a wife, for men are cads with no taste for domesticity who must be financially bound. Deserted, Nafeisa would be damaged goods without any support for herself and her children. However, Ali was too distraught about his own clouded future to bear her lectures or even to care if his engagement was teetering on the brink of a debilitating antagonism.

Forbidden by Mustafa from returning to Cairo, Ali slowed his pace to that of the village, but time hung heavy on his hands. The tiny house was crowded with 15 bodies of various sizes and ages. Sister Amina's five month old baby Rokaya curled up in a blanket on a mattress, but each time she dozed off her three-year-old brother Maggot pinched her. Six-year-old Sa'id chased cockroaches with a broom. The Salahs were squabblers. They had been over the same arguments, hurled about the same accusations and dredged up the same misguided memories a million times before, so the harangues never ended. Ali had always been high strung and full of spirit, but he was but a shell of himself. Deprived of Cairo, his robust friends and their dangerous but stimulating activities in the Jamaat, he was listless and solitary. Not even arguing politics in the tea stalls seemed to interest him anymore. He took to reading popular novels or sleeping hours on end.

Sourly, Auntie told Nafeisa, "Ali gets more tired out with the least amount of activity than anyone I know. Why is he not working on your house? I was already pregnant by the time I was your age." Nafeisa turned to gaze at Ali with longing; she saw the strain it put into his face, but she couldn't stop herself.

"I haven't got the bride-price; our house is not finished." Ali gave his shoulders a hitch to convey the impossibility of this conversation, which they'd had a million times before and would have, he was sure, a million times more. When Ali could no longer bear his aunt's squawking and his fiancée's pleading looks, he would flee out of doors.

Every morning at sunrise the people stirred with the *muzzin's* call from the mosque. As the village gradually wakened, tourists wandered down to the beach. With most of the soldiers gone, a tranquility permeated the shoreline. On warm days boys in their BVDs dove off the seawall, and men came down to fish from the shore. Mid-mornings, Ali would amble down to the breakwater to dive for small fish and shells. Nafeisa would later come upon him laughing and conversing with the vagabonds from Europe, showing off his shells. These human relatives of crocodiles lazed in the sand with their jaws agape, and Ali would lie next to them, baking in the hot sunshine to his heart's content. He spoke with glowing enthusiasm of the scuba divers, beach boys, fishermen, and sun worshippers who congregated at the Club Med just a few kilometers down the beach, and Nafeisa was astounded.

Like most of the local residents, Nafeisa viewed these foreigners with more than a little trepidation. Their cocky ways constituted an alien intrusion into her staid birthplace, and she didn't know what in the world could possess these highly peculiar women to flounce around in costumes that were really no more than two thin strips of cloth and a shoelace. Plunging necklines, no bras, shorts revealing a slice of their buttocks, wide brimmed hats sporting fake fruits and flowers, eyes the color of faded denim jeans, golden hair tumbling down in undisciplined folds around their faces and shoulders, exhibitionistic flashes of arms, legs, and faces—Daughters of Satan! And it was more than just the eye-popping way they clad their tight little backsides. Their behavior was equally bewildering. She had seen them, possessed by a devil-inspired energy, swim and play volleyball or toss Frisbees all day. Then in the evening, they would slap on lipstick, smoke hashish, enter cafes and sit right down next to their men, even hugging and kissing them in public and shocking all decent onlookers with their debauchery. Nafeisa didn't know what to make of all this. Nor did her parents, who were often heard raging against the intruders for their leisure and money, their lack of dignity and lasciviousness, the bad influence they were having on good little Muslim girls and boys.

"Brazenly, these infidels flaunt themselves and their freedoms," Nafeisa said to Ali one day as she squatted next to him on the sand, her face covered by her white scarf so that only her heavily *kohl*-lined eyes showed. "They can hardly keep their suits on. Everything bulges out." She spoke with irritation, but quietly. Her pose was outwardly serene, eyes looking down at her palm, cupped inside the other in her lap.

Not far from them a Norwegian woman was sitting cross-legged on a rice mat absorbed in a newspaper. Purple lips shone from under the shady hat, half obscuring her fine features. Her batik skirt was hiked up to her hips and almost touching her thigh was a bottle of dark Aswali beer from Aswan. A portable stereo poured out a Caribbean beat. Ali had chatted with her the day before. He could talk with her in King's English, then turn around and greet a passing *fellah* in colloquial Arabic—all without missing a beat. She didn't realize that Salah could look and sound more cosmopolitan than he really was. Ali himself was blissfully unaware of his own contradictory nature. He appeared in his own eyes as a typical Egyptian male—as indeed he was.

"They flaunt themselves," Nafeisa repeated, pantomiming a

flagrant feminine gesture. She couldn't forget how Ali acted with the Norwegian yesterday, laying back on his elbows, positioning his face in the shade of her body, gazing up at her. Now, prickles of jealousy crawled over Nafeisa's flesh, a feeling intensified when her cousin failed to get as upset as she.

"They do love the limelight, don't they?" responded Ali—a man who knew titillation when he saw it. As though mesmerized by the music, his eyes followed the graceful movements of the Japanese as they slammed a volleyball back and forth across the net. His voice was low-pitched with a cool, drawling sound. "Perhaps they don't realize that their actions offend us," Ali finished like a man half asleep. He was lying on a long beach towel, his head resting comfortably on his rolled-up jeans, his eyes partially closed, luxuriating in the warmth of a brilliant midmorning sun.

Nafeisa was unable to read his face. He wouldn't look up at her. If he did, would she see pleasure in his eyes? She didn't know what to do. She'd begun the conversation in a voice of condemnation, expecting to be praised, but she feared at any moment he'd denounce her as an ignorant person. She stared at him and the frown line deepened between her brows, though she could not point out that his present attitude differed considerably from the one he had exhibited so short a time ago—for he had, in a flash, snapped out of his lethargy, jumped up and run down to the water. Nafeisa watched him, wanting to understand, but at the moment all the solid rock of reason had turned to vapor beneath her feet. Upon his return from the States, Ali had told her that women there were motivated by insatiable vanity and a desire to lead men astray. A more disagreeable, egomaniacal, selfish, and dissipated people you would not want to meet than Americans, at least as Ali had portrayed them. And only yesterday when she'd stepped out of the courtyard without her *tarha*, her scarf, Ali's eyes had turned suspicious, angry, and he had accused her of going on a wild ego binge—whatever that was. He had quoted sutra after sutra to her trying to convince her that unrestrained female vitality was too much for any orderly society to control. That is why Egypt must become an Islamic Republic.

Outwardly, Nafeisa attended to what Ali said with an expression of reverence in her big brown eyes, but, in truth, his arguments only made her more confused than ever. Sometimes he would tell her, "We must struggle to change our society; that is the revolutionary's task." In the next breath, he'd say, "Everything in life is preordained; inexorably, we are destined from birth to move toward our eventual end."

When Nafeisa was five years old her mother had brought in the incisor to remove her clitoris, for that, according to Islamic tradition, was her female destiny. She had sunk into a stupor of pain that she could still vividly recall even now, ten years later. It had to be done, her mother insisted, it is a custom handed down by our wise ancestors. Otherwise, a girl would grow up wild and untamed and no man would want her for a wife. Female circumcision maintained an orderly society.

What, then, was this crying need for an Islamic Republic, this need to struggle and die for something that was already a given? Nafeisa thought bitterly as she remembered the terrible pain—a pain inflicted upon her by her mother, the one person she had trusted above all others!—that ancestors were no wiser than the living, and their being long-dead had added no luster to their wisdom.

14

Nafeisa walked down to the water's edge. Despite the bright sun, a refreshing breeze came in from the sea, bringing the not-so-fragrant odor of fish with it. She sought Ali's head bobbing in the Red Sea among the other swimmers, but the glare of the sun on the surface of the water prevented her from distinguishing his from the foreigners. Standing there, Nafeisa toyed with thoughts of her wedding night. She knew what it would be like, for her married sisters had told her all about it: "You'll be taken into a back room. Grandmother and the aunties will place you on the bed and hold your legs. Ali will wrap one of his fingers around a white cloth, then stick it in down there. If it comes out with blood, he'll know you're still a virgin. Father will be at the door. Ali gives him the bloody cloth and he puts it on a stick and shows it all around. It's a sign of the family's honor, and when the guests see it, they fire their guns into the air."

"Why in heavens name do you come here?" Nafeisa demanded of Ali when he got out of the water, still bewildered by the contradictions she saw in him. And then she motioned outward. It was a motion that took in Infidels full of fun and popping out of their skins with sex, boats with red sails like triangles of fire in the sunlight, windsurfers and guitar players—all the vivid conspiracy of sensual detail that Club Med encouraged to attract the wild and sinfully monied foreigners here to Magaweesh.

Ali wiped away the droplets of salty liquid clinging to his skin. Without opening his eyes to catch a glimpse of her, Ali knew Nafeisa had a look that demanded answers, but he didn't care. To him, this place was a source of life. Hurghada looked like a ghost town by 9 a.m. because most of its residents had a well-earned reputation for going to bed on the same day they got up. Oh, to be in Cairo again! The sun beat down unmercifully. The sweat was forming at his hairline and on his lips. He wanted to strike out, but all he said to Nafeisa was, "This place is preferable to staying around your mother. You say she's got a good heart, but I have never seen it up close."

"You're shouting," Nafeisa pouted. Ali had toweled himself dry and lay down in the sand. He rolled over on his stomach to expose his cold back and legs to the hot sun, cradling his head on his arms. Nafeisa moved over so that their bodies barely touched. Her eyes swept up and down the beach. Then quite innocently she asked him, "Where is Betty—that old woman you were talking with yesterday?"

"Don't stand there with your mouth open," he said abruptly, "like a stupid person who knows nothing."

The skin on Nafeisa's hands had broken into blisters from picking artichokes and she picked one now. "She tells everyone she is Egyptian, but they say she is really an Israeli. What do you think? I notice you're with her a lot." There was a thin vein of bitterness in her words.

Ali shuddered, chilled to the bone despite his sweat. He would have to think up some plausible reason why he'd been speaking to the Scot, but his improvising cells were napping. Would it help to say, "I need to keep practicing my English so it doesn't grow rusty?" Or how about, "Five minutes is not a lot, for Godsake!" At last he settled on, "Anyone who's different is talked about one way or another. A woman's knee shows for two seconds and the market hums for a week."

"Hah!" Nafeisa exclaimed with a short laugh, feeling a sliver of fear pierce her heart. "Betty shows more than her knee."

With a nervous gesture, Ali brushed back the lock of hair that slipped in front of his eyes every few seconds. Several sea gulls floated gracefully down from their airy heights, landing hungrily at their feet. Purposefully, Ali rolled over. Although he could not be fond of Nafeisa, he felt a certain sense of duty towards her that precluded sharp exchanges of this sort. Inspiration struck. "I will tell you about Betty if you promise not to tell anyone else. You know how the British feel about their privacy."

Delighted to have her cousin's confidence, Nafeisa put her finger to her lips and swore they were sealed forever. "As Allah is my witness."

"She is here visiting with her two grandsons." Ali pointed to two big English teenagers frolicking on the sand some twenty yards away. Nafeisa looked confused. "Now, please bring me some lemonade," Ali concluded, his request muffled by the towel under his head.

Her footsteps dragged away. He shut his eyes and youthful memories assailed him, of hiding with the other boys behind the dunes and crumbling walls, peeping and leering at bodies the color of fresh, wet pink marble—although the owners of those bodies never paid them the least bit of attention. Curiosity turned into painfully unfilled sexual hungers as he and his friends started to display the early signs of new black moustaches. The females almost made you suffocate from the joy they brought. He remembered how he and his friends had pounded the sand with their fists and badly bruised their knuckles hitting the wall, for anger had flooded over the youngsters when they thought that these great, juicy, mouth-watering females were teases, provoking and feigning blindness while enjoying every second of their anguish. Ali had been the one most ashamed of his lust, yet after he saw his first Raquel Welch movie his hyperbolic imagination took flight, and he dreamed nightly of falling in love with a maiden wilder than a jungle lioness and running off to Darkest Africa. Females who were a bewitching mixture of primitivism and sophistication were central to his fantasy life.

Not surprising, then, it was *ajaanib* (foreigners) who most often strode out of the breakers of these teenage delusions— until the day she had glided out of the summer haze in all her magnificence and fantasy became reality. It had been right here on this beach that he'd met the woman of his imagination, an enchanting Swede with her waist-length flaxen hair pulled back, her blue eyes hidden by an intellectual's rimless glasses. She wore coral jewelry, and Indian scarves tied

around her hips to make her look like a gypsy, and she was so
beautiful that her family should have kept her locked up.
Monica Thalmann had translated a book that her father had
written on the Bedu of the Sinai and was a student of a well-
known American anthropologist. Being Swedish, she was part
of the human race that didn't have critical worries about food
and clothing and medical care, a person who could spend her
hours worrying about, "am I happy?"

"Are you happy, Ali? Will we be happy together coming, as
we do, from different backgrounds?" It irritated him no end,
and one day he told her that "we Egyptians are too busy
planting and tilling and harvesting our crops to indulge in
such endless emotional pulse-taking!"

Summer drew to a close and Monica would soon be going
back to graduate school at the University of California at
Berkeley. Ali decided he would follow. And in time he did,
though a foulup in paperwork landed him on the Santa Cruz
campus instead. A sense of destiny seemed to surround his
meeting with Maria Luz Gracida. He had left Monica and
Hurghada on an evening when twilight was firing the reds of
the pepper trees into a spectacular blaze to travel half way
around the world and find another coastline, other pepper
trees and underneath them, walking towards him in the twilight, a dusky beauty with a scarf tied around her hips, gypsy-
fashion.

"What are you thinking about?" Nafeisa's query cracked like
a whip in the silence. She was holding a jar full of tea in the
crook of her arm. Could she ever hope to overcome his
resistance to talking to her about what's on his mind?

"Nothing," Ali breathed tremulously, thrusting his memories sharply aside.

15

The alarm went off at five A.M. In a fog, Leonard turned it off and lay flat on his back, listening to Luz's shallow breathing. The curve of her back glowed like alabaster, and he ran his fingers down it. He smiled happily, remembering their love making on the *falucca*, then in this bed. Her body had been a miracle. "Are you up?" he whispered into her ear.

"Do I have to be?" came the muffled protest.

"Time to rise and shine," Leonard coaxed, nudging Luz gently. Then he slipped his arms around her waist. She purred, curled up in a ball like a well-fed cat, and appealed for more sleep. "We leave in 20 minutes, sweetheart." The words, while insistent in her ear, were accompanied by a kiss on the shoulder. "Let's paste our armpits with an Arrid Dry stick, polish the pearlies, slap on some after-shave, then hit the highway on schedule. We've got a long drive ahead of us today."

Leonard rolled out of bed and stretched with the quiet power of movement that suggested someone confident of his own physicality. He swung his arms around and touched his toes ten times. Rummaging around in his bureau drawer, he found clean shorts and a T-shirt and started to put them on.

Stretching, Luz shook away the cobwebs. "What time is it?"

"High noon, gal," Leonard mimicked a Gary Cooper drawl.

With the room illuminated only faintly by the blue bathroom light through the slightly open door, Luz scrutinized him carefully, her eyes barely visible above the sheet. Although he was well-developed, his biceps didn't call attention to themselves, and he looked the scholar even in his BVDs.

The little flat was located in a quiet cul de sac, and it was fresh and comfortable and a pleasure to be in after a week in a rundown hotel perfumed by male pee and a thousand odors of cooking floating up from the streets. Leonard's windows were directly opposite those of his neighbors' so the shades were always drawn, which made it hard to see the marvelous Roberts prints and African masks on the walls, *flokati* rugs on the floor and Indonesian wooden statues on the dressers. But the dusky lighting gave the place an eerie Alexandria Quartet ambience. Luz was immersed in it, swept into another time, another place, another era where time stood still.

The few photographs were revealing: a young Leonard with violin, formally posed, his blond locks sentimentally curled; his mother and aunt, both in their 60s, thin boned and fragile as china and with guarded, quizzical looks; his aproned father standing next to a bar-b-que and gazing at the camera with an Oriental calm just before his death at 27. There was a small snapshot of Karen, the ex-wife who foolishly loved Italians. In her black aerobic leotard and tights, her sunglasses pushed atop her hair, she looked like a blond Anais Nin. "I never knew my father, *alevasholem*," Leonard told Luz. "But my mother says he was the best dressed man she ever saw and a perfect gentleman."

"A condition he didn't pass on to you." Luz paused when she noticed the look of dismay on his face and elaborated, "Well, you took advantage of me, didn't you? And you weren't wearing a tux when you did it."

Leonard thought it had been less a one-man show than a matter of inspiring each other. "Together we rose to new heights of mutually satisfactory perversion."

When Luz asked how he rose from poverty to a political officer's slot, he said, "It was my mom who was determined I'd be somebody. She was always rooting me on. I wasn't exactly blessed with musical talent, but when I was five she bought me that violin and a Fauntleroy suit to go with it. It cost her four paychecks. Man, when I had to go down the street to my lessons with that violin case, I ran as fast as I knew how. Ever since then I've had a frenzied fear of virtually everything in existence. You know, when I moved in this flat, it hadn't been cleaned since it was built in 1923, and it was the grungiest place on earth. I wanted to just blow it up. But a fortune teller who read my palm predicted one day you'd come along and want to move in with me, so I dug in and got it fixed up and here we are. Feel free to alter the environment if anything doesn't suit you."

He was beaming at her, grinning from ear to ear. His calm exterior gave no hint of the turmoil he was feeling. Should he come right to the point, say, "Let's go get your bags, check you out of the hotel?" He went out to the kitchen and returned after a while with two cups of instant coffee.

"I want to make this legal," Luz told him silently. She rose up on an elbow and took a sip of coffee, grimacing as the steam curled around the corners of her mouth. The idea of marriage had come to her a moment ago in the half-sleep of waking, creeping in like a night prowling cat at dawn, making its presence known to her with a gentle pounce. And so, Luz acknowledged to herself now that she was awake, it is an idea that comes from emotion rather than thought. But she had a heartfelt intuition about Leonard Berg. It was more than just delight and lust she felt for him. They belonged together, Len and Luz, linked, a molecule without surname. She glanced over at Karen's picture. This was as good a time as any to ask Lenny if he thought there'd been more to the collapse of his marriage than a predatory Italian.

Leonard tensed. That was the sort of question one didn't ask casually. If Karen had had her way, they would never have gone five blocks beyond Georgetown. She'd have spent her days in her atelier, her evenings doing the gallery scene, discussing nihilism with people wearing black lipstick. Lenny admitted to Luz that he and Karen had never fortified each other, even in the States, and living in the Middle East only made it painfully apparent.

"We Foreign Service Officers aren't any prize," he volunteered. "We spend our days screaming at secretaries and telecommunications clerks who take our beautiful prose and turn it into gibberish, toe-dancing around a bunch of inflated egos, yelling at the host government for not running the country the way Washington wants it run. We spend our nights doing more of the same and womanizing a little on the side, when we have a spare moment. What I'm saying is that we're already married to our jobs, so marrying a woman just makes us bigamists."

"But Foreign Service Officers do marry," Luz reminded him, "and a good thing too. Marriage keeps you from getting a social disease or impregnating the local belles or destabilizing the local government."

"It's true," Leonard agreed, "that we sometimes get married. But usually it's only to another Foreign Service Officer or a stewardess or a bartender. Those are the only women we ever meet. Thing is it takes a saint to be married to a diplomat. Better you should marry a rigger of oil derricks or a guy who wears your dresses."

Luz ran her tongue over her lower lip. "Thanks for the warning."

When he ruffled her hair and said, "Cum'on, babe, up and at 'em," she threw off the sheet and lay very still. "I can't move my legs, *querido*," she announced in a mournful tone. "Think I may be paralyzed from too much screwing?"

The sunrise had turned the Eastern sky to a great spread of pale silk. The light inside the bedroom was a diffuse golden-yellow as Leonard sat down next to her, then bent over to kiss the inside of her thigh. "Let me see." He ran his hand up her ankle to her knee, soaking in the sight of her dark body, strong breasts, supple legs, sleek belly, and the Virgin of Guadalupe medal resting in the valley between her breasts. He could spend a lot of valuable travel time concentrating on those breasts.

Luz stared into his hazel eyes, plying her fingers in the fringe of hair above his ears. "How did you get to be so good in bed?" The mellow intensity of her voice was enchanting. "Practice?"

"No." Leonard's breath was warm against her skin. "Correspondence course." He was stroking her leg just above the knee where the muscles start when her arms flew around his head, pulling him down and pressing herself hard against him. "We're going to miss the bus, Ramona," he protested as he attempted to rise.

But Luz would not let go and Leonard was too enraptured to deny her anything. Pulling him down and rolling over on top of him, she said airily, "*Mallesh*, we'll hitchhike."

They were showering together when Luz asked him if he'd marry her. Leonard blinked his wet lashes with unexpected surprise. "But, ah? Why?" he stammered, feeling absurdly tongue-tied.

Luz's dark eyes took on an impish twinkle at the incredulous expression her proposal brought to Leonard's face. She handed him the green bar of Irish Spring. The shower stall was a swirling, whirling mass of steam. As she brought her face in close to his sandy moustache, it was dim and dreamlike, as if she were coming towards him through a thin, refractory mist where depth and focus were out of sync. Luz, her eyes locked onto his, said, "I can't give you reason, *caro*. It's too early in the morning for reasons. But I know it's the dead solid correct thing for us to do."

Luz cocked an eyebrow, waiting for a response. Leonard was thoughtfully scrubbing her breasts. "Well, I don't know," he began, then faltered.

Luz, arching and preening as he soaped her body, willed herself to be calm. Why was Lenny so hesitant? Her faith? She assured him, "I avoid church religiously, ever since they put that Polish calamity in charge."

Lenny rubbed his mouth nervously. "It's just that when I get married I usually like to be engaged for a week or two," he objected, though he didn't sound as if he quite believed that excuse.

"Are there any foods you don't like?" Luz asked.

"Sure. I don't care for lima beans. I don't like parsnips and brussels sprouts, either."

"Neither do I!" Luz threw her arms around his neck and kissed his wet cheek. She liked brussels sprouts and hated rutabagas, but that could be sorted out after the wedding. After all, they both liked cheese blintzes and tacos. "We're perfect for each other," she declared, lips caressing the nape of his neck.

Families: the word flashed through Leonard's mind. He

demanded to know just exactly what kind of a family she came
from, if any. Luz had two wonderful parents and three terrific
brothers, but she deadpanned, "What's to know? My mother
was named Fort Hood's Catholic Laywoman of the Year. Dad
took it the wrong way and beat her to death. But he only did it
once, and he was drunk at the time."

She waited for Lenny to be amused, but his face sagged
into seriousness as he fumed, "I'm not firing on all cylinders
yet and you hit me with this. Do you realize that ours may be
my shortest courtship on record? What will the Ambassador
say? 'You're irresponsible,' probably. That's Tuck—very main-
stream. Maybe he'd even put it in my PER."

Luz frowned and Leonard explained the unfamiliar expression. "My personal evaluation report. Yep, ole Tuck'll say,
Berg's too flighty to promote; pack him over to the consulate
and set him to handing out visas. You see it all the time; a guy
has a little flirtation and bingo, he's exiled to Perth. If I were a
gossip what tales of misfortune I could tell. Those damn
Foreign Service Review Boards are sticklers for propriety.
That's because anyone assigned to a review board has to prove
he went to college back when they wore ties to football games.
Yep, if Tucker only would throw away his plaids and wear
pinstripes, he'd be living in style in the Residence in Vienna
instead of here. It's his Rodney Dangerfield wardrobe more
than anything that's got him screwed, blued, and tattooed in
Cairo even though Mrs. Tucker is always properly turned out,
Palm Springs casual wear in the daytime, Belle Epoque at
parties, you know, pearls and feathers and rose satin." He
sustained this anxiety-ridden verbosity for the next ten minutes, undeterred by the fact that Luz had stuck her head
under the faucet.

"I never wear anything outrageous," she finally responded,
coming out from under the water. "Eccentric maybe, but not
outrageous. You said you prefer me naked anyway, so why are
you carrying on about my clothes? Never mind, let's get back
to Tucker. What about telling him I got you in a family way?"

Then came a barrage of words. Leonard rambled, philosophized about marriage and the family, needled about the
perils of a life lived among the packing crates, the absurdity of

having to carry on a normal life in 120 degree Saudi heat, pausing only to let a point sink in or to tack on a dramatic flourish. Finally, "Oh, I've lost it," he conceded, as if the thread of his argument was pretty thin to begin with. He stood right under the faucet and opened his mouth.

Luz jammed her fists on her soapy hips and feigned exasperation. "Don't just stand there with your tongue hanging out, *hombre*, answer me yes or no."

Leonard threw his hands up in a gesture of surrender. Then he grabbed her tightly to him, gave her a big, wet, juicy smack on the lips and roared, "You're on, sweetheart. But remember, I'll be living overseas for the next twenty years. There's no life for me without the Service."

The striking black eyes in the brown face met his soberly. "Then I'll be an expat too. There'd be no life for me without you."

There were parents in the States that had to be notified. The Gracidas were ecstatic, Mrs. Berg less so. Leonard had to hold the receiver away from his ear to soften the buzz of objections. Bella wailed, "I can't believe this is my son talking, a child of my loins," before breaking down into deep, gulping sobs. She could no more accept Luz than she could breathe under water.

When he'd replaced the receiver in the its cradle, Luz asked Leonard if his mother had found the idea of a lapsed Catholic daughter-in-law hard to swallow. He seized her finger and held it tightly. "Maw was—" he'd almost said "hysterical" but his tongue couldn't wrap itself around the word and the truth remained unspoken. Ever the diplomat, Leonard patiently counseled his wife-to-be, "It'll take a while."

Luz raised an eyebrow at him and said, "By a while, you mean: try a lifetime."

16

Later that morning, Leonard released the clutch and the Range Rover slid out of the shadow of the petrol station and into the bright sunlight of the highway. He smelled the moisture in the air. The road from Port Suez to Hurghada ran in a southwesterly direction for about 30 miles, all the while following the coastline; then at Ain Sokhna it swung to a more southerly direction, ran a few miles along the Gulf of Suez and then began to climb to a plateau with high barren hills on their right. The landscape, once they had left the coast and the heat haze shimmering on the rusty waters that fringed it, was bleached, stony, and arid. Except for an occasional palm or shrub, there was little vegetation.

They were driving off into a mystery, a potentially dangerous one, but *mallesh*. Leonard was singing joyfully, turning the wheel to the curves of the narrow winding road, oblivious to the bugs splattering on the windshield. Three days on the Red Sea was just the cure for his disenchantment with Tucker. Stressed-out, feeling like a prophet without honor in his own country because of his failure to make Haig take his pungent comments seriously, the political officer needed to recuperate. Tucker had been as thrilled to get rid of him as he was to be out here on the open road. The Embassy was on the other side of the moon. Dressed in sandals, baggy khakis, and an easily removable loose red jersey, he was with the woman he loved and—Blessed be the Good Lord!—up there ahead of them lay a beach.

Luz found this land of stark plateaus and rocky canyons fascinating. "*Bella!*" she said on a breath of rapture. "*Bellisima!*"

Leonard took a curve, murmuring a compliment. "Those tones were worthy of the Chamber of Commerce." An audaciously brilliant sun poured through the windshield and the sea was a calm stretch of glitter under an immense blue sky. Leonard was determined to put his problems aside for the time being and enjoy the radiance of a perfect day. He pushed his sleeves up past his elbows and slapped a Nitty Gritty Dirt Band tape into the deck. But Luz wanted to talk about her assignment, so he turned off "Ripplin' Waters" and gave her his attention.

"In the States, Anwar Sadat is a household word, like Tide or Folgers Decaf." Luz was fulminating with an edge of desperation in her voice. Her natural optimism was turning sour before her disbelieving eyes. "I don't suppose that the Virgin Mother herself could take his saintly reputation down a notch or two. But what else can I write, except what I see and hear? To be honest with you, *caro*, when I sit down at my typewriter it's like pulling teeth, getting the truth down on paper. Try likening it to saying in a high school textbook that Benjamin Franklin had a bastard son or that George Washington liked to diddle his neighbor's wife when Martha wasn't looking. Jesus Mary, if I say Anwar Sadat, the man who flew to Jerusalem, has warts I might as well come out and publicly disavow motherhood. My editor is always less than an inch away from firing me as it is."

Luz dug the carbon copy of one of her articles out of her handbag. A sudden and unexpected breath of wind ruffled the still air inside the vehicle and sent the pages flapping in her hands. The article was the one she had written after seeing the film at the USIS library and then discussing it with a group of Egyptian students from the American University of Cairo. They said in their own words much of what had been expressed by others, pointing to the cynical manipulation of the film, its dishonesty. One intense young man by the name of Moshen had accused the American press in general and Luz herself in particular of being conspiratorially and conspicuously silent to save the skin of a lout who was good for the United States, but terrible for Egypt.

"You try to paint a rosy picture of things," said Moshen

accusingly, "when there isn't one. Sadat's income is so vast, his lifestyle so lavish, that you tend to overlook the fact that there's 45 million other Egyptians on an altogether different boat."

During their discussion, Moshen's eyes blinked wildly and his impassioned declarations caused his thick glasses to bounce up and down on his nose. Now, almost a week later, Luz could still picture him in her mind and hear him saying, "The problem of poverty is already awesome, and it's growing by leaps and bounds. Sadat has a glib tongue, but nothing new in dealing with Egyptians who need jobs, housing, pride. He gives us oratory instead. Even when things are going to hell, he thinks what we want to hear is the rhetoric of triumph. What we really want to hear is the echo of his words in Boulak, a slum where people don't have shelter, don't know how to read or write, and there is no possibility to live anything but a rat's life. And there's no getting around the fact that Sadat sold the Palestinians down the drain. And he is very much responsible for the torment of the Lebanese. The Israelis would not have been free to waltz into Lebanon if Egypt were still a confrontational state. Sadat's deal with the Zionists has castrated our armed forces. Haig might have given Sharon the green light, but Sadat's flight to Jerusalem certainly turned it amber."

"Betrayal and treachery," Moshen had said, red-faced and bellowing. That might have been overkill, but Luz got his drift and she'd quoted him, anonymously, of course. Now, she asked Lenny how accurate were the charges. Weren't the students laying it on a bit thick?

Leonard lifted his foot from the gas pedal. "Yes and no," he answered, taking the descent cautiously. "Sadat's willingness to retire his forces from the field was a boon to the Israelis; there's no question about it. But you gotta give Begin his due. His obsession that the Jewish state will some day occupy all the Biblical land on both sides of the Jordan River and north to the Litani is the kind of notion that draws a loyalty out of him that other men might feel for a woman or for a family. The Biblical landscape is imprinted somewhere inside his skull. It was Begin's pipedreams, and the ruthlessness of his bully boy

Sharon, that caused Israel to come unglued in Lebanon. When those lame brained Swedes gave Begin the Nobel Prize I had to refrain myself from physical abuse. For a little while I was cheered up by thinking the doctors would tell me that I had something terminal, which would free me to go assassinate him."

Luz was shocked. Who was this man she planned to wed, Arnold Schwarzenegger, the Commando? "You'd never do such a thing?"

"No, I wouldn't." Leonard immediately regretted his flash of *macho bravado*. "Another one of my favorite quotes is from Freud: Civilization began when the first man hurled an insult instead of a spear at his enemy. So I hurl insults while Sharon hurls missiles, but at least I haven't descended to his level."

Luz glowered at him under her thick fringe of lashes. "Well, I still think that Sadat and Carter deserved it," she said, a trace of aggression in her voice. The Rover was quiet, quiet enough to hear a pen scratching across the page, quiet enough to hear her breathing and thinking. "I just wish we'd learn something about supporting these dictators. We stand by with a finger up the nose while the Shah steals 20 billion dollars from his people, while Ferdinand Marcos steals around the same amount, while Mrs. Suharto in Indonesia and Baby Doc in Haiti steals Lord only knows how much. We should tell them, Listen here, *ladrones*, you can take 10 million out of the till, but that is the limit, *basta*! Exceed that and you're all washed up with us. That's not being too harsh, is it? I could live on ten million, couldn't you?"

"Only for a year or two," Leonard answered promptly. "After that I'd have to go out and get a job. So what exactly did you write about Carter and Sadat?"

"Tarnished Knights on slightly soiled chargers" is what she called them in her article. Luz read a few lines of what she'd written. "Under the sanctimony is a sense of decency and a sincere desire to do what's right. It humanizes them and lends them a certain nobility as they sally forth in the quest for peace in the Middle East." She looked up from the pages, her expression a far cry from that of a cocky and confident newshound, and demanded, "Well, how does that grab you?"

The road went over a small bridge where the sun was reflecting off the stones and boulders in a dry wadi. Leonard kept his eyes on the road as he offered in a broadly bantering way, "Well, hon, it tells me that the woman who wrote it read Don Quixote as a child."

Luz laughed, her laughter tumbling in on his. "My Boss Al Haig would love it," Leonard assured her, "if that's any consolation. No one has ever found more silver in darkening clouds than he. The conventional wisdom is that Egypt is the heart of the Arab World. And now with Camp David, the way is supposedly clear for 150 million Arabs to fall in and send their ambassadors to Tel Aviv."

Luz shoved the pages back inside her bag. "And you think that's wishful thinking?"

"Totally out of touch with reality!" Leonard slammed the heel of his hand on the steering wheel for emphasis. "Not that I wouldn't jump with joy if détente came to pass. I want to see Israel at peace with its neighbors so badly I'd do a Faust number with the Devil, if it'd help. But you don't get anywhere chasing rainbows or by limiting the debate either. Under Haig's rule we can't talk about Palestinians, we can't talk about Arafat's peace feelers, we can't talk about or talk to the PLO. All those things should be up for heavy and protracted ventilation, but we're operating on the fantasy that if we don't say the words, four million people will blow away in an evening breeze."

Picking up on this, Luz sang out, "Gloryoski, Berg, we're gonna wake up one sunny morning and they'll all be gone, taking the Mideast conflict with them. Then it'll be a Burger King job for us both."

Leonard shifted gears and thought how much alike they were. He was developing a reputation for being hard to work with, and apparently, Luz was not known for being an editor's day at the beach either. A perfect match! "You know what makes a Foreign Service Officer a good political officer? He's the one who digs in the heels and says, 'This is it.' I've always believed that there are times when you have to risk everything. And you have to say to yourself that the worst that can happen is that they transfer you to Mali. You have to have that kind of courage. My all-time favorite quote is Anton Chekhov, although I don't recall the words exactly."

Leonard glanced at the barren hills with the disorientation of a man who is usually never more than a corridor away from a reference library and always able to reach for this or that tome, turning to just the right page and reading it aloud. "Chekhov," Leonard suddenly remembered, "said it's not the business of the writer to offer a solution to any great dilemma. All he does, all he owes his readers, is to describe a situation truthfully, to do justice to it so no reader can evade it. You can borrow it, if you like."

Luz leaned over and kissed his cheek, loudly. "Thanks, *companero*, I needed that."

Leonard went on, "I bristle at opposition just like the next man. Death and disease worry me. I'm afraid of upheavals, wars, arsenic in my Tylenol capsule, and the sound of goose-steps on the cobblestones. But the way to deal with them is not by looking away and saying they don't exist. You have to look right into the face of a thing and see what it is and what it isn't."

Luz offered as quickly and gently as she could, "I gather you and Alexander Haig don't see eye to eye then."

"To put it mildly," Lenny sputtered while echoes of Ambassador Tucker's rosy remarks and Secretary Haig's bombastic demands for recantation darted through his mind. Another one of his favorite quotes was: The trouble with my superiors is they think they are. "The General likes to present himself as a hardheaded battlefield realist, but invaders who try to sneak in and disturb him in his hammock on Fantasy Island get blasted." He stopped and pushed his hands through his hair in a gesture that was somehow boyish and acerbic. "Just ask me; I'll show you the holes in my hide."

"Anybody takes a shot at you, *caro mio*, has Gracida to deal with," vowed Luz, moved by an intense feeling of oneness with him. "How much does your being Jewish have to do with your becoming an Arabist?"

"A lot," Leonard replied cheerfully, as a stiff wind from the Gulf raised yellow dust from the asphalt and swirled it against the vehicle. "My intern post was Singapore, which is a won-

derful city, but when I heard of an opening at the Arabic
Language Institute, I felt a pull to go there and find out about
my cousins. It feels more natural to me now, more real. And
what I've discovered at this post, and Qatar too, is that you
just can't read about the Middle East. You have to be here. If
you're a Jew and you're concerned about Israel's fate and the
potential for a nuclear holocaust sparked by this endless Arab-
Israeli conflict, you have an obligation to do something. In the
1973 round, Israel had about 5,000 killed. In a three million
population, that's a rate of one in 600 killed in a sixteen-day
war. It's almost seven times as bad as the American dead
during years we were in Vietnam, 57,000 out of a population
of 230 million, which is one dead in 4,000."

Luz cut in, "Then there's been the additional loss of nearly a
thousand in Southern Lebanon."

Leonard nodded sadly. "For some American Jews, Israel is
their religion and so they're willing to shut their eyes to the
dark side of Likud's policies, but I'm not one of them. Likud is
spilling Jewish blood for no good cause that I can see. My
family bleeds each and every time another Israeli life is lost,
and they're not alone. After the Holocaust there is tremendous pain and grieving in the Jewish community created by
these deaths in Lebanon. They make donations, but it also
helps them to see me out here on the front line, so to speak,
putting in something apart from money. They feel less impo-
tent in the situation."

Luz's brown hand fell to her chest, and she began to toy
absently with her Virgin of Guadalupe medal. It suddenly
dawned on her that being Mrs. Berg meant spending her
future not "overseas," but specifically in this very troubled
part of the world, for Leonard would stay on in the Near East
Bureau, doing honest reporting and honorable labor until it
was emptied of all but the Huns. Luz had always seen her
place as being in Latin America. The irony of her career
seemed to be that when she was facing in one direction, fate
was turning her in another.

Leonard pressed on the accelerator and gave vent to a self-
deprecatory laugh. "Of course, I don't expect to solve all the
Middle East's problems. I'm just putting in my two cents,

which includes communicating to the home office what Likud's greed for more land, more military adventures, is costing all of us. Needless to say, I get a lot of static from Haig on that score because he is such a big friend of Israel's. Friend my foot! Whenever Sharon gets the urge to shoot himself in the head, Haig's there to hand him the gun. You'd have thought the sonofabitch had amply indulged his jocko-machismo in Vietnam, but his stupidity turns out to be practically limitless."

Luz wondered, "Is Ambassador Tucker connecting the dots? What I mean is, does he know what a precarious position Sadat's in?"

Leonard shrugged. "Tuck knows so little it's hard to keep up with what he doesn't know."

The Rover crawled up the road. It was narrow, rough, and hazardous even when well maintained, which in spots it was not. Leonard was gingerly negotiating around a pothole when the insistent blare of a horn caused him to look up in the rear view mirror. A truck with a dozen live camels in its bed was trying to pass. Leonard tried to get over as far to the right as he safely could, but the road wasn't wide enough. The horn blasted insistently as the truck came abreast of them, crowding them onto the shoulder. Leonard stomped the brake and the Rover skidded for a breathtaking moment on the gravel and dirt as its treads failed.

Luz clutched the dashboard and cursed. By the Virgin and her glory, there's a man who learned to drive in Mexico City! Shifting down, Lenny lost sight of the truck racing its unknowing passengers to ritual slaughter.

They came once more to the Gulf, and Luz let her gaze drift across the rustling waters. "You get along with these people very well on a human level," she remarked, remembering the ease and friendliness with which Lenny communicated with the clerk in the pharmacy, the waiters in the restaurant, Masoud on the *falucca*. Did he not feel, in the circumstances, some resentment against Muslims? With some awkwardness she asked, "You don't exonerate them for their share of all this bloodshed, do you?"

"Of course not." Leonard bent forward, shoulders hunched

to the wheel. "Pull my shirt away from my back, honey. Thanks. Some of those Palestinian splinter groups are wild men, and the fanatics among the Shi'ites make Charles Manson look like a cutie pie. But no matter how many Jews they kill, they'll never catch up with the Christians. We've had centuries of being murdered in the name of Jesus Christ."

The frown was suddenly back on Luz's forehead. Leonard's glance went swiftly from the twisting roadway to her scowling countenance, and he laughed again, a laugh that was as warm as a bedside embrace. He put a hand on her knee and finished, "But you and I certainly get along well on a human level, don't we? Did I ever say thank you for last night?"

The breeze fluttered her hair as Luz assumed a Southern Belle expression of injured innocence and a Magnolia accent. "Why Ah guess ya'all should thank me, Colonel. Ya had a whole night with yore hand on mah knee."

Leonard's lewd chuckle ended in a long sigh. "It's my knee you'll be turned over in a minute if you don't pay attention to the scenery and stop scribbling in your notebook. This is supposed to be a vacation, fer Pete's sake."

The traffic had thinned out considerably since they had left Ain Sokhna, but there was a roadblock up ahead, and Leonard brought the Rover to a halt before the barrier. He stuck his head out the window and spoke with a soldier in Arabic, quickly and efficiently. After inspecting the vehicle's registration papers, the soldier waved them through. Off to one side of the road was the truck that had flown pass them earlier, its four-legged passengers granted a stay of execution while a young soldier leafed through the driver's documents.

When they were on their way once more, Luz asked Lenny if the CIA thought that Ali was mixed up in something to do with commando daring and dash. "Yep," Leonard's lips rolled tight. "The spooks think Salah and his buddies want to knock off Sadat. And, as we all know, the CIA is never wrong."

"What?" Luz could hardly countenance the accusation enough to credit it. Besides, had she tried to say more, it would've choked her.

Leonard ran a finger along his moustache and amended, "Or to be more precise, this heavy by the name of Hikmat a.k.a Ibrahim wants the President wasted. He's a very dangerous man. He eluded a police dragnet recently. If Ali's involved with Hikmat, he's way out of his depth. Hikmat is playing for high stakes but he won't be the one to pay when the points are tallied up. It'll be some poor *putz*—"

The sentence hung unfinished in the air. "Like Ali" was implicit.

17

They stood for a while, getting properly oriented. The beach was deep-shadowed ocher. There was a strong perfume of flowers and trees on the night air. The sky was a ferocious pink. Overhead a gull cart wheeled and sang. "Which way, Senorita?" Leonard asked. Luz peered up and down the beach and then decided to head south. It amazed him that she'd picked right without knowing it. He tucked her arm under his, and they started strolling leisurely away from their Club Med bungalow. Except for the waves breaking on the beach the evening was still and silent. Luz could feel the sand damp and faintly sticky under her feet.

After they'd gone a few hundred yards, Luz and Lenny came upon a campfire. Two female figures were huddled around it. The blonde's hair was punk-styled into a big spiky puff and slicked back along the sides. The younger woman, who had coiffured her black hair like a schoolmarm and covered herself in an *abayas*, had nevertheless put enough *kohl* around her eyes to turn on a raccoon. They turned to look keenly at the Americans. The blonde jumped up and began waving her arms like someone demented. "Yahoo!" she shouted, the sunset casting a pink glow over her full figure.

Leonard took Luz's hand and they picked their way through the rocks and tar to the fire. "How nice to see you," gushed the blonde unfurling a large towel for them to sit on. She smiled broadly at Luz, revealing perfect teeth. Her red lips shone with gloss. She looked at Leonard and their eyes met in quick and intimate recognition. But when Leonard made no move to introduce her to Luz, the woman layered the awkwardness over with a rush of words. "I suppose you two came here to wallow in the lap of Club Med luxury. Four days and three nights of unlimited beverage beads and unlimited erotic pleasures, if you trust the glossy brochures." She stopped suddenly and coughed in an embarrassed manner. When she spoke again, it was with the authority of a woman once very beautiful. "Please do come and join us for a while."

"Well, ah—" Luz stalled. She was disarmed by the mysterious communication between Leonard and the strange woman. Her eyes had met his with a look that said something like, "It's about blooming time you got here!" or "Thought you might get cold feet and not show." Luz couldn't pin it down, but she knew her perceptions were close, for she could see an amused twinkle in the woman's eye, the look of someone holding tight to a juicy secret. Could she be an old paramour of Lenny's or perhaps an agent sent out by the same unseen authorities that had dispatched Gourdjaw and the man in the silver sports car?

The silence stretched out interminably. Leonard jumped in with a compliment for the blonde. "This fire looks very inviting. You are a Good Samaritan, but I don't need to tell you that, do I?"

He broke off at the sight of a wiry Napoleon-sized man coming through the palms. He seemed to be built entirely of solid power, and his face was both instantly recognizable and unfamiliar. Luz was thunderstruck. "Ali!" When she finally spoke his name, it came out as an exclamation. "I can't believe it's really you." Ali answered only with his stare.

She and Leonard had come here hoping to find Ali Salah, but Luz had assumed it would take them hours of searching. She wasn't prepared for this, nor for the change in him. The goatee had disappeared as had much of the hair on the top of his head. He sported a polite moustache and beard and a calm demeanor, as though he'd exchanged his Benzedrine for Quaaludes. He was broader in the chest than she recalled, and his sun-crumpled skin made him look older and wiser. Immediately, Luz wondered if this brassy blonde had anything to do with helping Pete Sanchez and Lenny set up this "chance" meeting with Ali. Could all these manipulative per-

sonalities believe that Gracida was the instrument that would
pry Salah's lips open? Neither she nor Ali had given them any
reason for such hopes. Santa Cruz was a million years ago.

Finally, Ali said, "Noor!" as though coming to consciousness after having been stunned with a brick. Ali Salah
had imagined himself to be beyond surprise. He'd seen it all,
been there and back several times, but now he was astounded. Luz, or so Mustafa had told him, was supposed to be
the Trojan Horse that would get Khalid and one of the Muslim
Sisters into Mrs. Sadat's tea party. How did Khalid let her get
away? And how did she find him? Being here in the flesh, Luz
appeared to be living testimony to what all pessimists believe
in their hearts: the best laid plans of mice and men always go
belly up. Yet, he allowed no sign of concern for the mission to
disturb the expression on his face as he remarked, "It has
been a while, hasn't it?"

"A while and a half," Luz agreed.

Luz's long-sleeved tunic was cut in a deep V that deliciously
revealed her bust when she moved her arms in a certain way.
She saw Ali watching her intently and she smiled, a smile that
made her face glow. She walked right up to him, her hands
outstretched, her round hips rolling under her jeans and tried
to kiss his cheeks. A look of horror crossed Ali's face at this,
and it didn't leave as he backed away. "Hey, quit that, Noor,"
he muttered. "This is Upper Egypt. They've got laws here."

Only one hand dropped to her side. "*Santamaria!* We're old
friends, aren't we?"

Ali gazed on Luz fearfully, not knowing how to answer. He
couldn't begin to guess at what kind of game she was playing.
Had Khalid told her where to find him? If he had, Mustafa
would throw him into a sack of snakes and pull the top tight.
The muscles around Ali's mouth tightened, but he moved
automatically to take her hand. "Who's the guy with you?" he
asked in English, and Luz found herself looking into a pair of
eyes that were unmistakably hostile. Suddenly, she was un-
reasonably angry at Leonard for suggesting they come to
Hurghada. Who needs this? She heard Ali insisting on an
answer. "Is he a ... friend or something?"

Luz's face flushed. The light was dim, but enough to make

out the Mr. Lumpenproletariat message on the T-shirt stuck
to his chest: Nuke the Whales. In a tightly controlled voice,
she made the introduction: "Ali, this is my fiancé, Leonard
Berg."

Ali stared with narrowed eyes at Berg, not totally convinced. Marriage had held no appeal for the Luz he once
knew. The men's hands barely touched as they exchanged a
ritualized greeting, a few words about the journey down from
Port Suez, the weather in Cairo, the latest bulletin on
Zamalek's win over a Polish soccer team. Some of the shock
had worn off Luz's face and, following Leonard's example, she
took off her thongs and sat down on the towel. Leonard
stretched out full length. Nafeisa offered him some lemon
squash. He smiled and shook his head, crossed his arms
behind it and stared up at the sky. "Fantastic," he whispered
joyfully. "I've never enjoyed any place in Egypt more than
this."

The blonde was Betty MacGregor, a middle-aged woman
with a commanding presence. In actuality, she used to be on
the stage, and her flamboyant acting style could fill a theater.
She spoke directly and with the clipped accent of someone
born in Fayid in the Canal Zone and educated in British
schools. She referred to herself as an Egyptian, though she
was only one-eighth of one. Although she wore the long gown
that was traditional among women of Upper Egypt and around
her neck clanked the usual silver jewelry, something about
her reminded Luz of those gabacho women who migrate to
New Mexico from New York and go about with long braids
falling down a Mexican peasant blouse, turquoise rings, and
huaraches.

The curtain calls were far behind her, but Betty had a
pension from a late husband. "Now I'm just going where the
ride takes me, with no destination in mind. I've been meeting
some very interesting people." Betty beamed around the
circle at everyone, then elaborated stoically, "Being a free
woman in Egypt is a lot like being an early Christian."

Nafeisa, who had been listening in the background, spoke
up nervously. "Ali?" He had made no attempt to introduce the
woman whom he had referred to as Noor, but turned instead

to her male companion. Unable to contain her curiosity, Nafeisa interrupted to ask, "Who is this woman?" She'd inquired in Arabic, thinking she would not be understood by the strangers.

There was something in Ali's manner that suggested she'd better not question him too closely. "Just someone I once had the misfortune to meet," he said succinctly, knowing Luz would catch the barb.

Luz laughed. Her laugh was not the sort of tittering giggle that you hear in the villages of Egypt. It was a belly laugh, an American laugh. Then Luz embarked on an animated English conversation with Ali that, judging from the direction of her glances, referred to Nafeisa. "What is she saying?" Nafeisa asked Ali.

"I am saying," Luz repeated in Arabic as fluent as Nafeisa's, "that you are a very pretty young lady."

"*Shukran.*" Nafeisa said thank you with the strained politeness she felt was due this stranger who spoke to her in a gentle accent not very dissimilar to her own. Was she an Egyptian?

Luz was conscious of the fact that "pretty" was not the word she would have used to describe Nafeisa in an article. Movie stars like Ishahane and Nagwa Fouad were beauties, but most poor Egyptians have faces ugly enough to make them pull the curtains shut and lock themselves indoors forever, and Nafeisa was no exception. Denied well-balanced diets, soaps, emollients, creams, shampoos, sun shields, vitamins, dentists, orthodontists, and bathtubs, their complexions are as bad as their breath, and their smiles full of overbite and missing teeth. With her dowdy dress and unwashed hair parted severely in the middle, Nafeisa looked like a runaway from the cast of "Saturday Night Live," Egypt's own Roseanne Roseannadana. Yet she looked out at the world with curiosity, and there was a warm inquisitiveness in her eyes when she asked Luz if she had ever been to the cinema.

"Now and then," Luz admitted. "And you?"

Nafeisa was entranced. "Oh yes!" She rocked back and forth, as though she were still reeling from the experience. "Once Cousin Ali took me and my sister Aza to the cinema in

Safaga. It was our first time to see a film, and we just sat there
and watched this magical thing unfolding: sumptuous villas
with swimming pools, a long motorcar with a canvas top and a
side-mounted spare tire, and Fatin Hamama, five meters tall
in a spangled dress. No wonder Omar Sharif married her!"

Nafeisa's voice had an odd, disjointed rhythm all its own
which was lulling Ali into a kind of dreaminess. He faced East
and felt that the Red Sea beyond, the dark beach around them
and the way they all fit into it, had imbued a haunting,
elegiacal quality to the evening. He looked over at Leonard
thinking, "I view just about everything under the sun from a
180-degree opposite point of view from you. I am opposed to
your government and what it is doing in the Middle East, but
somehow it is right that you are here."

"To me," Nafeisa was rattling on breathlessly, "the film was
absolutely awesome, and it touched the three of us in a very
magical way. I wish it had been my fate to pass all my days in a
cinema. For years afterwards Ali said he'd dreamt of having a
motorcar just like that."

That brought Ali to himself sharply. Idiotic girl! Humiliating
him in front of other people! "I've never wanted things for
myself, Cousin. Only liberty for our country and you damn
well know it." He stopped, trying to find something to say,
other than what he might not say in front of this bastard Berg,
who was probably an agent of the CIA. He shut his eyes,
folded his legs lotus-like, and shivered slightly. If Berg took
him to be a mystic and an epileptic given to meditation and an
occasional fit of depression, so much the better.

"Sorry." The voice was sweet and deferential, but her large
brown eyes stared with an unexpected self-assurance. Nafeisa
knew from long and painful practice when to sluff off a Salah
outburst and a Salah act. "Another time we saw a double
feature, one with a Miss Alice Faye and the other with a Miss
Joan Blondell. I don't remember which one of the blond
ladies wore a bathing costume, do you, Ali?" Getting no reply
from the yogi, Nafeisa hurried on. "Well, it was really a rather
modest affair, nothing as shocking as you can see at Club Med
today, and when we got home Aza told my mother who told
our grandfather. He ordered Ali to get his belt. You can still

see the marks across the back of Ali's legs and his left thigh.
Show them, Ali."

"Not now." Ali coughed and his hand fluttered in a feeble
attempt to stop the chatter. His brooding eyes fixed on Luz.
Would she remember the scars?

When Ali didn't move, Betty MacGregor rose from her
towel and came to sit close to him. With easy familiarity, she
reached down and pushed up his pant leg. The scars were
there, although the man who had put them there had long
since passed away. Pointing to the long line, Nafeisa said Ali
had to be taken to a clinic to have 18 stitches put in it. "It
looks as though he had at you with a cat-o-nine tails, ducky,"
Betty crooned, compassionately. "Had this same incident
happened in the MacGregor family the results would have
been quite different. Papa would have been killed. Push a Scot
and he pushes back. I learned early when I saw a brother
make a fist to dive for a foxhole."

"No one in my family ever makes a fist," said Leonard
ruefully, sitting up and locking his hands around his knees.
"Bergs are all neurotics or hypochondriacs."

Luz was intrigued with Grandfather Salah and why he'd
visited corporal punishment upon Ali, not that the same
thought hadn't crossed her mind once or twice back in Santa
Cruz. Nafeisa explained that it had something to do with sin,
haram. Betty swung around and grabbed Ali's toe. She dim-
pled her cheeks and affected a coy pose. "Doesn't everything
that's worth doing?" The lightness of her laughter hung heavy
in the air.

Nafeisa was shocked out of her wits by Betty's remarks,
though it confirmed what she already knew about wayward
Englishwomen. Her chin elevated virtuously as she said, "If
my mother heard you, she would wash your mouth out with
soap."

"Really?" Betty's voice drawled with an upward inflection,
mocking and questioning. "I didn't realize you people had
soap."

Ali had told Betty earlier that his cousin Latif was supposed
to have wed Nafeisa, but he ran off to Manchester to work.
Betty's first reaction upon meeting Nafeisa was that this un-

seen cousin was a wise, wise man indeed. She let go of Ali's toe as Luz said to Nafeisa, "What was Grandpa's problem?"

Nafeisa gave her a curious look. Noor spoke Arabic, but not quite like a native. You could pick out the occasional discordant phrase. She was a stranger, yet obviously a woman Ali had known. Nafeisa rocked back and forth, as if she realized she should be keeping the information about her grandfather to herself, like a good Arab woman, but the story was too tempting. She said Abu was a moralist in whom the blood of his Upper Egyptian ancestors ran strongly. He believed with all his heart that women should be held in safekeeping, cosseted, and revered by men. As a young husband he once caught his wife riding down a desert road on the donkey cart of a neighbor. Abu tied his neighbor to one wheel of the cart and castrated him. Involuntarily, Leonard's hand went to his groin. No one likes to hear such things about another man, even one you'd never meet, but once told, it is impossible to resist the gory details. Did he bleed to death? Or do an Abelard number and join a monastery? Commit suicide? Ali, who appeared to be sliding between nervousness and apathy, said nothing, nor was Nafeisa eager to fill in the blanks. "It has to do with female fragility," she explained with bogus loftiness, adding, "It is ever a *Safagi's* firm conviction that the rest of the human race with the misfortune to live beyond the boundaries of Upper Egypt lead wickedly immoral lives, which, as we all know thanks to the cinema and Club Med, they do."

There was a long silence as everyone stared into the flames. Nafeisa had strained, yearning eyes that reached out as if she wanted something to rise from the ashes, but was not sure how to recognize it if it did. Because she was engaged to Ali and he was in the Jamaat, Nafeisa mouthed Ali's line, but Leonard suspected the girl might be fed up with having sutras poured into her ears and listening to a parade of homilies— "Oh Virgin, God's noblest work on this earth!"—delivered in cadences so august as to border on the Confucian; and, in truth, she was fascinated by these foreign devils around her. The heat from the fire gave a waxy sheen to Leonard's forehead as he said to Nafeisa, "You speak about your grand-

father's noble deed as if you were nominating him for
president of the world."

"Our grandfather was a man of his time," Ali offered in a
reasonable voice. "He wore a red fez with a black tassel,
brushed his teeth with twigs and—"

Nafeisa shut him up. "Our family is a fine family and very
devout," she said hotly. "We are True Believers. The only
reason Ali got put in prison was that the Cairo police are
Zionists. They live inside a bordello and see sins where none
exist." Ali shook his head in warning, but she prattled on like
the typically loose-lipped Egyptian female she was. "And as
for our cousin Talaat dying of an opium overdose, well, that
can happen to anybody. Look at J.R. Ewing. You Americans
make him into a demigod, but we can see the skeletons in his
closet." She turned to Ali for support.

A log broke on the fire, shooting sparks upward so that Ali's
eyes glinted red as he growled, "Be quiet, Nafeisa." He had
been drinking beer with Betty and some Danish tourists all
afternoon long. It was not a strong drink, but he sat glassy-
eyed on the sand trying to maintain his dignity. Betty Mac-
Gregor was not exactly a Oui centerfold, Ali thought; too
much smoking caused her to cough through sentences now
and then, and her face carried the memory of too many smiles
and too many sunny days. Nonetheless, for the past week his
repressed sexuality had been enflamed by the excitement and
vitality of her uninhibited ways. That afternoon she'd asked
him to come to her after seeing Nafeisa home. He remained
uneasy about the wickedness, but Betty knew he would forget
it once they were in bed—he always did.

Time apparently hadn't dulled in the slightest the feelings
of desire Luz aroused either. She smelled as fragrant as a
flower, and Ali wanted to press his fingers into the denim
swelling on her hips. Alas, he mused, if only he had been
born soon enough in human history to rush across a gigantic
harem like a Caliph in his palace, trailing sparks of inspiration
which court poets could use to immortalize him. Today, his
sex life was understandably constrained by the necessity of
avoiding any step that might offend his aunt, by being faithful
to the tenets of the Brotherhood, and by taking advantage of

any small opportunity Nafeisa's momentary inattention offered. Yet, he had to admit, his relatives' certain outrage and Ibrahim's violent disapproval lent a splash as invigorating as a dip in the early morning sea, making their brief encounters that much more bracing.

Ali felt the pressure of Betty's hand on his leg ease up, and he turned to contemplate Luz. It was clear that she felt no love for him. From time to time she looked at him with frank friendliness, but nothing more, no nostalgia even for their long lost, potholed love affair. Feeling rather rejected, he asked Luz if she ever missed Santa Cruz. She felt him cup her chin, forcing her to look into his face. "Sometimes," she answered evenly. "It's okay to look at the past, *companero*. Just don't stare at it."

But Noor was staring at him now. All the old talkative vitality, the exuberance, and the flair Luz remembered in Ali seemed to have vanished, replaced by a sullen restlessness. Even when conversing with Leonard about nothing much, Ali stumbled for words, jumping and darting from one topic to the next without completing his thoughts. It was as though the black and white instructions he usually followed—"Be an Egyptian with Egyptians, an Arab with Arabs, a Westerner with Westerners,"—had gotten all jangled up in his not knowing who she was: Luz or Noor or both, and not knowing what brought her here, but fearing the worst.

Dropping his hand, Ali turned back to Betty. Her dress was hiked up, exposing her bare leg, and he lit one of her Benson and Hedges. Berg was telling a funny joke in fluent Arabic, but this night suddenly seemed impossible for Ali. His worry about the future, his and the Jamaat's, seemed to gnaw at him, and the laughter only grated his nerves. How dare they be so carefree when the fate of the world hung in the balance! For the next hour the air was filled with physical awareness and a submerged torrent of feelings and memories and jealousies and evasions—all glossed over by smoke and small talk.

Or was it so small? Ali could see that being a couple was the most important thing about Luz and Leonard as they sat together on the towel. That connective spirit was almost palpable in the roll of sentences that began in one mouth and ended in another, in the mix of joking and attention that surrounded his or her remark, in the touching, the leaning into warmth, the hugs that came so unconsciously. Where in heaven's name did she meet him? Did their families give their blessings? A jealous rage was rising inside him, but Ali could not ask any of the questions that rushed to his head. He merely wished a tidal wave would crash in on Club Med tonight and carry them both out to sea. Cursing silently, he fumbled for another cigarette.

Betty struck a match, but Ali didn't see it and the flame burnt out. Nafeisa was still center stage and Ali wanted to tell her that she was talking too much, but it would appear boorish to the Westerners. A biting sea breeze drifted across the dying fire, causing the shadows of the palm trees to undulate on the sand like bodies in bed. Ali shivered with chill and anticipation.

His cousin's voice broke into his reverie. "It is a disgrace for women to have authority in a country. We have all the authority we need in the home." Nafeisa had adopted the lecturing tone Ali always used with her. "Women cannot rule; we are weak. Power here is always the man."

Leonard laughed, a dry, harsh laugh. "That's just what President Sadat preaches: Egyptians are one big extended family, of which I am the indispensable head. My rebellious son, be obedient, submit. Who are you to question your father?"

Betty pitched her voice loudly, puffing herself up to the performance level of a talk show guest. "It is clear as glass that Sadat's unforgivable sin was to get up on the telly and admit he thinks his wife has opinions worth listening to. The tea stall hoot that greeted this egalitarian statement echoes in every criticism of his regime. He respects his wife? Why that filthy bugger! Egypt is a country that sentimentalizes women or dismisses them, but we do not take them seriously. Nor do we have much regard for a man who does."

"Jihan behaves as the complete opposite of an Egyptian woman," Nafeisa protested. She and Betty stared hard at each other. Nafeisa went on, "Jihan misbehaves by challenging men. We exist to satisfy our man, to give him sons, and to serve him. We mustn't struggle against that. Struggling is just a nicer word for postponed obedience."

Betty cut in, "Please, old sweet, lay off Jihan. The only real difference between Jihan and everyone else is the degree of her match-making. She married her children into rich families, and that makes her a successful woman in her line of work, which is being a mother. What goes on in the Sadat family goes on, in varying degrees, in every family from the Sudanese border to the Mediterranean Ocean. You show me an Egyptian mother who would let her daughter wed someone with one chicken if she can stoop to games of skulduggery and come up with some bloke what's got two bloody chickens and a bag of cotton seeds."

Betty wiggled her toes and finished in those round English vowels, "His character, his intelligence, has nothing to do with it. Let him be a miserable sodding thief if he's got a few bob more than the next prospect. It is shameless opportunism, pure and simple. It sticks in my craw a bit, that."

"You seem to forget," rejoined Ali, not liking her tone, "that it is the duty of a family to make sure a bridegroom has money, as well as a sworn obligation to honor the contract." Ali took a long draw on his cigarette. A ripple of smoke drifted into his eyes. Squinting at Betty, he challenged, "Who are you to talk? You are a Western woman, for whom pregnancy is no more a threat than frostbite would be for a Fiji Islander. Nafeisa will be a mother nine months and three minutes after we get married. It can't be helped." The grim look on Betty's face cut him off.

In that look sat all the disgust it was possible for a woman to feel. "No romantic pretensions! Put the economic right up front!" MacGregor had a way of making everybody shape up all of a sudden. "Isn't that the Muslims way? You bet it is! Yet someone has only to mention Jihan's name and you turn positively livid. I dare say she's hardly out of place. Perhaps her dresses aren't long enough to suit your taste or her hair shows. You deal with these peccadillos as if the lady were dropping an atomic bomb on a kindergarten. And you never let up for a minute on poor Anwar. I grant you he cuts his corners on occasion, but only a babe in the woods could

suppose that unflawed marble is the stuff of which effective
leaders are made."

Ali's head fell into his hands. Nafeisa found herself on her
feet, standing as straight as if her back were in a brace. She
was suddenly angry with Betty, who had just said something
that appeared silly to Nafeisa, but she could see it possessed a
painful meaning for her cousin. Ali blew hot and cold when
this obnoxious woman, this English, was around. Nafeisa was
not so blind as to be ignorant on that score. All evening long,
but surreptitiously, she had watched Ali watching Betty, her
breasts, her legs. The fact that he'd squeezed her hand a few
seconds too long did not go unnoticed by Nafeisa. His infatua-
tion was obvious, though at first Nafeisa closed her mind to
the thought. All evening long she'd struggled hard not to
believe it and felt sick at her inability to do so. Now, she
buried her nails in her palms in an effort to control herself,
but the fierce whisper escaped her lips. "Ali, do you know this
woman in that way?"

Ali pressed his lips and remained silent. He looked so
guilty that no answer was necessary. Nafeisa felt as if she were
awakening from a long dream. She looked at MacGregor with
dull loathing. Betty laughed. Ali was biting his lower lip and
shaking his head at her without even realizing it. Nafeisa's
temper rose once more, but this time it was directed at Ali. In
fact, she was so furious at him that when Luz asked Ali what
he did for a living these days, Nafeisa piped up to say, "As little
as possible." A second later she wanted to protest that her
remark had been made without thinking, but a pounding
heart had urged her to say exactly what was on her mind.

Shadows and firelight played on Ali's face as he poked at
what was left of the logs, sending sparks into the darkness.
"Philosophy," he began, but his tired brain declined to fur-
nish him with a more credible answer.

Ali had barely spoken all evening, but afterward, walking
down the beach toward their hotel, Leonard had the feeling
that he had directed the course of the conversation and
headed it away from dangerous ground. Luz had tried to ask
him about Khalid, whom she'd not seen for several days, tried
to solicit a few political opinions, but he'd simply waited until

Nafeisa's mouth saved him a reply. Berg kept asking himself, why did Salah have to leave Cairo in the middle of the night? Cairo was where the action would be, but Salah was beach-bumming. What was going on here? Had he seen the light? Had he been chastened by the sight of Hikmat in flight? Had it dawned on him that while the sheiks and ayatollahs might be gifted orators and politicians, trained in the roughest school imaginable (the mosque), at the center of their vision of change there lies an ill-defined and perhaps empty core?

Sitting next to Ali Salah, Berg decided, was a little like sitting next to styrofoam; neatly bearded styrofoam. You could get no feeling for him either way, not liking, not disliking. Ali seemed solid and not over-excitable, easy to be around for an hour or two, but an enigma. Luz had advertized her affair with Mad Ali as a bubble in her champagne and a departure from the small beer altar boys of her youth, but was it really? Salah appeared, instead, to have the sort of nebbish person-ality usually associated with bank tellers and flight attendants. His chief virtue as a rebel seemed to be a chronic stupor and a clichéd anti-American stance.

The sky was growing black, the stars small and far away. Luz sighed and turned to look at him. She wanted an accounting of Betty MacGregor. That she and Lenny had had a history with each other was apparent to Luz, although there was more than a hint they'd gone their separate ways. Leonard pasted a look of surprise on his face. "You don't like Betty?"

"I have nothing against Betty as a person. I'm sure that when she's not leading one-woman assaults on eastern culture, she's nice enough. But she helped you set up this little get-together, didn't she? I can tell from the way you eyed each other, your faces full of unspoken words, that you know her from somewhere before. So don't try to wiggle out of it."

Leonard stared at Luz, and the pale light showed a deep crease between his brows. "Am I that transparent?" he asked, his hands flapping at his sides. "Yeah, well, we met at a party in Alex about six months ago and we had a few dates, a roll or two in the hay. There wasn't much to it, though I'll have to confess I sort of enjoyed the air of innuendo that attached itself to the relationship. Perhaps because Betty has a bit of a rep for being a femme fatale and, being a bit of a romantic myself, I was attracted to that quality in her, of Holly Golightly gone to seed. But that grandiose presentation of self gets old fast. I think she works for a friendly country's intelligence agency, but I can't say for sure. Mac offers everything and gives nothing. All she adds up to is *tsuris.*"

Luz prodded, "What kind of trouble?"

"I mean, Betts could be playing her own game, one so utterly mad and private that it's invisible to the rest of us. Her family's property was pretty extensive before the Free Officers confiscated it all. She might have some old scores to settle. Her interest in me was pretty basic. She wanted to know everything I knew about the security situation here. She told me that everyone in her outfit seems to be searching desperately for the inside skinny on what the opposition will do and when it will do it and who will do it. For where it'll be done, they've got their eyes on Assyut."

Puzzled, Luz broke in again. "Why Assyut?"

"There's an old Egyptian saying that only two crops are grown in Assyut, opium and dissent. But we think the lid will blow off in Cairo. So much for The World According to J. Bond." He kissed her temples. "All that fooling around is behind me now that I've found you. You are a great traveling companion, sweetheart."

"Recommend me to your friends."

"Like hell I will."

18

Shirley Anne Grady was lying in bed reading when Joe Dooley came in from the kitchen humming, "Biddy Mulligan." He sat his whiskey and water down carefully on the beside table. Shirley Anne looked at the glass with that tight-lipped expression that he was beginning to hate, but he held his tongue. She was very desirable in her heavy way, even though there were times when she had the amorous instincts of a Carmelite nun. He reached out and caressed the fleshy part of her arm. She gave him a languid smile and his loins trembled, anticipating exertion.

"Faith and you're a fine lassie," Joe chortled, stripping off his underwear. He had a lot of auburn hair on his body and a little on the top of his head. He fell across the mattress, burrowing his face into her crotch and making growling sounds. Shirley sat up and shifted to rest her back against the head of the bed, watching him as he grabbed her ankle. He slid his hand up her leg, around her thigh, to let it rest on the spot where the taut flesh of her leg joined the lips of her vagina.

"Cut it out, Joey," Shirley giggled, making a half-hearted attempt to push his hand away. The glow of anticipation on his face didn't quite dispel his harried look. He was singing a love song, but there was a clumsy determination in the way he was stroking her. He rose on his knees.

The buzzer rang as she was guiding him into her, and Joe quickly decided, "Nobody we know, sugar. Ignore it,"—he was easing in—"and they'll go away."

Shirley squirmed away. "Have you forgotten I've got the

duty this week-end?" Her gaze held onto his bloodshot eyes
and she wondered if he remembered her name. He never
called her anything but sugar—which was close enough to
Shirley when you come right down to it. "Some sumbitch
tourist could've lost his passport or had a heart attack. They
take a perverse delight in messing up your week-ends. Or we
could be going to war."

"We're always going to war," Joe grunted, his body slick
with sweat.

The buzzer was rudely insistent, as if someone were leaning
on it. Shirley rose and slipped her feet into her big pink
bunny slippers. "I gotta answer it."

Shirley Anne Grady came out of the bedroom shoving her
arms into a terry cloth bathrobe and tying a loose knot in the
belt. She peered through the peep hole. The delivery man
had a slight build, dark glasses, a thin black moustache, and a
black and white *khaffiyea*, and he was carrying gladiolus the
color of blood oranges in tissue paper. He took off his sunglasses and smiled—it was a winsome smile. Then he lifted up
the bouquet so she could see it.

"Flowers," the messenger announced when Shirley opened
the door.

Her eyes lit up. "For me?" Thomas Joseph was a gentleman
of the old school, obviously. Enchanted, she reached into her
purse, intending to tip the delivery man. When she pushed
two crumbled pound notes in his direction, he suddenly
slashed out at her with a knife—a knife that looked to her as
long as a beheading sword as it came plunging downward,
closer and closer.

In the bedroom, Joe Dooley was sipping his drink when he
heard Shirley scream. It was a scream that made his blood run
cold. When he hit the front room, he could see a man stabbing his girlfriend. Without a split second's hesitation, he
hurled himself forward. The man saw him coming and ran
down the stairs. Joe, naked as the day he was born, gave
chase. An elderly woman who was climbing up to her flat on
the fifth floor heard the roar coming her way like a flash flood
in the desert; she flattened herself against the wall and
prayed. A young man, his face hidden behind his *khaffiyea*,

darted by. The old woman couldn't believe her eyes when she saw Joe Dooley coming after him. Her false teeth chattered and she clenched them on her lower lip. Surely, she must be having one of her dizzy spells. "Oh dear, oh dear, oh dear," she groaned as she lowered herself tenderly to a marble step.

The young man was cutting in between the parked cars, hips swiveling with the agility of someone who had played a lot of soccer in his lifetime. He was heading for the compound across the street. He lunged at the black wrought-iron fence, trying to scale it. But before he could gain the top, Dooley nabbed him by the belt and jerked him hard. He fell from the fence and landed atop a snarling Irishman. The young man struggled, but Joe was wrestling him to the pavement, pinning an elbow behind his back. In the fight, the *khaffiyea* had come off. So had his thongs and his dark glasses. "Stop it, Joe," he said, turning his head around in an awkward angle to be heard. "It's me."

The voice sounded familiar. Joe rolled the man over and stared into a friendly face, a face belonging to one of the young men who'd met him at the airport in a Sun Tours Fiat and brought him and Luz into town: Khalid.

Dooley was paralyzed with shock. He worked his mouth to speak and finally managed a few words Khalid could understand: Holy Mother of God! Khalid pushed him off and sprang to his feet. Looking down from height at his pale baby-smooth skin, Khalid said in a scolding tone, "You shouldn't be out here in public with nothing on, Mr. Dooley. You are surely going to get yourself sent to jail, and then to Hell." A quick squeeze on the shoulder. "Your injuries looks like they're healing real good."

Ambassador Roland Tucker notified his two bodyguards and his driver at 9 p.m. that he did not intend to ride in his limo to the cocktail party. It was a tender evening, one made for strolling. His wife Paulette joined him at the Embassy; together they set off on foot for the Meridien Hotel which was right on the Nile. With one bodyguard in front, another in back, and the limo cruising slowly along side, they began walking along the far edge of the British Embassy. It was just

9:20 when the guard who was out on point stopped at the edge
of an angry crowd, his hand reaching in his shoulder holster.
The driver, seeing him withdraw his pistol, radioed the Marine Guard on duty. As Ambassador Tucker came to a halt, the
driver could see that he was white around the mouth and
breathing hard. He lunged at a naked man, his fist raised, but
was held around the waist by Mrs. Tucker, who was wailing
something in a voice that sounded like a vibrating bed.

With Khalid gone, Joe Dooley staggered to his feet and
looked around. Passersby had stopped dead in their tracks to
gawk and jeer at this bellicose oaf who was clad only in air and
sky. Shirley Anne Grady was advancing on him with a
blanket, holding it out to him like a matador with a cape. Her
arm was swathed in a towel. "For Godsake, Joe," she called
out frantically. "You're naked as a jaybird. Where do you think
you are, India?"

Joe turned and found himself staring at the business end of
two handguns. "Oh no," he howled at the Ambassador's
bodyguards. "Not again."

Shirley Anne Grady was treated at the Anglo-Egyptian
Hospital for cuts on both hands and several scratches. Six
stitches and some mercurochrome did the job. Police re-
covered a five inch kitchen knife on the stairwell, a bunch of
gladiolus and two crumbled bills on the door mat, and a
Palestinian *khaffiyea* off the fence. They ruled it an attack by
al-Fatah.

19

Leonard Berg greeted the doorman's young daughter with a warm *Salaam* as they entered the building. "That was a wonderful trip," said Luz as they headed for the elevator. Before they reached the door, the little girl affably informed them the electricity was off in parts of the building.

"Home Sweet Home. Let's hope," Leonard prayed as he put his foot on the first step, "that these stairs don't conk out too, or we'll really be in trouble."

The climb didn't bother Luz. She was glad to have put the long and tiring journey—and Ali Salah—forever behind her. She was looking forward to a hot shower, an hour spent with her freshly washed hair on a soft pillow, an interesting book in her hands, chilled white wine and French herbal cheese on a tray nearby. "Thanks for talking me into it, *querido*. Now I can tell people I've seen the Red Sea without lying."

"Rest assured I won't say I told you so." Leonard looked sanctimonious as they reached the landing, and he hoisted the bag to his shoulder. Sounding like all the Oak Ridge Boys rolled into one, he started singing, "Elvira." In his mind's eye he was already picturing Luz's soft breasts pressing against his chest, her hips lifting to meet his. With his free hand, he dug into his pants pocket for his key ring. The light above the door was burning brightly, illuminating both the bluestone charm to ward off the Evil Eye and the *mezuzah* in its slanting position beside the doorjamb. "Oom papa mowmow," he sang the refrain of the song in a gay voice.

Instantly, Leonard had come to a dead stop, his eyes blinking, his moustache quivering like the whiskers on a startled muskrat. "What's wrong?" Luz asked, instinctively wary.

167

Leonard's head pivoted back to her. "My front door's ajar."
He kicked it gently with his toe and it swung open. "Stay
here," he whispered insistently as he put the bag down
quietly on the doormat. Tense and alert, he took several steps
into the foyer. Luz was right behind him, holding her breath
and close as his shadow.

Little light penetrated the dark recesses of the flat, but as
her eyes became accustomed to the gloom she could make out
the shapes of furniture in the middle of the room. They moved
as stealthily as guerrillas through a jungle trying not to trip
over anything.

Luz could imagine him at Fort Bragg with the other reluctant conscripts on night manuevers among the spooky pines in
the red clay scrublands of North Carolina. Walking his fingers
like a crab across the wallpaper, Leonard sought the light
switch; he flicked it to on, but no illumination came from the
chandelier. Of course, the *boab*'s little daughter had said the
electricity was off in parts of the building.

Feeling his way like a newly blind man, Leonard made it to
a small table at the side of the couch where candles and
matches were kept on hand to be pressed into service during
Cairo's electrical blackouts. "Ouch!" He'd stubbed his toe and
uttered a few obscenities as he lit a candle. He held it up and
out, in the manner of a vestal virgin marching into the temple.
The clap-clap of his sandals sounded unnaturally loud.

"Shit!" Rage potent as electrical volts erupted when
Leonard caught sight of the upheaval around him. Chairs
were upended, the sofa pulled away from the wall, lamps were
on their side on the floor, and potted plants had been up-
rooted and strewn about. The family photographs had been
knocked off their perches, the glass splintering into the rug. A
painting was torn from its frame.

Leonard took a tentative step and his toes connected with
something on the floor. He bent to retrieve a cedar box inlaid
with an intricate arabesque of mother-of-pearl. A hinge was
broken. He recited a litany of Yiddish and Arabic curses on
the perpetrator of the crime, stopping only when Luz put a
hand on his shoulder, and with the other hand, pointed to the
color television set. Amazingly, it had emerged unscathed.

They stared at each other blankly. Leonard just shook his head
and stared at the TV set, owl-eyed. Dispiritedly, he wondered, "How do you suppose they missed that?"

"They didn't take the stereo." Luz was standing very still,
her voice filled with amazement. Another detail caught her
eye: the eight-branched candelabrum was resting safely on
the sideboard, not on the floor. "Your menorah wasn't
touched, either," said Luz, parking the cooler and the oranges
on the carpet until she could find her way safely to the
kitchen.

Leonard disappeared. "Goddamn their testicles!"

"*Momento*! How do you know it wasn't a whoa-mann bur-
glar?" Luz's skin became damp, her mind a turmoil of mixed
thoughts. Could the men who killed Talaat have anything to
do with this? She stood without moving, breathing heavily,
filled with anxiety. Things were closing in on them.

Leonard overrode her. "A thief with tits wouldn't have
passed up your bottle of Chloe perfume, would she?"

Suddenly, Luz's throat was dry and she could feel the blood
pulsating in her ears. She started walking flat footed and
slowly in the direction of the cursing and found herself standing next to Lenny in the bedroom, looking at the perfume
bottle in his hand. The drawers were pulled out, their contents emptied onto the *flokati* rugs, the clothing in the closet
yanked off hangers and tossed around the room as if they'd
been caught up in a tornado. The mattress and blanket had
been torn off the bed, the pillows slashed open. The sheets
were ripped to shreds, as if Rapunzel had attempted another
getaway. The clothes in Luz's suitcase had been doused with
molasses. When she discovered that, Leonard anticipated a
wail, perhaps tears. Instead, Luz shook her fists in the air and
let loose with a torrent of abusive Spanish that made him
chuckle.

The mirror above the bureau had been shattered, throwing
their reflection back at them a hundredfold. The sight made
Luz's stomach churn like a washing machine. "*Madre mia!*"
she gasped. "Have you ever thought about quitting and collecting your pension, *caro*? You know, while you're still
around to spend it?"

Sweat was forming on his upper lip and he felt queasy with fear, but Leonard gave her his fiercest stare. The buzzer sounded. It was the doorman, the *boab*. Grabbing him by the arm, Leonard agitatedly described the disaster that was his flat. With loud protestations, the *boab* told the *effendi* he was in no way responsible for this contretemps. Not once during the last 73 hours had he shut his eyes. He'd even missed meals, so as not to abandon his post (he grabbed the sides of his *galabiah*, which was doing a good job of cloaking any evidence to the contrary.) Yes, it is true, as Allah was his witness, eternal vigilance was his manner, you have only to ask everyone in the building, every single one of whom has known him for at least 190 years.

Berg was not one to tolerate such perjury and he raised his voice. Luz finally managed to position herself in between the two furious males and convince them that there was little to be gained from a shouting match. The *boab* growled out the old Arabic proverb that a woman's counsel isn't worth much, but only a fool ignores it. Luz searched the man's face for mockery; there was none.

As a peace offering, the *boab* gave his flashlight to Berg. They distributed more candles about. Once they were lit, the apartment was luminously dim. After the *boab* had scurried off, Leonard called the Embassy's Chief of Security to report what had happened. Then Leonard began to range about the flat, peering into corners, moving things with sharp exclamations of scorn and disgust. Luz followed behind him, anxious to stay close to his biceps—just in case. Together they undertook a painstakingly minute inventory. It took them several hours. When they finished, they stood and stared and tried not to let their imaginations run away with them.

"Not a damn thing missing," Leonard announced in a baffled tone, his bewilderment acute. "Damn! I'd feel better if this were your garden variety robbery, I really would. You could understand it."

There was a noise at the front door and they both jumped. An enormous man with lips like two whooppee cushions and muscular arms yelled, "Lenny, where the devil are you?"

Composing himself, Leonard went forward to met Ted

LaGrange, the Embassy's Chief of Security who was holding a large flashlight. "Hiya, Ted. That was quick. I called you less an hour ago. Hope you weren't sitting down to eat."

Ted drawled, "You're close. We was sitting down to play bridge with the neighbors, but it can wait." His eyes went from Berg's face to circle the room. "You wanna tell me what happened."

Leonard took a deep breath. "We were out of town for four days, took a flying trip down to Hurghada. This is what we found when we got back. We haven't moved a thing."

Ted rubbed his neck, which was short and tubby, a description that aptly suited the rest of his body as well. Unzipping his jacket, he revealed a yellow T-shirt stretching heroically across a more than ample girth. He seemed to wear a perpetual smile on his fat face as Leonard took him on a tour of the apartment. Luz stayed in the shadows of the front room as the two men went from room to room, conferring in low tones which she could not make out. In the bedroom Ted bent over her suitcase and fingered a pair of lacy black bikini panties. Slyly, he asked Lenny, "Yours?"

Keeping his cool, Leonard explained that his roommate had transferred her gear from the hotel just before they'd departed for the Red Sea. "So I noticed," Ted said. Once back in the front room, LaGrange moved to an upturned wing chair. Putting it right side up, he sunk down and spread his big arms over the armrest. He gave a smirk and said, "So who's we?"

"Excuse me. I was so eager to show you the scene of the crime that I've forgotten my manners." The beam from the flashlight hit Luz in the face. "My fiancé, Luz Gracida." Leonard volunteered, "She's a reporter for a Spanish-language newspaper."

Ted touched one finger to the tip of his baseball cap. Then he came to meet her with a broad smile and a handshake. "Pleased to met ya, Mizz Grace." Ted beamed at her, while out of the side of his mouth he said to Leonard, "She's a mighty fine woman, ole buddy. Much too fine for you."

When Luz offered Ted a drink, he said, "Okay, if you've got a beer."

Leonard handed her the flashlight and she set off for the

refrigerator. Before she was out of hearing range, she heard LaGrange say in a low, hoarse whisper, "Whadda ya know about her, anyway?"

Leonard's stern hazel eyes met his. "What the hell is that suppose to mean?"

Ted wasn't the sort to laugh a lot in a room dark as confessional box, but he giggled when he said, "You can bet your sweet ass that door jam would've splintered when the intruder forced the chain. Kinda leads you to suspect an inside job, doesn't it?"

Leonard reproved him. "Ted, you *putz*! I promise you Luz could be trusted with our code books and the combination to our classified files." Ted made no comment so it was hard to say whether he'd be prepared to go that far. "Trust me, Ted, I know this woman," Lenny swore.

Ted held up a restraining hand. "All right," he said slowly as if he weren't convinced. "I gotta ask, see, for the record. But don't get your balls in a uproar, Len, I'll approach the subject with discretion. Okay, tell me, where'd you met this dame?"

Luz got the bottle of Michelob from the fridge. It was warm. Though the electricity had been off for some time, the rest of the building seemed to have lights. The two men sat and talked for a while, sipping their warm beers, Ted speculating on the identity of the culprit while Lenny listened with what seemed interest. Ted described the knife attack on Shirley Anne Grady by a deranged Palestinian terrorist. Luz overheard the word "ex-Congressman," and thought that this was definitely not Dooley's year. His injury and Talaat's death continued to prey on her mind. Luz made herself a cup of hot tea and took it into the bedroom. Throwing off her slacks and blouse, she put fresh linens on the bed and stepped into the shower.

When she got out, LaGrange was blessedly gone. Standing in a puddle on the tiles, she asked Leonard if the man had gotten her name right, for the record. "When you've got a secretary," said Leonard, tugging playfully at her towel, "spelling doesn't matter."

Luz blurted out, "What kind of a jerkwater mission are you folks running anyhow? Grady opens the door to a stranger and

Tucker strolls the streets like somebody's Uncle Wiggly. You agree to marry me, and I could be a Mexican Trotskyite for all you know."

Leonard gave it some thought. "Well, you could say we haven't had to throw anybody out for drug abuse and it'd be the gospel truth. Of course, we haven't done any testing either." Suddenly, the lights went on. "Hey, the *boab* got us electricity."

That night, after they had climbed into bed, Leonard noticed Luz was still upset and he told her to wake him if she couldn't sleep. "You could knock me out right now, Doc," she purred. "And save yourself a poke in the ribs at midnight."

Leonard wrapped his arms around her. They lay toe to toe, hip to hip. "Better to poke than get poked," he leered, already hard against her, his fingers probing and tickling.

Shivers were fanning out from between her legs, engulfing her belly. She asked him in a breathless voice," Did you just make that up?"

"No," he said with a laugh, "that's an old Irish proverb." Then he took her more urgently than before, clinging to her with a kind of desperation, as if he couldn't get enough of her.

A few hours later, a little after midnight, they were awakened by a sharp, high-pitched cry, as from a lonely wolf out on the tundra. They bolted upright in bed, wide-eyed, staring at each other and sat there in startled silence for a little while. "What was that?" croaked Luz, leaning against Leonard. He turned on the lamp to dispel their uneasiness.

"Must've been my neighbor, Vittorio," Leonard improvised, wanting to spare her any more worry. "Forgot his key and his wife Maria won't get up and let him in."

Luz could hardly mutter, "I've heard that one before. Just prior to the victim's death he says, 'It's good ole Vittorio.'"

Tearing himself out of her arms, Leonard went into the front room. Nothing there. He checked the door, the windows. Before returning to the bedroom, he went into the kitchen. Nothing there either. He was beginning to feel silly. This, he scolded himself, is how ten-year-olds act at summer camp after one too many ghost stories in a darkened cabin. At that moment he felt a furry form crawling around his calves and his heart skipped a beat.

"Meow," purred the cat. Leonard scooped it up and threw it out the back door. Then he went back to bed where Luz waited expectantly. "The cat," he explained cryptically as he crawled in between the sheets.

Luz noticed the beads of sweat on his upper lip. Somberly, she reminded, "But you don't own a cat."

"No, but Vittorio does." Leonard cuddled against her, moving so that their legs touched from knee to hip. "I love you, Lucy."

"I love you too, *querido.*" Luz buried her face in her arms so that he couldn't see her eyes crinkling in amusement, and said, "We sure get a lot of mileage out of Vittorio, don't we?"

20

The next morning, there was a sharp rap on the doorjamb, then Pete Sanchez stuck his head in the door of Leonard Berg's tastefully-appointed office. "Got a minute, Lenny?"

Berg didn't look up. "Just about. Siddown."

It was one of those golden days in October, a warm sun shining and a light breeze off the Nile. Sanchez was in a cable-knit Portuguese cardigan, with not a hair out of place, and shod in Gucci loafers with little metal buckles. His brown face was distinctive and strong, set off by a square jaw and a warm smile. "I haven't been able to sleep a wink all night," he teased as he leaned back in his chair and drove his hands into the pockets of his bulky white sweater. His voice projected a sense of locker-room fellowship. "So, *compadre*, let's hear about your trip to Hurghada. Details, please. Exactly when did Salah the Rebel Boy get there? What's he been up to, who's he hanging out with? Conversations, impressions, everything."

Leila Shawaari, Berg's shy Egyptian secretary, approached hesitantly with an offer to bring coffee, then—getting no takers—she disappeared. When she'd shut the door behind her, Leonard told Pete all he could remember about Salah while making only the briefest references to Betty MacGregor and Luz.

"Impressions," Pete repeated the word. Sanchez's blood raced on rumors and gossip about the local populace and his attitude at the moment clearly said, Get on with it. "Did you get any hint as to Salah's potential as a Muslim Brotherhood hit man, a Jamaati killer? Whattaya think?"

Leonard struggled to take stock, still uncertain in his mind about Ali Salah. He was either the most accomplished scoundrel he'd ever encountered, and he'd met quite a few, or he was innocent of everything but guilt by association. Pete was giving him a searching look. Leonard pointed to the brevity of their meeting and asked rhetorically, "How much can you learn about someone when he doesn't say ten words all night? But I'm pretty sure Ali would never deliberately cause that kind of lethal harm."

A mop of black hair fell across Pete's forehead. He tugged at it thoughtfully. "I suppose the word to be emphasized in that sentence is deliberately."

Both men were choosing their words with care, circling each other and sizing up the matter. A gooseneck lamp illuminated the chaos of scattered papers, reports, and yellow pads. Leonard sat hunched in the circle of light, frowning slightly, shuffling a few papers on his desk. "What about these plots against the President's life? Have you heard anything more?"

"Nary a word. We're keeping our ears open, of course. But let's get back to Salah. What does he think of Sadat, or did he say? Just hit the high spots."

Leonard grinned. "He thinks Sadat is a family man."

"Yeah," Pete returned the grin, but his voice quickly lost its humor. "That bastard would shoot a daughter to protect his reputation as a family man and bet which way she would fall."

"Now, now," Leonard admonished gently. "That's no way to talk about the President."

Sanchez rushed on, "I wish the police had Hikmat in jail. But that *hombre*, he's a hard eel to trap. Just when you think you've got him cornered he'll stage a breakout, like Houdini. The Jamaat has obviously infiltrated Security and the police." Pete brooded for a while, rocking his chair to and fro until it creaked. His face had the look of a golden retriever who's just smelled a quail in the bush and presently he was interjecting sharply, "Hey, Lenny babe, when did you start keeping your head down in the trenches? You've always come through for me. What's holding you back?"

"Nothing." Leonard leaned forward, indicating a sudden switch to the offensive. "You know, you bring me all this information about Salah and his buddies, but where's the evidence? And if I saw it, how would I know it's on the up and up and not manufactured? Are you getting set to shoot a mosquito with a Stinger?"

"Lenny baby," Pete wailed, composing his face to read, This is me, Agent *primero uno* you're talking to. Whenever Berg started to play the water-cooler philosopher, Pete was ready with the clincher, references to top secret classified information unavailable to all but those with a need to know. The Agency did have the low-down on these self-styled revolutionaries, by cracky, Lenny wasn't to lose a second's sleep on that account. The unvarnished truth was even worse than anything you could imagine. "Meantime, I'm telling you as much as I can tell a civilian. And when I tell you I don't want you to sit there like one of the three wise monkeys, the one with his paws on his ears. 'Cuz we're on the same side, okay? *Basta,*" a tone of exasperation seeped into Sanchez's voice, "I don't have the time for a replay of our usual conversation."

"I'm not as wet behind the ears as you think, Pedro. Fact, I suspect you haven't got a wisp of proof about Salah except he's a dissident, a label you could justifiably pin on ninety-eight percent of the angry Egyptian population at the moment. This whole subject of subversion versus dissent is a big ball of fuzz. You spooks, you take yourselves so seriously that everything you think becomes a fact. Dissidents become malefactors; critics of the Sadats are called traitors. And you have so many wrong ideas, like running guns to that sonofabitch Pol Pot, hiring Fat Tunas to bump off Dictator Twiddledee so you can put Dictator Twiddledum on his throne, creating the Contras when we haven't had a declaration of war against Nicaragua, haven't even broken off diplomatic relations. This isn't the glory days of Allen Dulles when you could slay a dragon every day, overthrow a democratically-elected leader like Mossadegh in Iran or Arbenz in Guatemala and leave everyone cheering."

Leonard paused as though catching up with his own thought process. How, he wondered, could Pete's job trigger no ethical skirmishes in his mind? "Gangsters can do your dirty work one day, and turn on you the next. Mark my words,

Pedro, you stay with the Agency long enough, and you're going to end up with your legs sawed off, floating in a barrel off Malta."

"Jeezus!" Pete looked outraged. "Did I ever steer you wrong, *amigo?*"

"You've steered me into eight car collisions," Leonard replied, a calm smile concealing his desperation.

Pete was staring at him intently, taking his measure. At length he drawled, "Did you ever think of becoming a diplomat, Lenny?"

"Every morning when I wake up, Pete, but I don't know. I meet a cowboy like you and blow my cork."

A red light flashed. Berg looked at it, postponing the moment when he must hear the message at the other end of the line. Finally he reached over to the intercom and smashed a button down. "Yes?"

The intercom murmured back at him, "Ambassador Tucker wishes to see you in his office, sir, as soon as Sanchez leaves."

Leonard snapped off the intercom and fell back in his chair. "Tuck is probably eager to know what two lowly peons are gabbing about. You haven't been keeping him in the dark, have you?"

"The Ambassador is always fully informed." The lie came automatically to Sanchez. Besides, what did Tucker even care to know? His own analysis of a situation usually went something like this: Sadat's popularity will go up, unless it goes down or stays about the same. Pete stared at Lenny, reading the depths of his feelings for this old flame of Salah's. "Forgive me for asking these questions, about Gracida. But you see, we think this dame—"

"Not a dame, a woman." And a Chicano like yourself.

Pete waved off the distinction. "Lenny, Lenny, don't be a chump. Gracida, she's more than just another newshound with a nice set of knockers. But please, will ya quit sidestepping the issue."

Leonard bent his head, studying a paper, for the slightest eye contact with the CIA agent seemed somehow to be dangerous. "Listen, Pedro, I've got a ton of work here and—"

Pete returned the front legs of the chair to the floor with a bang and stood up, grinning good naturedly. "You get into her pants?"

Leonard found himself aware of a hidden sinister note in what Pete was saying. A furious anger tightened his lips. "Why ask me? I'd have thought by now you'd have dusted her body for my fingerprints. Have you gone dainty on us? Behaving properly and minding your manners and keeping your nose out of other people's business?"

Pete wanted to answer with a long stare but he couldn't keep from smiling ruefully at the blind trust of a man in love. When at last he spoke, his words were but a footnote to what his sudden militaristic expression conveyed. "*Momentito*, Leonardo, this is war. We haf'ta keep our dicks hard, our powder dry and all pull together if we want to be home by Christmas. Hellsbells, I don't have to tell you that we can fight this thing better if we fight together, do I?" Pete's face was hard, somber, his muscles contracted with implacable determination. "Listen up, Lenny, we gotta find that bastard Hikmat and pile on."

"I know, I know," Leonard laughed bitterly but didn't stop. "Keep our shit wired together, saddle up, nail the coonskin to the wall." Leonard's head sunk into his shoulders, the muscles flexed at the corners of his mouth. John Wayne was not Berg's idol, and he had to stifle a repugnance for the Return to Bataan dialogue coming at him.

"Yeah, well, just keep knowing, funny pants. And be careful." Pete's solicitous tone became sharp and assertive. "Your pretty lady reporter-friend spells trouble. Forgive me, Lenny, but it's my obligation to put this to you as directly as I can because I can absolutely guarantee you that those rags she write for are as radical as Mother Jones and then some."

The advice stung. "All right already, I get the picture." Leonard slammed the paper down on his desk, grabbed Pete's elbow hard, and started for the door. He was beginning to develop a profound distaste for the Agency's silly cloak and dagger games, for the 'Nam lingo, and he wanted to put as much distance between himself and Agent Sanchez as possible. "Gimme a break, Pedro. Go find someone else to entertain you, James Bond. Go on over to the Marine House and watch Debbie Does Dallas on video. Find the Gunny and chew over old times in Saigon when the rats fattened while good men died, but who cared? You expected some casualties while killing Commies for mommy."

Pete's jaw dropped and he stared at Berg as if he'd lost his marbles. Realizing he'd gone against his intention to lift Lenny from his barely concealed depression, Pete abruptly turned sympathetic. "Is something bothering you, *compadre*?" he asked in a soothing voice, feeling as if he were humoring a drunk.

"You're bothering me," Leonard flashed. "The break-in bothers me." A feeling of utter exhaustion came over Leonard and he muttered spiritlessly, "Sorry, Peter. You and I keep trying to be friends, but there's too much water over the dam, eh? Your Agency has never gotten over State's thinking well of the Cuban Revolution in '52. We're all limpdick liberals in your book."

It brought a forgiving smile to the Agent's face. "Semi-limp, Leonardo," Pete offered as he turned to the door.

Drained of strength, Berg sank back into his chair in a cold sweat. He couldn't have risen if his life depended on it. Thank God, Sanchez was finally gone! How could he explain to Pete that it was the "nothings" that had him sick with worry? A montage of disjointed images passed through Leonard's mind with such rapidity that he felt dizzy and unable to put his thoughts in order. To begin with, there was the trip to Hurghada where they had found Ali Salah. The most they could ferret out was that Salah was doing nothing more than beach combing and diddling Betty MacGregor. Then they returned to find his apartment turned inside out and nothing was missing. A top priority cable from Washington demanded to know the whereabouts of ex-Congressman Joseph Dooley. Rumor had it Ambassador Tucker's very own secretary might know something. But when asked, Shirley said nothing.

So many rumors chewed over like *qat* leaves, and so many nothings were starting to add up to too much. Berg felt like a pimply teenager sitting home alone on a Saturday night. He suspected everyone else was doing something, and he didn't have the foggiest notion what it was. Question marks kept springing up in front of his eyes like hungry crows above a barren cornfield.

Nonetheless, Leonard put aside his worries long enough to get married. With Khalid and his wife, Masoud the boatman and Leonard's secretary Leila in attendance, Berg and Gracida were joined in a religious ceremony performed by a Baptist missionary. The next morning Leonard had the marriage registered at the Consulate. He also obtained a black diplomatic passport for the new Mrs. Berg. There was no time for a honeymoon, but as Luz pointed out, they'd already had one, so to speak, on a romantic *falucca*.

21

"Yahoo, Luz."

The sound of her name abruptly called out as she was coming out of the American University compound startled Luz. Swinging around, she saw Betty MacGregor coming through the lines of stalled traffic at a fast trot. "Luz," she was saying, as a believer who sees a vision might say, It's the Virgin Mary. Very dramatic. "When did you move in with Leonard?" Betty demanded abruptly as she reached Luz's side.

"After he married me," Luz replied, walking on at a determined pace.

Betty ran to keep up. "Slowdown! What is this, a sprint?" When they'd stopped, Betty congratulated, "How wonderful, even though Leonard is fizzless compared to an effervescent Egyptian man, as you well know. *Mallesh*, this calls for a celebration. You two must come to my place tonight. I'll invite a few of Leonard's friends, and we'll all toast you with chilled champagne."

"Why, thank you, Betts," Luz responded with a grateful smile. "That would be very nice."

Betty didn't offer directions to her flat, so apparently Leonard knew the way. "Lenny is such a nice man," said Betty, as if to atone for calling him dull. "And of all the American officials I know, Len is the only one who honestly likes Cairo, even though it is a clapped up, murderous mess."

"To some people, Cairo is just traffic jams and cockroaches. Lenny's not like that. What he came to see was the camels."

It took Betty a moment to realize that Luz was joking, but when she did, she slipped her arms around her, hugging her

as though they were the only two surviving members of an
Arctic Expedition to finally reach the pole. MacGregor had
the stagy bravura of an actress whose only audience was her
friends and acquaintances, the self-exaggeration and grand
gestures of someone who thrives on melodrama, always acting
out scenes, living on nerves and emotion. The two women
indulged in a few more pleasantries as they waited on the curb
together. The sun was at its height, but there was a cooling
breeze and the dry air was pleasant. When the light changed,
Luz started to move away, but Betty caught her by the arm.
She looked at the journalist for a moment, gnawing at her
lower lip. Tiny droplets of perspiration fell from her corkscrew
curls to her red cotton dress. Etched into her face was a
certain sourness that comes from dreams lost. Luz had a
million things to do, but Betty was so eager to talk about Ali
that she hardly noticed.

"Um, Luz, uh, look, I hate to sound as though I'm behaving
like a stupid big sister, but I can't help it," Betty began in a
halting voice. She finally blurted out, "You're a busy reporter
so I won't waste your time. My maid Suhar came in this
morning and told me there are rumors floating around town
about another batch of arrests. Apparently, the Citadel is
bursting at the seams with prisoners. By God, the last thing I
needed with my tea and toast was a dose of Suhar's fears about
a widening dragnet."

More arrests? Luz cocked an eyebrow. "Could that be
true?"

Betty found it possible to somehow grin impishly. "Anything could be true, unless you read it in the papers. Listen,
old girl, you haven't seen Ali, have you? I'm fairly sick with
worry about him."

Luz shook her head vigorously. "Not since Hurghada," she
replied, scanning the line of moving vehicles. Fending off her
own apprehension, she added, "What's gone wrong?"

Betty took a long shuddering breath. "Just about bloody
everything. Ali came back with me yesterday, got a bit tiddily
on beer, then he disappeared, taking all his belongings with
him. Of course, that doesn't prove anything," Betty concluded in a manner that was both offhanded and intense. "But

then again, when it comes to Ali, nothing is ruled out." She shot Luz a sideways glance with a burlesque lift to her eyebrows. "It could be another woman, you never know."

"You never know," Luz repeated. "When it comes to being true blue, you can't expect anything from Ali."

Betty gave Luz a forlorn look. "I expect nothing but trouble. Ali has a gift for it. I'm afraid it's too late to expect him to change his ways. I might as well save my breath."

"Yet he looks saintly," Luz remarked with some irony.

"Ho-ho!" Betty laughed sarcastically. "Ali isn't a saint just because he has a beard. There's quite a few Egyptians who fall into that category, but none falls as deeply as Ali. I'm a good sport, but enough is enough. He is a thoroughly heartless brute anyway you look at it." Betty's voice was shaky as she nervously plucked on her collar.

"What about his grandmother?" Luz suggested. "Could she help—or better yet, his cousin Mustafa?"

"I'll get nothing from them," Betty answered coldly. Security had already been to Grandmother's house, turning it upside down, but Ali was gone, his whereabouts a mystery. Betty turned away with bitter thoughts. If she had believed Ali's "I love you," it was her own fault; sheer moonshine, all of it. Deep pain lines etched her face. Luz tried to take her hand, but she snatched it away. "He is such a miserable sodding Casanova! But I don't suppose I have to tell you that. I knew from the start it could only end in misery, but that didn't stop me. And now here I am, alone. A pretty fix I've managed to get myself into."

For a moment, Luz thought Betty was going to cry, but she squared her shoulders and added with a certain resignation, "I won't die from lack of love, though I'll certainly wilt." She paused again. "Ali had a lot of good things to say about you," Betty went on with an envious edge Luz couldn't help but notice. "What a memory! He has not forgotten a moment of his life since the day he was born. To be honest with you, at 25 I swore I'd never take a lover younger than myself. At 35 the idea was more acceptable. Hell, I was always very mature. I was 48," the number slipped out unintentionally, "the day I was born. Which means I ought to know men and their propensities by now. They're always after innocence."

At that moment two young women in Islamic dress brushed by them. Betty glanced thoughtfully at them and said, "It used to be you were on the outside looking in if you weren't in Western skirts and blouses. But today it is the Western dressers who find themselves badly positioned. More and more Westernized women talk about being social pariahs, about men refusing to marry them. This is becoming a very powerful force, much more powerful than the religious creed itself. They're such foolish, frightened creatures, giving up their right to independent action in exchange for social position! Oh well," she wound up, sounding listless and defeated, "do you suppose if I'd taken the veil, I could've held on to him?"

Luz made a guess that MacGregor saw a good deal more in Ali than his relative youth and sexual stamina. Was she flattered to be the great exception to the rigor of a fundamentalist's single-mindedness? "I don't mean to pry," she began with a disclaimer, "but can you tell me what Ali and his friends are up to, more or less?"

"Certainly," Betty replied without hesitating. "Agitation. It's usually preceded in your newspaper articles by the word 'student.' If this were Paris, they would most likely be tearing up the cobblestones while a Jean-Paul Sartre clone cheers them on. But since this is Egypt, you get toxic level doses of Islam. Rather like Poland, wouldn't you say, with all those crucifixes and Solidarity priests having a good thrashing about?"

Luz shifted her feet and said to MacGregor, "Tell me exactly, would this mean an attack on Sadat?"

"It might mean any number of things." Betty's answer was vague, her thoughts never wandering far from Salah. "Doesn't Ali rather remind you of Karl Marx, a revolutionary talking sacrifice, yet loving the good things of life? He's an idealist willing to die for mankind while possessing such an egotistic inhumanity in his own character. His little Nafeisa makes a perfect Jenny von Westphalen, too, wouldn't you say, a slavish buttress for his megalomania? What is all this shouting about change, sweeping away the old order? Right or left, men are pashas."

Luz had never scoffed at Ali, or anyone else, for such failings. In addition to a reporter's detachment, she had a culture that treasured monks who made fine brandy and homosexuals who painted chapel ceilings for the Popes. Paradoxes, contradictions and ambiguities—they came with the human composition. Before Luz could say as much, Betty turned and flagged down a passing taxi. When it stopped, she got in and slammed the door. Quickly the driver swerved into traffic. Betty stuck her blond head out the window and instructed, "See you at seven."

Luz remained where she was, feeling bewildered. Underneath the stagy mannerisms, Betty seemed to be a decent, intelligent, but fundamentally ordinary Scotswoman who had made the great mistake of falling in love outside of her social circle. A more conventional person might have a less dramatic life than the aging actress, but it was unlikely she'd end up like Betty, loving and hating her missing Egyptian neo-revolutionary in equal measure.

Betty MacGregor lived on the 24th floor of a high rise across from the Sheraton Hotel. From the balcony, you could see land stretching toward Libya to the West and the Sinai to the East. With such a breathtaking view constantly available, Betty confessed that it was rather like living in a bubble helicopter. There were drawbacks, however; namely, the water didn't flow from the faucets and had to be brought up in jerry cans, nor did the elevator reach to this stratospheric height. *Mallesh,* several dozen hardy souls had climbed up the 24 floors to extend a *"Mahbruk,"* a *"Mazel Tov,"* or a "Great going!" to the newlyweds and to partake of the lavish buffet that Betty's cook had laid out on a fine white linen cloth. Luz knew none of the guests besides the spook, Pete Sanchez, but they appeared to be officials from the various legations with a sprinkling of theater folk with whom Betty had worked over the years.

At one point, Luz found herself chatting with an ex-matinee idol by the name of Ramses, a paunchy, slope-shouldered man

who had much to say—and none of it good—about the watch-
dog censorship activities of the sheiks of Al-Azhar. To demonstrate their seriousness of purpose, they insist that when an
actor plays the role of a Chosen Person of Holiness and
Dignity in a film, he must not mar this image by later playing
the role of a killer, a gambler or a smuggler in a future film. A
professional actor can seldom afford to cut himself off from
future offers. "After all," Ramses explained in his sensible way,
"acting, not suicide, is our bread and butter. Consequently,
the role of the holy man invariably falls to some bloke they
drag in off the streets. He is usually someone whose acting
skills could qualify him as a good camel driver with a face
begging to be smacked by a custard pie."

That being the case, Luz wondered if the sinners didn't
steal the show. "Always," Ramses nodded, grinning. He fell
back lazily into the cushions. "The unintentional message that
comes across on the screen is that being an idiot is a prerequi-
site for holiness."

Ramses was taking a handful of peanuts from a heaped dish
when Betty joined them. "Speaking of the devil, I was once a
member of a witches' coven. Did I ever tell you that?"

Ramses lowered the corner of his mouth in contempt. "If
you were half the things you claim to be, *cheri*, you'd be 200
years old."

Betty's hackles perked up a bit. "You decline to take me
seriously." She looked hurt for a second, then she threw
Ramses a stagy smile. "I know the secrets of the human
heart."

Ramses gave a dry and abrupt laugh. "My dear girl, don't
you know by now that humans are heartless?" He patted
Betty's arm affectionately as he told Luz, "*Mallesh*. She is a
true article, our Betty."

As the evening wore on, most of the officials had congregated in one corner of the room where they were deep into
heavy political talk. Luz was content to eavesdrop, but Betty
had something more interesting in mind for all the women. A
Zar party was going on in an apartment on the 18th floor. If
Luz had never been to one, she shouldn't miss it. When
informed he was losing his bride to another gala, Leonard

waved nonchalantly and told her he'd put the key under the mat.

A flashlight in hand, Betty descended the dark marble stairwell, followed by five excited and curious Western women. As they went, she told them that an evil spirit had taken possession of Mrs. Nasharat Sarwat, the wife of an electrical engineer and mother of six children all under the age of ten. She was a pious woman who had made the pilgrimage to Mecca not once, but twice—to no avail. The wily jinn had crept into her body one night while she was sleeping, rendering her paralyzed. She could not get up the next morning; she could do no housework, no child care, no marital duty, no nothing. She could only lie abed and weep. Nasharat's relatives had put her on a stretcher and taken her out to a saint's shrine on the outskirts of the city. Once there, the poor woman spent the day rolling around in agony on the floor, screaming her lungs out, tearing at her clothes and her hair, babbling incomprehensibly in unknown tongues while having her face mopped with damp compresses, her limbs massaged, and her feverish brow stroked by her mother, her sisters, and her aunts.

Troubled by his sister's ordeal, her brother Muhammad Chatti entered into negotiations with Nasharat's husband, Mr. Sharfiq Sarwat that ended with Sharfiq's agreeing to engage the help of a maid, plus giving his wife a specified sum to buy some bracelets and rings from a goldsmith in the *souq*. Nasharat, in turn, would cease keeping a cool connubial bed and talking in tongues. After the settlement was reached, the jinn miraculously vanished. It was a happy ending that called for a *Zar* party—which was now in progress as the newcomers were shown in through the door. The flat was packed with Egyptian females of all sizes and ages, the majority in traditional Islamic garb. Hospitably, they made room for the Westerners who sprinkled themselves among them. After they were all settled, a pretty young girl in polyester print took a ceramic bowl filled with little balls of hashish around to all the ladies to put into their cups of steaming hot tea.

Everyone sat conversing demurely as they sipped the liquid. Only Mrs. Sarwat displayed an exuberance, which was more or less excused on the grounds of her being stage-center and with a purple heart won in battle with the evil jinn. She rose and started singing a popular ballad, even though she couldn't sing.

Betty, who'd placed herself next to Luz, told the Chicana that her naturally black hair was dyed blond more for reasons of disguise than cosmetics. In truth, she, Elizabeth Jane Mac-Gregor, was a dead ringer for Queen Farida. But more than that, the two of them were soul mates in a very special and very mysterious Egyptian way. When Farida was consort in the King's palace, Betty was doing well in her career and her marriage. Then, one fateful day, Farida walked into the royal bedroom and found King Farouk in dalliance with a French opera singer. Farida was cast off by the two-timing monarch and Betty suffered in her own way. One day they had both been decked out in silks and satins; the next day they wore the divorced woman's wardrobe of holey undergarments, orphaned stockings, cotton blouses with frayed collars and missing buttons. As she described the 180 degree turns of her life, Betty waggled an upturned hand back and forth, a gesture indicating helplessness in the face of unreason.

Betty brought her hands together. "Farida is my sacred sister," she whispered fiercely, "even though we have never met in the conventional sense. You see, there is your Occidental way of knowing, very pragmatic and structured. But there is another wealth of knowledge that only we Oriental women can know. It is very mysterious, very ancient, and totally resistant to scientific inquiry. So you needn't ask."

Nasharat Sarwat finished a song to polite applause, actually an expression of relief that the off-key wailing of a recently possessed woman had at last ceased. After everyone had a second cup of the relaxing brew, several women began slow, steady rhythms on their *tabulas*. The beat commenced low, like something heard in a distance, up river, and then it got louder, sounding like some weird initiation rite among the blue-black Nubians of Southern Sudan. The drummers hands went straight up and down, but their upper bodies moved in many directions.

For a while, all the women just sat quietly, listening to the beating of the drums, trying to strike cool, inscrutable poses. The beat was contagious, and they had to struggle, so loath were they to surrender their brow-furrowing attitudes, their dignified reserve. But there were fissures, a deterioration inevitable in hot and muggy climates. Even with the Cairene traffic audible in the streets far below, the *tabulas* were able to summon up a lush, exotic imagery of birds of paradise, red sunsets, and faraway jungle islands with all their virile teeming abundance. The drummers' pounding went on and on in a deeply felt ritual outpouring, their insistent rhythms navigating the women up a Nile River of the mind. The tone was foreboding, edgy, the atmosphere in the dimly-lit room all sinewy and humid black-magic darkness. One woman stood up, then another and another. They began moving around the room, shuffling in time with the drum beat. The steps were not intricate and soon all the women joined in, moving to a slow, steady beat. As the drummers increased the tempo, the dancers threw off their scarves, shawls, and sweaters and became more and more unrestrained in their movements.

For a while Betty sat watching the dancers, her eyes as calm as a lion's; then, feeling a fire within herself, she joined them, stomping her feet and raising her voice with the others. More hashish was consumed. Soon, they were all caught up in the tantalizing fragrance of sin and temptation. Faster and faster Betty danced to the rhythm of the drumbeats, until she could no longer keep going and broke off, collapsing on the rug next to Luz. The floor was rocking to the pounding of the most uninhibited group of female dancers Luz had ever seen. She sat mesmerized by the sight. As sweat poured, garments were unbuttoned, going-to-church shoes discarded, stockings torn off and flung about. Vibrating bodies were in a frenzy of total release, screaming, thrashing, jumping, stomping, whirling like dervishes, crashing and spinning themselves on the floor like breakdancers. No dancer in a strip joint in New York City could have performed a more frankly sexual number, nor could a Dolce Vida orgy contain more erotic vibrations. The women danced and danced until they collapsed exhausted, falling asleep where they dropped.

In the wee hours of the morning, Luz stepped over the prostrate bodies and went home to wake her husband with the news. "Flaming lesbians on LSD!" she yelled into his half-awake face. "No joke, *caro mio*, I haven't seen anything like that since your Hell's Angels initiation."

Leonard pulled her next to him. "Sounds like you had a good time," he muttered, slipping back into sleep.

What made that jinn-inspired fandango so incomprehensible to Luz was the kind of women who were there. She wouldn't have batted an eyelid to see Rolling Stone groupies letting it all hang out. But she was stunned by the unrestrained abandon of such devout Muslim women, who in their daily lives would not dare to be seen out on the street with their hair or ankles showing, would never attend a cinema even to see Mary Poppins, or go out in mixed company, even with their husbands. And what in the name of the Virgin Mary and all the saints was one to make of that loon, Betty Farida MacGregor?

22

The Sixth of October had finally arrived and it was a tourist's fantasy. The city was calm, the sky was bright blue and the sunlight carried a crisp, clear edge of chill. This particular morning, the heavy flow of traffic heading out to Nasser City, a new suburb of Heliopolis on the northeastern edges of Cairo, was due almost entirely to the scheduled parade celebrating the eighth anniversary of the 1973 war. At 8:30, two burly policemen left their patrol car to monitor the thin stream of vehicles turning into the site of the parade. The younger cop was named Hanie, the older man was Halim. The early arriving vehicles were carrying television crews. After setting up their equipment at the edges of the reviewing stands, the crews lolled around, rather like bus riders, staring blankly, smiling to themselves, lazily stretching out on the cement railings for short naps. The 2,000 guests began arriving around ten and distinguished they were: cabinet officials, foreign diplomats, dignitaries, and military attaches. In no time, the congestion had become impossible.

Police officer Halim was busy trying to keep the traffic moving, loudly shouting out commands, and signaling with his gloved hands, but his mind kept wandering back to this day eight years ago when he had been a corporal in the army, an apprehensive infantryman with his ears stuffed full of cotton wool, charcoal smudged on his 19-year old face, ready to go into combat. At 2 P.M., with the sun at their backs, the Air Force had launched a strike against the enemy's positions with two hundred and twenty-two jets. It was followed by an artillery barrage from more than two thousand guns. Five army divisions and over a thousand tanks crossed the Suez Canal and broke through Israel's Bar Lev Line. It had been one of the proudest moments of Halim's life, and now, eight years later in the midst of honking horns, petrol fumes, and short-tempered drivers, Halim's smile was as big as the split in a watermelon.

A mile away, a yellow Fiat with the words Sun Tours on its sides took a sharp right turn and entered the highway leading to the parade grounds. The driver pulled into the passing lane at once, winding the engine too tightly for second gear. "Slow down, Ali," cautioned Khalid from the back seat.

"Okay," said Ali, who had the attention span of a flea at the moment. He was electrically charged, worried, feisty, pugnacious, spleeny, and determined, it appeared, to live up to every preconception Mustafa had of a do-or-die race car driver. Mustafa's big brown eyes bulged and he reached for a handle, as if he might be getting ready to parachute out the door. They almost sideswiped a Mercedes SL180. When he rolled down the window, Ali could feel the bracing wind against his face. He had the accelerator pressed all the way down to the floorboard. They rushed up to the intersection, and only at the last possible second did Ali brake the Fiat.

Fear was crawling out of the cave in Mustafa's stomach. "You are going to attract notice if you keep driving like this," he grumbled, as angry with himself as he was with Ali. "I am crazy to let you take the wheel. You drive like you are trying out for the Grand Prix. You will surely get us all in big trouble, Don Juan."

The Don Juan tag rankled, but Ali decided to let it go. There was no time to waste bickering. "When have I ever gotten anyone into trouble?" Ali answered his own question: "Never."

Khalid heaved a sigh of exasperation, like a harried father with two bickering tots on an outing.

"You really want me to do this?" he asked Ali, his tone plaintive, hoping that Ali would announce a change of heart at the last minute.

Grinning cockily, Ali was ready with another one word reply. "Yes."

For a while Khalid watched the utility poles go by, reading the advertisements they carried: Marlboro, Dunhill, Olympia Airlines, Fly PIA, Rothman's king size cigarettes. He reached over the seat and squeezed Ali's shoulder. "It might not be possible to get both of your old girlfriends out in time." A long silence followed those words that were as much a conclusion as an inquiry. A shaft of sunlight had turned the lenses of Ali's glasses opaque, and Khalid was annoyed that he couldn't see his eyes. "Which one do I go for first?"

Khalid waited for a response from Ali, but Ali was in too great a turmoil to articulate his own thoughts. It was Mustafa who spoke. "For Godsake, Khalid, you are the one who is going in? Why can't you decide?" After this long a time together, they all asked questions for which none of them expected answers.

Without turning around to face Khalid, Ali said with a little flourish, a pointed exclamation of the hand, "Both." Salah's conscience was large, but his heart was larger. And the whiff of danger had his juices flowing.

Dark waves rose and swelled in Khalid's head, and he could feel his knees grow weak, but he gave him an impudent stare. "And what do you plan to do about Berg?"

"Pray he has better luck than he deserves," Ali replied, laughing boisterously, feeling the jealousy once more.

"I could be killed—" Khalid stopped, feeling the full weight of those words he had never dared speak aloud.

"Not you, Khalid. You are too young to die." Mustafa spoke the rote assurances forcefully. With a smile, he joked, "Notice I said, too young, not, too good."

"Thanks." Khalid brightened.

Policeman Hanie shouted to his partner. Halim turned his head slowly and looked at Hanie as though he were awakening from a deep and wonderful sleep. Caught in a shaft of bright light, he pointed to his breast as if questioning the command to check out the Fiat that had come to a screeching halt in front of the barrier. Finally reacting, Halim motioned the Fiat over onto the service road that ran parallel to the main road. Mustafa slumped down in the seat. "Policemen," he whined shrilly. "God, they make my flesh crawl."

"Quiet!" Khalid shusssshed. He was sweating, the beads of cold sweat running down his backbone.

Halim stuck his head into the window and glanced at the occupants of the Fiat with a fierce, disapproving imperiousness. When he demanded identification, Mustafa reached into the glove compartment. His lips were drawn together as though they'd been cobbled with surgical thread, and he fought to control his breathing, calming himself, passing the papers out the window. "They are right here, Officer." Taking the papers, Halim looked directly into Mustafa's eyes and was disarmed by the way the big man returned his hard, searching look.

It was 11 A.M. and Joe Dooley was mostly sober, although Paulette Tucker didn't think so. They were sitting next to each in the second row, off to the left of Sadat, sizing each other up. Paulette Tucker was a native Oklahoman with a practiced smile and short hair greying at the temples. The lines around her mouth and above her eyebrows were still fine and her face taut, although she was nearing 60. The Tuckers had met Dooley when he had first arrived in Washington as a newly-elected member of the House of Representatives. Paulette continued to chat with Joe while watching him carefully, trying to take in the changes that the last ten years had brought to him—the thinning hair, the broken blood vessels in his eyes, and the big nose that looked as if it had been set by a spastic surgeon. Gravity, she noticed, had tugged at the corners of his mouth, bringing it more in line with the faint stoop of his shoulders. He wore a navy blue blazer with gold basket-weave buttons and a mysterious bulge in one pocket.

When Dooley took an airline miniature of bourbon out of this pocket and twisted the cap, Mrs. Tucker inquired with some disapproval, "Why must you bring that miniature out here?"

"The airliner wouldn't fit in my pocket," Joe wheezed defensively, not quite sure if her question had been a plea to share or a sarcastic remark. He squinted at her and wondered if she'd had plastic surgery. The skin was pulled back behind

her ears and gathered up with huge clips—or were they
earrings?

Paulette leaned over and picked a piece of lint off her
husband's sleeve. Even among so many dignitaries, America's
Ambassador Roland Tucker loomed large in a baggy blue suit,
puffing on a pipe and projecting a Bohemian air of
gemutlichkeit that Günter Grass might have envied. He was
upset by the tension vibrating between ex-Congressman
Joseph Dooley and Paulette and, to change the subject, he
asked Dooley what he was doing so far from Boston. Joe
swallowed and coughed, then explained, "Jimmy Carter, one
of the nicest fellows to ever get himself hauled up in front of an
Iranian firing squad, asked me to represent him today."

The diamond in Paulette Tucker's finger winked in the
sunlight as she lifted her hand to shade her eyes while she
peered at Dooley. "You mean to tell me," she said indignantly,
"that you're the only thing the Democrats could come up with
for an important occasion like this?"

Ambassador Tucker was shaken by his wife's unexpected
outburst, but Joe continued as easily as if she hadn't spoken.
"Jimmy asks me to represent him today and I'm supposed to
say no?"

"She's only joking," the Ambassador assured Dooley with
an empty smile.

"Says who?" The very soft voice of Paulette Tucker hard-
ened. Her disgust was palpable, her controlled aloofness in-
tact. The smell of Dooley's breath still in her nostrils, Paulette
drew a lace-trimmed hankie from her purse and fanned her
face. In no time the faint odor of Anis/Anis surrounded her
like a protective mist. The noise of the parade seemed to
recede, becoming only a soundtrack for her confrontation
with this Irish lush. "If you're going to drink like a fish,
Congressman, you should drink what fish drink: water."

A Dooley hoot greeted her remark. "In Egypt, drinking the
water will kill you."

An Egyptian woman, stout and matronly in indigo jersey,
stepped on Joe's toes as she moved toward the aisle. Joe
grunted, then gazed about distractedly. The band was playing
a rousing John Philip Sousa march. Explosions of sunshine

bounced along their instruments. For Dooley, it brought back sweet memories of so many political campaigns that for a moment he felt a physical pain. "You have any idea when this here parade's going to end?" he asked Paulette in a hopeful voice.

"Can't rightly say," Paulette smiled. She loved parades and it wouldn't bother her a hoot if it went on till nightfall. The sparkling weather, the sunshine and the cloudless skies held the promise of a glorious day complete with music, marches, stirring speeches. Just her luck to get stuck next to the fly in the ointment. "But this is what you're here for, Joseph, so sit back and enjoy." Crisp as the crunch of a new fall apple, a cool breeze from the north tugged at her hat. "Dadgum it," she swore, "one damn thing after another."

Roland Tucker reached up and began rubbing his hand back and forth on his wife's shoulder, as though he were sandpapering wood. Getting the message, Paulette fell sullenly silent. At that moment Tucker saw his Political Officer Leonard Berg making his way down the row of seats toward him with a beautiful young lady in tow. Berg was dressed in an immaculately tailored black pinstripe suit with a pale pink oxford button-down shirt. A couple of days in the Red Sea sun had tanned his face a ruddy bronze. His Latin female companion was a traffic-stopper in a red wool Chanel suit. Curiously, Tucker lumbered to his feet. "What have we here, Lenny?"

Leonard looked up. The Ambassador was blocking his way, smiling indulgently, as though he'd caught him in some venial sin. It was time to set the record straight. "I'd like you to meet my wife, sir," Leonard said with a touch of pride, "Maria Luz Gracida."

Roland Tucker was a blustery man who like to pretend he was hard to impress, but he was impressed. Still, he managed the faintest smile as he began the litany of "where from":

"Mexico?

"Spain?

"Puerto Rico?," he questioned.

"Everywhere," said Luz, an army brat. "But mostly Texas."

Leonard explained to the Ambassador, "We met at Columbia when I was getting my master's degree."

Tucker stared into those summer earth brown eyes. Luz put
her hand out and the Ambassador shook it. His quizzical look
made it clear that he was trying to recall if anyone had told
him that Berg was even engaged. "Well, I'll be!" Tucker finally
exclaimed in a mellifluous voice, "Sandbag the rivers, lash
yourself to the mast! Find two of every creature, male and
female, for the flood's coming." To his wife, he said brightly,
"Did you hear that, Paulie? Lenny went to the altar again."

Before Mrs. Tucker could offer the pair her best wishes,
Luz caught sight of Dooley. In her most formal voice, she said,
"How do you do, Congressman?"

Joe dead-panned, "None the better for your asking, lassie."
From the way Joe moved his body, Luz surmised his back
wounds were mending well. There had been other changes as
well. His thick neck was adorned by a gold *kartoush* he would
have scoffed at as a faggot's trinket before coming to Cairo, and
his glasses were the yellow kind favored by aviators and skiers.
For a second Luz wanted to scold Joe for running out without
letting her know where he was going, but she was too glad to
see him to waste time on old hash. Instead, she told him she'd
gotten married. "Have you now?" said Joe in his lovely lilt. He
started drifting animatedly into reminiscences of his own marriage, which ended in divorce, when he halted in midsen-
tence.

A squadron of Soviet MIG-17s were doing acrobatics in the
air, drowning out all speech. There was prolonged applause
and when they peeled off to regroup and Luz could be heard,
she asked Joe with sincere solicitousness where he was staying
now that he'd left the hotel. He told her that he had moved in
with someone who works at the Embassy, a gal he had known
since their overlapping tours in Washington. "Don't go talking
it around," Joe warned Luz in a low voice, "because Shirley
hasn't told a soul yet."

The afterburner of a jet kicked on not far off, and Tucker
sucked in a breath. Could he have just heard his secretary's
name mentioned above the deafening roar of a low-flying
aircraft? He looked from Dooley to Berg, his expression that
of a *duena* at an orgy. Hurrying in, Leonard asked him, "Is
primero uno here?"

The Ambassador nodded and pointed to a spot in the middle of the front row of the reviewing stand. Vice President Hosini Mubarak was on Sadat's right, Defense Minister General Abdul Abu Ghazala on his left. A shallow-curved wall formed the front of the stand. At each side, the wall fell straight back for several yards. It was rather like Berg's moustache, thinning and drooping at the tips. At each tip, a flight of steps ran back up to the stands behind.

Anwar el Sadat was decked out as the Supreme Commander in a blue field marshall's uniform that perfectly matched, in color and brightness, the day. Luz's interested eye missed no detail of his orthodox attire: gold stars pinned to a broad green silk sash over his shoulder, the Star of the Sinai and two wheat stalks on red velvet at his throat, rows of campaign ribbons over his left breast, crossed swords on his cap. Leonard's thoughts were running in the same channels as hers. "Men fight for baubles," he started to say but hesitated, searching his memory for the line that preceded that famous piece of Bonapartic cynicism, but Napoleon eluded him today.

Tanks were rolling by, both Soviet T-55s and American M-60s. He and Luz found their places. When they were seated, Leonard took her hand and directed her gaze to the monument directly across the way from the reviewing stand. It was a modern stone pyramid, perhaps one hundred feet high, that bore a resemblance to the Eiffel Tower. "It is the Tomb of the Unknown Soldier," he explained solemnly, "who is, but one of the more than 5,000 dead that were brought back in body bags from the Sinai eight years ago."

Next to Luz was a stout Milanese from one of Italy's leading newspapers, *Corriere della Sera*. His name was Ugo Biagiotti and he wore a Pucci suit and longish hair styled to camouflage his prominent ears. When he found out that the Chicana reporter spoke Spanish and thus could understand his Italian, Ugo immediately struck up a conversation. He spoke in a graceful, almost oratorical way, Luz translating, and Leonard answering with equal flourishes. A half dozen other reporters, mostly from European news agencies, eavesdropped around them. The sun flashed on Ugo's glasses as he sang the President's praises: Sadat has put Egypt back on the map, revived

the moribund tourism industry, got back the oil fields at Ras
Banas, thumbed his nose at the Palestinian die-hards, told the
Saudis to take their lira and see how far they could get with it.
He has stood up to that *cretino* Qaddafi, too, a nomad made
mad by his sudden wealth. "Put a beggar on horseback and he
will ride straight to the devil," declared Ugo, who clearly
regarded Sadat's regime as a Camelot on the barbarian plains
of the Arab world.

Frankfurter's *Allgemeine Zeitung* had sent out journalist
Hans Stolz, a conservatively dressed man with a scholarly air
and perfectly cut features. He spoke a mixture of French and
Arabic, sometimes turning to an interpreter for assistance.
"Sadat has many enemies," he began. His voice was very soft
and heavy with the throaty accent of his German heritage.

But Ugo didn't allow him to continue. Turning up the heat,
he said, "What do King Hussein and the minnow have in
common? They are both tiny, both brainless, and neither of
them has made it to Jerusalem." Despite the clunk-clunk of
the passing half-tracks, he got the chuckles he was after, and
Luz wondered if Ugo had a joke or a pithy aphorism for every
situation.

"Miss Noor! Miss Noor!" Luz turned toward the speaker, a
blue-helmeted guard who was standing in the aisle and motioning her to come with him. Leonard tightened his grip on
her hand, but Luz pulled it away. She got up and followed the
guard as the October sun edged its way up in the sky.

"Hold on!" Leonard piped to Luz, which didn't stop her for
a second. She made a patting motion of her hand, telling him
to stay put, she'd just be a minute. A man standing by the
railing was watching her strangely, his eyes slit. It was Pete
Sanchez, and his eyes looked at her with the absorbed gaze of
the voyeur. Ambassador Tucker was demanding his political
officer's attention, and Leonard had to stifle the alarm he felt
seeing Luz go off without him.

"There's a man from your office who needs to talk with
you," the blue helmet explained to Luz now that they had
descended from the bleachers and were walking around toward the rear.

Up ahead she saw a familiar figure with close-cropped black

hair and wraparound glasses. He was standing in the shade, dishevelled, and smoking a cigarette. It was Khalid. Luz could hardly mask her dismay at seeing him here. As he came forward, he paused, as he always did, slowly appraising the people around them, to see if she were being followed. He seemed disoriented by the spectacle of uniforms and custom-made suits. "Is something the matter?" inquired Luz when she reached his side.

"You shouldn't be here." Khalid's mouth was pulling on his cigarette the way a hungry baby would suck on a bottle.

"What are you talking about?" Luz asked belligerently. Then, calm, composed, and icily polite, she informed him, "I am a reporter, and this is what I do for a living."

"And maybe it is what you do for a dying," Khalid murmured, hoping the softness of his voice would give Luz the hint that she was talking too loud. He reached out a hand and drew Luz absently into the curve of his arm, without turning his head. He continued to stand quite still, holding her against him, staring skyward and drawing greedily on his cigarette as though his mind were several hundred miles away—as indeed it was. It was the first time Khalid had ever touched her and Luz was stunned. Was he trying to deliver a message with his touch that he couldn't convey with his body? After a time he looked down. "There are more important things in this world than a job," he declared, releasing her.

"*Santamaria!*" Luz breathed. Thin rays of pale yellow light streamed down through the bleachers. A rowdy group of children ran by, gaily waving little paper Egyptian flags. A boy of no more than five or six thrust his at her, and she smiled warmly. The flag was like a French tricolor with a gold eagle in the center of the white band. She slipped it into a button hole in her white shirt.

Khalid pushed the sunglasses up on his head. The storm clouds on his face had fled. It was hard for him to stay mad at a person he was risking his life to save. A futile endeavor, he thought bitterly as he blew a smoke ring at the bleachers above his head. He had trashed her boyfriend's apartment, trying to scare her into leaving Cairo before the parade. For the sake of Joe Dooley's life and limbs, he had dressed himself

up as a West Bank exile with a knife hidden among the
gladiolus and slashed at a women he had never laid eyes on
until that moment. And Luz and Joe wouldn't leave! The
moral of it all seemed well-nigh inarguable: you shouldn't lean
on people, but if you do, lean hard. Unfortunately, Khalid had
no stomach for violence; it wasn't in his nature. He wished he
were on a different planet.

Luz looked searchingly into his eyes. "Where is Ali?" Her
whisper was suddenly sharp. "Is he with you? Did he send
you?"

Khalid dropped his cigarette butt. "Ali is getting worse," he
said, his voice like a hedge clipper. "Sending him to
Magaweesh was not a good idea. He gets crazy every time he
goes there. Talaat was right about him, he is seven different
people in the same body." His voice faltered as he grew tense
and nervous. Luz could see the strain in his face, but did not
pursue it. She simply watched him closely, worried and feeling intuitively that something unusual had happened or was
going to happen. "Listen to me, Noor," Khalid continued
with dogged perseverance, wiping his nose with the back of
his hand, "there has been a some trouble. It is urgent that you
call Doctor Qaddus' daughter." He put his hand in the small of
her back and started toward the parking lot, moving with
obvious apprehension.

Luz stopped short, yanked Khalid to a halt and, turning
him around, looked resolutely into his face. "What does she
want with me?" she asked carefully. "What's going on?"

Inspired, Khalid began to improvise. "It's about one of your
articles," he began. "Apparently, the police must have put two
and two together when they read them, and they picked her
father up two days ago." He paused to give his words more
weight. "And, well, you know how dissidents are treated here.
This is no joking matter."

Her lips compressed ever so slightly. That, plus her silence,
were the only reactions that hinted at her perplexity. Physical
beatings, electric shock, partial asphyxiation by plastic bags
over the victim's heads, exposure to extremes of hot and cold,
squirting chili pepper in carbonated water up a man's nose—
Gracida had reported from Ferdinand Marcos' Philippines,

Roberto D'Abussion's El Salvador, Baby Doc Duvalier's Haiti, the generals' Guatemala, she'd heard it all. The thought that anything in a article of hers might bring torture to Doctor Qaddus made her ill. *Madre de Dios!* What could she do to stop it? Khalid's eyes went to Luz's haggard, yet open and trusting face and his own face changed abruptly.

"Please listen to me, Noor, we must get out of here right away," Khalid pleaded, and she noticed his expression, not understanding, but trying to respond to his urgency as she edged to pull away. "There is no time to lose. Come with me. We've got the Fiat right outside. Ali's double-parked."

Luz raised a palm to stop him. "*Momentito*, I've got to tell Mr. Berg first."

In the distance came a muffled pop-pop, then from the parade ground, an eerie din. Luz cocked her head, thinking it sounded like a cross between a hurricane, a vacuum cleaner, and a firecracker. She turned to ask Khalid, but the spot where he'd been standing a moment ago was empty. He had vanished, floating off like a wraith in the steam from a witch's cauldron. Mystified, Luz started back to her seat. Khalid had called her out for a reason. Was it really Qaddus' arrest? No, she realized now that he had pulled that one out of a hat. Quite suddenly, an answer slipped into Luz's head as though it had been whispered into her ear by a little bird: someone was laying a deadly trap for Leonard. She had to get back to him. Whirling on her heels, she dashed back to the lip of the reviewing stand as fast as her legs would carry here, screaming, "Lenny, Lenny."

Before she could turn the corner to the stairs, Joe Dooley grabbed her arm. "Hey, Luzzz, you got any idea where a man might get a beer around here?"

"Let go!" Luz's voice was breathless with panic, her body numb. But Joe wouldn't release her. With a strength Luz didn't know she possessed, she rammed her fist into Joe's stomach and sent him sprawling in the dirt. She shook her hand to dissipate the sting, then guilt set in, forcing her to help Joe back on his feet. The end of the barrel of a pistol reared at her. A policeman had seen her knock Dooley to the ground.

"There you are," exclaimed Pete Sanchez, shouldering his way towards them, his smile as open as daybreak. He made a rapid explanation in Arabic to the policeman and the pistol went back in the holster hanging from a webbed belt. In his best law-and-order voice, Sanchez reminded his fellow Americans they were not in their proper slots. "You keep messing around like this, and you're going to miss the fly-over."

Dooley, dusting off his trousers, begged off, citing his need for "a terlet." Pete informed him there were none available within commuting distance. Dooley would have to use the trunk of a tree just like everybody else. Joe glared at three or four Egyptians who were standing nearby as though they were personally responsible for this terrible turn of events.

A flight of six French Mirage 5-Es was buzzing over everyone's heads. A column four deep of Soviet Zil-151 trucks were moving, ponderously as dinosaurs, in front of the stand towing Korean 130mm anti-tank cannons. Suddenly, the truck leading the artillery column pulled slightly out of line and stopped about 25 meters from President Sadat. It was the third breakdown of the day, and few of the notables in the stands looked its way. Their chins were pointing up at the sky as if pulled up by some invisible puppeteer, their eyes squinty on the Mirages. A man in a crisply-pressed uniform jumped down from the passenger side of the stopped truck.

It was a young lieutenant, looking sharp and fit and competent at handling his job. He was no doubt coming over to salute the Supreme Commander. Sadat was standing to take the salute. Respectfully, Mubarak and Al-Ghazala stood up with him. The lieutenant's arm swung back and in a flash he flung a grenade and then another. Both grenades landed inside the President's viewing stand, but did not explode. Instantly alert, Mubarak and Al-Ghazala were clawing frantically at Sadat, pulling him down. Three other soldiers were standing up in the back of the same stationary truck, firing on Sadat with their Kalashnikov AK-47 automatic rifles. They jumped down from the flat-bed and charged in, throwing more grenades and firing their rifles.

By the time Joe Dooley and Luz Gracida reached the

reviewing stand, people were diving head first, tumbling over one another and their chairs, pathetically seeking cover that wasn't to be had. The first soldier had run back to the cab of the truck for a submachine gun. He attacked the President and the security men who were frantically trying to cover Sadat with chairs. Luz's heart raced, the scene pooled in her eyes, and inexplicably, what she saw was "The Martyrdom of Saint Ursula" by Caravaggio. The Saint, accepting the destiny she'd been accorded, looks down in sorrow and resignation at the arrows that had pierced her breast while the executioner rushes forward with his bow still vibrating to see whether he's hit the mark. Behind Ursula, Caravaggio himself raises his hand in vain protest. Then, as if from a great distance, Luz heard a voice call piteously, *"Mon Dieu!"* Acrid smoke filled the air, and she knew she was not in a museum looking at a painting. She slammed her eyes shut against reality.

Someone close by cried, "Jesus, Mary, and Joseph!

Luz jerked Joe Dooley under a falling chair, and he suffered a painful blow to the rump. He lay without moving a muscle, panting, his throat as dry as if he had a hangover. Luz had dropped on all fours and was crawling toward Leonard, who was sprawled belly down on the ground. She tried moving faster but the air wrapped itself around her knees like heavy, viscous liquid. She called Leonard's name, and he raised his head a fraction. Their eyes met: "Get down, get down," his pleaded.

"No need to tell me twice," her eyes answered.

Paulette Tucker fainted. Her husband shielded her body with his. Roland Tucker was trembling violently, and his teeth chattered as though he were freezing. He watched as a gunman ran up the stairs on the right hand side of the stand. Turning swiftly, the man began firing directly into the disarray of bodies covered with nothing more than their garments and their chairs. Two security men fired their pistols at him, giving as well as they got, but they didn't bring him down. Another presidential guard was firing at the Lieutenant who was sprinting towards the front of the wall. He raised himself on tiptoes and fired downward. Two of his comrades in this murderous adventure made it into the stands, where their rifles rained bullets into the people huddled on the floor.

"Stop, you animals, stop!" Tucker shrieked, his hands clapped to his ears. "In *Gottes namen*, stop!"

Leonard had flung himself face down. He could hear the burst of automatic fire whizzing just inches above his head and the ricochet of bullets. He could hear someone calling, "*Nejdah*," Help me! His head was muddled with fear, but he tried to sort it out. This must be a coup, he thought as he waited for his doom. God help us, the planes will dive bomb us next! He could hear a babble of Italian nearby. Was it prayer or curses, he couldn't tell. He decided to risk a glimpse of Ugo Biagiotti. There were beads of sweat on the man's forehead that ran down and mingled with the tears that disfigured his round face—then the silence, followed by a stirring of human life, tentative and numb. "Luz," Leonard said the name as if invoking a prayer, then closed his eyes.

Less than a minute and it was over. A woman with a thatch of blond hair and a sunburnt freckled face crept past Luz, her fist stuffed into her mouth, blood splotched on her tartan skirt. It was Betty MacGregor and she didn't recognize Luz, who was too stunned, in any case, to greet her. When a gentle Hungarian major helped Betty to a seat, she sat down and howled and sobbed until she exhausted herself while he babbled in his strange tongue that no one could understand.

Paulette Tucker swam slowly up out of blackness into the haze of the afternoon sun. Someone was pouring iodine down her throat and she choked and spit. "It's Scotch, Missus Tucker," volunteered a soft voice.

Joe Dooley, white as a sheet, was looking down at her with compassion. He called through tears he made no move to wipe, "Here now, Missus Tucker, a wee sip."

Paulette stared up at him with frightened eyes, at a momentary loss to know where she was or what she was doing or why this strange man was trying to poison her. She shut her eyes, then opened them. He was still there. "What happened?" she asked faintly.

"World crashed apart," Dooley answered grimly, lifting her to her feet. She put her face against his shoulder.

And then suddenly she remembered. "Oh, dear God! Where's Tuck?" Paulette shouted out with all her strength, clutching at Dooley's sleeve. He tightened his embrace as she whimpered, "Find him, please."

The Ambassador had just sat up, his breath coming short, and opened his mouth to call for his bodyguards who were already at his side. When he saw that they were unscathed, he waved them away and reached for his wife. She fell into his arms, sobbing. He stroked her hair and crooned, "Now, now, Paulie, it's all over. It's all over." Her frantic fingers digging into his back told him she didn't believe it.

The bodyguards brought chairs while Dooley rose from his knees, and Paulette finally relaxed her grip on her husband. Dooley leaned down and jerked the Ambassador ungently to his feet. "Thanks, Joe," Tucker said gratefully; then he helped his wife to a chair and massaged her shoulders slightly.

Grasping, Paulette Tucker announced to everyone, "It was the worst sight I've ever seen." When her husband interrupted to say that she hadn't seen it, she begged to differ. "I didn't faint, Tuck, really. I was riveted to that young officer. I don't think I could have been more shocked than if I'd watched Lee Harvey Whatshisface kill John Kennedy." Again, the Ambassador put a comforting arm around his wife's shoulder. "It's like history repeating itself," Paulette sobbed emotionally, clenching her fists by her side.

Ambassador Tucker continued massaging, his fingers extended down over her collarbone. "Now, now, Paulie," he crooned. "The lesson of history is that it does not repeat itself." But his wife wasn't listening to his lecture; she was busily craning to see Jihan Sadat. When she finally caught sight of the First Lady clutching a tearful grandson, Paulette's eyes filled with sympathetic tears. She had always loved parades, but now she knew that she would never be able to attend one without being afraid.

All this time, Leonard had not moved. "Hail holy Queen," Luz whispered, "Mother of Mercy, our life, our sweetness, our hope." Stumbling and praying, she crawled on hands and knees past Hans Stolz who lay in a tangled heap. She saw blood gushing from his swollen, horribly discolored face and his chest streaked red. Ugo was buffeted to the point of insanity as he touched the slack hand and stared at the lolling tongue, the glazed, protruding eyes.

"They got him, the *barbari!*" Ugo spat the curses through his teeth. "*Gentaglia, ruffiani!*" He let the lifeless hand drop back onto the floor. Something his mother used to tell him kept running through his mind, *La morte e solamente una porta*—death is only a door, a passage to a better life. But Ugo had never wanted to go through that door, and he doubted that anyone else did either. Not Hans, not the poor Egyptian lying a dozen yards away, his body obscenely gutted like a fish on a slab.

Breathlessly, Luz rose to her feet and pushed through the confusion until she reached Leonard. "*Querido?*"

The use of her Spanish endearment nudged him. He lifted his head and stared at Luz's beautiful face, magically next to his, and said a silent prayer of thanksgiving. By now he was sitting up, his face as pale as a winter moon except where the blood was streaming out of a cut in his eyebrow. He looked around at the chaos with a dazed expression. "Who could imagine just sitting here watching the tanks roll by and the air planes flying overhead, listening to band music, then—" Leonard threw his hands up in the air. "Madness, utter fucking madness!"

Luz took his face in her hands. "Are you all right?"

Leonard's immediate reaction was to deny the severity of personal danger once it had passed. "A little frazzled around the edges, *bubeleh*, but all in one piece." His smile was uneasy, an attempt to be reassuring that didn't succeed.

Not caring in the least what Muslims felt about public displays of affection, Luz drew him close to her, his body smelling of Dove and cologne and sweat and terror. Lenny buried his head against her shoulder. Luz held him tightly, arms like steel bands, and he could hear her heart pounding right out of her blouse. She kissed him fiercely, joyfully, then buried into him like a tick. It began to register that they'd been lucky.

Leonard started to massage his numb joints to restore circulation. He felt a terrible pain in his side. But they were damn lucky! "Perhaps, my luv," he suggested with a crooked grin, "we ought to chop ourselves up into small pieces and sell 'em in the form of amulets." The grin vanished. "What if this is a coup attempt?"

Luz shivered. "I wish you hadn't mentioned it."

"I wish I hadn't thought about it." But he smiled. As if the warmth of his wife's touch was able to transmit strength from one body into another, Leonard suddenly realized that he was no longer afraid of anything.

General Al-Ghazala radioed for a helicopter to take the bleeding President to Maadi Military Hospital, and its landing was almost as dramatic as anything that preceded it. Rotary blades stirred up a throat-stabbing dust. Coats and hats and skirts swirled about as though a great whirlwind were brewing, its vortex, the risen Supreme Commander on his stretcher. Each man, woman and child in the crowd had an individual pose. Some, compelled by the compulsion to view the horrific, were craning to see the inert and bloody form. Others were turning away as if overwhelmed by the sight. Seven people were dead and 28 were injured. Ambulances were summoned.

"Oh, Egypt," the announcer tossed his head and bellowed to rent the sky, "Oh, treachery." His words coming through the PA system were scarcely audible over the roar of three Czech jets. Flying low overhead like an angelic choir, they ironically raised their wings in celestial praises. No one had told them the parade was over.

23

Luz felt a slight shove and turned around. Leonard was ten feet away, deep in conversation with Ambassador Tucker, Pete Sanchez, and several other men. They were already considering the consequences of Sadat's assassination for the United States, for its interests in the Middle East, calculating what to say and how to say it. Luz was half-listening, half-wondering if Tucker remembered his mocking assessment of Leonard's reports. Suddenly, she remembered why she was here.

The world changes; the gods crumble before your very eyes, and a journalist's work never ends. Reaching in her bag, Luz sought her notebook and pen. With the tools of her trade in hand, she approached an Egyptian admiral, a tall man with a strong nose and chin and dark eyes who was furiously fighting back tears. When Luz tried to elicit a comment, the Admiral didn't answer. She started to move away, but he restrained her with a light hand on her elbow.

"Forgive me, Mademoiselle, but it is really quite impossible for me to arrange the avalanche of my feelings in any orderly way." The Admiral faltered, swallowed, and trailed to a miserable halt. His eyes were lifeless, his face drained of all color. His thick black moustache seemed to be flourishing on a corpse. Luz stood very close to him, feeling his pain, and waited. At last, he managed to say, "Assassination was something that happened in other countries. It is foreign to Egypt. Now, after this, we are filled with more than grief. Right now, I am asking myself why Allah willed that Adam and Eve should have appeared on earth. There is no answer."

His comely wife Inayat jumped in to lend him a hand. "My

husband thinks it is a stunning and terrible shock for the whole world." Her voice sounded strained and raw. "Don't you?"

"Yes, of course, I'm very sorry." Luz winced even as she said that, aware of how insufficient those words were to express her feelings.

Inayat had a delicate jaw, dark liquid eyes, satin skin. She wore red round-toed patent-leather pumps and swung a handbag with the same shine. A strong, neat, composed woman, with a gracious manner, and a low cultivated voice, she went on, "What I mean is that Sadat gave himself to peace, and because of him, we Egyptians are well-regarded around the world. Singlehandedly, he succeeded in discrediting the bloodthirsty Arab myth and showed that we are decent people who will choose conciliation over confrontation."

The Admiral interrupted crisply. "Providing, of course, that our homes and families are not threatened. What happened here today plays right into hands of the stereotypers and makes us look like desert nomads once more." Luz's hands flew across the page.

The Minister of Finance and his teenaged son passed by, and the Minister recalled vivid memories of a man he'd known for 48 years. "Anwar had a kind and caring heart. He touched the lives of more people than any other man I have ever known. You hear about individuals with charismatic gifts, able to evoke loyalty, gratitude, admiration, and affection. I have only known one, but I have known him all my life." He paused to make the full weight of his feelings felt. Brokenly, he added, "Anwar was unforgettable."

As the gunmen were being roughly hauled away by security forces, the Minister gave a baleful glance at them and said, "May Allah the Merciful forgive them, for no one else will ever be able to."

After father and son moved off, a French colonel stopped beside Luz and offered an intriguing comment. "People are going to say Sadat tempted fate with Camp David, and fate was not to be delayed. But it is a little more complicated than they would like to think. For better or worse, Sadat made Western values his own. That might have been his undoing even more than his peace treaty with Israel. The people's perception was that their leader was more comfortable with outsiders than he was with them. That was very dangerous." He took Luz's hand and brushed the knuckles in the Gallic manner; then walked away.

Luz turned back to find other Egyptians to query, grateful that they were such a talkative people. Even in their grief they gave you all they had. To them, the questions of what dissident faction the men who killed Sadat belonged to seemed a distant puzzle. *Takfir wal Hijra*, Atonement and Holy Flight; *Shabaab Muhammed*, The Youth of Muhammed; *Jun'Illah*, The Soldiers of God; *Mujahideen*, Holy Warriors—did it make any difference? More visible was their anguish over the fact that it happened at all, and that the world had been looking on.

Seeing Leonard coming toward her, Luz put her notebook away. As they walked to their car, they were joined by Betty MacGregor looking as if the bottom of her world had fallen out from under her. "Thank God you're alive," Luz exclaimed.

"Just barely." Betty's eyes were red-rimmed, the veins in her temple had swollen like the roots of a banyan tree, and her mouth twisted with a misery that almost throttled her capacity to speak. Luz's brown eyes were full of worried concern as she took one arm, Leonard the other, comforting Betty with their touch. "I am afraid Egypt may really be dying," Betty brooded, dabbing at her nose with a tissue.

Her remark met with such a silence that she felt obliged to support it. "Of course, I know it is the oldest cliché in the Middle East. Egypt has been dying for years and years, since before I was born and my parents were born. Only this time, the prognosis might be terminal." Anger had compressed the glossy lips into invisibility. "Do you have any idea of the consequences if these rabid Islamic revolutionaries were to take over Egypt? What would happen to women like me? It would be another Iran. The prospect is enough to set any civilized person's teeth on edge."

Luz took note of the conviction with which the woman spoke, the obvious feeling. Betty looked as if she might burst into tears again as she added, "The Muslim Brotherhood, the fundamentalists, they have no use at all for tolerance, for moderation."

"That seems pretty well established," said Luz, looking back at the parade ground.

Leonard's hands were pressed against his temples as if he were trying to keep them from exploding. "Knock it off, Betts, will you? I don't know where you got that idea and I don't want to be enlightened, but I find you morbid. You sound just like a Colonel Blimp pissing and moaning because you didn't get your way at Suez."

Betty grimaced, "A right old cock-up we made of that; but never mind, I still say this country is on its last leg."

"You're letting your imagination run wild," Leonard insisted, then he stopped. Luz was staring at him with an odd expression. He raced on, advising MacGregor to reject gloomy portents. Cheerless forecasts have a way of becoming self-fulfilling prophecy. Betty colored, but her eyes were empty as a winter sky. Luz was still staring at him, her lips grim and drawn, so he asked, "What's the matter?"

Luz reached for his arm sympathetically. "For a moment there you sounded exactly like your ambassador. I didn't mean to eavesdrop on your conversation with him, but I got the impression that Tucker really knew all along you were telling the truth about Sadat's decline and fall. He just couldn't bring himself to say: Lenny, you're right as rain."

"It all came true." Leonard protested, "Though I wrote my cables as a warning, not as a prophecy."

24

Leonard had to go to the Embassy, and Luz planned to go home and cook dinner. When she got there she found Khalid sitting in the lobby, dressed in a black *galabiah*, chatting and munching on pumpkin seeds with the *boab*. Her eyes widened in amazement. "What in the hell are you doing here?"

Khalid sprang up so quickly that his wooden stool skidded back from him across the tiles. "I thought you might want to go out, Noor. *Yanni*, sniff around for more stories. I know I would. So I give you my fire and you give me your light." His mouth twisted a little wryly at the pun.

Luz had braced to give Khalid a steely brush-off, but now she turned, her brow furrowed at the unfamiliar expression. "It means we scratch each other's back," Khalid explained, grinning.

Not a bad idea, thought Luz, to find out what the streets are saying, get a feel of the city's pulse on this historic occasion. The *boab* was eavesdropping, and he warned them that a state of emergency had been declared. Anyone caught out on the streets could be shot or worse. This was no time to be foolish. The *effendi* would have his head on a platter if anything happened to his new wife.

Luz considered for a moment. Egyptians would never stay inside on a night like this. The streets would be filled to the brim with people, their wailing renting the indigo sky. It'll be a great story. "Okay," she told Khalid, succumbing to the temptation. "I'll change into something anonymous and be right down."

Cairo was strangely silent. Luz and Khalid walked down

one empty street after another, listening to that silence. The
scruffy buildings looked back at them, composed and watchful. Kasr el Eini, usually so crowded with workers and knots of
AUC students, was utterly deserted. The noises of traffic and
crowds were an integral part of Cairo, and the city seemed an
altogether different and unfamiliar place without them. Luz
looked around with a certain air of detachment; she wanted
very much to understand what she was seeing. Unable to
decipher her feelings, Luz confessed to Khalid, "My first
thought was to liken what happened today in Cairo to what
happened in Dallas when Kennedy was shot."

Khalid said sharply, "You flatter yourself to call that thinking. That is exactly why I brought you out tonight." He
grabbed Luz's arm. They faced each other. "What were you
doing when you heard the news? That is the question every
American can answer, even twenty years later, but next week,
Egyptians will have to stop and think."

They walked around Talaat Harb Square. There was no sign
of anyone except Suleiman Pasha in his bronze form, and they
stopped to gaze at the statue. The old hero looked as Egyptian
as Farouk in his *tarboosh*, but he had started out his life as a
Frenchman. He had married an Egyptian, fathered many
Egyptian children, spoke Arabic, and modernized the Egyptian army. "Suleiman Pasha was French," mused Luz. "Sal-
adin was a Turk. Glubb Pasha, behind that title bestowed
upon him by King Abdullah of Jordan, behind the fluent
Arabic and the flowing robes, was really Sir John Bagot
Glubb. Have you ever wondered just how many great Arab
heroes got an equally bad start in life?"

Khalid laughed. "I can't say. I have a habit of never asking a
question for which I don't already have an answer. It comes
from all those years I spent in mosque school."

Early on in their friendship, the perceptive Gracida had
accused Khalid of being a cradle Muslim, but not a True
Believer. Only after she'd seen the fury of his denial had she
known it was true. Khalid had joined the Jamaat, but he
hadn't struck an attitude of his own yet, and he hung sus-
pended between his contempt for the sterile orthodoxy of
religion and his love for the Muslim Brotherhood and what it

was accomplishing. It ran the best schools, clinics, and community services in Egypt, and it ran them honestly and efficiently. And when he said as much, Luz began to understand what a religious revival meant to progressive-minded individuals like Khalid. They were going to Islam for the sense of hope and continuity it gave them. It offered them a past from which a better future might come.

Luz heard a sound and the hairs on her skin prickled. "What's that?" she asked with a scared break in her voice. "Police?"

Khalid didn't answer. He was gripping her shoulder so hard that it hurt. "Down," he ordered in a harsh whisper as he thrust her roughly to the grass.

A military truck was coming close. Their knees cracked on the stone at the base of the monument as they fell to a kneeling position as the truck went by. Khalid threw his body over hers, like a blanket. It had not gone far when the driver braked and turned around. The truck came closer—Khalid shut his eyes and mouth tight, his breathing stopped, and his fingers tightened convulsively on Luz's shoulder. They lay sprawled downward as a searchlight swept the area nearby. Khalid's heart jumped. They put their noses into the grass and prayed softly, he in Arabic, she in Spanish, until the searchlight went off and the truck was out of sight. Getting to their feet, they brushed themselves off and looked down the Kasr el-Nil. Groppi's ice cream parlour was shut up tighter than a drum.

Khalid grinned at Luz and said, "I think we make a good team."

Luz's nerves were raw, but Khalid seemed cheerful as they walked on, as if his good spirits had been untouched by their close call with danger. Luz asked him how he managed to seem so calm and unruffled. "I've learned how to die," Khalid said matter-of-factly. "I don't get depressed; terror-stricken, afraid, and all that, but not depressed."

They went down to the Nile. The surface of the water, splattered with moonlight, was as flat as polished steel. Luz looked over the stone railing at the river, and she spotted a young man squatting by the bank, defecating. Since he didn't seem to notice the fact that he was in a public place, it seemed only good manners to take no notice of him. But Khalid's teeth were grinding, and Luz sensed a fury in him that she would not have suspected. The assassination was more than she could think about at the moment. Still, she asked solicitously if something was wrong.

"How will we ever get rid of these damn diseases," Khalid thundered, enraged by the ignorance, if not the impropriety, "when people won't stop shitting in the river?"

They started legging it back to the flat. "I can't believe this city," marveled Luz. She started to pant as they jogged by the Orisis Building across from the American Embassy. "This is worse than *On the Beach*; after all the nuclear bombs have gone off and everyone's dropped dead."

"I missed that movie," interjected Khalid, puffing. The hem of his *galabiah* was held between clenched teeth to free his legs for the sprint.

"Fred Astaire wasn't dancing anymore," Luz recalled, smiling thinly. "It was that bad. Do you suppose people are staying inside because this is the eve of *'Eid el Adha?'*"

She was referring to the feast celebrating Abraham's sacrifice. There were huge meals to prepare, visiting relatives, tales about nieces, nephews, and cousins to catch up on. "That's it," she went on, "the family-loving Egyptians are just too busy to come out and mourn. Or maybe they're just so numbed by catastrophe that they can only react as if nothing has happened?"

Khalid ran across the street against the red light. "No," he said immediately, remembering what had happened when Nasser died of a heart attack in 1970. "When Nasser died, the whole country went insane with grief. People spilled out into the streets to mourn him, sobbing buckets full of tears, ripping their clothes, slapping their faces, beating their breasts. There isn't an Egyptian alive who doesn't remember exactly what he was doing when Nasser died. Afterwards, when the new President Sadat tried every which way he knew to get the people to spit on Nasser's grave, they wouldn't. No," Khalid repeated, emotion swelling his chest, "if this had been Nasser who had been shot today, the people would have come out, *eid* or not, a state of emergency or not, in a raging flood or a howling sandstorm. Nothing could have stopped them. They just don't care enough about Sadat to mourn him. They are treating him in the same indifferent way that he treated them. That's what these empty streets are telling you, Noor. And that's what you have to tell your readers."

25

The distant muffled noises of jets, tanks, and gunfire that had reached the ears of the anxious members of the Jamaat had died down into fitful, barely audible sounds. The attempt on Sadat's life had been a success or it had failed. Fearfully, Hikmat el-Din waited inside the dingy room to learn from the BBC what it might be. He was slumped down in his chair, hands folded across his chest. His life and all his energy seemed to be centered in his fiery eyes which never left the television screen. The afternoon sun poured in on a framed likeness of Ayatollah Khomeini hanging above his desk. There was a verse from the *Qur'an* painted in black on a pottery plate, across from six inch-high crossed swords in brass, and alabaster objects, photographs, and calligraphy. These attachments of a lifetime would not follow him to a prison cell—or to the gallows.

His sister Zenaib was too much the cynic to ever respond to his fancy flights of idealistic passion. Her misgivings apparent, she was pacing up and down, and she came to a dead stop in front of him. Hikmat cared not a fig who was mowed down so long as he got his way; he always did what he wanted and devil take the hindmost. What did he care if the whole family was made to suffer? What did it matter to him that they all had to live from moment to moment in desperation, like cockroaches able to show themselves only in the darkness of night? What will people think if they never see her in the streets? They are probably all talking about them, whispering with glee, saying, "Hikmat has really done it this time!"

"I hope you are satisfied." Zenaib shot her brother a venomous look, then continued with her pacing.

"We are trying to save this nation." Hikmat's expression bordered on anger, but his voice was low. As he spoke there was little of the rhetorical fire that marked his appearances before huge gatherings of his follower. Hikmat's desire for domestic tranquility led him most times to retreat cowardly from his sister's temper, but at the moment, he needed a target for his anxiety.

"And what difference will it make?" Zenaib challenged him boldly. This was not the first time that Hikmat had chosen her as the focus of all his frustrations and anger. She gave as good as she got. "The Turks, the French, the British, King Farouk, the Nasserites, the Muslim Brotherhood, the Army, Sadat—whoever rules this country ends up with the booby prize. You are naive if you believe otherwise."

Hikmat gave her the travesty of a smile. "My dear sister, I do hope you will change your way of thinking." Despite the supplicant statement, there was a hint of the imperial in it. "And please sit down. Unless you are afraid you will not be able to rise again."

Zenaib stood, immobile, staring back at him with her droopy eyes like two gloomy bloodhounds in a cage. Hikmat rose. Tiny beads of perspiration now had begun showing on his high forehead. How was it he could be a great leader of men, and yet, at times his older sister could make him feel as unsure of himself as when he rode in the scarf tied around her back? He stood very still, looking down at her, his mouth a tight line. "It is your unbelief, dear sister, that has made you so unattractive." He spoke with a precise, formal syntax, but a slightly pained pitch, as if his undershorts were too tight and his tea cold. "Had you but faith, you would be a handsome woman—and a married one."

Some of Ibrahim's young disciples were gathered in knots in the courtyard, speechless, with clasped hands, their necks stringed into knotty cords, eyes closed in concentration or prayer. From time to time, they talked quietly. In the neighboring buildings, people thrust their heads from windows or climbed the roofs to catch a glimpse of the planes. With pounding hearts they hoped for the success of the suicide squad, their heroes. Twenty-two-year-old First Lieutenant

Khalid el-Islambouli and his brave comrades were the champions of their religion. And it was out of these corrugated-roofed shanties that so many fighters had come to the cause. "The weak will fight to secure their interests," Ibrahim said, righteous in his conviction, "even if they have to spread chaos throughout the whole world. This, the Ayatollah has promised us."

Zenaib wasn't up for her brother's ringing proclamations— or his new Iranian idol. Who was this Khoemini anyway, but another Rais, another Pharaoh? True, he could be merciful to those of the old order—he'd debate a while before deciding to execute the Air Force General, and some of the new rulers would have sent assassins out to eliminate the Shah's two sons. But women were a different kettle of fish, eh? With the monarchy gone, the way was clear for him to kill as many women as he liked for the good of their souls and the general welfare of the country. Zenaib considered herself a good Muslim, but ever since childhood she had been a troublemaker, asking questions for which there were no answers. She stood now, looking at the Ayatollah's picture and asking him silently, "If you execute an adulteress, why not an adulterer? Why punish the woman and not the man?" And what did Hikmat know of marriage? He had been wed to their niece Leila for two years, during which time Leila suffered horribly from asthma. Hikmat divorced her for her barrenness, and her asthma attacks went away. Remarried, Leila had five children in four years.

Voices from the courtyard interrupted Zenaib and she wailed, "They are all so young! A revolutionary or a criminal, what does it matter if they die before they get a chance to marry and father children?"

"Martyrs go straight to Paradise," Hikmat countered. Of this he had not the slightest doubt. "I tell them that all the time."

Zenaib cut him short. "I know you do." She also knew her brother had a habit of stating things in such a way that suggested benefits to the person he was trying to convince, rather than to any ambitious agenda he might have for himself. The young men outside hero-worshipped Hikmat and tried to model themselves after him, unable to see the dark side of his character for what it was. Once before when he was in hiding, desperate and ready to cut his throat if someone gave him the knife, Zenaib had overheard him talking to a cousin, confessing that he was frantic with fear and wracked with worries. The cousin suggested prayer. "Prayer is for mullahs," Hikmat scoffed. "By Ali's blood, I will have you know we are men of action."

Now, Zenaib stopped her pacing. "You could be taken from us, brother." She steeled herself to mention it without a tremor. "What happens to us, women alone and without, ah—"

"Without protection?" Hikmat supplied with deceptive gentleness. "Dear, dear Zenaib. Everyone knows you need protection like a lion needs protection."

Water trickling from a broken faucet made a grating sound, but now that the sun had gone down, the scent of jasmine and lady of the night filled the air with fragrance. On nearly every roof of the crumbling buildings pigeons cooed and fluttered as they settled in for the night. On local radio and television there was nothing but endless music, as if even a "No comment" would be telling much too much.

They jittery cooing of the pigeons, the somber, dirge-like music from the radio, the nervous babble of human voices that trailed off into heavy silences, the lack of horns on the highway—Zenaib was shifting through the hundred sounds that formed this unusual chorus. Suddenly, she heard a commotion at the front of the courtyard. Someone began banging on the gate, yelling something about *El Jihad el Jedid*, the new holy war. She saw Hikmat leapt to his feet, shout *"il-Hamdullilah!"* and throw open his arms to Rashed, who was running in with good news straight from Maadi Military Hospital. Ibrahim's face broke into its first grin. Quickly, he lifted up his arms in thanksgiving to Allah. Then he turned to Zenaib. "What did I tell you, sister?" he crowed triumphantly. "Such a change is coming to Egypt as you have never witnessed." Turning to Rashed, he said, "Now we must put our own affairs in order."

Later that night as Hikmat knelt in prayer with his disciples, his face had the faraway, but altogether blissful smile of someone watching the last reel of a movie with a happy ending.

26

The American Embassy was a beehive of activity for the next week. The funeral would be attended by a star-studded cast for whom the local Mission would need to guarantee food, lodgings, transport, parleys, and safety. Jimmy Carter and Richard Nixon would be on hand, as well as Doctor Kissinger, General Haig, and numerous lesser lights. That meant huge entourages and a press corps; that meant entire first-class hotels to be taken over; that meant armies of security-*wallas* and fleets of limos to coordinate so that they didn't bang into each other. "A truly awesome responsibility, folks," Ambassador Tucker told the staff, "which we will discharge without a single fuck-up, right?"

Leonard had broken three ribs during the shoot-out in the stands that took Sadat's life, but as soon as he was x-rayed and taped up, he went back his office. It was too interesting to miss—being at the center of events, watching things unfolding. Luz brought him several Anaprox tablets for pain relief, along with a picnic basket of fried chicken, fruit, yogurt, cookies, a huge thermos of black coffee, and several cold beers in the cooler. Lenny touched his bandages gingerly, saying, "Maybe I shouldn't be eating so much."

"Go on," Luz urged. "I'll send for the rabbi if need be."

In return for her tender, loving care, she got a quick kiss and a whispered tidbit: "Ted LaGrange had a premonition that Sadat was going to get it on October Sixth."

Luz asked in a voice as low as his, "Did he tell anybody about it?"

"No." Leonard's lips twisted into a wry smile. "He didn't

get it until the Seventh." Suddenly, Leonard's smile stretched out, reaching from ear to ear and he grabbed her. "By the way, Ms. Overseas Correspondent, there's an Ambassador's Wife luncheon in Sana with your name on it. No kidding, *bubeleh*, you will have your work cut out for you these next two years. I've been nominated to be the Ambassador to Yemen—or North Yemen to be exact."

Luz cheered lustily, *"Olé! Mazel tov!* They had you pinned to the mat and you bounced back up."

"Crazy, huh?" Leonard dipped his head modestly. "It's rather like falling off a roof and finding out you're Superman."

"By the Virgin and her glory, we're going for the big bucks and the bright lights." Luz clapped her hands and pressed her forehead to his. "Yemen's a rather primitive place, isn't it?"

Huffily, Leonard said, "I'll have you know, *señora*, that I like primitive places. Trekking over the rope bridges, riding the high dunes by Land Rover, humdinger desert sunrises, the lonesome tinkle of a faraway camel bell in the stillness of the night, the whole Banana Republic schmeer. It'll be a welcome change after Cairo."

The world could keep them in primitive places for the rest of their lives, thought Luz, if that's what Lenny liked. Rubbing his neck, she asked him, "So how did this assignment come about, or can you tell a civilian?"

"Haig's memoirs," Leonard replied. "General Bonehead can run my cables through the shredding machine once I'm out of here; then re-write history to suit himself. No matter, I'll probably get a Presidential award when I'm 86. They'll wheel me out with my colostomy bag and say, 'For fine reporting when you were a little shaver and nobody gave a damn.' Tuck wept, but I suspect he'll be glad to see the back of me." He glanced at his wristwatch; then he put his hand around her waist and guided her to the door. "You'd better get out of here, angel, while the getting is good. Your tight T-shirt and my thick rug are giving me ideas, and this is no time for ideas, at least not those kind of ideas. Be sure to lock the door and bolt it, and don't go anywhere without Khalid. It worries me to think of you wandering all over when things are so unsettled."

The danger was something Luz tried not to focus on. "I'm a working stiff, Mister Berg," she said with dignity. "And I'll going on being one even though you've finally made an honest women of me. We'll both have to learn to wave each other off in the morning, greet each other in the evening, and try not to think about the evil jinns in between." Excitement lit up her eyes. "Hey, I just thought of something. When you're the ambassador, it'll be the first time I've slept with a source."

They stopped talking when they saw a tall man with a whiskey face and tape recorder approaching. It was a Baltimore Sun reporter, striding toward the DCM's office so quickly that his bush jacket was flapping. After he had flown past, Leonard placed a forefinger on Luz's cheek and traced her chin. "How are you going to be an envoy's wife and a journalist? Have you ever thought of that?"

"*No problema, caro mio.* I'll fake it." Luz gave him a big kiss. Then she turned on her heel without further comment and walked away, humming.

Outside in the compound, Luz ran into Paulette Tucker, all dressed in black. Luz gave her a cordial smile, which she noticed Mrs. Ambassador didn't return. It wasn't snobbishness. The melancholy which had been stealing in on Paulette since the assassination had settled around her like a robe. "Tuck is just exhausted," Paulette said in a lifeless voice. Around her neck was a rope of green malachite which she fingered like worry beads. "It's just nonstop now, one thing after another. They put a rollaway bed in his office, but he couldn't sleep. It's the lumpy bed's fault, he says, knowing it isn't. Poor man, I don't see much of him."

"Don't worry." Luz grinned, hoping to inject a cheering note of humor. "Leonard's keeping an eye on him—and on that bed."

Paulette looked blankly at her. "It's such a terrible blow for the Egyptians," she explained to Luz, taking her hand. "I know you haven't been here very long, but I can tell you that these are very gentle people and they are grieving. I had a neighbor come to the Residence after he'd heard about the assassination. He said, 'Madame Tucker, is it true our father has been killed?' And tears began to roll down his face."

Luz's fingers pressed sympathetically. Remembering what Cervantes had advised ("Patch grief with proverbs."), she searched for something Islamic and came up with, "Death's a path that must be trod, if man is to pass to God." It wasn't the *Qur'an*, but it was close, and Paulette smiled.

27

Ali Salah stopped to look up at the row of tall, flat-roofed apartment buildings that ringed the cul-de-sac, one of which contained Leonard Berg's residence. The French windows of the Berg flat looked on to a tiny iron-railed balcony wherein hung several drying lines of laundry. He waited a while until he saw a woman open the windows and collect some stockings. Her mouth was moving, but the distance was too great for him to make out if she was talking to someone behind her or if she was singing. Berg himself would be in his office, but perhaps there was a maid or a friend. He would have to take the chance. He crossed over and entered the building. An old man was sitting on a stool, his hands crossed over a cane, talking to himself. He glanced up and said that his son, the *boab*, would be back in a jiffy. Perhaps he'd care to wait?

Ali leaned against the wall, uncertain whether to stay or not. There was a click of heels on the marble floor behind him, a babble of Arabic, and an old woman wandered in, loaded down with her morning's marketing. She was carrying two string bags filled with groceries. They weren't large, but Ali could see that she was straining. Quickly, he took the bags in a possessive grip. "Let me, Auntie," he offered in a dulcet tone, sweeping her up the stairs. "These are much too heavy."

The old woman was flustered. "Who are you?" she demanded, lunging at her bags. There was panic in her voice.

"A friend of the American gentleman who lives on your floor," Ali replied smoothly. "Please forgive my appearance. I've just been tinkering with the engine of my Mercedes SL190." He smiled as she relaxed.

Luz was shocked when she saw Ali materializing in the
front room. "You never though you'd see me again, I suppose," he greeted her with a big smile. "Well, I found you. I
picked the lock on the door."

Ali Salah was hardly recognizable as himself; his clothes
looked as if he had just been cleaning out the septic tank, and
his face showed signs of intense and prolonged strain. There
were deep lines around his eyes and mouth that Luz didn't
remember seeing as they'd sat around the campfire in
Magaweesh. What had he been up to? He looked around the
flat with caution and curiosity. His voice barely above a whisper, he demanded, "Is this place safe?" Luz was speechless,
and he asked again, "Is this place bugged?"

"Cockroach infested, yes and then some. Electronic listening devices, no." Luz's affected calm only exaggerated Ali's
apparent anxiety, which didn't displease her. "At least, I don't
think so."

Luz wore a short Japanese happy coat that barely covered
her bottom, and it was at once obvious that there was nothing
but herself underneath. Ali let his eyes feast on the sight of
her voluptuousness, her night-dark hair. She asked him, "Do
you find me repulsive, Muhammad Ali?"

Ali laughed uproariously. "You really ought to be forbidden
by law to be within a kilometer of a boys school, you know?"
and laughed again. There had been no malice in the remark
and she smiled at him.

There was a sound, as if a metal pot had bounced on a
terrazzo floor. Ali took a swift stride toward Luz, and the palm
of his hand was hard and warm over her mouth. She watched
as he tossed a glance to the right and left. His wide, haunted
eyes searched her face with a desperate intensity. Then he
heard an Arabic exchange between two maids on the floor
above, and he drew a short breath of relief. Dropping his
hand, he apologized contritely. "Sorry, Noor, I'm on edge.

"I can tell," Luz nodded with a touch of reluctance, licking
her bruised lips.

"I'm in a jam," Ali announced, though of course she knew
that already. His face was scored with lines of weariness and

fatigue, and his voice sounded as if he'd smoked 60 cigarettes in the last hour. Inside the room, his pale eyes wandered, as though checking for exits. Luz questioned him about the events at the parade ground and he replied in a quiet, strained voice that was entirely unlike his usual loud and incisive tones. Changing his tone, he reached his hand out to touch her shoulder and crooned, "I've come to you as a bee to honey."

"Where's Hikmat?" Luz asked.

"Who?" Ali made a disgusted noise in his throat. "Oh, Ibrahim. I haven't seen him, not since our falling out."

In a quickened voice, Luz repeated, "Your falling out?" He nodded coldly without speaking. She hesitated, then asked, "I gather, then, you've broken with your partners in crime?"

She had touched a sensitive nerve and he reacted swiftly. "Completely." As Ali spoke, he straightened to his full height, all 5 feet 6 inches of him, and raised his hand as if taking an oath. Hastily, he added, "The crime, if you will, is only what the criminal in the Presidential Palace says it is."

Luz's face was a study in speculation and Ali prayed she would not betray him, as Fathi had tried to when he went to his flat—putting a sedative in his drink, then calling the police. He'd only managed to get out of there by the skin of his teeth. Ali was a wanted man, wanted by both the security forces and by Hikmat; he'd be in a terrible mess if he allowed himself to be captured. Hikmat's men would be on to him like a hornet's nest; the police would send him prison where he would die. He needed rescuing. Somehow, Luz thought of poor Nafeisa. Isolated in Hurghada, illiterate, her dream house no more than a cracked floor and scattered bricks, making thrilling noises at other girls' wedding festivities, but with no marriage prospects of her own. She faced a dismal future. Coldly, Luz asked, "Why did you come to me?"

Ali moistened his lips, but he couldn't begin. After a long silence of just looking and breathing, Luz said, "You want me to help you?" The question choked her. What was he going to ask for? What answer could she give him? Money? An airline ticket?

Ali began quickly by saying, "I have a little scheme that might do both of us some good. Are you game?"

Cautiously, Luz asked, "What sort of scheme?"

"You could drive me through some roadblocks." His voice heightened as the idea took hold, as though it had only now occurred to him. Her look was one of total disbelief. "We could do it, Noor. It won't be easy, but together we could do it. I know we could." Ali took her hand and held it for a brief moment in a hard grip. "Wasn't it you who used to tell me, I can do anything if I've got the gumption? Have you forgotten that we were once—" he groped for a circumlocution—"the best of friends?"

Luz was so astonished by his audacity that her manner turned icily formal. "If my memory serves me accurately, you once told me your religion frowns on suicide and I said, So does mine." Ali started to interrupt and she held up her hand. "I am sorry to disappoint you, Senor, but what you're asking me to do is much too incompatible with a decent respect for my own safety and well-being." She let her words sink in, then added, "The answer's NO."

Ali cupped her face in his hands, just as he did long ago in Santa Cruz. Then he added a little awkwardly, "Please, Noor. I don't know where else to turn. And I will be eternally in your debt." He was thinking that nobody loves a good story like a reporter. They are drawn to one in a way that makes lemmings look indecisive. Give a reporter a lead and they'll take it. His hand dropped, and in a firmer voice, he concluded like a man playing an ace, "Of course, there's an article or two in this for your paper—an interview with a real live rebel. You can scoop the rest of the herd on this one."

"Hm." Luz hesitated. Was there really a story? Was Ali telling the truth? Her mind clutched at the possibilities for getting out of Cairo with Ali Salah wrapped up in an Oriental rug in the trunk. No chance at all if they went in the Sun Tours Fiat, only slightly better if they went by bus or taxi. But what about a Land Rover with diplomatic plates? The roads were crawling with police, and no doubt they were dealing with suspects with considerable firmness—arc lamps, electric prods, and God knows what else. Ali paced around the room like a small, taut tiger, very much on edge. Something squeezed her heart: again she stood in that reviewing stand, watching those gunmen, remembering the bloody scene before her eyes and the terror that flooded her when she thought Leonard might be dead. Coldly, she asked Ali, "Did you have anything to do with Sadat's murder?"

"What's he to you? Bruce Springsteen?" Anger flooded Ali. He wanted to say, "Yes I did and I am proud of it," but better be tactful for now. Taking the deep breath of a man who's decided to make a confession, he dove in, giving her the outline of a story, avoiding details, of how he'd joined what he thought was a group dedicated to non-violent change, the philosophy of Gandhi and Martin Luther King, and, of course, of Badshah Khan, the Pathan nonviolent soldier of Islam. They had misled him—here he added a blast of self-abasement—and now he was in an appalling fix.

There was the sound of a braking vehicle and footsteps on the stairs. Luz thoughts drifted back to the countless times in Santa Cruz when Ali would pound on her door in the wee hours of the morning with an excuse so elaborately improbable that she would be charmed into opening up, letting him in, loaning him her car. He'd certainly had the knack of dazzling her. Now, ten years later, she was staring into those same eyes, layered in depth upon depth, like the sea, and hearing once again, "By the souls of my dead father and mother, I swear I meant you no harm. You must believe that, Noor. You know I never let politics intrude on my personal feelings. The minute I heard rumors, I drove Khalid right over. I sent him in to get you out of the reviewing stand, didn't I?—to talk you into coming out, but you were stubborn. Admit it." He nearly grabbed her shoulders to shake her. "You can't say I don't give a fig for you."

Slowly, "No, I can't say that."

Having won his point, Ali's tone changed from pleading to bitterness. "And when Ibrahim heard what I had done, he said he'd see me hanged and pray for the health of the hangman."

Luz's smile was sour. "Yeah, well if Lenny ever finds out I tried to spirit you out of Egypt under the nose of the whole frigging security force, he'll call me everything but a white woman."

"He won't find out, unless you tell him. What do you say?" Ali waited expectantly.

With a painful expression, Luz mimicked Bogart's famous line. "Of all the cheap gin joints in the world—"

"—why'd you have to go and pick mine?" Ali finished for her, a reminder of how each of them had always been the other's kind of person. His brain working busily, Ali raised his wrist slightly and noted the time: 9 a.m. It was perilous to linger. Security was sniffing around; they'd clap him in irons the minute they saw him.

If Ali Salah's explanation was unclear, his anxiety was not, for it swirled about them like thick Northern California fog. Luz looked at him in silence for a moment, perplexed by her inability to simply sweep this old lover aside. "Haven't you any friends left in this city?" Her dark brown, inquisitive eyes hadn't left his face.

Ali chuckled bitterly. In Cairo only the dead are considered faithful. "Certainly I've got friends. And both of them begged me to stay away." The bitterness evaporated as quickly as it came. "Hell, I don't blame them. Harboring a fugitive can get you detained indefinitely. You can face up to ten years in prison, or risk being shot on the spot. Of the two alternative, instant death is the more merciful. Yes, by God, it is true. The goddamn police have total license to act in any way they choose against suspected friends of suspects. They have never showed any reticence in the past, and now it is open season. They will jail some, hang some, boil others in hot oil, and bury the rest alive."

Ali damned his emotion and stopped. A harlot he'd called her, and yes, she had her weaknesses. But what he wanted now was her strength. "You are my only hope, Noor." His voice had climbed up into the whining range. "Please, my life is hanging by a thread," then slid back down the register to decision. "Listen, you've got to help. Your goddamn CIA is working hand in glove with Security. I know because last night that bastard Sanchez came over to Rashed's house with a

Chicano Marine. I couldn't see them, but I knew it was Sanchez because I heard him speaking Spanish."

Luz looked doubtful. "You're sure of that?"

"Positive."

Luz said something in a language that Ali didn't understand, then asked him, "All right, señor, what was that?"

Ali didn't know, but he figured she was trying to trap him. "Italian," he shot back, his smile triumphant.

"It was Portuguese."

Ali grabbed her hands with his own. "Please, habibti!"

There was another moment of hesitation, then Luz sighed and nodded slowly, aware of what all this would mean. "Well, I suppose whether you're into Gandhi or armed struggle or whatever; it doesn't figure in what's going down between you and me. I owe you one and that's for sure. But get this straight, amigo, I won't be so helpful a second time."

But she would be helpful this time. And that, thought Ali with a sigh, is all that matters. An expression of gratitude crossed his face. "I thank you with all my heart." Spreading his hands wide, he said, "What can I say?"

Until they got clear of Cairo, there was a moodiness about Ali, a disinclination to converse. The quiet inside the Rover suited Luz, who was into her own thoughts. Before leaving the apartment Ali had taken the time to wash up, and his black curly hair was tousled and damp at the ends, his features clean and his bloodshot eyes hidden behind Leonard's extra pair of sunglasses. "You look much better," Luz complimented, enjoying the luminous sea air floating in through the open windows. They were heading westward at a normal rate of speed.

Ali pulled the visor down and studied his reflection in the tiny mirror cautiously. "I look horrible," he decided. Then he let his eyes sweep over the beach. He saw nothing to give him cause for alarm, but he pretended to be anxious as he grumbled, "I don't know if I should trust my life to a driver who's got such bad eyesight."

"Beggars can't be choosers," Luz reminded him, and the

ghost of a smile tilted his lips. They were overtaken by a
military jeep that paid them no mind. Several other vehicles
approached and went on by. She was starting to think, this is
going to be easier than I thought.

"But what if we come upon a roadblock?" she asked.

Ali answered in an offhand sort of way, "Bribery, *yanni*, a
little money goes a long way in this country. Don't worry, it'll
be all right."

"Maybe." Luz smiled as one who tries to do so. "That
remains to be seen."

They'd been blasting down the highway for hours, talking of
old times, while making good time on a road that was almost
entirely free of traffic at this hour. Without warning, Luz
slammed on the brakes and shouted, "If that is Cleopatra's
Bath, we've made it."

Rudely jolted to attention, Ali followed the direction of her
finger which was pointing to a far distant rock jutting into the
water. Like Joseph's coat, the sea around it was a kaleidoscope
of colors: purple, blues, greens. They should be in Marsa
Matruh in 45 minutes. Once you make it to the resort where
the passable road ends, there are only two ways a non-military
person can go west: by plane or boat. Planes get shot down
regularly, but boats carrying contraband are sometimes willing to take passengers for a price. Luz said, "I've never been
to Marsa Matruh."

"Neither have I." Ali slid down in his seat, his knees resting
on the dashboard of the Rover. He shaded his eyes and looked
at the water speckled with shafts of late afternoon sunlight,
and in a lazy voice, he added, "I will stay in the Rio tonight,
then head west in the morning. You can travel for miles out
there and never see another soul. Just rocks and maybe some
wildlife."

Luz looked out across the expanse of desert, letting the full
force of Ali's predicament land squarely in her lap. Heat waves
shimmered like transparent yellow veils, and there were no
comforting sounds like the tinkling of camel bells, the chatter
of monkeys. The shores of the Nile River were lush and
verdant, but this land was a dusty, beige emptiness where
only a few resourceful lizards had learned to exist without

water. Luz told Ali, "Offhand, I'd say there isn't much wild life here, apart from you."

Suddenly the motor broke into a fit of coughing. Ali bolted upright in his seat. "Bloody hell! What's that? What's wrong?"

"Not to worry," Luz snapped, cutting off his stream of anguished questions.

The same thing happened once or twice on the way down to the Red Sea. Leonard had explained to her that the locally brewed gasoline was like a watered-down pot of coffee. When the Rover needed its caffeine fix, it just wasn't there. Another motor cough and Ali sought more reassurance. Luz said, "It's nothing,"—at which point the engine gave a final gasp and fell silent. "Shut my mouth," she swore as the vehicle coasted to a full stop. She turned the key in the ignition. The motor sputtered and died almost at once. Uttering an Arabic imprecation, Ali flung himself out, lifted the hood, and stared at the engine in disgust. Luz leaned over the fender, muttering a Spanish curse.

Ali pointed to a dangling wire. "Look, this wire has been torn in two. Can we fix it?" The pronoun was to be used loosely. Fixing cars was supposed to be part of a male's repertoire, but Ali knew how to put petrol in the tank, water in the radiator, and air in the tires. Beyond that he was lost. But he had faith that Noor could perform black magic under the bonnet; she'd done it before in Santa Cruz.

"Bring me the tool box on the floor in the back seat," Luz directed, "and we'll give it the old college try."

Ali retrieved the box and a baseball cap with "U.S.S. Nimitz" stitched in gold thread. He put the cap on, then brought the box to Luz. She opened a button of her shirt in the heat, then rummaged through the tools until she came upon the electrical tape and a pair of pliers. "*Bueno*! Just what the doctor ordered," she said cheerfully as she began stripping away an inch of insulation from each end of the severed wires. Luckily, the wire was long enough so that both ends would still meet. Her hands moved swiftly, but without haste. She was meshing and twisting the ends together in a methodical way when Ali called out suddenly, "Noor." She rose quickly, banging the back of her head on the hood. "Aiiee, what is it?"

Ali was peering with squinted eyes at a cloud of dust. He
heard the motor first, a faint sound coming from the southeast
along a narrow dirt road, and his heart sank. Luz heard it and
stood in silent anticipation of she knew not what. Ali skirted
the rear of the Rover, and walking backwards, came beside
her. "A military truck is coming from out of the desert." A look
of intensity came into his dark eyes and he began to sweat
profusely. He pulled a damp handkerchief from the hip pocket
of his jeans and wiped the beads from his face, which gave him
little relief. "Oh Lord, what if they decide to stop?"

Luz could hear the panic in his voice. She handed him the
pliers. "Here, you finish this," she encouraged, trying to
ignore the anxiety that clutched her. "I'll see if I can get rid of
them." The truck was getting closer now, no more than a
minute away. Moving with the lithe grace of a cat, Luz went to
fetch their passports—hers real, his bogus—from the glove
compartment. "You keep your sunglasses nailed to your face,
companero, and your head buried inside the hood. And for
godsake, don't do anything to attract their attention." Ali
acknowledged her instructions with an unsmiling nod.

As Luz watched, the truck slowed down while still keeping
to the center of the road. Her mind cleared of all extraneous
thought. She saw a fierce-looking sergeant with a full, flowing
moustache. He could leave them free or take them captive.
Before he could open the door and jump down, Luz put both
palms flat on the door and her lips began to curve upward in a
smile. "What is it, Colonel?" she inquired sweetly in lightly
accented English.

Various nationalities ran through the Sergeant's mind: Italian, Portuguese, Greek? It was hard to say; her long-lashed,
mestizo-slanted eyes gave a certain mysterious quality to her
face. In thickly-accented English he asked her where she was
from and was surprised when she showed him the American
passports. A half dozen young recruits in the back of the truck
were hanging over wooden bench that showed the scars of
much hard wear, eyeing her full breasts appreciatively. When
they voiced their appreciation, loudly and in Arabic, the
Sergeant snapped at them to watch their tongues and their
manners, least the foreigners report them all to the tourist

police. Then, with his own eyes on her cleavage, the Sergeant sputtered, "Ah, yes, Miss, is there some problem here?"

As Ali bound the raw copper with the electrical tape, he heard Luz saying in an unbelievably calm and phlegmatic voice, "A minor matter, Colonel. My husband has it under control. But, we thank you for your concern." She gave the man a full 100 watt smile.

The driver, his black hair cut short to resemble a helmet, was sitting slumped at the wheel and taking no notice of her. His unit, like every other one in the army, had been on around-the-clock duty ever since the assassination. Dusty, tired, and hungry, he was eager to get back to camp. He could see a dust storm coming.

Adrenalin sent blood pounding through Ali's veins. He tried tightening the connection at both posts, but his palms were so moist that he let the pliers slip. They clattered to the ground, sounding in his ears like a locomotive crashing into a stainless steel wall at 170 kph, but no one looked at him. At the Sergeant's harsh rebuke, the soldiers had petulantly turned their backs on the unfolding drama. Ali bent down to retrieve the pliers, keeping his back to the truck. "I have a mechanic who can take a look-see at that motor for you," offered the Sergeant. He'd spoken in the tone of someone very distracted by other business.

Luz gave him a 50 watt smile this time. "That's very kind of you, Colonel. But I'm sure Albert—my husband, that is—can manage. He and the car are used to each other by now. We've come all the way from London in it."

There was a squeal of brakes as a boxy little metallic silver Lancia came to a stop behind the truck. The man behind the wheel wore a Pierre Cardin suit; his thin face was arrogantly aristocratic. It took less than a second for an impatient horn to blare. "Good day, sir," bid Luz, stepping back, smiling and waving one hand loosely at the Sergeant. The bored truck driver didn't wait for the usual shouted directive. He put his foot down heavily on the accelerator and the vehicle shot ahead.

Ali was amazed at Noor and when both the truck, with its hubbub of youthful male voices, and the Lancia had passed

into the distance, out of sight, he showed it, slapping her
shoulder with a chortle of glee and telling her she was wonderful, absolutely wonderful. Luz tossed her head back to
loosen a stiffness in her neck and said, "That just cost me ten
years of my life, *hombre*. I'm getting too old for this sort of
thing."

Ali lowered the hood. "If Allah wills, the engine will start."

As they climbed back inside, Luz made the sign of the
cross. "In the name of the Father, the Son, and the Holy
Ghost." Ali asked her if she did that from right to left or left to
right. "Times like this," she replied solemnly, "I do it both
ways."

Agreeing they needed all the help they could get, Ali
crossed himself too. She reached for the ignition key and
turned it. The engine caught, coughed, and died. To their joy,
it caught on the second attempt and held. "We did it!" Ali
cried, feeling a tremendous surge of exhilaration.

Luz's tension dissolved into laughter. Truly, that was
Christ's miracle of miracles. "If that doesn't convert you," she
said, activating her four-wheel drive, "I don't know what
will."

They were moving through a haze of sand that the wind,
growing stronger by the minute, raised in swirls that reduced
visibility to less than ten yards. Luz turned on the yellow fog
lights. With one free hand, she removed the Blessed Virgin
Mary medal from around her neck and gave it to him. Ali was
reluctant to accept it. What if he were walking out across the
barren desert when he stumbled and fell into a ditch? Someone would find him a hundred years from now and think he
was a Christian saint. History gets made from skeletons,
trinkets, and fantasies. Luz attempted to smile when she
asked him, "What's wrong with being a saint, besides the fact
you've never tried it before?"

Ali smiled at Luz, enjoying her gallows humor. "There are
no saints in Islam," he explained, tucking the medal inside
the pocket of his jeans. "Ah, I can just see it now. The heat will
cook the flesh from my bones, and they will lie there for
hundreds of year. Then some fool will see this medal and
bring my bones out of the desert and make them into holy

relics, Saint Alex the Short, or San Alijo del Sands. Maybe
they'll even display them in a glass case in some church in
Spain."

"That's one way to get there." Luz's eyes were laughing,
vibrant. There was nothing remote about her; her mestizo
face was lively and alert. Then her eyes lifted to the rear view
mirror and clouded over. A Chevy was following them. A man
in sunglasses and a *tarboosh* was behind the wheel. A veiled
woman sat beside him in the passenger seat. Traffic on the
road was sparse and it had not escaped Luz's notice that they
sped up and slowed down each time she did. She leaned
weakly back against the seat, aware of the feeling in her gut
that would not be ignored.

Ali turned once to stare at the Chevy. But he didn't imagine
any assailants lurking behind the dark glass and gauze. "Most
likely Saudi tourists," he said, and Luz momentarily relaxed
her vigilance somewhat for many Gulf Arabs did come to frolic
on this stretch of beach. Still, best to be cautious.

The westerly wind moaned as it moved across the long
sweep of shoreline, and Luz's lungs echoed with the sound of
her arguments. "Best bet," she told Ali, "unless you're absolutely determined to get out of the country, is to dig in for a
while at a small hotel. Act like an Italian tourist, drink vino,
and sing *La Tarentella* in a lusty baritone."

Ali wouldn't consider it. The sooner he got out of Egypt,
the better. "And then what?" Luz wondered.

His plans were vague, no more definite than the morning
mist that burned away in the sunlight of a new day. He said,
"After Cairo, all I need is clean air and sunshine, and perhaps
I'll grow tall, become prosperous, meet a nice virgin, marry,
and raise a family, and return to take over as Minister of
Mining and Mineral Exploration." Humbly, he amended,
"*Ins'challah*," if God wills.

A virgin he wanted? "Did you feel guilty about our affair?"
Luz asked promptly.

And just as promptly Ali answered, "No. You felt guilty
enough for both of us, always going to the priest to confess
your sins."

Luz no longer went to confession, and seldom to Mass, but

Salah hadn't changed much since Santa Cruz. He still relished the sight of a great drama unfolding and the prospect of playing an important role in it; he was a buyer of dreams. Ali picked an olive canvas bag up off the floorboards between his feet and started checking out his supplies: the *baladi* bread, his grandmother's herbal remedies for headaches, blisters, and stomach cramps, Dristan nasal spray, and a plastic sandwich bag filled with *doq-qa*, the protein powder and salt mixture which nomads carry when trekking through the desert.

With bravado, Ali told Luz, "I will try and cross over into Libya." He spoke the plan in oratorical tones, as if this were the act that would alone accomplish his purpose.

"That's loco!" Luz let out a low sigh. It's easier to get to than Brazil, she supposed, if you're a man on the run and without a Lear Jet in your hanger. The Chevy was still reflected in the rear view mirror. She glanced at it; fear spread throughout her body, diminishing her strength. She studied him with troubled eyes. "Of all the possible scenarios I'd worked out for you, revolutionary wasn't even on the list."

A wave of anger washed through Ali, and he was momentarily on the point of responding heatedly. He shook his head faintly instead and looked at her for a long quiet moment, the flash of anger disappearing almost as quickly as it came. "The last I heard, revolution was a perfectly respectable occupation."

"Who told you that?" Luz asked suspiciously.

"Tom Paine." Ali darted a sly look at her. "Or was it Thomas Jefferson?"

"Bravo," Luz said in dismay, her eyes on the road ahead. "I can remember your telling me, 'no windmill can be brought down with a well-placed lance, that's the theme of Don Quixote.' So when did you abandon Cervantes for those two tomcats?"

Ali watched her hands playing on the steering wheel. "*Naseeb*, destiny," he said shortly. The Rover was confining, but Ali gave it the most dramatic gesture the space would permit, flinging both arms out. "Destiny. Allah calls the shots and we cannot change what He decides for us to do. When He opens the door, our duty is to be ready to pass through." Ali was working up a good head of steam, diving into his favorite subject, the universal anti-colonial impulse. "The Crusaders came to a sterile stop in less than seventy years. In the end, the French had to quit Algeria. The Brits, too, left and went home to tend their rose gardens. The glory days of Zionism are waning. We are a patient people, we Muslims."

Ali had begun a speech, and when even he heard it as such, he paused. Luz, unwilling to prolong the discussion, pointed to a squat cinder block building up ahead and announced, "I'm hungry. How about you?"

They stopped at the small roadside cafe for a bite to eat, and Luz was happy to see the suspicious Chevy whizz on by. They had not been its prey after all. Sea gulls circled above the patio, their screams piercing the air. Despite the bright sun, a refreshing breeze came from the sea, bringing with it the not-so-fragrant odor of sewage. Luz ate the lamb in her dish of *kibbeh* slowly and methodically. A few sips of the wine that was put before them quelled their nervousness.

There was another roadblock on the outskirts of town that they had to pass. Mustafa had supplied Ali with an American passport to go with his American jeans, slang, and traveling companion, and they did the trick. Once past the checkpoint they continued their journey down a shoreline that travel writers liked to call the Egyptian Riviera. The scenery was beautiful, and they drove on in silence, but each was aware of the charged field between. Luz finally said, "Must change always be so brutal?"

Ali laughed scornfully. "Ah, Noor, you must have been born in a lily. Heaven knows I would like it to be easy without bloodshed, but my experience has taught me the odds. People with power and possessions never want to share them. They get a little and then a little more and it corrupts them." His voice began to rise with evangelistic fervor. "All they want is more and more, which means the rest of us have less and less. When you complain they shrug and say, La-de-dah, life is unfair. It's not like we were running around Cairo with a beheading sword in one hand and a Molotov cocktail in the other. We wanted a dialogue. We wanted more than a rubber stamp Parliament. Look here, Miss College Girl, even the Vatican recognizes that armed struggle, as a last resort, is allowed by church teaching. Ambrose, the Bishop of Milano in the Fourth Century, argued that Christians have a moral duty to oppose injustice, by force if necessary."

"If you're saying your head is back in the Fourth Century, you'll get no argument from me on that score." Her smile maddened.

With strained patience, Ali reminded her, "You're Catholic, Noor, so why are you ignorant as to what the Pope says about just wars?"

Luz was being lectured again. Her face darkened, and she yelled, "The Pope says no birth control and no abortion and no divorce and no ordination of women. He's wrong about a lot of things. *Madre mia*, I can't tell you how much the self-righteousness of the purists gets to me! The highmindedness of the moralists, the bluenoses, the fanatics—" she grimaced. "Any woman who would allow 500 men in dresses to control their lives, their bodies, is a wimp in my book."

"I am not a fanatic." Ali's palm pounded his knee. Luz took her eyes from the road long enough to look at his face. The lines around his mouth tightened as he declared, "I just want my people to have a chance, Noor. Islambouli and his men have put them on the field. I don't care if they lose. At least they will have a feeling of being there. And if they win, we will have a World Cup." Impassioned, his eyes alive, he was speaking with the voice of a mystic visionary. To clinch his argument, he took her hand in his moist palms and told her, "Since you never grew up in a mud hovel, you have no call to have an opinion. And besides, Lieutenant el-Islambouli never executed anybody who didn't deserve to die."

This remark infuriated Luz, but she jerked her hand away, channeling her surge of anger into her grip on the wheel. Biting off each word sharply, she said, "There were seven other people whose only sin was to be standing in the line of fire."

Ali's head jerked around. He shot her a venomous look. "Talaat was murdered and many, many others as well. Our lives were imperiled. We tried to have a discussion, but they wouldn't talk with us. Now, we do our talking with the edge of the sword and the mouth of a gun."

Sadat was executed while Talaat was murdered?—an interesting distinction. "I'm sorry about Talaat."

"He is in Allah's hands," said Ali, his expression pious. "He is happy at last; we are glad for him."

His eyes scanned the horizon. Ahead lay an undulating beach that stretched as far as the eye could see. Ali started to sing in Arabic. Years ago, Luz remembered, Ali tried to explain Eastern customs to her. If you try and kill somebody and fail, you are guilty of nothing for it is God who didn't wish it so. Somebody stabs a friend with a dagger, and he is in exactly the same fix as somebody who's had an accident on the highway and kills a pedestrian. The Muslim mind doesn't distinguish between intentional and accidental acts. Had Allah not wished Anwar Sadat to be taken from the Egyptian people, He would not have allowed it to happen. Events speak for themselves and death is easily justified—*Ins'challah*, God's will.

Ali's thoughts were running in another direction altogether. "Look at China," he directed, in his debater's voice. "First year Mao Zedong was in power, he killed three million people, landlords, Mandarins, and their ilk. And people said, 'Jesus, what a horrible man!' They conveniently forgot that the year before 17 million Chinese died of starvation. They were landless peasants, poor folk in the slums of Shanghai, opium addicts, and crippled veterans, so they didn't count. It's the same here. Infants die every day in the City of the Dead and who notices? Who cares? Certainly not Americans. You mention Cairo to them and they say, 'Isn't that somewhere near where Indiana Jones was searching for the ark?'"

"Don't knock our entertainments, *amigo*," Luz cautioned. "When it comes to hard news, Dan Rather tells us what we need to know."

"Well, did Rather tell you Sadat didn't do a damn thing for the people in the City of the Dead? I bet not. Jihan is trying to make herself into the richest woman in Egypt, but you see only the glitter and the glamour and remain loyally blinkered. It's the Shah and his gorgeous Empress and their big tent show extravaganza all over again. You guzzle their French champagne and hear the music and think when women get the vote, happy days are here. But beneath the Rais' medalled chest and his wife's fur coat there was nothing but self-indulgence. Lieutenant el-Islambouli had plenty of nerve, let me tell you. I wouldn't have cared to do what he did. I wouldn't have been able to do it. But I am grateful he did it. He has given us hope again."

A soccer game was in progress in the middle of the street. Luz leaned on the horn and gunned the engine threateningly. The boys made way. She drove on mutely, but the white knuckles on the steering wheel gave her away. Suddenly, her inaccessibility infuriated Ali, but he kept his voice gentle when he apologized, "I didn't mean to upset you."

"You didn't," Luz replied automatically. She stopped as a group of pink-skinned Germans crossed the street. They wore bikinis and tossed their heads, displaying their long blond hair. Off to the side, a pregnant Egyptian woman was trying to quiet the toddler in her arms. Her weathered face was crumpled like a brown bag, her chin covered with blue tattoos. The child refused to stop crying no matter how she jiggled or cuddled it. Luz drove on, thinking once more of Nafeisa, who perhaps would never marry, never be a mother. "What about Nafeisa?" Luz asked Ali. "Does leaving her trouble you in any way? Does her docile acceptance add to the guilt?"

Ali was not an insensitive man and he exploded, "What do you really know about our family, Noor? You have jumped to a conclusion that is completely unwarranted and, I might say, unjust. There are other cousins, a few uncles. Anyhow, marriage is for better times. Who can think of it, living on a volcano that never stops bubbling?"

The Rover turned into a narrow dirt lane. Huge overhanging palms cast delicate shadows on the ground. "This might be my last night in Egypt," Ali said in a cracked voice. Only by a fierce act of will did he turn his mind away from that horrible thought. Putting a cigarette to his lips, he appeared pale in the glow of the flame of the match, the lines of his young-old face deeply etched, and for a moment she thought he was going to cry, but he rallied immediately and exclaimed, "*Mak-tub*," it is written. "I won't be gone long. I believe that." And he did. He had to.

Luz took her eyes off the road long enough to give him an encouraging smile. Ali bit his lip in a fierce air of concentration as they circled the blocks trying to find the Rio Hotel. Luz took a few wrong turns and he became fidgety. He began to talk faster, but in an increasingly desultory manner about the first time he went for a ride in a car, of Swedish socialism as his first girlfriend Monica had explained it to him, about hearing Nasser speak over the radio and how it had changed his life, about what a dead-end life he would have married to Nafeisa in a tiny Hurghada dwelling with no piped water, no television, no sewer.

After a long draw on his cigarette, Ali alluded to his recent falling-out with Ibrahim. "He said if I run away he hopes I'll be captured and tortured and put to death. I am willing myself to survive just to spite him. I should have been more wary after his sister Zenaib told me he how he has always tailored his ideology to fit his ambitions. Even though he hated Nasserism, he quickly picked up the socialist language when Nasser gave him a high position in the Ministry of Education. He turned against the socialists after the Iranian Revolution, when it looked as if Khomeini would be the new bearer of the true flame. An opportunist forever bending with the wind, that's Ibrahim. He is going to be found out some-day."

Ali pushed his hands through his hair in a gesture that was somehow boyish and despairing. Luz felt an inexplicable rush of sympathy for him. Ali closed his eyes against the Egyptian sky and declared with feeling, "I am an excessive being. I've always been capable of extraordinary emotions, you know that. How many chairs did I break? How many windows did I sail through? Sometimes, after you left me, Noor, I drank and I would drink to such a point I no longer knew who I was. When I think of the things I did, the people I hurt, I can't recognize myself in those acts. Such anger! I don't suppose my temperament has changed with age. The only difference is that I know how to channel it, where to put it to do some good—in the cause. Politically, I have this great capacity for rage. And so long as I have it, I will never be a sheep, led around by the nose like the rest of my family."

Luz questioned, "Do you believe in God, *amigo?*"

"Yes," Ali replied without hesitation, rubbing his dark-ringed eyes. "But He is not off the hook for grinding me down for all these years. He has been on an opium holiday, and I don't know when I'll forgive Him." Ali leaned back. "You know, five years ago I'd have been depressed about what happened between me and Ibrahim and between me and Fathi. But that's not fair—to myself or to the people I love, Mustafa and Rashed and my niece. You grow up, you do the best you can, you try and be brave."

Ali launched into *The Streets of Laredo*, and Luz joined in. "I see by your outfit that you are a cowboy...." Her black hair was rolling gently on her shoulders. Ali reached over to grasp a lock between his fingers, opened the scissors on his Swiss army knife, and quickly snipped off a lock. Stopping his song, he said quietly, "For luck."

The lowering rays of the sun, filtered through a latticework of clouds, cast a soft yellow hue over the town and turned the sea into liquid fire. After winding through several crowded streets, they saw the hotel in front of them. Across the street, under a pepper tree, sat the Chevy. Luz stared at it, wanting to get away from there as fast as possible. "You have an overactive imagination," Ali chided her. Then he turned to face her. He was seeking what he'd last seen in her face ten years ago, and he supposed she was doing the same. He made a motion of the head toward the hotel. "Are you coming in?" There was a twinkle in his eye, and despite her efforts to prevent it, Luz laughed. She was mightily amused by the image of Ali as another reformer in the mold of King Ibn Saud, preaching puritanism yet never stinting his appetite for what was it?—300 and some women. Ai, what marvelously complex men the Arabs were!

"I'm going to stay at the rest house in el-Alamein tonight," she answered. "Do a story on it to cover my tracks. Leonard will be in a panic when I tell him where I've been and the

desperado I've been with. God forbid, I don't want to scuttle
his becoming the ambassador to North Yemen."

"Leonard?" Ali had forgotten him entirely. So Berg would
be the next US envoy in North Yemen? The State Department
was certainly giving him a hard acre to plow. Luz's future
suddenly seemed as inauspicious as his own.

Off in the harbor a boat sounded its horn. Ali leaned over
and their cheeks brushed. His mouth moved on hers for a
moment—a brotherly kiss, a kiss of goodbye. Ali gave his
blessing on her marriage. "That new husband of yours, Noor,
is a civil man with great wit and a very lucky man, too." He
added softly, "I envy him." Then he opened the door and
jumped down. Luz handed him his small satchel into which
she had stuffed a wad of dollars. He smiled the smile of a
thousand farewells and started to walk away.

The door of the hotel flew open and a woman yelled,
"You're here!"

Ali looked in grateful astonishment at the sight of Betty
MacGregor. She looked frazzled in a wrinkled skirt and blouse
and damp, yellow hair in corkscrew curls.

"Betty," Ali cried, reaching for her hands and kissing both
of her cheeks.

"This place is all the way to hell and gone," Betty complained.

His hands dropped to his sides. "Nobody said you had to
come along."

Betty's mood changed immediately. "Oh, darling," she
gurgled, her voice deliberately gay and flirtatious as she caressed his cheeks, stroking his silken black whiskers. "How
could I stay in Cairo without you? I was so afraid I'd never see
you again." She sunk against him, her face upon his shoulder.
"When Rashed came over and I saw the look on his face, I
thought you might be dead and he had come give me the
awful news. But you're alive and you're here with me. Thank
God, it is a miracle!"

Luz stared at Betty MacGregor. Was this the same woman
she'd seen in the stands at the parade ground, an admirer of
the slain President who'd been so utterly devastated by his

assassination that she could scarcely walk or talk? Was she the
woman behind the veil in the Chevy? Surely by now, Betty
knew that Ali had a role in that crime, however minor. But
she'd come here with what—relief or rescue or redemption?
     Ali, too, was taken aback. Betty had seen Rashed? That
surprised him, as he had said nothing to Rashed about his
leaving the city and coming here—unless Mustafa said something to Khalid, who in turn had let the cat out of the bag. For
a moment, Ali found her presence vaguely menacing, but
Betty held tight to him, endearments spilling from her lips,
her ample breasts pressing into his chest. She had more
makeup on than you could sink a stick in, and her Cleopatra
earrings banged wildly against her cheeks. "I got a boat for us,
ducky," Betty announced excitedly. "There is nothing to
worry about. But let's go up to the room. Thank God you
made it; you're out of Cairo. I'd have died if something had
happened to you."
     "A boat?" Ali repeated the word with a trace of awe. Just
then he noticed her navy blue shirt. Her blouse had ducks on
it. Her eyes were as blue-green as the Adriatic Sea. Everything about her was nautical.
     "Yes, a boat," Betty repeated, lifting her chin slightly, show-
ing him the soft hollow of her throat. "It wasn't easy, but I
know some people. If all goes well, we will take off around
midnight." She flicked her wrist aggressively in Luz's direction, a gesture both of farewell and dismissal.
     Luz had never thought she'd see the crazy Scot as Ali's
guardian angel, and come to think of it, she was not too sure
she liked it. If Ali and Betty didn't exactly boil—their romance seemed more like the fondness of an orphan boy for a
kindhearted aunt—they obviously did percolate. Reluctantly,
Luz put the Rover in gear. "*Vaya con Dios*," she called to Ali's
back. Then she turned the Rover around and headed east to
Cairo.
     Ali Salah had not become the mover and shaker that their
friends back in Santa Cruz predicted, but he surely deserved
some sort of immortality as one of Egypt's outstanding female
manipulators. Very little of his life passed without the need for
some woman to haul his chestnuts out of the fire—his grand-

mother, his elderly English tutor, his aunt, Monica, Luz, Nafeisa, Betty. And he knew how to hit the right note, or so it would seem, since nearly all the wounded kept coming back for more.

The room MacGregor had rented for them was small and on the top floor. Betty hurried up the rickety stairs, moving swiftly despite the restrictions imposed by her skirt. An open window let in the sea breezes. In one corner of the room a tap dripped cold water on the dirty tiled floor. Ali put his bag down, still not fully able to absorb his good fortune. There was a boat waiting to take him away to safety. As if reading his mind, Betty teased in an exotic voice, "I think you really need me now, you sod."

Ali kissed her tenderly on the lips. "Shows you how wrong you can be. I've always needed you."

After bolting the door, Ali turned to see Betty pulling her skirt and blouse over her head. Closing in on 50, she was still a sensuous woman, easily belying her age by a dozen years or more. For sure, her left ear didn't work as well as it once did, and her hair was gray at the roots. Liver spots competed with the Hurghada tan on her hands. Still, she had the soft, approachable femininity of a loving mother. Past all fears for their safety, Ali began to want her. He began to remember the slow hands caressing him, the warmth of her fleshy body, the security of her embrace.

"There might be some rough sledding ahead, *habibti*," Ali warned in fidgety English as he unbuttoned his shirt.

"We bloody well can handle it." Betty got into bed, watching the crack of light along the edge of the door, making sure they were alone. "Hurry," she gave him a ribald laugh, pulling the blanket up against the chill breeze. She seemed to be trembling with anticipation, her breathing short and shallow.

Ali stood there, momentarily conflicted. "Hurry," she repeated, throwing back the blanket and spreading her legs invitingly. He tore off his clothing and was on her. Inside Ali's head, he could hear Hikmat's scolding voice, but the warm softness flat against him had aroused him and they began to make love.

28

When Luz let herself into the apartment, she was met by a stack of suitcases. Beyond them stood one very angry husband. Lenny already knew, she could see it in his face. He was confused and it made him angry. "*Caro?*" Luz stammered, a lump of fear rising in her throat, thinking, Dear God, do we pay for our falls from grace, every one? Leonard was yelling now in a mixture of Yiddish, Arabic, and Lord only knows what else, standing right in front of her. She was afraid he might hit her, but she just stared him in the eye, marshalling her arguments like a general preparing a battle strategy. The words started to tumble out, the condemned confessing right before the execution.

Leonard intervened, "Pete Sanchez's told me everything. It blew me away, totally. I've never been in a 747 that hit an air pocket and dropped 10,000 feet, but when Pete told me you were with Ali, I thought I could appreciate the sensation. Christ almighty, what are you trying to do, get yourself killed even before our first child arrives? What am I supposed to tell the kids if you do that?"

Wearing his most ferocious expression, Leonard pantomimed strangling her neck, then he grabbed her to him, kissing her lips, her eyelids, her temples. Luz clung to him, her eyes moist. She loved this man so much and never wanted to hurt him. Had she scuttled his ambassadorship? No, she hadn't, but she'd shortened his lifespan by ten years. She wanted to explain what had happened, but she had yet to explain it to herself. She tried to apologize, but Leonard silenced her.

"That brand-new black diplomatic passport of yours," he said, "is going to keep you from getting arrested, for either helping Salah to get to out of Cairo or for murdering him. But we've got less than an hour to catch the plane to Athens. If we miss it, God only knows what the police will do." He handed her a bag, but she couldn't hold it.

"Murdered?" she asked, her voice strangled.

"I'm afraid so."

"*Madre de Dios!*" The word burst out of Luz, the news piercing her, leaving her dizzy.

Leonard put his arms protectively around her shoulders and nodded. "They found his nude body washed up on the beach this morning near Marsa Matruh, a knife between the ribs."

He turned to let the *boab* in the door. The two men hoisted the luggage. Leonard wrapped his own brown suede coat over Luz's shoulders. With the edge of a suitcase, he tried nudging her out the door. "Step on it, honey." He spoke swiftly, trying to impress her with the urgency of his request.

Ted LaGrange yelled up the stairwell that he had an Embassy van double-parked outside; they'd better shake a leg. Luz took a breath, summoning up her energy, and took one of the bags. Leonard said, "Good girl."

Ted smiled up at her, a smile that suggested that once more womankind had justified his worst suspicions. In the foyer Luz stopped, a sleepwalker hunched into her sweat shirt and jeans, and felt another prodding suitcase against her leg. She found her voice when they reached the van. "The minute I saw her there, it struck me—" she started to say, but Ted interrupted.

"You two hop in back," he ordered. "I'll sit up front with the driver."

There was little conversation on the way to the airport. Spikey palms were twisting in an uneven breeze, causing Ted to break out into song. "It's a long way to Tipperary, it's a long way to go...." When the Bergs declined to join in, a look of disappointment crossed his face. He turned around to say he didn't expect any trouble, but he could be wrong. "There could be a lynch mob outside the terminal by the time we get to the airport." After a moment of silence, Ted offered conciliatorily, "Just kidding, folks. I'd like to believe that the local Security boys are out frying bigger fish than Missus Berg."

Luz sucked in a breath. Leonard squeezed her thigh and asked, "Did you ever hear me tell a lie?"

"Not a big one." Luz grinned, trying to appreciate Lenny's humor and stop thinking about Ali.

Leonard gave Luz an encouraging smile. "If they decided to investigate, we can tell them that Ali, the bastard son of a one-eyed camel, put a gun to your head or a knife to your throat or whatever and forced you to help him. I'm sure they'll buy that and let the matter drop."

"Think so?" Luz said, hoping against hope.

"The Ambassador doesn't want to see you stretched out on the rack, Mrs. Berg." Ted curled his lips to make clear his own quite different preference. "He says he doesn't relish the Embassy's good name and all that getting dragged through the mud. That's why we have to get you two out of here pronto."

Leonard took comfort in looking forward to staying in Athens that night and getting a little shnockered in some rowdy cafe in the *Platka*. Luz felt wrung out and disembodied. She lifted her head and gazed out at her surroundings, at the thin minarets rising from out of a crumble of dwellings to pierce an early evening saffron sky. She could hardly believe she'd been in Egypt less than a month. It seemed more like a lifetime, ten lifetimes, in fact. Leonard squeezed her hand and offered, "A penny for your thoughts, sweetheart."

Luz sank deeper into her sweat shirt, tucking her hands into opposite sleeves. Lenny tucked her under his arm. She lifted her face to him. "Tell me, *querido*, why'd she do it? She wanted Ali above everyone."

Leonard shook his head. His voice was strangely soft and mellifluous. "Women like her never want anyone. Ali, the poor shmuck, he never had a prayer. Superman wouldn't have had a prayer."

Unexpectedly, Luz decided that in some indefinable way Lenny was right. Shaken by the thought, she looked away. "The whole idea of killing another human being, especially

someone you've made love with, seems so—" Luz was unable
to come up with a sufficiently evil adjective.

Leonard shrugged fatalistically. "Betty obviously had her
reasons. From the minute I met her I could see she was
harboring a grudge as big as the Giza Pyramid, but I thought
it was against Nasser and Sadat. She fooled me or she changed
her associations. Now, we all have to pay. Everybody wants a
piece of Egypt, Qaddafi, the US, Israel, the Brits, the Rus-
sians. My guess is you could put in eight hours for one agency,
moonlight for another, and be rich before you know it. *Mallesh*, we'll be in Yemen this time next week, so it's not ours to
worry about any more. Leave it to the gods Isis and Osiris to
judge her—and Ali too. It's the Egyptian way."